Dirty Like Brody

TITLES BY JAINE DIAMOND

CONTEMPORARY ROMANCE

Dirty Like Me (Dirty #1)
Dirty Like Brody (Dirty #2)
2 Dirty Wedding Nights (Dirty #2.5)
Dirty Like Seth (Dirty #3)
Dirty Like Dylan (Dirty #4)
Dirty Like Jude (Dirty #5)
Dirty Like Zane (Dirty #6)
Hot Mess (Players #1)
Filthy Beautiful (Players #2)
Sweet Temptation (Players #3)
Lovely Madness (Players #4)
Flames and Flowers (Players Novella)
Handsome Devil (Vancity Villains #1)
Rebel Heir (Vancity Villains #2)
Wicked Angel (Vancity Villains #3)
Irresistible Rogue (Vancity Villains #4)
Charming Deception (Bayshore Billionaires #1)

EROTIC ROMANCE

DEEP (DEEP #1)
DEEPER (DEEP #2)

Dirty Like Brody

JAINE DIAMOND

Dirty Like Brody
by Jaine Diamond

First Edition June 2017

ISBN 978-1-989273-70-8

Cover and interior design by Jaine Diamond / DreamWarp Publishing Ltd.

Published by DreamWarp Publishing Ltd.
www.jainediamond.com

Jessa

I WILL NEVER FORGET the first time he spoke to me.

I remember everything, right down to the music that was playing on the Discman I had tucked into the back of my jeans. (It was my brother's new Chris Cornell album, and the song was "Can't Change Me.") When the bullies started taunting me I turned it up, but I still heard what they said.

I was eight years old, and the last girl on the playground anyone would ever guess would grow up to become a fashion model. Every day I came to school in clothes that were worn and usually a couple sizes too big for me, hand-me-downs, either from my brother or from Zane. When I wore their baggy clothes, the other kids didn't spend so much time telling me how skinny I was.

But they said other things.

I was sitting alone in the playground after school when it happened, up on top of a climbing dome; my brother and his friends called it "Thunderdome" because they'd made a game of dangling like monkeys from the bars inside and kicking the crap out of each other. The bullies were standing at the bottom of Thunderdome, so I couldn't even run away. They were big bullies. Fifth grade bullies, and while my brother, who was in seventh, would've intervened, he wasn't there.

"How come you got shit stains all over your jeans?" the dumb-looking one asked me, leaning on Thunderdome and looking bored. "Doesn't your mom do laundry?"

"You got a shit leak in those saggy diapers, dork?" the even dumber-looking one asked, and they both snorted.

"Yeah, she's so full of shit her eyes are brown."

"What's wrong, baby dork? You gonna cry?"

No. I wasn't going to cry. My brother had a lot of friends and while they were never *that* mean to me, twelve-year-old boys could be relentless. I knew how to hold my own. I'd cry later, at home, when no one could see me.

Besides... the new boy was coming over, and I definitely wasn't crying in front of him.

He was in seventh grade, but the rumor was that he was thirteen or even fourteen and had flunked a grade or two. Obviously, he was super cool. He wore an actual leather jacket, black with silver zippers, like rock stars wore. He smoked outside the school, hung out alone at the edge of the school grounds, and spent more time in the principal's office than the principal. I never knew what he did to get in trouble, but whatever it was, he did it a lot.

The other kids in my class thought he was scary. I just thought he was sad.

Ever since Dad died, I knew sad when I saw it.

The bullies saw him coming and they started getting squirrelly. I thought they'd run but he was there too fast, closing the distance with his leisurely, long-legged stride.

"You guys're so interested in shit, there's some over here I can show you, yeah?" He stood with his hands in his pockets, his posture relaxed, as the bullies started going pale.

I slipped my headphones off.

"Naw, I don't wanna—"

"Sure you do, it's right over here." He toed the ground at his feet with his sneaker. The grass was still damp from a bit of rain in the afternoon and mud squished out.

The bullies started shaking and sniveling, babbling apologies and excuses. There was a brief, almost wordless negotiation, at the end of which they ended up on their knees in front of him.

He hadn't moved. His hands were still in his pockets.

"Just have a little taste and tell me if it's fresh," he told them, in a tone that brooked no argument, squishing his foot in the muck again.

Then he looked up, his brown hair flopping over one eye, and winked at me.

I stared from my perch atop Thunderdome with unabashed, eight-year-old awe as the bullies bent forward, shuddering.

He was going to make them eat shit!

For me!

I was ninety-nine-point-nine percent sure it was just wet mud, but those bullies were scared enough to believe it. And ate it, they did.

He then told them to apologize to me, which they also did, eyes downcast and shaking, spluttering mud. One of them was crying, snuffling through his snot and tears. Then he told them to beat it and they ran away, blubbering and tripping over their own feet.

I stared down at my savior as his unkempt hair fluttered in the breeze. He wore a Foo Fighters T-shirt under his leather jacket and his jeans were ripped, like mine. "You can go home now, you know," he said, like maybe I was slow.

I just sat there, picking dried mud from my jeans.

"Aren't your parents waiting?"

I didn't answer. I knew better than to answer questions like that.

When other kids found out what happened to Dad they either made fun of me or worse, they felt sorry for me. And Jesse said not to tell anyone Mom was sick again. He said if they knew how sick she was, they might take us away from her.

So I said, "I'm waiting for my brother."

He glanced around at the empty playground. "Who's your brother? And why isn't he here kicking those little shits up the ass?"

"Jesse," I said. "My brother is Jesse. He's in detention with Zane."

He took a step closer, teetering on the edge of the sandbox. "Yeah? How come?"

"They... um... got in an argument with Ms. Nielsen because she said I can't come to school in dirty clothes. They do that a lot," I mumbled, wishing maybe I hadn't said all that, except he looked kind of impressed about the detention thing.

He looked at my jeans; I'd gotten them muddy when I sat in a ditch to listen to music before school. I could pretend it didn't hurt me if he said something mean about it, but that didn't mean I wanted to hear it.

Why didn't he just go away?

"Well, you can come down. Those little shits aren't coming back."

I picked at the hole in the knee of my jeans, where my kneecap was poking through.

He leaned over, resting his elbows on Thunderdome. "What're you doing up there?"

"Playing Thunderdome."

I knew how stupid it sounded when no one else was there. It wasn't like I didn't have *any* friends to play with when my brother wasn't around, but they all had parents who picked them up after school. Anyway, I thought it might impress him. Thunderdome was outlawed by the teachers and we only played it after school.

He stepped into the sandbox. "How do you play?"

"It's quicksand!" I squealed. "You can't step in it!"

"Oh. Shit." He jumped up on the dome. "Almost lost a shoe." He looked up at me and his hair fell over his eye again. Blue; his eyes were a deep, dark blue. He climbed to the top of the dome and sat across from me.

Maybe he wasn't making fun of me; he just didn't know the rules of Thunderdome.

"It's okay," I told him. "You're safe up here with me. I'm the princess."

It was true; my brother and his friends always let me be the princess so I'd stay out of the way while they played, and sometimes they let me decide on the winner in case of a tie. But I figured it sounded more important if I left that out.

He pulled out a cigarette and lit it with a shiny flip-top lighter that had been scraped and dented all to hell, and started smoking. His hands were scraped too, his knuckles split and scabbed over. His fingernails were too short, chewed all down into the nail bed, his cuticles all ragged and blood-encrusted. They were a mess. But his face...

He was so... pretty.

"What happened to your hands?"

He didn't answer. Just smoked his cigarette and looked out across the school grounds, his arms wrapped around his knees, watching as parents picked their kids up in the distance, along the road in front of the school.

"A princess, huh?"

"*The* princess."

"So who's the prince, then?"

"Don't need one."

He looked at me. "Then who's gonna save you if you fall in the quicksand?"

"I will."

"What if you can't?"

"Then you can," I said. "If you want to. But you might get stuck in there, too."

He stared at me for a minute. Then he smiled, slowly, and it was like the sun coming out from behind the clouds.

"Then I guess we'll sink together." He took a couple of drags of his cigarette, his eyes squinting through the smoke. "You got a name, princess?"

"Jessa Mayes."

"Jessa Mayes," he repeated. "Don't ever let those little shits talk to you that way, yeah? Next time they try, you make a fist, like this." He showed me, clenching his fist until his split knuckles looked like they might burst. "And you hit 'em, right here, in the nose, as hard as you can. You do it hard enough, they'll go down.

Then you run away. You do that once, they're not gonna bother you again."

I shook my head. "I'm not supposed to hit people. My brother says sticks and stones—"

"Yeah?" He flicked the ash off his cigarette and spat on the sand below. "Well, your brother's a pussy who doesn't know shit."

I gaped at him.

No one talked about Jesse like that. The other kids all thought he walked on water because he could play guitar.

"I can't make a fifth-grader eat crap." My face was getting hot and I looked down at the sand. "Maybe you can. I can't."

When I glanced up again, he was taking something off his jacket. He held it out to me. "Take it," he said.

I took it from his outstretched hand and examined it. It was a little silver pin shaped like a motorcycle. It said *Sinners MC* on a banner that wrapped around the tires. There was a woman on the motorcycle but she wasn't riding it, exactly. She was facing the wrong way and reclined back, her back arched, shoving her boobs out.

I was eight.

I had no idea what *Sinners MC* meant, so it never occurred to me to wonder why he had a pin that belonged to an outlaw motorcycle club.

"You wear that," he said, glancing over my shoulder, "no one's gonna mess with you." He was looking in the direction of the school, his eyes narrowing as he dragged on his cigarette.

"Smoking on school grounds *again* Mr. Mason?"

I turned to find a teacher stalking toward us, one of those shit-eating bullies in tow, red-faced, looking anywhere but at us. "What will your parents have to say about this?"

"Can't wait to find out," he muttered. His blue eyes met mine as he tossed his cigarette aside. Then he smiled at me again.

I smiled back.

He leapt to the ground, jumping over the quicksand and landing in the grass.

"See you around, princess."

I watched him shove his hands in the pockets of his jeans and walk away. But it wasn't true; I didn't see him around. He never even came back to school after that day.

Not for two whole years.

Those bullies never bothered me again, though. None of them did. And I was pretty sure it wasn't because of some pin. It was because of *him*.

Because he'd made two fifth-graders eat shit for being mean to me, and no one wanted to eat shit.

The next year, when a new girl in my class asked me about my motorcycle pin, she didn't believe me when I told her where I'd gotten it. As if I'd made up the whole thing about the badass boy in the leather jacket who saved me from a couple of bullies—then mysteriously vanished from school, never to return—just to impress her.

But I knew he was real.

I had his pin, and I had his picture. In the seventh grade class photo in the school yearbook he was standing right next to my brother, staring down the lens of the camera like he was ready to take on the world... and make it eat shit.

His name was Brody Mason.

He was the love of my life.

If only I'd figured that out a lot sooner than I did.

CHAPTER ONE

Jessa

I WAS LATE. For my brother's wedding.

And because I was late, the universe seemed to be conspiring to make me even more late. All three legs of my flight had been delayed. The last was the airline's fault, the second, the fault of the weather, but the first... well, that was all me, so it was kind of a domino effect.

Once I'd finally touched down in Vancouver—thirteen hours late—it seemed to take an unusually long time for my bags to come down the carousel, and by the time I'd gathered my things, piled them onto a baggage cart and steered my way to the exit doors, I'd been traveling for over twenty-four hours. More than enough time to ponder how pissed off my brother was going to be.

I was weary and uncomfortably hot, sweating in my leather boots and faux fur jacket. I'd worn a thin T-shirt layered over a tank top and knit leggings with the jacket and boots, not sure what to expect with the weather. Vancouver was having a weirdly cold winter but the snow and ice was now gone, replaced with a faint, drizzling rain. The air that greeted me was cool and fresh but not cold as I walked through the sliding glass doors. And everything felt... familiar.

Much more familiar than I thought it would.

I took a breath and tipped my face up to the cloud-bruised sky. I glimpsed the peaks of snow-dusted mountains in the distance. And I felt an overwhelming sense of... *joy*.

Aside from the fact that I didn't actually want to be here, that I was carrying the burden of a gut-gnawing sense of dread—the kind that came with knowing you were about to come face-to-face with things you'd never really figured out *how* to face—it felt good to be home.

Home.

I grinned as the wisps of rain hit my face...

Then I saw him.

Him.

Several feet to my left, there was a queue for the taxis, which I'd planned to get myself into. I'd get my ass to the ferry where I'd meet my old friend, Roni, my "date" for the wedding. On the ferry over to Vancouver Island, she and I would catch up and I'd generally get my shit together for what promised to be the most difficult weekend of my life. In the winding, four-and-a-half hour drive across the island, I'd run through the various tidbits of conversation I'd prepared in my head to get me through this; inconsequential, impersonal stuff like the latest celeb gossip, fashion trends from the front lines, and if I was really desperate, the weather. Canadians were always game to discuss the weather; it was kind of a way of life. Of course, I'd throw in a few decent jokes, too.

My old friends were always good for a laugh.

At the end of the road, maybe Roni would flirt with the boat guy and he'd let us grab a super-quick drink (or two) at the last bar we could find before heading out. On the private boat to the very posh and very remote resort up the coast where the wedding was taking place, I'd give myself the little pep talk I'd also worked out, in preparation for coming face-to-face with the man I'd painstakingly avoided for the last six-and-a-half years.

Basically, my entire adult life.

Along the way, Roni would provide distraction, entertainment and comic relief, as she always did. And when I saw him, *him*, she'd be by my side, drawing attention and generally providing a loud and lovely buffer.

And everything would work out just fine, right? Because no way seeing him could possibly go as badly as I feared it might.

Right.

That was the plan.

Instead, I was alone. I'd taken all of two steps into my hometown. I was weary and jet-lagged. I'd had not one drink. And my little pep talk? Completely out the window.

Because a dozen feet to my right, he was standing at the curb in the rain, staring at me... and my world fell apart.

"Brody," I breathed.

Then I more or less went into shock. Because he was *right there*. In jeans and a black leather jacket, his dark eyebrows furled as he stared me down, rain droplets dripping from his soft brown hair and his full lips... the smoldering, overcast sky casting shadows in his eyes... looking just like he used to look, only... better.

"You're late," he said, his voice flat. He took a few steps toward me, then stopped, his gaze flicking down to my breasts. "Is that my shirt?"

I glanced down.

It was an old Led Zeppelin tour T-shirt. It said *United States of America 1977* and had a rockin' angel on it, a naked dude with outstretched wings. It wasn't the kind of T-shirt you paid too much money for in some hipster boutique because it looked old and distressed. It *was* old. It was large on me to begin with and was now so stretched out I tied it above one hip to make it fit. The neck fell off one shoulder. It was worn to hell and had a few holes.

And yes, it was his.

I'd picked it up off his bedroom floor one sketchy morning when I was eighteen, and never gave it back. He'd never asked for it back. And even if he wanted it back after I'd worn the hell out of it, I wasn't giving it back.

It was a piece of him. The only piece I had.

"No," I lied, pulling my jacket shut. Butterflies skittered in my stomach as he reached past me, scooping my bags off the cart.

"Had a shirt just like that. Disappeared around the time you did."

His blue eyes met mine and I felt the almost-electric jolt all the way down my spine. I felt it *between my legs*.

Holy *hell*.

I *still* felt it.

That same thing... that thing that should've died with all the years and all the miles between us... all the silence... all the time I'd *wasted* trying like hell to fight it, to deny it, to just plain numb it out. Coiling fast, hot and tight at the base of my spine... in my lungs, at the back of my throat, every cell of my body catching fire... as every nerve, every fiber lit up in protest of every second we'd been apart.

It was exactly the same. Only... worse.

It was *more*.

That crazy, irresistible pull I'd felt around him back then had only grown stronger.

His eyes darkened as his pupils dilated... and I knew he felt it, too. Then his gaze dropped to my lips. He breathed in, his nostrils flaring. His jaw clenched.

Then he turned and walked away. With my bags.

Oh my God.

I just stood there, watching him go, the air between us stretching thinner and thinner the farther he got, until I couldn't breathe. At all.

I allowed myself two-point-five seconds to freak out. Then I forced some air, shuddering, into my lungs.

Then I went after him.

I caught up only when he stopped to toss my things in the back of a black Escalade parked at the curb, hazard lights flashing. I stood there, awkwardly, waiting for him to turn around, every part of me throbbing with the force of my heartbeat; my lungs as I fought to breathe, my brain as I fought to think, my *clit*.

My knees were shaking.

No man had ever made my knees shake before.

Well, no *other* man.

This was not how my body had ever reacted to other men.

And yes, I was aware that deep, deep down, there was still some part of me—maybe larger than I'd like to admit—that was still that skinny, dorky, lonely girl who'd been bullied on the playground. But making my living as a model over the past decade meant I'd grown a thick skin. Very thick. I'd also learned that no matter how I felt inside, the world did not see me as that skinny, dorky girl; that men, in general, found me beautiful. Way more beautiful than I'd ever felt. I still had a hard time reckoning *me* with those pictures of model-me in designer lingerie, my long brown hair highlighted with caramel and honey, my eyebrows perfectly shaped, my cheekbones and chin all somehow grown in to balance what I'd feared would always be an awkward nose, my full lips and long limbs somehow all working together to create an image that was something far and away from that girl inside. Even so, I'd learned how to carry myself with confidence, how to compete, perform, win and even lose with grace. I'd learned how to keep my cool under intense scrutiny, and mercifully, how to handle rejection. Because the world I lived in, even for beautiful girls, was rife with rejection.

What I'd never learned how to do, apparently, was look Brody Mason in his deep blue eyes and not lose my shit.

Lucky for me, he barely spared me a glance as he slammed the back of the truck shut. "Get in," he said, disappearing around the driver's side.

I walked up to the passenger side door as he got in the truck. Then I stood there, in the misting rain, still kind of in shock, just trying to get a handle on all the reactions set off by his sudden presence.

Because how could I still react to him like this? After all this time?

It was like no time had passed at all.

Worse; I knew exactly how long it had been, and according to my body, I had six-and-a-half years without him to make up for. Preferably immediately, nakedly, and repeatedly.

I took a deep breath, fumbled with the door handle and opened the door. "Thank you for the ride," I managed.

He didn't smile. He just swiped a hand through his damp hair and stared me down with those intense blue eyes. I started to register how much older he looked than the last time I'd seen him, though his eyes hadn't changed. Time had been good to him. Very good.

Six-and-a-half years.

It hit me like a kick in the gut, all at once.

It wasn't something I'd ever allowed myself to fully process: the agony of missing him, of wishing things had gone differently for us. If I did, I'd probably curl up and die, right on the spot. Because how could I live with it?

Now that he was here, though, right in front of me... all my carefully constructed walls, the armor I'd built up over the years against my true feelings, against *him*, cracked open, and everything came surging into the light. Every moment between us. Every breath I'd taken on this Earth since Brody Mason sauntered into my life.

And it was in those deep blue eyes, that he remembered, too.

He remembered everything.

"Get in," he repeated, and started up the truck.

I got in.

As we pulled out into traffic he was silent, and I tried to think of something to say to fill the void. It was the perfect time, really, to tell him. The perfect opportunity to explain why I'd left, all those years ago.

I could tell him everything. Just come clean, like I'd told myself I should do... could do. Might do, while I was in town for my brother's wedding.

Instead, I stared at his handsome profile, afraid to speak. The arch of his brow, his high cheekbone. The strong line of his nose. His square jaw, clean-shaven but slightly shadowed. His stylishly unkempt brown hair. The battered leather of his jacket.

I hadn't laid eyes on him in years. Not until my brother's well-meaning fiancée started texting me photos of her and Jesse, and Brody happened to be in some of them. I should've deleted those photos, but I didn't. Instead, I'd gazed at them a thousand times. And now he was *here*.

So close to me.

I watched his throat move as he swallowed. I watched his knuckles turn white on the steering wheel as the wiper blades beat an angry rhythm against the rain.

I stared at the familiar tattoo on the back of his right hand, a mess of entangled vines that wound around his thumb and wrist and belonged to a small, black rose on his palm. So familiar, like we'd never been apart. How many times had I traced the pattern of those vines with my gaze?

A million, at least.

That tattoo, just one of the many things about Brody—the many small details that made him *him*—that I'd tried to forget over the years. But I hadn't forgotten. I knew I hadn't. And despite all my preparation for this moment, I wasn't prepared at all.

I wasn't ready.

Would I ever really have been ready for this?

Maybe I was totally kidding myself to think I'd ever be able to face him, those blue eyes staring me down, and come clean.

Maybe I'd just always be dirty and there was nothing I could do about it.

I looked out the window. "It's raining," I said. Yeah. Brilliant. But since I was a total chickenshit, I was going with it.

"Seven years," he said. I looked over at him, but he didn't look at me. "*Seven fucking years*, and all the times I've tried to talk to you and you shut me out, and now that's all you've got to say? It's fucking *raining*? It's January. It's Vancouver. Where you were fucking born. So yes, it's raining, like it always does in January. What the fuck else do you want me to say about it?"

Okay...

So much for my Canadians-love-talking-about-the-weather theory.

I was judging by the number of F-bombs in that little tirade that he was pissed. At me.

Not that I hadn't expected him to be a little mad. Among other things.

But the fact that he obviously *was* mad just proved that he still cared, right?

"Six-and-a-half years," I said.

"What?"

"It's been... six-and-a-half years," I repeated, my voice fading, "since we... saw each other."

He said nothing.

It's just because he cares, I told myself. *And he probably won't be the only one who gives you attitude this weekend, so get used to it.*

But I couldn't get used to it. I had no experience with mature, pissed-off Brody. I'd barely been able to deal with the Brody I used to know. Young, wild, too gorgeous for common sense and angry at the world.

At all the world... except me.

We took a turn to the right, continuing back into the airport, and I struggled to get my bearings; it had been years since I'd been here, but this was definitely not the way to the ferry terminal.

"Where are we going?"

"To your brother's wedding."

"But... I'm supposed to meet Roni at the ferry."

He shot me a look that could only be described as scathing. Come to think of it, it was the first time he'd looked at me since I got in the truck. "And I'm supposed to trust you not to skip out on the dinner tonight, or the wedding tomorrow? You're already missing the rehearsal."

Oh.

Jesus.

That's what this was about?

He didn't pick me up at the airport because he wanted to see me?

I studied his angry profile and it all became so clear.

No. He didn't want to see me.

He'd only come to get me because my brother, the big rock star, had asked him to drive out here in the rain and deal with me. Brody was one of my brother's best friends, so why not? Worse; Brody managed my brother's mega-successful rock band, Dirty, so this was probably some sort of business deal. Like somewhere in his contract, my brother had snuck in a clause that it was Brody's responsibility to deal with all the most tedious bullshit in his life, up to and including escorting his little sister to his wedding so she wouldn't bail.

Definitely something my brother would do.

Well, if they had a contract. In their many years of working together, Brody and the band had never had a written contract between them. Because that's just the kind of friends they were. A verbal deal, then.

You deal with Jessa. I'll owe you one later.

"It's really none of your business," I told him, "if I go to my brother's wedding or not." And it wasn't. Brody wasn't *my* manager —much as he'd wanted to be, back when I was writing music with the band... but that was neither here nor there. He wasn't the boss of me either, any more than my brother was.

Yeah, try telling either of them that.

Whatever. This was ridiculous. Offensive, actually, that they both seemed to think I needed some kind of chaperone for this event. That they were treating me like I was still a fucking teenager.

Yes, I'd screwed up six-and-a-half years ago—and okay, every day since then—but today was a new day, right?

"Jesse *is* my business," Brody ground out. "Literally. If you skip out on his wedding or any of the other romantic bullshit Katie has planned for the next forty-eight hours, that shit will not fly."

We made a sharp turn into the small parking area in front of the Flying Beaver, a little restaurant and bar on the water where the floatplanes docked, and panic started to rise. This whole thing was spinning way, way out of control. Because apparently I was about to be trapped in a very small plane with a very pissed off Brody for the next couple of hours, and *he didn't even want to be here.*

"I told Jesse I'd take the ferry to the island. He was going to have a car meet me—"

"Yeah, well, you're *late.*" He parked us at the curb and cut the engine, popping off his seatbelt.

"I was at a shoot, Brody. It ran late. I couldn't just bail in the middle of—"

"Do not say my name."

I blinked at him.

What?

"Go ahead and say and do whatever the fuck you're gonna do," he said, "but you do not get to say my name." When I just gaped at him, he turned to me and leaned in, so close I could see the silvery-gray flecks around his pupils, and said in a low voice, "You wanted it, I'm giving it to you. Exactly what you've been asking for the last *six-and-a-half* years with a whole fuckload of silence. *Consider me dead to you.*"

I stared at him, speechless. At the lines of repressed rage on his handsome face; the coldness in those dark blue eyes.

"You're... you're angry with me," I stammered.

He grunted derisively. "We can't just go from being strangers to best friends, princess. Doesn't fucking work that way."

Princess.

He used to call me that, when we were young. It wasn't a derogatory term, the way he said it now.

I looked out the window and sniffled a bit. It was the rain making me sniffly. It wasn't his words that were making my eyes itch and blink, my stomach twist itself in knots.

When had Brody become such an asshole?

Right... Probably around the time I "disappeared."

I knew that. I knew this was my fault. That I'd treated him badly.

No, not badly. Badly was when you forgot to tip a really decent waiter. Badly was cutting someone off in traffic.

I'd treated Brody horribly.

Horrendously.

I took a breath and looked at him again, watching him pocket his keys and generally ignore me.

"We are not strangers," I said softly. "We never have been."

He looked at me briefly. "I don't know you," he said, and my heart crushed in on itself.

"If you don't know me now," I told him, trying to keep my voice from wavering, "you never did."

"You're right. I didn't." He started to open his door.

I reached to stop him, catching his leather sleeve, and he stiffened like I had the fucking plague. Those ice-cold eyes locked on mine.

I shrank back in my seat, letting him go. "You don't need to do this, you know. I can just take a cab to the ferry."

He slammed the door shut and swore under his breath, an angry muscle ticking in his jaw.

"Let me tell you what I know," he said, turning to me, his elbow on the steering wheel so his broad shoulders seemed to take up all the space in the cab. "What I know is exactly how fast and how far you can run. What I know for fucking sure is exactly what it does to the people you leave behind when you do, and I am not spending this weekend scraping together a trail of shit when you ruin Jesse's wedding. So if you wanna hate me for it go ahead and hate me, but if you think you're going to the ferry, you've got another fucking thing coming. You're doing this my way and that's all the fuck there is to it."

Holy shit.

Not only had Brody become much more of an asshole than I remembered... he was kind of scary when he was pissed off. Colder than he used to be; harder. Bigger, too. A lot more muscular; I could tell, even with the leather jacket.

"*Unless* you want me to arrange to get your ass on a plane out of here right now," he went on, leaning his big, muscular, pissed-off self into my space, "and we pretend you never landed. Because if anyone finds out you showed your ass in town and then you turned tail and took off, sweetheart, I am not gonna be the one telling Jesse to back off and give you space. You hear me on this? I'm fucking done with covering for you and making excuses for you and waiting for you to get a clue. Your brother loves you and the least you can do is show your face at his motherfucking wedding."

My gaze dropped away from the accusation in those cold eyes. I studied the muscle ticking in his jaw, the veins standing out on his neck, and realized I'd been wrong. He wasn't pissed.

He was *seething*.

And no, this was definitely not going as badly as I feared it might. It was much, much worse.

I felt the burn at the back of my throat, the stinging behind my eyes, but I took a deep, shuddering breath, willing myself not to do this... not to fall apart. Not in front of him. But *shit*. I totally felt like a teenager.

Maybe because the last time I'd been this close to Brody, I was one.

His hand went to my hip and I heard the click as he released my seatbelt, felt the straps slide over me as he reached across me.... his nose almost bumping mine as he pulled the latch on my door, opening it.

"Get out," he said.

I didn't move. Instead, I bit my lip.

I didn't realize I'd done it until his gaze dropped to my lips, then flicked back up to my eyes. His eyes darkened and a slow, aching minute passed between us.

If he was any other man, I might've thought he was turned on.

As it was... he looked kind of disgusted.

The rain pattered down on the truck, encasing us inside, and yeah; it was just like I was eighteen and he was twenty-three all over again, sitting in his truck in the rain—except that day, he wasn't telling me to leave. He was asking—no, *begging* me to stay.

But back then, Brody didn't hate me.

Now...?

I couldn't blame him for being mad at me. I'd expected things to be difficult between us. I did not expect this.

I did not expect hate.

But it was definitely hatred I saw in his eyes. Pure, ice-cold loathing, with a hefty side of revulsion and resentment.

And Brody Mason hating me? No amount of preparation could've helped me with this. Even if I'd told him everything I thought I might tell him, my harrowing confession... I didn't think he'd hate me. I thought he'd like me less, and that was bad enough— bad enough to keep me *gone* for six-and-a-half years. I couldn't even imagine how hard it would be to come crashing down off the pedestal he'd put me on so many years ago... but I knew it wouldn't feel good. I knew it would be painful.

But this? This was pure hell.

"Are you getting out," he asked in that stone-cold voice, "or do I have to drag you out?"

Um... no.

That would not be necessary.

Mostly because the thought of him putting his hands on me right now, in any way, was making my clit throb, because apparently, pissed off Brody turned me on about as much as he scared me. Because I was screwed up like that.

Yeah; pure hell.

"I'm here," I managed. "I'm here for the wedding, okay?"

"Believe it when I fucking see it."

"So you're just kidnapping me, is that it?"

"I'd call it damage control, but if that's what you wanna call it," he said, "go right the fuck ahead."

Then he opened his door and stepped out into the rain.

"I'm sorry," I said to his back. Because I couldn't think of anything else he might want to hear from me right now.

He looked at me but he didn't say a thing. He just slammed the door. I watched him stalk over to a big, dark-haired man who'd appeared on the sidewalk in front of the restaurant.

Oh, Jesus. *Jude.*

This was serious.

My brother's best friend and the head of Dirty's security team, Jude was pretty much permanently glued to my brother's side. If he was here to accompany us to Jesse's wedding, they really were afraid I might bail.

There was no way I was getting out of this.

Never mind that I'd actually been looking forward to the ridiculously long drive across the island, the time on solid ground to acclimate to being home and to prepare myself for two days at a remote resort with Brody.

Clearly, that wasn't going to happen.

I climbed out of the truck as Brody got my bags from the back, handing them off to the pilot.

"Picking up Amanda," I heard him say to Jude. "We'll see you up there." Then he was off, without a glance in my direction, heading back through the rain to his truck.

We.

I tried to squeeze out a smile as Jude grabbed me up in a hug, all muscles and killer dimples, and planted a kiss on my forehead. At least someone was happy to see me. I hugged him back, grateful for his solid comfort. He asked how I was doing and how my flight was and I did my best to answer, but I wasn't sure my words made any sense.

Brody wasn't even coming on the plane with us.

He was going to get Amanda.

Amanda.

I felt every letter of her name stab my heart.

I had no idea who Amanda was. Unfortunately, as far as I could guess, bimbos were never named Amanda. Smart, beautiful girls were named Amanda.

Amanda, who was going to my brother's wedding with Brody.

Fuck. He had a date.

A girlfriend?

Which meant... No. Fuck, no. I wasn't going to tell him. I watched him peel out in his truck, and I made the decision, fast; I wasn't going to tell him anything.

What good would that do? He was already pissed at me for what I'd done—for leaving the band, for leaving everyone behind six-and-a-half years ago. For leaving *him*. He wasn't going to be any happier about the reason I did it.

He wasn't going to hate me any less.

"Jessa! Fucking! Mayes! You beautiful AWOL bitch, get your ass over here!"

I turned to find Roni stepping out of the restaurant. She strut toward me through the rain, arms held wide.

"Roni!" I gave her a big hug and she laughed, jumping us both up and down with little-girl joy. Fair enough, since Roni and I had been friends since high school. And I really hadn't seen her in a long time. Like most of my friends back home, I remembered her looking younger than she actually was, but time had been good to her, too.

Tall, dark and the sort of sexy that had been known to cause at least one major traffic accident, if anyone could take focus off my arrival at my brother's wedding, it was this girl. A girl who could turn any situation into a party; whether it was booze, drugs, or an epic hook-up you were in the mood for, Roni was your girl... a girl who'd once hooked *herself* up with Zane Traynor, my brother's life-long friend-slash-nemesis and the insane—and insanely gorgeous—lead singer of Dirty.

When I'd asked her to be my date for the wedding, she was incredibly keen, and I wasn't naive as to why.

"Zane is in the wedding party," I reminded her as she hooked her arm through mine and we followed Jude down the walkway toward the float plane dock. "Can I trust you to behave somewhat? This is a wedding, not an orgy. I think my brother's new wife will be a little perturbed if the two of you turn it into one." I didn't worry that she'd take offense at the warning; we both knew it needed to be said.

"My orgy days are long behind me," Roni lied with a grin. "Anyway, been there, done Zane. You know I never go back for seconds." Then she winked at Jude as she climbed onto the plane. I watched Jude's gaze fall straight to Roni's ass in her skin-tight jeans.

Yeah, with Roni in the room, no one was even going to notice me.

One could hope.

I followed her, taking one of the leather seats and shaking the rain from my hair. Jude climbed in behind me and the pilot welcomed us on-board, launching into the safety spiel. I really should've paid attention, since crashing into the Pacific Ocean in a tiny floatplane was probably one of those life events I'd want to be prepared for. But I just couldn't do it.

Picking up Amanda.

Shit, this was going to be a long fucking weekend.

Luckily, Roni pulled out a flask before we'd even hit the air. I took a swig of her infamous home brew—blackberry vodka—then a couple more, and tried really hard not to care.

So Brody had a date for the wedding.

So he hated me.

What the hell did it matter? I was never going to see him again.

As soon as the wedding was over and my brother and his new bride headed off on their rock star honeymoon, I was getting the hell out of here. And nothing would really change.

Okay, so Brody would hate me instead of liking me. But for all I knew, he'd hated me for a while now; I just didn't know it yet. So now I'd be *aware* that the only man I'd ever loved couldn't stand me —couldn't even stand for me to say his name.

But so what? I'd be gone.

And this time, I was never coming back.

CHAPTER TWO

Brody

THE FLOATPLANE LANDED in the calm waters of Cathedral Cove just as the sun was setting at our backs, the light fading over the seemingly-boundless waters of the Pacific Ocean. The cove, a tiny inlet lined with towering spruce, hemlock and western cedar trees, was tucked up along the coastline of Vancouver Island, accessible only by water and air.

Even I could admit it was an epic location for a wedding.

The main lodge building, where the ceremony would take place, appeared through the trees on a rocky promontory, overlooking the water with its towering front walls of glass and what I could only assume were heart-stopping views of the cove and the Pacific beyond; it wasn't called Cathedral Cove Resort for nothing. I could already see why Katie chose it.

And why her best friend, Devi, had sent flowers and steak dinners to my house for a week after I called a guy I knew, who knew the owners of the resort, and twisted a few rubber arms. Really wasn't all that difficult to convince them to book out the entire place for Jesse Mayes' rock star wedding on semi-short notice. Turned out, they were fans. But I enjoyed the steak anyway.

As the plane growled up to the docks, it occurred to me that I really hadn't been out of the city, into nature, in far too fucking long.

This wedding would be a great excuse to—mostly—forget about work for a couple of days, unplug, and breathe some clean, green air.

I should really be happy right now.

Or at the very least, looking forward to spending the next couple of days with my best friends, my friends who'd become, over the years, my family, at what was sure to be one of the best parties of the year, probably the best party of Jesse's life—because we were celebrating his marriage to Katie Bloom, a woman who made him ridiculously happy.

But I wasn't happy.

I was far from happy.

Fortunately, the loud drone of the plane and the distractingly stunning view made convenient cover for the fact that I couldn't manage conversation with Amanda, much less look her in the eye. But as the plane settled and we climbed out, the crisp, cold wind off the water smacking me in the face, I knew I had to get my head together. I couldn't exactly mope around like some adolescent asshole for the next two days.

If you don't know me now, you never did.

Jesus, that girl knew what to say to piss me the fuck off.

No; not girl. Woman.

No mistake, she was a woman now, and didn't that just drop-kick me right in the guts. Because I'd missed it. All of it.

Everything Jessa Mayes would become... she'd gone and become it without me.

And now, with one shitty little comment, she thought she could just wipe away the years I had known her? All the time we'd spent together as kids, and then, as we got older... She could just take that all away from me?

Well, fuck her.

Maybe it meant nothing to her, but she didn't get to decide what it meant to me. She didn't get to tell me what I knew or didn't know, and she sure as shit didn't get to tell me how I felt about it.

You're angry with me.

Yeah. No shit.

I was also more than a little pissed at myself for losing my cool. But I just couldn't fucking handle it. Being that close to her... every caveman urge I'd ever had rearing up in violent protest that I had her, *that* close, again, and she was gonna slip through my fingers, again.

Consider me dead to you.

Jesus. What a fucking asshole.

Amanda turned to me and smiled, her short blonde hair dancing in the breeze. She looked like a Canadian beer commercial with her white teeth, tight jeans and short bomber jacket, her plaid shirt tied above her navel.

I smiled back.

Our bags were whisked away as a guide from the resort gave us a quick tour of the grounds, which pretty much consisted of a maze-like cedar-planked boardwalk winding through the ancient trees. It was suspended over the rocky, uneven ground, and far below, a stream that meandered through the rainforest, feeding the hot springs on the rim of the cove. We were already late, so once we'd stopped off at our cabin and changed into our dinner clothes, we headed straight up to the lodge. The tiny amber lights that had been strung along the boardwalk had begun to sparkle in the dusk; I had no idea if the lights were always there or if they'd been hung for the wedding, but it was beautiful.

Along with the scents of cool, damp cedar, fresh spruce needles and moss, the bird calls and chirps among the trees, the water crashing on the rocks below... the whole scene was pretty breathtaking. So breathtaking, I was pretty sure Amanda hadn't yet noticed that I hadn't said a word to her since the plane hit air.

Or maybe that was wishful thinking.

The scents of cooking—lemon, dill, something buttery and something else kind of sweet, like fresh baking—wafted out from the back of the lodge, and the scent of a wood-burning fire, smoky and inviting, clung in the slightly misty air off the water. I took a few slow, deep breaths, just trying to soak it all in, collect my thoughts the way I might before a particularly unsavory business meeting.

But this unease had nothing to do with business.

As we approached the lodge, I could make out the thump of bass and the unmistakable, bittersweet rhythm of The Black Keys' "Never Gonna Give You Up." Which was really fucking unfortunate, since a Black Keys song had once imprinted on me in a way that I'd never be able to separate hearing this band from the memory of dancing with Jessa Mayes on a shitty summer night in the dark.

But really... was there anything left on Earth that didn't somehow remind me of her?

Amanda caught my hand and leaned in, resting her head on my shoulder. I could hardly blame her. It was the perfect setting for romance, never mind that it was a wedding. Katie and her girls had done well planning this thing, and if my goal was to get my date in the mood to spend the next couple of days screwing in front of a fire, mission accomplished.

Except that I was suddenly wondering why the fuck I'd brought Amanda to this thing at all.

Maybe because it would've seemed weird if I didn't bring her? Maybe because, when she heard that Jesse Mayes—lead guitarist of Dirty, the band I'd managed since they and I were little more than kids, and one of my best friends—was getting married, she just assumed she'd be coming with me.

Or maybe because, when she'd assumed she was coming, I let her go ahead and assume, because deep down I'd wanted to send a big fat *Fuck you* to Jesse's sister by showing up with the pretty blonde at my side.

Yeah, that sounded about right.

Not that I was proud of it.

As we stepped from the boardwalk onto the wraparound deck of the lodge, I took another fortifying breath. One of the catering staff opened a door for us, and as we stepped inside, I saw them.

Jesse and Katie.

In the middle of the room, dancing slow and kind of making out, laughing as they pawed at each other like no one else in the lodge, or the universe, existed. Pretty much their usual mode.

Everything was as it should be, then.

A few other people were dancing; most were talking, drinking and snacking on hors d'oeuvres. Besides the lodge staff, the catering team bustling in and out, and Jude's security guys, there were about forty or so guests, all VIPs—close family, members of the wedding party and their dates—here for the rehearsal in preparation for the wedding tomorrow, which would be attended by another sixty or so guests. All of whom I knew.

But as we started across the room, despite all the familiar faces, I had eyes for only one person; one person who clearly wasn't here.

I didn't see her. Anywhere. And Jessa Mayes was pretty fucking hard to miss.

I didn't see Jude either, so I couldn't even ask him where the fuck she was. Saw Roni in the corner, flirting with one of his security guys, though, so at least their plane had landed.

"You wanna dance?" Amanda asked, just as the Rolling Stones' "Wild Horses" started playing.

Christ. What was with all the soul-sucking love songs?

Right. Wedding.

"After I introduce you around," I told her, steering her past the dance floor. The more people she knew, I figured, the more likely she might have a good time—despite the fact that she was here with me.

I took her over to greet the other members of Dirty—also pretty hard to miss. Zane, our lead singer, with his white-blond mohawk, demonic beard twisted into a braid, eyebrow piercings and ice-sharp blue eyes with just that little bit of crazy in them—wearing jeans and a black leather vest, because that was semiformal wear for Zane. And Dylan, our drummer, his six-and-a-half-foot frame making him the tallest dude in the room; add to that his unruly, flaming auburn hair and athletic build, poured into leather pants and a cashmere sweater, and even if I hadn't seen them, all I'd have to do was follow the batting eyelashes.

Wherever these guys went, a trail of drooling women was sure to follow, and there were about a half-dozen flocked around now, including Katie's mom. Yeah; we probably could've made these guys a decent career in music even if they had zero musical talent.

Lucky for us all, they had it in spades.

Both of them were grinning like fools as Amanda and I waded through the pheromones. They looked just a little too happy, which in my experience was rarely a good thing. When these two got up to shit they were like a couple of idiots on the playground; neither of them could back down from a dare.

"No bullshit at Jesse's wedding," I told them, straight-up. I didn't have it in me to deal with their shenanigans on top of everything else.

"Nope," Dylan said. "Just saying how good it is to see Jessa. Jesse's so fucking happy. Kinda feels like a reunion."

"Yeah, we could get her to stick around for a bit, we could actually make it one," Zane said. "You know, get her out to jam, write some killer shit."

"Yeah," I said. "If we could." I looked around for someone to introduce Amanda to, so I didn't have to tell Zane, here and now, that was a shit idea. And never gonna happen.

Jessa Mayes' days of songwriting with Dirty were over.

Long over.

She'd made her choice, six-and-a-half years ago. She'd walked away from the band and never looked back. Fucking thing was, I knew for a fact every member of the band was more than willing to let that slide if she'd just come back and write with them again. Especially Jesse; he'd loved that girl from the second she came into the world, and he wasn't about to stop. When Jessa was born, her four-year-old brother had named her—after himself—forging a bond that would never be broken. He would always have her back, would never turn against her, no matter what shit she pulled.

Not me.

It was my job to look out for the band, and I was never gonna let Jessa Mayes fuck us all over again.

"What's your deal, Bro?" Zane looked from me to Amanda and back with a devious grin; clearly, something wasn't adding up.

People could say what they wanted about Zane being a lunatic, but the man wasn't stupid.

"Yeah, man," Dylan said. "I'm sensing a general aura of funk."

Great. If it was that obvious something was off, even to Dylan, by far the most laid-back—and least nosy—of my friends, this was gonna be a long fucking night.

"No deal," I said. "Just airsick. Floatplane."

Total bullshit, but the best I could do just now was spit out a few two-word sentences and turn away before they asked more questions.

I was glad to find Dolly when I did, waiting for a hug. Zane had brought her as his date, though she would've been invited anyway. Dolly was Zane's grandma; she was also the woman who'd raised him from the time he was two years old, and it was her garage that Zane and Jesse jammed in with all the shitty little garage bands they formed before we put Dirty together.

Grandma Dolly had also helped raise Jesse and especially Jessa while their mom battled her illness. When she died, it was Dolly who'd taken Jessa in, given her stability, a sense of family and three meals a day so Jesse could pursue the gonzo life of a musician on the brink of superstardom.

I had big, big love for this woman. We all did. Tiny and white-haired, she was pushing ninety and still going strong; at least, strong enough to take the flight out here, be a part of this crazy shindig, and keep putting up with Zane's shit.

I wrapped her up in a careful hug and kissed her soft cheek. "Zane taking good care of you, Doll?"

"Oh, he always does." I could hear the joy and the pride in her scratchy voice. "Everything has been just lovely, and all my babies together." She patted me on the back before letting go. "Everyone's so happy that Jessa's come home. Have you seen her yet?"

"I picked her up at the airport, actually."

"She looks like she's doing well, don't you think? Such a beautiful girl."

"Yeah," I said. "Beautiful. Dolly, this is Amanda."

I introduced Amanda around to all the usual suspects, including Dylan's "date," Ash, lead singer of the Penny Pushers, one of the bands Dirty often toured with. Dylan and Ash had been besties since they'd met playing a festival about five years back and because he was Dylan's plus one, Ash was the only Pusher who'd be attending the wedding. That's how selective the guest list was.

I'd told Jesse not to sweat it. If anyone was pissed about not getting invited—and they would be—I'd deal with it.

The only member of Dirty who wasn't here yet was Elle, our bass player and Jesse's ex-girlfriend. She was invited, of course, but wasn't in the wedding party, so she wasn't here for the rehearsal. She'd be arriving sometime tomorrow with the other guests. Awkward, sure, but this was Jesse and Katie's thing and that's just how it had to be.

I'd be checking in with Elle and I knew my partner, Maggie, would too, to make sure she was doing okay. But this was what it was.

Jesse was happy as fuck, he was marrying Katie, and Elle just had to deal.

As long as it didn't fuck with the music, we'd be fine.

Maggie had materialized to greet us, looking pretty as usual in a silky gray cocktail dress that matched her striking eyes, her dark hair slicked back in a ponytail. Even in her heels she was petite; I had to lean down to kiss her cheek. Despite the pretty package, Maggie was pure kick-ass. I'd never met anyone who could rally people and bend them to her will the way she could—not even Jude's security guys, and they often carried guns.

She showed us around the room, essentially a giant yet cozy banquet hall, with a massive fireplace at one end, opposite the towering windows overlooking the cove. She gave us the lowdown on where the ceremony would take place—in front of the windows— and showed us the stage toward the back of the hall where Zane's side project band, Wet Blanket, would play tomorrow night. The floor in the middle would be used for seating during the ceremony, then dinner, and later cleared for dancing. Right now it had a cluster of eight round tables set for the rehearsal dinner. The tables were lit with dozens of candles, chandeliers glowing above.

If Maggie ever decided to quit the music business, she could probably make a solid career as a wedding planner. I wasn't gonna tell her that, though; I needed Maggie taking on more work, not planning her escape. On paper, she was my assistant, which was fucking ridiculous. In reality, she did a lot more for all of us than her fair share. I'd been trying to officially promote her for years, but apparently she didn't want any more "responsibility." Which I translated as: *I already put up with enough of Zane's shit, don't make it any easier for him to abuse me.*

Katie's best friend, Devi, joined us, and the two of them chattered on for a while about wedding stuff. Jesse had given them a blank check to do whatever they wanted—meaning whatever Devi thought Katie would want, and what Katie wanted, evidently, was an intimate yet glamorous wedding in the Canadian wilderness. Glad no one asked me how to pull that off, but somehow, Maggie and Devi had.

The both of them had been obsessed with it over the past five months, calling me ten times a day with inane questions. I gave them the best answers I could, but really, I did not give the last shit about weddings. Weddings, and marriage in general, were, in my limited experience—as the child of not one but *three* ugly divorces—pretty much a farce.

I did give a shit about Jesse though, which was why I'd agreed to be one of his groomsmen when he asked. And what Jesse gave a shit about was Katie Bloom, that cute-as-all-hell girl in his arms with the dark hair and blue-green eyes. Apparently, the spoiled fuckwit she'd almost made the mistake of marrying a few years back—or rather, his fuckwit parents—had insisted on a big, grandiose summer wedding, but Katie had always dreamed of a cozy winter wedding. So a cozy winter wedding was what Jesse was giving her.

Pretty sure he'd give her any-fucking-thing, if she asked.

Thing about Katie was, she never asked. Which was one of the many things I liked about her. Refreshing change from the other women Jesse had dated over the years, who were, for the most part—other than Elle—opportunistic airheads.

The man was brilliant on guitar; not so brilliant in his choice of women.

When I saw him with Katie, though, I could say he'd finally gotten it right.

He was smiling ear-to-fucking-ear when they came off the dance floor; he let her go long enough to give me a bear hug, lifting me right off the floor. It struck me, when he smiled, how much he resembled his sister; the both of them kinda dorky as kids, all lanky and over-serious about music, now tall and statuesque, more than their fair share of beautiful, with their flawless, chiseled features, big, dazzling smiles and soulful brown eyes.

"Brody. About time you graced us with your presence. Had to stop and get a new tattoo on the way, brother?"

"Just a quick one, of Katie's name," I poked back.

Where normally he might've dropped me on my ass for that, he just laughed. Of course, he had Katie. He had Jessa. The two people he loved most in the world were here, and nothing was gonna piss on his parade.

Even my general aura of funk.

I gave Katie a hug and a kiss and told her she looked gorgeous, which she did. I'd been informed that she wasn't wearing a white dress for the wedding, so the little white cocktail dress she'd chosen for tonight was a nice touch. "Luckiest groom around," I told her, and she smiled her sweet, disarming smile at me.

Then I introduced Amanda around to Katie's family; I'd had a chance to meet them at the engagement party back in the fall. Nice people. Solid. Loved Jesse something fierce. And they took to Amanda right away, like everyone did.

Why wouldn't they?

Amanda was charming in a genuine way, and easy to talk to. Not to mention easy on the eyes. Definitely deserved better than some distracted asshole who couldn't even fucking see her.

Because the entire time I introduced her around the room, eventually landing at the bar where she got chatting with Katie's parents, playing on repeat at the back of my mind—actually, at the front of it —was: *Where the fuck is Jessa?*

Where. The Fuck. IS she.

I would've liked to believe myself when I explained to myself that my interest in the answer to that question was purely for Jesse's benefit. That as one of his best friends and groomsmen, not to mention his manager, it was my duty to help make sure this thing went off without a hitch, that Jesse was happy, that Katie got the wedding of her dreams; that as soon as they got back from their honeymoon, Jesse was going back into writing mode for the new album and it was important he not be distracted or dealing with the fallout of some bullshit family drama, courtesy of his disappearing-act of a sister... or some such shit.

But the truth was, I had to see her again.

Had to.

One glimpse of her, standing in the rain at the airport, her face tipped back as she grinned at the sky like she didn't have a fucking care in the world, wearing my shirt—or at least, a shirt that looked a fuck of a lot like a shirt I'd once had, that she'd been wearing the last time I saw it—and I was done.

Done.

Sitting all of two feet from her in my truck? I was well and truly fucked. Because I'd forgotten how many colors there were in those soulful dark eyes. Forgotten how fucking pretty she was; how painfully fucking pretty. And I could still see the little girl she once was in those eyes—the little girl who'd looked at me like I ruled the fucking world.

I could barely look at her, could barely fucking breathe—that smell of her, *fuck me*, the smell of her that hadn't changed in all the years since I'd met her, sweet and pure, like apples and blossoms and rain and fucking stardust and moonbeams; I couldn't say what it was, but yeah. All I could do was grip the wheel and concentrate on driving and just try to keep from foaming at the mouth when I lit into her—try to pretend that none of it mattered; all my pissed off, miles-deep frustrations; all the disappointment; all the repressed agony and the pent-up clusterfuck of rage... that none of it destroyed me at all... that *she* didn't destroy me, when she so fucking did... all of it, just broiling beneath the surface, ready to blow.

And her *voice*.

That fucking voice I hadn't heard in six-and-a-half years, melodic and soft and so fucking *her*.

I had never in my life had to jack off so badly that I pulled my vehicle off the road, onto the shoulder of a fucking highway, and took my cock out while cars blasted by and I did not give one fuck who saw me.

But I did just that.

Not five minutes after dropping her off with Jude, on my way to pick up Amanda... because no one needed to see me like that. So totally fucked up.

Christ, who does that?

A maniac, that's who.

And if I was a maniac, it was because Jessa Mayes, once upon a time, turned me into one. But shit happens, yeah? I was a kid then. Since then, I'd become a man. I wasn't gonna unravel at Jesse's wedding.

And I didn't.

I was good. I had this.

Until I heard her name, just somewhere in the ether, and I knew she was here.

Jessa.

Someone said it, somewhere, and I turned to look across the room like a dog tossed a scrap. Pretty sure I salivated. My wine glass broke in my hand. It made an audible popping sound, and both Amanda and I looked down to find the delicate bowl of the glass, still in my hand, cracked, wine dribbling out.

At least I wasn't bleeding.

"Omigosh," Amanda said, and grabbed a bunch of napkins from the bar to help me. "Um... I think you're supposed to finish drinking the wine *before* you break the glass." She smiled at me, then got the bartender to whisk the broken glass away and hand me a fresh one.

While I just stood there.

Staring across the room.

Because Jessa Mayes had just walked in wearing a dress that couldn't possibly be legal on that body.

Not that there was anything scandalous about the dress on its own. It was fitted to her goddess-like curves, but it was longish, ending just below the knee, the neckline dipping no lower than her collarbone, with half-sleeves. It wasn't exactly an upstaging-the-bride sort of dress. It wasn't white, slutty, or showing miles of leg— and Jessa Mayes had miles and miles of leg under that thing.

It was just what it did to my brain when I saw her in it.

It was made of what looked like thick, bunched-up silk. Not quite peach, not quite pink... salmon? Iced-rose-cantaloupe-sorbet? I had no idea what the fuck a chick would call it, but it was mother-fucking hot.

Along with her silky, slightly wavy hair that reached pretty much exactly to her nipples, worn smooth, the ends curled under and one side tucked behind a perfect ear, she looked like a screen siren out of some old black-and-white movie—but in vivid flesh tones, like some technicolor wet dream.

Hard to tell when I'd picked her up at the airport in that furry jacket, but now I could see how she'd changed since she went away —in all ways holy and good. As a little girl she was cute, a little dorky, scrappy, with her mane of wild brown hair and those big brown eyes. As a teenager, she got lithe and limber, swanned right out into an angel-faced beauty.

As a woman...

I'd seen photos of her these last six-and-a-half years. Professional photos from high-end shoots for major fashion brands. It was pathetic how often I'd searched her on the web, found new shots of her from some swimsuit shoot or lingerie campaign I hadn't yet seen, and saved them.

None of those photos came close to capturing what I was looking at right now.

Jessa's eyes found mine across the room... and that wide-eyed look of hers went straight to my dick.

Christ.

She turned away, hastily. Then she bent down to give Dolly a hug, giving me a first-rate view of her perfect, heart-shaped ass, and I just about broke another wine glass.

It was fucking official. The woman was trying to kill me.

Wasn't enough that I was dead to her; she was actually trying to end me.

As I watched her across the room the most fucked up thing was, after being that close to her again—close enough to breathe the same air, close enough to smell her, close enough to glimpse all those colors in her eyes—I'd probably let her.

I put the wine glass down on the bar and stared at my hand wrapped around it, afraid if I let go the whole thing would fall apart. Stared kind of blankly at the tattoo on the inside of my forearm, a single line of runes that read *abstinence.* A tattoo that only I, or someone who happened to know how to read ancient Germanic runic writing, would understand. And for the life of me I couldn't remember what it was supposed to mean or why the fuck I had it permanently inked into my arm, other than the fact that it had nothing to do with abstaining from alcohol or any other such substance—and a lot more to do with the goddess across the room in the silk-sorbet dress.

I let go of the wine glass and ordered up a beer from the bartender. Why the fuck was I drinking wine anyway? I didn't even like wine.

Amanda. Amanda liked wine.

My gaze fell to her. She was standing next to me, sipping her wine and watching me over the rim of her glass. It really wouldn't take a genius to match my line of sight to Jessa Mayes' ass and Amanda was far from stupid, so I wasn't even gonna pretend that wasn't where I was staring for the last half minute.

"That's Jesse's sister, right?" she asked lightly, like what I'd been staring at didn't bother her at all. But yeah, it did.

Because perfect, heart-shaped ass.

"Yeah," I said, trying to keep my tone business-neutral. Like, *Yeah, that's the sister of one my best friends, and isn't that nice she made it to the wedding? I haven't seen her, or even thought about her, in six-and-a-half years. Have you tried the crab cakes yet?*

No idea if Amanda knew me well enough yet to see through that shit. But she smiled softly and the uneasy, suddenly self-conscious look in her eyes made me feel like that much more of an ass. "Maybe you could introduce us?"

Yeah. I'd get right on that.

"Have you tried the crab cakes yet?" I asked her. "I'll get you some."

Then I took my beer and got the fuck out of there.

CHAPTER THREE

Jessa

THE REHEARSAL DINNER was served at five o'clock sharp; afterward, I was told, both the bride and the groom were being whisked away to their respective stag and stagette party. The food was amazing, the room was beautiful, and my brother wasn't even pissed that I'd missed the rehearsal. No one was.

Which kind of just made it worse.

Both Jesse and Katie were just so thrilled that I was here, I felt like such an ass for everything I'd ever done to make them think maybe I wouldn't be.

I was seated at their table along with Roni, Devi and Grandma Dolly, next to a table with Katie's family, which consisted of her parents, a sister named Becca, her husband Jack and their two children. Since Jesse and I had no family to speak of, it was truly lovely to see him so embraced by hers. They were warm and friendly people and Becca was hilarious, an older, more boisterous version of Katie.

But as nice as they all were, as welcoming as they were, as much as they tried to include me in conversation and asked all kinds of genuinely interested questions about me, about my life growing up with Jesse, about my time writing music with Dirty, and about my years as a model, I couldn't hold up my end of the conversation. I really, really tried. I tried to steer the conversation back to any one of them, any chance I got, to keep them talking, because I simply could not keep up a coherent line of thought.

How could I, when Brody was *right there*?

He was sitting across the room with his date, and all I could see was Brody talking, Brody laughing, with people who weren't me.

Brody with his serious blue eyes, with the laugh lines permanently etched at the corners.

Brody with the slightest glint of gray in the hair at his temples, which I'd only noticed up close, in his truck, in the daylight. Brody who hadn't bothered to color his hair, who didn't give a shit his hair was beginning to turn gray at age thirty, because why would he? Brody would be gorgeous gray-haired or bald.

Brody with his short-sleeve button-down shirt and his rocker's tattoos, the mashup of business-meets-pleasure that had always done me in. His sleeves rolled up to reveal the same tribal guitar tattoo he'd had on his left bicep at fifteen, a bicep which was now larger, the guitar surrounded by tribal symbols that swirled down his arm in a partial sleeve. The same *grace* tattoo, spelled out in Danish runes, that he'd had on the left side of his neck at eighteen. And a tattoo of runic letters spelling something I couldn't read down the inside of his right forearm.

I wondered if Amanda knew what those runes said. And there was something so devastating in imagining her knowing, and seeing his tattoos up close, touching them... like she was accessing some intimate part of him that I had never been able to touch.

I should've just looked away, but my eyes kept landing back on him.

On her.

She was very... compact. Muscular, in a good way. Apparently, she was a yoga instructor with her own yoga space in Kitsilano; I'd learned more about her than I ever cared to know in casual conversation over pre-dinner drinks. Vancouver was lousy with yoga instructors and yet I couldn't even quietly roll my eyes.

So she was all Zen and fit and flexible and had her own business.

She had Brody.

And even if I didn't envy her Zen or her flexibility, there was always something to envy, and something to loathe, about a woman who was with the man you secretly wanted for yourself. So I let myself envy her, and loathe her.

And then I tried to forget her.

It wasn't easy.

I did not know how Elle did it. Watching the man you always thought you'd end up with in the arms of someone else. I'd met up with Elle a few times for drinks while I was in L.A. these last few months and I knew she was still hurting over the breakup with my brother, even if she didn't say so; she didn't have to.

At least Brody wasn't marrying this one.

I took a glass of the port that was offered after dinner, even though I didn't particularly like port. Would it be wrong to get blind drunk at my brother's wedding in hopes of blacking out and forgetting the whole thing entirely?

Yeah. Most definitely.

Which meant I was just going to have to grow the hell up and deal with the fact that Brody had moved on. Which, as it turned out, was a really hard pill to swallow.

I knew he wasn't mine. Had never really been mine.

But that didn't mean some selfish part of me, deep down—or maybe not that deep down—didn't still want him. And want him to want me.

Which, until a few hours ago, I actually thought he did.

How stupid was I?

Somehow I'd convinced myself that when I went away, everything had stayed the same. Including Brody's feelings for me, as evidenced by his continued text messages and voicemails over the years. But clearly, that wasn't true. A lot of things had changed.

Even the band had changed without me.

Seth Brothers, Dirty's original rhythm guitarist, was long gone.

Zane had stopped drinking. That was a big one; he'd gone into rehab soon after I left the band, after Seth was kicked out because of his drug addiction, and managed to stick it out.

And my brother... he was so, so happy. Not that he wasn't happy before. Jesse had always been a pretty happy guy. Like me and like our dad he was prone to brooding, but unlike the both of us, Jesse's periods of brooding were usually brief and few and far between, and he tended to bounce back to happiness without the traumas of life making much of a dent. He was more like our mom that way—at least, how she was before Dad died.

But this... this was different. This was the kind of happiness that only the truest, deepest, most lasting type of love could bring.

So maybe it was only me who'd failed to change.

As Roni and I mingled over post-dinner drinks I watched my brother with Katie across the room, chatting with Brody and the lovely Amanda, all four of them smiling, laughing, and looking happy. No; happy wasn't even the word. Joyful. Brimming with life and love. The way you looked when you were surrounded by the life you belonged in. And how fucking jealous I was, of all of them.

Because it was supposed to be me standing over there, with them; not her.

It was always supposed to be me.

My brother had always dated around and never seemed intent on settling down; not until Katie suddenly came into his life. Meanwhile, I just knew I'd fall in love and get married and look as happy as my brother looked right now, and my husband would look at me the way he was looking at Katie. I'd be the perfect wife. I'd make my husband happy and he'd never even think of leaving me.

That was my little girl fantasy.

Oh, and in that fantasy? My husband was Brody.

As I watched him across the room with another woman by his side, a woman that—who knew?—maybe he *would* marry, I realized I couldn't even be upset about it. I had no right to be. Because I was the one who'd let him go.

He was right; I ran away.

However... that didn't mean that when I saw Amanda hop up on her tippy-toes to say something in his ear and lingeringly kiss his cheek, I totally kept my cool. No. In fact, I lost it.

Big time.

As in my knees started to give out and I reached back, grabbing onto what I was sure was a sturdy but empty banquet table to sit my ass down—and sat my ass right in the cake.

The ladies around me gave a collect gasp... and wouldn't it be just perfect if Brody chose that moment to look over?

Yeah. He did.

Maggie grabbed my arm and hauled me up and I turned, mortified, to find a dent in the shape of my butt, dead-center in the cake. Some of it had slopped over the edge of the table and smushed down my leg. There was icing in my open-toed pumps.

At least—thank God—it wasn't *the* cake. As in, the wedding cake.

This was just a simple, single-layer thing that had been set out alongside a mountain of other dainties, and in my Brody-induced daze, I'd failed to notice the catering staff setting up behind me. Nobody would even miss this cake, I told myself.

The cake, I told myself, would be a multi-tiered deal that would be served tomorrow, after the ceremony, and would be so big there's no way I could fail to see it and accidentally back my ass up into it.

"Shit," I said, because really, what else could I say?

"Look at me." Maggie got in my face as the attention of the room converged on my icing-coated ass. "Don't worry about it. You should be charging for that service. It's a great ass." Then she snickered and yanked me from the room.

I did not look back.

Since I had icing and cake smeared all down my leg and inside my Manolo Blahniks, I kicked off my shoes, did my best to wipe them out with some damp toilet paper and set them to dry. Then I got in the shower. I turned on the water and let it pummel my backside until my dress was cake-free.

It looked like the butter in the icing was going to leave grease stains, which was a damn shame, because I loved this dress. It was a gorgeous, pale coral—my favorite color.

I peeled it off and cleaned the rest of me off, lamenting my inability to get through a couple of hours in Brody Mason's presence without doing something lame. It was as if, when I'd climbed into his truck at the airport, I'd travelled back in time... and regressed into a complete and utter dork.

I was just stepping out of the shower and wrapping myself in a towel when Roni strolled into the bathroom with a freshly-opened bottle of wine. Since Maggie had stagette party business to attend to, she'd tasked Roni with walking me back to our cabin to help me clean up. Though Roni's idea of helping was pretty much helping herself to the fridge in my room.

"Why are you acting like a freak?" she asked, leaning back against the sink and taking a swig of wine.

"Huh? Oh. No reason. You know, sometimes I'm clumsy."

"Right. How about a tall, blue-eyed reason who keeps trading fuck-me stares with you across the room."

"What?" I feigned utter confusion. "What blue-eyed...?"

"'Fuck me'... 'No, fuck you'... 'Uh-uh, not if I fuck you first'... Does any of this sound about right? I mean, I wasn't exactly involved in the conversation. Just a witness. But I'm pretty sure that's more or less how it went."

"Fuck-me stares...? I don't even know what you're talking—"

"Save it, Mayes," she said. "Never bullshit a bullshitter." Then she turned to fluff up her hair in the mirror. "Better move that ass. We've got a stagette to attend. Although if you wanna go fuck Brody, I found a closet at the lodge that would do and I can cover for you. Just don't take too long. I wanna call dibs on one of the strippers, if they're fuckable, before the other girls do. I've got some chocolate lube in my bag if you want some."

I looked at her like she was loony. Which maybe she was.

My brother's friends hadn't nicknamed her "wild card" years ago for nothing, and apparently, the nickname still fit. Because now all I could picture was Brody Mason's dick, slathered in chocolate-flavored lube.

Not that I'd ever seen Brody's dick. But I had felt it up against me—hard and ready—enough times over the years, I had a pretty good idea of what he was packing.

Roni grinned triumphantly.

"Um, no," I mumbled. "I'm good."

"I also have peach," she said. "They're sugar-free."

"No, thanks."

"And strawberry."

I sighed and pointed toward the door. "Still no."

Roni rolled her eyes and said, "Boring." Then she handed me a clean pair of shoes and strutted out.

CHAPTER FOUR

Jessa

AFTER DESSERT, Devi ran through the details of tomorrow's wedding ceremony with me—and with Brody and Jude, who were also in the wedding party but had missed the rehearsal. Because of me. Which was horribly uncomfortable, since Brody was dead to me and all, which apparently meant he wasn't talking to me or even acknowledging my existence.

Fun.

At least I could thank God for small favors when I learned I wasn't paired up with him in the wedding. He'd be escorting Katie's sister, Becca, down the aisle, while I'd been paired up with Zane.

When that was done, Devi and Becca hustled all the ladies under thirty-five off to Jesse and Katie's luxury cabin, which they'd decorated for Katie's stagette. The cabin itself was huge, with a loft for the master bedroom and a wraparound deck—a weirdly fitting combo of rustic and posh, with exposed wood, giant windows, designer furniture and a giant, three-tiered deer antler chandelier, dripping with crystals, in the center. If Kanye West had a cabin in the great white north, this would be it.

"Wow," Roni remarked as she sauntered into the middle of the room and gazed up at the glittering chandelier. "There are a *lot* of rubber dicks in this room."

There were. Aside from the penis-shaped balloons that were dangling on ribbons from the chandelier, there was an anatomically-correct male blow-up doll laid out on the dining table, serving as a sushi platter, penis party trays filled with snacks, and penis drinking straws standing in the cocktail glasses along the bar.

There was also a handsome gentleman with slicked-back hair and large, perhaps steroid-induced biceps, standing behind the bar in a sleeveless tuxedo shirt, mixing drinks.

Devi rolled her eyes a little. "You can thank Becca for that."

"You're welcome," Katie's sister said. "I put myself in charge of penis-shaped party favors."

"Katie's just kissing her man goodbye," Devi informed us, "which could take a while, obvs. When she comes in, the order of business is girl talk and drinking."

"And not necessarily in that order," Becca put in.

"Where're the strippers, though?" Roni turned in a slow circle, like she expected a bunch of oiled-up, g-string-clad hunks to pop out of the woodwork any second. "Please tell me you got strippers."

"Katie wants girl talk," Devi said as she started handing out cocktails, "so that's what we're going to give her. Tomorrow will be a little difficult for her, so get yourselves lushed up and let's make her feel the love."

Difficult?

Why would it be difficult?

Before I could inquire about that, Roni asked, "Where're the guys going?"

And I was glad she did, because it was kind of killing me that I didn't even know where Brody was and Amanda most certainly did. She'd probably just kissed him goodbye.

I glanced at her face, like I might see traces of him there, evidence of the kisses he'd given her only moments ago. She caught my eye and smiled.

I tried to smile back.

Holy hell, this was going to be awkward.

But I could fake my way through it, right? I was pretty much a professional faker. Act like these ugly-ass panties are the hottest undies ever designed? No problem, I'm your girl. Look happy and sexy while frolicking in the waves on an ice-cold beach? Do it all the time.

Pretend it's no biggie to share some girlie bonding time with the woman who's sleeping with the man of your dreams tonight?

Easy-fucking-peasy, right?

Fuck.

"The guys are hopping into helicopters," Devi was saying as I sipped my frothy strawberry daiquiri through a penis straw. "They're taking off up the coast to some remote rescue service cabin. Some guy Brody knows is letting them use it." She waved her hand in the air, like this was redundant. "You know, Brody knows everyone."

"They're gonna chop fire wood or throw logs or some such shit," Becca explained. "You know, be manly."

"We should've gone up there," Roni said, shooting me a look over her drink.

"You," Devi said, pointing her finger at Katie's niece, Sadie, "get one drink from the nice bartender man, and then you're going to bed."

"Why?" Sadie whined.

"Because," Roni answered, "after that your mommy and aunt Katie and aunt Devi are gonna talk about penises, and they don't want you to hear it."

"Yucky!" Sadie cried.

"*Roni,*" I warned her.

"What?" Roni shrugged. "She's like ten. She knows what a penis is."

"She's seven," Becca said, "and yes, she does."

"Why are you talking about penises?" Sadie asked her mom, horrified.

"Because sometimes," Becca said, handing her daughter a virgin cocktail, "that's what mommies do."

"Have any of you hooked up with a member of Dirty?" Becca asked, all giggly and flushed. "I mean, besides Katie."

I bit my lip and made a weird hiccuping-gagging noise before bringing my penis straw to my lips and sucking on my daiquiri.

Everyone looked at me.

We'd all been lushed up with a few drinks by now. Sadie had been carried off to bed by her mom a while ago, and Becca had quickly returned, jubilant to be kid-free for the night. Then all seven of us had changed into our bikinis, which Devi had instructed us to bring, and piled into the massive hot tub in front of the big, round window overlooking the cove, frosted cocktails in hand, and got to drinking.

Roni suggested we go in naked, but the rest of us vetoed that.

Beck's "Dreams" was getting us in the party mood as it pumped over the surround sound system, and spirits were high. The nice bartender man was keeping the open bar, courtesy of my brother, flowing. And even though he seemed to be keeping an eye on us—because really, seven bikini-clad girls drinking in a hot tub—as did the big dude Jude had assigned to stand inside the front door and look surly, we forgot about them, more or less, and got to the girl talk.

It started on a casual note, chatting about how happy we were for Katie and her big day tomorrow, about our dresses and how we were going to wear our hair... which led to those who didn't know the scoop asking for the details on how Katie and my brother hooked up... which led straight to sex.

"Yeah, I really don't need to hear about my brother's sex life," I'd put in, which was probably a mistake. I would've much rather heard about my brother's sex life than answered Becca's question.

In the wake of that question, everyone had gotten really, really quiet, and Katie's eyes went wide.

Devi looked intrigued.

Maggie looked like she needed another drink.

"Oh, this night just got interesting," Roni said.

Katie eyed me across the hot tub. I avoided her gaze, suddenly fascinated with the sugar crystals on the rim of my daiquiri. "Jessa?" she asked sweetly. "You ever hooked up with anyone we might just love to know about?"

"Hooked up? What do you mean, hooked up?" I tried to look as incredibly blank as possible. Or possibly drunk. So I couldn't be expected to keep up.

"Hooked. Up. It's a universal definition," Becca said. "Meaning any part of his body down your pants."

"Or up your skirt," Roni added.

Okay. Safe there.

"Wrong," Katie said. "Kissing is hooking up. I'm the bride here. I make the rules."

Uh-oh.

"We know Jesse's out," she added with a grin when I didn't respond. "So that leaves Zane or Dylan."

"Or Elle," Roni put in helpfully.

Yup. That girl was all kinds of helpful. Which was kind of why I liked her; Roni nudged me out of my comfort zone. If she had to, she'd kick me the hell out of it. Right now, though, it was a little more than inconvenient.

"I don't think I'm her cup of tea," I offered.

"Please," Roni said. "Bikini model much? You're everyone's cup of tea."

I rolled my eyes.

"Does Brody count?" Amanda inquired, sipping her drink and not looking at me.

"Brody's not in the band," Devi pointed out.

"Hells yes, Brody counts!" Maggie put it. "I need some dirt on that man. If any of you besides Amanda have hooked up with Brody, I wanna know."

"As do I," Amanda said, sounding half-intrigued, half-apprehensive, and still not looking at me.

"C'mon Jessa." Katie's words were starting to slur. "'Fess up. Any Dirty romances in your past? Or present?"

Now everyone was looking at me again.

Even Amanda was looking at me.

"I hooked up with Zane," Roni announced. This news was greeted with a collective gasp of delight, tinged with perverse curiosity.

Roni didn't know much about my history with Brody, though obviously she'd picked up on *something* tonight, and maybe she'd felt the need to save me. Or maybe she felt like bragging. Maybe she was just bored and trying to get this chat moving along. But I wasn't exactly relieved she'd spoken up.

Not when I caught the look on Maggie's face. She tried to hide it behind her giant cocktail glass, but it was there in her eyes—the same thing I felt when I saw Brody with Amanda.

Stone cold envy... and just that little bit of loathing.

Maggie and I had been friends for a long time. I knew she had a crush on Zane, years ago; or at least, she pretended it was years ago. But I'd seen the guarded way she looked at him tonight, and I'd suffered enough longing over the years, over a man who wasn't mine, to understand that look. And while I knew Maggie wasn't really the type to act on that attraction, or whatever it was, because of how seriously she took her job with the band, I knew it couldn't exactly be fun for her to come face-to-face with women who *had* acted on their attraction to Zane... which I was pretty sure she did on a regular basis.

Zane had always been a slut.

"Was it... good?" Katie inquired.

"Of course it was good," Becca said. "Look at him."

"Shit, yeah, it was good," Roni said, thrilled with her rapt audience. "He does this thing with his tongue and his middle finger—"

"Jessa had a crush on Jude."

Shit. My gaze swung back to Maggie; never saw that one coming.

"Jude!" Katie exclaimed.

Sorry, Maggie mouthed at me, looking guilty for throwing me under the bus.

"It was a long time ago," I explained, before the blushing bride got all excited about the prospect of Jesse's best friend and I getting hitched and our babies playing together.

"I would so do Jude," Becca said.

Katie rolled her eyes at her sister. "Um, married much?"

"If I wasn't married," she clarified. "Do you think he does couples?"

"Oh, Jesus," Katie groaned. "TMI."

"Whatever." Devi shushed them. "I want to know what happened with Jessa and Jude."

"Nothing happened," I said. "From what I gathered, I wasn't his type."

Roni rolled her eyes. "Again. Everyone's type."

"What's his type?" Becca asked.

"Well... back then, he was fourteen years old and as far as I could tell, his type was voluptuous sixteen-year-olds. I was ten. I definitely never caught his eye." I shrugged. "That was such a long time ago... I almost forgot about it."

That was true, more or less.

And while Roni proceeded to regale the girls with detailed accounts of the other famous guys she'd had sex with—there were several of them, apparently—I zoned out, recalling exactly what it was that made me forget my crush on Jude. I could remember the day, the very moment Jude was forgotten.

The moment Brody came back into my life.

I was half-in and half-out of my new bra. It was my first bra, which my brother had discovered I needed after the first day of fifth grade, when Zane walked me home from school and bluntly announced, in typical Zane fashion, "You'd better get your sister's tits under wrap or you're gonna have a world of problems on your hands this year."

Hence a particularly embarrassing shopping trip with my four-teen-year-old brother to get my first bra.

I was trying to put it on, attempting to untangle the straps and figure out how I was supposed to do it up behind my back—or was I supposed to do it up, then spin it around?—when someone walked into my bedroom. I looked up, and there was Brody.

I was ten years old, so it's not like what I was trying to put in my new bra was all that impressive, but still. Naked boobs were kinda hard to miss, especially if you were a teenage boy. Which was maybe why he was staring at me.

I hadn't seen him since that day on the playground two years before. I never really expected to see him again. To my imaginative young mind, Brody Mason was an entity as magical and illusive as a unicorn, a fire-breathing dragon, or Eddie Vedder.

But there he was.

In my room.

"You're supposed to knock!" I cried, covering myself with my skinny arms.

"Why would I knock on the bathroom door when it's open?" he said, belatedly covering his eyes with his hand.

"Because it's not the bathroom!"

"I see that, princess. Maybe close the door next time you decide to get naked."

Princess?

He remembered me?!

"I'm not naked!" I shouted. "And you're supposed to knock on a bedroom door! Even if it's open!"

"I thought it was the bathroom!"

"Unless you plan to take a piss in my My Little Pony Show Stable," I screamed at him, "get the fuck out!"

Yes, in my panic, I'd dropped an F-bomb. It was the first time I'd ever done it, too. Because my brother and his friends used the F-word all the time I'd taken a stand against it, but not even my brother had ever made me that mad—or embarrassed. And yes, I had a My Little Pony Show Stable. It was faded and pink and sat at Brody's feet; before he'd died, my dad had often scavenged such treasures for me on his daily route as a trash collector.

It never had a pony to go with it, but I liked it anyway.

Brody's hand dropped from his face. He stood there in his faded

Weezer T-shirt, his ripped jeans and dirty sneakers, and grinned at me.

I would later find out that despite how he dressed, Brody came from a wealthy family. His father was self-made, the CEO of some plastics empire who was too busy battling environmentalists, counting his millions and managing his multiple affairs to find time for his son. His mom was little more than a trophy wife, too busy popping pills to care. As a boy Brody acted up in school, probably in an effort to get their attention, and even though he was so smart he'd ended up flunking seventh grade at his posh private school. His parents then dumped him into the public school system, which in their minds was probably some sort of punishment. And big surprise, he just kept disappointing them. The incident at my school, where he'd made a couple of fifth-graders eat shit (I would've sworn it was mud, but no one bothered to ask me at the time) was the final straw. After that, his parents yanked him out of school and sent him to a military academy on the other side of the country for the next two years.

He'd just returned to start ninth grade with my brother's class, already had a tattoo, and since he was obviously totally badass (and not just because he had a tattoo), Zane had immediately recruited him to their group.

None of which was knowledge to me in that moment.

I just stood there freaking out, completely at a loss as to why the universe was punishing me by depositing the coolest boy I'd ever met in my house, in my bedroom, when I had my new boobs out.

"See you around, princess," he said. Then he turned and sauntered out.

I ran after him and slammed the door behind him as hard as I could.

To my surprise, after that day, I did see him around. A lot.

And my crush on Jude?

What crush.

I'd never known a crush until fifteen-year-old Brody Mason sauntered back into my life, smiled at me, and called me princess.

From that day on I was ruined, *ruined* for every other male on the planet.

I was his.

Even if he didn't know it.

I took a breath, took a sip of my daiquiri, and decided not to share that particular story with the girls in the hot tub. Even if Amanda wasn't here, I wouldn't have shared that story.

My memories of Brody, good or bad, were mine. They were all I had, but at least they would always be mine; even if I had nothing else.

Memories, and a T-shirt.

CHAPTER FIVE

Jessa

SOMETIME LATER, the sexy bartender man was getting his flirt on with Roni—*and* Becca—and Maggie had started taking bets on who was going to make out with him before the night was through. Hopefully not Becca, since that probably wouldn't go over too well with her husband.

We were all gathered around on the designer couches in front of the big fireplace, and there was a general speculation going on about how much fun we were actually going to get away with having here.

Was the bartender just a spy? On Jude's security payroll? No one seemed sure. Not even Maggie.

Then the volume of the music went up. Way up. Ludacris' "What's Your Fantasy" started pumping through the room. The lights, rather suspiciously, dimmed. And the bartender, as he continued to make drinks, started to dance.

As it turned out, he was a pretty great dancer. Or rather, stripper.

Kind of reminded me of Channing Tatum's panty-wetting performance to "Pony" in *Magic Mike XXL*... but with liquor bottles instead of power tools.

"Does my brother know about this?" I asked, sipping my drink and trying to contain my laughter as the women around me dissolved into a whole lot of giggling, squealing and gasping.

"Who do you think paid for it?" was Devi's response.

We watched the dude peel off his clothes—all of them—to the rest of the song... at the climax of which he stirred—yes, stirred—the drink he'd just mixed with his semi-hard dick. Which was all kinds of wrong and yet, somehow, weirdly hot. Stress the weirdly. Most of us laughed until we cried. And *Jesus*, that felt good. When was the last time I'd laughed this hard?

Too fucking long ago.

Devi slipped a hefty tip in the stripper's little bowtie, which was the only thing he was still wearing. I didn't think Katie even looked. She was too busy stuffing a pillow in her face.

"Okay, ladies," Becca announced, holding the drink high in the air. "I've got two young kids, which means I don't get out much, therefore, I'm milking the shit out of this night. Which means whichever one of you tries to disappear to pass out first gets woken up—and you get to drink the dick drink."

"You mean the *cock*tail," Maggie put in, to a round of snickers.

"Look out," Katie warned her sister. "At the rate you're going it'll be you."

Then Roni stepped up, took the drink from Becca's hand, and unceremoniously downed it.

All of it.

After that, it was pretty clear all bets were off, and the party mood pretty much launched into the stratosphere. Which, if I knew Roni, was her intention.

Wild. Card.

The stripper, who'd managed to pull his g-string back on, dragged a chair into the middle of the room and beckoned Katie to it. Katie obediently took the seat of honor—after some cajoling—with her hands fixed firmly over her face.

"Oh, shit, you have to look," Becca told her. "You really have to look."

"I can't." Katie peeked out between her fingers, eying the security guy, who'd left his post by the door and was strolling toward her chair... just as the sexy, angsty, slow-grinding lament of The Weeknd's "The Hills" kicked in. "What about the security guy?" she stage-whispered, like he couldn't hear her.

"What, that guy?" Devi reclined back on the couch, tossed her pedicured feet up, and smiled.

Which was when our security guy—or more accurately, stripper number two—busted out some sexy-smooth dance moves... and started shedding his shirt.

After that, things got messy. Fast.

There was more drinking, a lot more dancing, a little more stripping—and not just by the strippers—and a lot of acting like drunken fools. There we were, a bunch of (somewhat) sophisticated women, between us a handful of established careers, money in the bank, even a couple of children... partying like it was our first spring break.

Which was when Brody walked in.

His blue eyes landed on me, where I was lounging with Katie on one of the couches, tonguing a Jell-O shot from a dick-shaped shot glass. I swallowed and smiled, because, well... I was kind of drunk.

He was followed closely by Jude and Zane, who strutted right on in... making it pretty clear it was their plan to crash our party all along. "Your men have arrived," Zane announced as he and Jude struck bodybuilder poses.

Next to me, a drunk bride-to-be erupted in giggles.

I would've laughed myself, and maybe thrown some pretzels at them, if I wasn't so busy watching the other little display going on. Namely Amanda, in her bikini top and low hipster jeans that showed off her tight, muscular butt, throwing herself into Brody's arms. Brody's arms, which went around Amanda. I watched, transfixed, as he spread his hands on her bare back, the thorny vines of his rose tattoo in my face.

And I wanted to trace every one of those vines with my tongue... taste every last inch of his tattooed skin.

Since I was pleasantly buzzed, this desire rose up hot and fast, unchecked, uncensored. I felt the rush of saliva in my mouth. I felt the butterflies in my stomach and the throb between my legs. There was no denying it.

Why bother?

I wanted to rub every part of me against every part of Brody Mason. Naked.

And I definitely wanted his hands off Amanda.

I wanted them on me.

I wanted his mouth off her, too, but she was up on her tiptoes again and he was leaning down to meet the kiss she was bent on giving him, and I had to look away.

There was only so much torture I could take.

Zane had sat down on the couch across from me, between Maggie and Becca. He threw an arm on the back of the couch behind each of them, his thighs spread wide in his shredded jeans. Which Becca seemed to enjoy. Maggie, on the other hand... I really couldn't tell.

He watched the floor show with us, which at the moment featured one of the strippers, naked, showing Roni some graphic thrusting moves. "Are chicks really into this?" he asked, like he was genuinely curious.

"Oh, yeah," Becca said, sipping her drink.

Katie giggled and looked elsewhere. I didn't think our guest of honor had even seen a dick all night, unlike the rest of us who couldn't seem to look up without getting smacked in the eyeball with one. We watched as the stripper lay Roni on the floor and dry-humped her, naked. Well... he was naked. She was still wearing her incredibly tiny bikini.

They could've been having full-on penetrative sex and we probably couldn't tell the difference.

"Okay," Zane said. "I think I get it now."

"Hot. Damn," said a male voice behind me. I glanced up; Dylan and Ash had arrived, and Ash was making a beeline for the front row.

"What's *his* deal?" Becca asked, checking out Ash in all his inky-haired, tattooed and pierced glory, as he checked out the show.

"Huh?" Zane said, distracted. "Oh. Ash is into dudes."

"Oh my God," Becca gasped, like she'd just been told unicorns were real. "*Really?*"

"Yeah. Chicks too, though."

"Really." Becca sipped her cocktail, eying the Pushers' lead singer over the rim of her glass. "Do you think he'd strip for us?"

"Say one more thing like that and I'm telling Jack," Katie threatened in her slurry, happy voice.

Becca eyed her sister. "We've been together eighteen years, little sister, you think my husband doesn't know what a perv I am?"

Just then, Becca's husband, Jack, walked in with my brother, and it was pretty clear he knew exactly what kind of perv his wife was when he took one look at the scene, collected her from the couch and backed her straight up into the kitchen—where they proceeded to make out against the fridge.

I watched for a minute without meaning to, but when his hand went up her skirt, I looked away.

"What is this noise?" My brother's eyes were bright with drink, a big, sloppy-happy grin on his face as he stuck a finger in his ear and wiggled it around like it was hurting.

This noise was Nelly, "Hot in Herre," the cabin was currently throbbing with it, and it *was* getting hot in here.

"What?" Katie protested. "I like it!"

My brother's eyes locked on his fiancée... and her white bikini top... and her skimpy cutoffs. Katie's cheeks flushed as he stalked over and dropped to his knees on the couch, kneeling over her. He then proceeded to strip off his shirt, to the music, his performance met by a bunch of drunken hooting and hollering.

"You like it?" he asked, his eyes only for Katie as he leaned in... making her lean back until I scooted out of the way. I didn't even think he saw me as he pinned Katie down and started giving her tongue like there was no one else in the room. Before I could fully process what was happening, he slid his hand up her side, right up under her bikini top and squeezed her breast.

"And that's my cue to get some air," I announced, to no one in particular.

As Katie moaned into my brother's mouth, I grabbed my furry jacket and headed for the patio doors. Unlike some of the girls, I was fully dressed. And maybe I was a little drunk, but as I pulled on my boots I definitely felt the dynamic shifting in the room.

Zane and Maggie were looking pretty cozy on the couch, his arm around her as they shared some kind of intense, whispered conversation. His ring-laden hand was on her bare thigh, his thumb smoothing back and forth beneath the hem of her skirt.

Roni was dancing on the coffee table, sandwiched between a shirtless stripper and a now-shirtless Ash. Ash had his hands on her ass, and while I watched, he leaned in with hooded eyes to kiss her, their mouths coming together in a slow burn.

Becca and Jack had retreated into a shadowy corner. I could see her fingers digging into the back of his neck as they made out. Her leg was wrapped around his hip, his hand still up her skirt... and I definitely heard her mewling little sex noises as I rushed by.

At least Brody had vanished; the last I saw Amanda, she was lounging in a recliner, alone, laughing and fanning herself with a wad of cocktail napkins as she watched Roni twerking it up between two shirtless studs.

I didn't even want to know what my brother was doing to Katie, but I giggled to myself as I stepped outside, overcome with that giddy, slightly envious feeling you can't really help but feel in the presence of all-consuming infatuation. *Jesus*, though. *Get a room.*

Well, it was their cabin. So technically, the rest of us were the pervy voyeurs crashing their pre-wedding sex time.

I walked around the corner of the wraparound deck, still smiling, and ran into Jude. "Hi!" I said brightly. The many cocktails I'd enjoyed had left me pretty damn giddy and really, all these happy, groping couples and swinging dicks, along with the feeling that everyone here, except me, was probably getting laid tonight, was making me feel like an awkward teenager at a party I didn't belong at.

Been there before.

Jude was on his phone, but he flashed his gorgeous grin at me as I walked on by. "Don't go far, bratface."

"Yes, sir." I rolled my eyes, even though he couldn't see it.

Bratface. There was one nickname I hadn't missed. Except that I kind of had.

I'd missed everything about my old friends.

Now that I was here, among them again—and I'd had enough booze to let my guard down a bit, and enough fun to start to remember how much fun we used to have—I could admit it to myself.

I'd missed them all, like crazy.

I wound my way around the deck and down a flight of stairs to the boardwalk in the near-dark. Then I burst into laughter in the fresh, coastal rainforest air under the stars. Seemed like a good idea. Therapeutic, even. A hell of a lot better than crying, which I would've thought I'd be more likely to be doing this weekend.

Then I heard a creak on the boardwalk. I turned around.

Brody was standing in the shadows, about three feet from where I'd just had my one-woman giggle fit. I'd almost walked right into him in the dark.

"Uh... hey," I said, breathing through the last of my laughter and choking a giggle back.

He just stared at me, his eyes seeming to glitter in the dark. Amused, maybe. Still pissed off, probably. I really couldn't tell.

So I shrugged and said, "So... dicks waving all over the place... not your thing?"

"Could do without," he said.

"Yeah. Um... me, too."

Then silence fell between us, fast.

I wanted to say more. There were six-and-a-half years' worth of things to say, and not one of them came to my lips. Instead, I pictured his hands on Amanda's bare back as she stretched up on her toes to kiss him.

"I guess, I'll... uh... just leave you..."

I started to turn away—but the next thing I knew, he'd grabbed me by my waist and yanked me against him. Hard. Our hips slammed together; so hard I felt the firm package in his jeans. My chest squashed against his and his warmth sank into me. His warmth and his smell... his musky, manly smell, a smell that had always reminded me of fresh air and deep, green woods, and still did, even when we were surrounded by both.

My heart pumped against his as I drew a shaky breath, my hands settling on his shoulders. I didn't push him off. My fingers, involuntarily, dug into his jacket.

I looked up into the dark of his eyes. He was scowling at me.

"You have any idea what you almost did?" he growled.

I swallowed thickly. "Wh—what?"

He jerked his chin, glancing over my shoulder. I looked back; over the edge of the boardwalk behind me... and into the abyss.

An ice-cold shiver prickled through me. There was no handrail behind me. None.

I'd almost backed right off the boardwalk.

The sudden sensation of tumbling into the dark, my body breaking on the rocks below, tore through me... and a chill shuddered up my spine, accompanied by a wave of nausea.

I'd be dead. If it wasn't for Brody's quick reflexes. If it wasn't for his strength. If it wasn't for him holding me right now, tight against him, I'd be dead on the rocks below.

I peered uneasily into the dark.

Okay, maybe not dead? I really couldn't tell how far it was down there, or what lay below. For all I knew it could be three feet to a bed of soft moss. But there were snarls of branches poking up out of the black, and I definitely wouldn't have escaped unscathed.

At the very least, he'd saved me from scrapes, bruises and embarrassment.

At worst...

I swallowed again, peering up into his eyes. They were in shadow, but I could just make out the dark pools of his irises as he looked back at me. His breathing wasn't right; it was quick and shallow, like mine. I watched in a daze as his full lips parted. He drew a deep breath, his chest rising against mine. I thought he was going to say something...

He didn't.

He didn't let go of me, either. His fingers curled, digging into my waist.

And a voice in my head said, *Just kiss him.*

It came out of nowhere. Well... maybe it came on the wings of those last few Jell-O shots I'd done with the girls. *Just tell him you're sorry*, it said.

Just tell him you miss him.

Tell him... everything.

But I didn't do any of those things.

"Thanks," I managed to whisper, my voice hoarse.

Brody said nothing. His mouth shut and his eyebrows furled. He still looked pissed, but there was something else in the shadows of his eyes. Concern?

Like maybe he would've cared if I'd just plummeted to my death?

So that was something.

Tell him you love him.

I opened my mouth, unsure of what would come out—but then he released me. He stepped back, shoving his hands in his pockets, as if to assure me—or himself—he wouldn't touch me again.

"Use the fucking handrail," he said gruffly, nodding toward the rail on the other side of the boardwalk, where the twinkly lights were strung.

"Right."

Then he turned and walked away.

I hugged myself, moving over toward the rail, still unnerved by my near-tumble into the dark... and even more unnerved by the feel of Brody's hard body against mine.

After a few steps, he stopped. He shook his head once, then suddenly turned back. "I owe you an apology," he said, not looking at my face.

"You do?"

"Yeah. You know, for kidnapping you. And generally being an asshole." He glanced at me briefly, then added, "I'm just looking out for Jesse," like that made it okay.

Maybe it did.

I knew the depth of friendship he had with my brother, the kind of friendship that had endured many years and many ups and downs; the kind of friendship I'd never really had with anyone, because I'd always been so afraid to let anyone get close.

I just stood there, hugging myself against the breeze coming up off the water, and breathed, "Okay."

Brody nodded shortly, then walked away. I opened my mouth to say something else, anything, but he was gone. He went back up to the party, leaving me standing there alone in the dark with his words... the music throbbing through the night echoing the throb of my heart.

I'm just looking out for Jesse.

I clung to the railing, grateful for the support. It was stunning how deeply it cut me to hear those words, to know that Brody was no longer looking out for *me*... even though I was the one who'd made it that way.

But there was a time... a time when Brody looked out for me, too.

It started sometime after I got my first period.

I could still see him, standing there at my front door with the little bag from the pharmacy in his hand.

I was thirteen, and it was the middle of the night. I knew what was going on when I woke up bleeding, but I wasn't prepared; despite my early development in the boob area, I was kind of in denial that this was really going to happen to me. My mom had no feminine products in the house, either. With her illness and all the medications, she'd gone through early menopause. She'd been sleeping for hours, so I wasn't about to wake her. She couldn't drive at night anymore, anyway.

There was nowhere open within walking distance at that time of night, and I was scared to take the bus. It was my first period; how did I know if I was going to bleed all over the place and everyone would see?

So I did what I did in any emergency. I called my brother and told him what happened.

His band had played a house party that night, and he was still there. I could tell he'd been drinking. His voice got all happy and slurry like that when he was drunk. But he told me not to worry; he'd take care of it. He was going to "send help." And before I could protest, he'd hung up.

I called him back but got no answer. I didn't even want to think about what kind of "help" he was going to send, but what could I do?

I was bleeding, for God's sake.

Forty-five minutes later, I was curled in a miserable ball on the couch, rotten with cramps, when I heard a motorcycle pull up. I knew only two people who rode a motorcycle. Neither of whom I wanted to see in that moment.

Jude, and worse... Brody.

I dragged myself up and opened the door to find my brother's super-hot eighteen-year-old friend, his forehead creased in concern, blue eyes staring me down, a bag from the all-night drug store in hand. In that moment, I silently vowed never to ask my brother for anything, ever again.

Brody handed me the bag. Then he proceeded to tell me, uninvited, how to use the tampons he'd brought—and that it might be difficult to "put them in" if I was, "you know, a virgin."

I could only hope the look I gave him caused him to wither and die while I was in the bathroom.

"I got the plastic ones," he went on, totally unfazed as I turned and walked away. "The lady at the pharmacy said they're easier to use. There're some pads in there too, in case—"

"Please stop talking," I said, as I shut the bathroom door behind me.

After I'd gotten myself cleaned up and came back out to the living room, I could still see his bike out the window. I slipped out the front door and found him sitting on the steps, smoking a cigarette.

I sat down next to him.

"You should quit smoking," I said, instead of thanking him like I should have.

"You should be on the pill now." He glanced over at the pin on my sweater, the one he'd given me when I was eight. "And you need to stop wearing that shit. Throw it out."

I watched as he mashed out his cigarette on the step, still reeling from that first comment. "I'm not having sex with boys!" I blurted.

He didn't react, just said, "But they're gonna want to."

I stared at him some more. "I don't care! That doesn't mean they get to." I hugged my knees. "It doesn't matter anyway. Jesse doesn't let me date."

He studied me. "You want to date?"

"I'm thirteen. Everyone else is hanging with boys."

"You hang with boys all the time."

"My brother's friends don't count. Anyone who calls me 'little sister' or 'bratface' doesn't count."

"I don't call you bratface."

"No, you call me princess." I rolled my eyes like it was worse, but secretly, I liked it.

He leaned in, bumping his shoulder gently against mine. "Don't worry, princess. By the time you grow up, men will be falling at your feet."

"Uh-huh," I said.

Then he got quiet, and something strange happened.

At the time, I really didn't know what it was. But he was looking at me. Looking at me in a way I'd never seen him look before.

And I just pretended it wasn't happening.

I looked away.

I held my breath as he leaned in, slowly. I felt his breath on my cheek. His lips, hot and soft, brushed against my skin, lingering for a moment.

He took a breath.

Then he was gone.

I watched him walk to his bike, throw his leg over and roar away.

Two days later, my brother gave me "the talk," along with a six-month supply of birth control pills and a box of condoms. Then he showed me a bunch of ghastly, gnarly pictures of venereal diseases on the internet.

He had a fat lip and some bruises on his face that he wouldn't tell me where he'd gotten.

And the next time I saw Brody, he had a black eye.

Even at thirteen years old, I could put two-and-two together on that one. And at that point, I pretty much decided I was never, ever going to need those pills, or the condoms; not with all the overprotective big brothers around. I was never even going to be kissed for real.

I was wrong about that.

I was wrong about a lot of things.

CHAPTER SIX

Jessa

"OH, no. I think she's gonna blow."

I was standing in a room at the back of the lodge with the bride and the other bridesmaids, when Becca backed away from Katie with a sneer of sisterly annoyance... and right into me.

I'd just been examining myself in one of the full-length mirrors, trying to make an eleventh hour decision on whether or not to dash back to my cabin for a pair of panties.

The bridesmaid dress I was wearing was a body-hugging, knee-length sheath dress in a rich champagne-colored satin, with asymmetrical ruching and a high neckline. It cut a killer silhouette and was flattering on all three of us who were wearing it. The back dipped low, and while I knew Devi and Becca had worn low-back bustiers, I'd skipped a bra altogether. I liked the feel of the fabric against my skin, and it was just thick, opaque and structured enough that I could get away with it.

Since I was already ditching the bra, Roni suggested, in her infinite, all-things-sex-related wisdom, that I go commando. No unsightly panty lines, she said, and there was such a "freedom" in it. A sense of sheer feminine power.

Well, sign me up. Anything I could do to empower myself on this particular day was a good idea, right?

Wrong.

I was starting to think this was a bad, bad idea, because going without panties did make me feel powerful. And sexy. Like horny sexy. And the very last thing I needed was anything making me hornier than I already would be in a room with Brody Mason and an open bar.

Yeah. Really bad idea.

But the eleventh hour was quickly evaporating and this day was not about me or my lack of panties. So I turned to the bride and put on a smile.

What greeted me was an image from the pages of a bridal magazine: Katie Bloom in a custom-made strapless champagne ball gown, a shade paler than the dresses we were wearing, with a fitted bodice and jaggedly-ruffled organza skirt layered over tulle. It was pretty, edgy, glamorous and perfect for her. Her thick, dark hair was piled in a loose, simple bun on the back of her head, a few strands framing her face, and she was wearing the rough-cut champagne sapphire earrings my brother had given her as a wedding gift. She looked like a total rock 'n' roll dream.

"What's wrong?" I asked, stepping in to get a closer look. Under her makeup, Katie's creamy complexion and rosy cheeks were taking on a definite greenish hue. Kind of like rotten cheese.

"I'm fine," she said, putting her hand on Devi's shoulder for support.

"You are so not fine," Devi said, examining her face. She handed over a bottle of water and Katie took a few sips, breathing slow, deep breaths in-between.

"Katie tends to blow chunks when she's nervous," her sister explained to me.

"Oh."

"I do not!" Katie protested. "I'm just excited. And maybe a little hungover," she added, squirming in her dress. "This thing is kinda tight. I think I ate too many cream puffs last night."

"Just tell me if this is gonna turn into a scene from *Bridesmaids* so I can get the hell out of the way," her sister said.

"Aw, shit," Devi muttered, and in unison, we all stepped back.

Katie leveled her sister with a dark look. "I hate you. And I was just about to say, if you'd let me get a word in, that I love you. All of you. And before we go... out there... I want to thank you for being here." Her breath hitched and her bottom lip started to quiver. "My last wedding was... a total disaster," she said, her eyes starting to fill with tears, "and you ladies are my team. If Jesse ditches me at the altar, I'm really gonna need you."

Last wedding?

If he ditches her at the altar?

Holy. Shit.

Someone ditched Katie at the altar?

I heard the sharp intake of breath as someone stepped into the room. We all cleared a path for Katie's mom and her niece, Sadie, the flower girl. Mrs. Bloom was staring at her daughter, open-mouthed, tears quickly forming in her eyes. "Oh, my girl," she gushed. "You look—"

"Don't say it," Becca cut her off. "You hated my wedding dress. I don't wanna hear it. Tell her later, when I'm drunk."

"Well, it was so short," Katie's mom said. "But this... Now this is a dress." She fluffed up Katie's tulle and fussed with the ruffles. "That white thing you wore, you know, last time," she half-whispered, "it wasn't you, with the stiff, straight lines and all the lace. This... this is you."

"Because we picked it," Devi said. "Last time, mother-in-law-zilla picked it."

"Almost mother-in-law," Katie's mom corrected her.

"Almost." Katie smiled as her mom kissed her cheek, but it was forced. Her lips trembled and her face started to crumple. "Mom... I am gonna feel so fucking stupid in this thing if he doesn't go through with this."

"Are you kidding me?" Devi said. "You look gorgeous."

"So, so pretty," her mom agreed.

"If he doesn't go through with this, I'll kill him myself and you can wear it to his funeral," her sister added.

Katie laughed and sniffled, hugging her sister.

"Stop it right now." Devi dabbed carefully at Katie's cheeks with a tissue. "You'll ruin your makeup."

As I waited my turn to give the bride a final pre-ceremony hug, I felt more than a little honored that she'd asked me to be here; that she considered me part of her team. I liked Katie. A lot. And the thought of her so nervous on her special day, or throwing up on that beautiful dress, her guts turned inside-out, just because some asshole walked out on her... I moved to stand in front of her and took her hands in mine.

"Katie."

She looked up into my eyes, sniffing. Her blue-green eyes were wet, shining, and pink at the corners. "Jessa," she said softly.

"Jesse is not going to walk out on you," I told her, squeezing her hands. "You know how I know that?"

"How?" she whispered.

"Because he loves you. And my brother does not walk out on people he loves." *Unlike me*, I thought, and a wave of something like nausea rippled through me. Katie wasn't the only one who'd drank too much last night. I took a deep breath to settle my stomach and my nerves. "I'm going to go out there and see him now, okay? Make sure the guys have their shit together. Is there anything you want me to tell him for you?"

Katie squeezed my fingers, tight. "Just tell him I love him, okay?"

"I will." I kissed her cheek and hugged her close. "You look beautiful," I told her.

Then I went to find my brother.

I found Dylan first, standing ready by the doors into the hall, smiling at me. I could hear music coming from inside. It was Ash and Paulie, one of Wet Blanket's guitarists, playing U2's "All I Want Is You" for the guests while they waited for the ceremony to begin. Just acoustic guitar, no vocals. And I got shivers, in a really good way.

This was happening. Right now.

"Wow, you clean up nice," I told Dylan, which was an understatement. He'd shaved and his wavy, chin-length auburn hair was tied back; he was wearing one of his trademark kilts, which he always performed in, with his white dress shirt and jacket.

In a word, gorgeous.

"You too, bratface," he said, kissing my cheek. "Though the cake on your butt was a good look, too."

I sighed. The guys weren't going to forget that anytime soon. "Have you seen my brother?"

Dylan cocked an eyebrow and looked over my shoulder.

I turned to find my brother, along with Jude, Zane and Brody, walking up, looking ridiculously handsome in their dark suits. They were followed closely by Katie's dad, her brother-in-law, and her four-year-old nephew, Owen.

"*Holy shit,*" I gasped, getting a good look at my brother as Jude and Zane each gave me a kiss on the cheek. I tried to pretend it didn't bother me at all—I didn't even notice, in fact—that Brody completely side-stepped the situation, heading straight over to Dylan like I wasn't here. "I don't think I have ever seen you in a decent suit," I told Jesse as he took his turn kissing my cheek. "I would say tone it down a bit, you know, give the ladies a chance..." I straightened the knot of his champagne silk tie, "... but you haven't seen your bride yet."

My brother smiled a smile so dazzling it could've blocked out the sun. "If I knew all I had to do to get you to come home was get married," he retorted, "I might have done it long ago."

"No, you wouldn't have. You had to find Katie first."

"How is she?"

"A little nervous. She told me to tell you she loves you. I hear her last wedding didn't go so well?"

My brother's face immediately clouded over, and he started toward the door to the ladies' dressing room. "Where is she?"

"No, no, no." I caught his arm and turned him back around, steering him toward the door to the outer deck, where Jude and Dylan were now waiting for him. "You get your ass down that aisle and you wait for her. And once she gets there, you let her know you're hers, for keeps. And you keep letting her know, every day, for the rest of your life—or I let Devi and Becca kick your ass."

He grinned at me, but his eyes shone a little wetly. "Not a problem, little sister."

I smiled. I had never been prouder of him. Which was saying a lot.

I'd always been proud of my big brother.

"But first, I have something to give you." I pulled the little stick pin from the ribbon on my bouquet and showed him the red stone set into it. "It was Mom's. Those earrings of hers, remember?"

"Sure. With the rubies."

"Garnets, actually. Passed down from Gran Ashton. She used to love them. I remember when I was little watching her put them on and look at them in the mirror. She never wore them out because they were so damn special." I shook my head and my brother laughed a little, remembering.

"Yeah, that sounds like Mom." His eyes met mine. "Or maybe she never wore them out because Dad never took her anywhere worth wearing them."

"Yeah." I bit my lip a little. "Maybe that."

"They'd be proud of you," he said, his eyes softening. "They'd both be so proud."

"Yeah, well." I sniffed a little. Damn my brother. Making me cry, already? Before the bride even got to walk down the aisle? "The jeweler who made this for me mentioned that garnet is the birth stone for January. And now here you are, having a January wedding... and it just seems fitting that you wear it today. You know, for new beginnings. And to remind you that even though Mom and Dad and Gran and Gramps and... well... pretty much everyone else are gone, we come from somewhere. We have history. And now you and Katie... you'll make new history. A new branch in the family tree."

I pinned the pin to his lapel and showed him the other stone, which I'd had mounted on a thin chain around my neck. "We'll both have them with us today."

My brother pulled me in for another hug. "This is the best wedding gift I could get," he said, "besides you being here."

"I wouldn't miss it." I released him. "Now get going, before your bride thinks you jumped out the window."

Dylan held open the door and my brother and Jude swaggered on down the wraparound deck. I watched them pause outside the hall. Jude said something to Jesse. Then they laughed, they hugged, and they went in through the glass doors, taking their places before the officiant.

Once Dylan gave the nod that they were in place, he went out the door himself to head up front and take his seat with Ash and Paulie. "All I Want Is You" faded out. There was a quiet pause, and Zane stepped into place beside me.

I took his arm, then took a breath.

Then the guys started playing another song. It was The Beatles, "And I Love Her," with Ash and Paulie on guitar, Dylan on bongos, and all three of them covering the vocal parts. It was a beautiful, slightly rocked-out arrangement I'd been lucky enough to hear them practicing just after lunch.

Taking his cue, Katie's dad opened the door to the ladies' dressing room. Katie emerged, followed by her mom, her sister, her niece and Devi, who were all fussing with her dress. Katie's brother-in-law swept open the doors into the hall, leaving them open for the rest of us. Then, as the guests seated in the hall turned to watch, he walked Katie's mom up the aisle.

Zane and I were next. I was really glad I got to go early, so I could see everything from up front; the setting was nothing short of utterly breathtaking.

It was a clear, early evening and beyond the cathedral-like windows, the last of a molten amber sun was melting into the horizon beyond the cove. It seemed unfathomable that they didn't do weddings here on a regular basis. According to Maggie, this was only one of a select few they'd ever allowed. I had no idea what magic Brody had worked to make this happen, but he'd done well. Better than well. And I wanted to remember every detail.

The music, the flowers, the people... the look on my brother's face; crystalize them forever in my memory.

Brody and Becca, who followed us up the aisle.

Devi, Katie's stunning maid of honor.

Owen, adorable as he strutted up the aisle in his little suit, the rings on his little blush pillow... followed by his sister, Sadie, with her basket of flowers.

Finally Katie's dad appeared, with Katie on his arm in that incredible dress. I watched her take a little breath as she stepped into place beside her dad, gripping his elbow. He said something to her and kissed her cheek. Then she looked up.

She looked straight down the aisle, like there was not one person in the giant hall. Not one, except my brother. And when she saw him waiting for her in his crisp suit and silk tie, grinning like a man in love, a sweet smile lit up her face.

My big brother, Jesse Mayes, married Katie Bloom just after five o'clock on a clear winter evening in front of their dearest friends and family.

He didn't ditch her at the altar.

She didn't throw up.

CHAPTER SEVEN

Jessa

"OKAY, all you single bitches—oops, sorry, Mom. All you single *ladies*... keep your horny asses on the dance floor!"

Katie's sister had strut onstage and taken over the mic, just as Wet Blanket was heading off. They'd wrapped up their set with a hot and heavy cover of The Kinks' "You Really Got Me," and a whole lot of blissfully drunken wedding guests were now screaming their appreciation of the night's entertainment—at the same time, screaming their lament of Zane and his band leaving the stage. Myself included.

Although after last night, I was pacing myself on the booze; I was currently rocking a mild but pleasant champagne buzz.

"If you're not already *on* the dance floor," Becca added, "you've disappointed me *and* Zane, but you've still got time to redeem yourselves."

As he departed the stage, Zane tossed a bunch of flowers stolen from the table arrangements into the crowd, laughing, and shouted, "Don't worry, kids, the party's just getting started!" As I was jostled about in the crowd, I could feel the effect Zane's stage presence, in particular, had on the women around me, and I had to grin to myself. It was still kind of strange to reckon that shirtless sex symbol in low-slung jeans and leather vest, all washboard abs and piercings, with that cute but annoying boy I grew up with.

But a sex symbol he definitely was, and the other members of Wet Blanket weren't exactly guys you'd kick out of bed. A super-group put together by Zane and several of his rock star friends from other bands, they'd get together now and then, usually in L.A., and put on a random show, playing cover songs for those friends and family lucky enough to get an invite—pretty much for shits and giggles and their shared love of music. The fact that they were here was pretty epic, and a testament to their affection for my brother.

Even better, I'd just learned that Paulie, one of their shit-hot guitarists, was joining Dirty as their new, permanent rhythm guitarist. Officially, no one was supposed to know yet; Dirty was planning to make the announcement at a special show in Vancouver next week—also a secret—but Elle had spilled both tidbits to me.

"You're Dirty," she'd told me with a dismissive shrug. "Jesse or whoever will tell you anyway."

And I was glad she'd told me.

Hearing those words—*You're Dirty*—went a long way to reminding me that I belonged here, and not only because it was my brother's wedding. I had more family here, after all, than just Jesse. And that reminder helped to counteract the incredibly opposite vibe I'd been getting from Brody all day.

After the cutting of the wedding cake—which, good for me, I did not put my ass in—I'd spent most of the night chatting and dancing with Elle. Maybe I figured she and I had some kind of special kinship now—like we'd made it into some crappy club. Elle had wanted my brother, but in the end she'd lost him, and now here she was at his wedding to Katie. And here I was, gazing longingly across the room at Brody, all smoldering in his dark suit, like some mute, adolescent dork.

Of course, Elle had no idea about my... issues... with Brody.

No one really did.

But aside from those issues, I was having fun. I was covered in a sheen of sweat, my hair and my bridesmaid dress clinging to me, my toes starting to throb in my shoes, but I didn't care. I was ready to dance all fucking night if it would save me from throwing a self-pity party.

Sure, Brody had grabbed me last night and yanked me up against him and held me, his fingers digging into me—sending all kinds of wicked signals between my legs. And he'd done it to save me from plummeting off a walkway into the dark, but that was a reflex; he probably would've done it for anyone.

Since then, he'd kept his hands the hell away from me. Like as far as he could get them without leaving the room.

"Crank the music!" Roni called out, jiggling up and down next to me, as eager as I was to keep dancing. But something was holding things up. I stumbled in my high heels as more ladies squeezed onto the dance floor; some of the guys were herding us together into a needlessly tight pack.

"Yeah!" I shouted, cupping my hands around my mouth so Becca could hear me over the crowd. "I want to dance!"

Then Katie walked onstage, twirling her bouquet in front of the cluster of women... as No Doubt's "Just A Girl" started pumping through the room—and it dawned on me what was happening.

Ah, Jesus. The bouquet toss.

All around me women shrieked in excitement, and Roni was one of them. Not that Roni cared to get married; she'd just take her fifteen minutes of fame any way she could get them.

"No one trample Grandma Dolly, okay?" Becca called out, as Dolly was led to the edge of the throng, all smiles. "That's a standing order. Jude and his guys are on hand if you bitch—I mean *ladies* get outta line."

A few ladies shouted some unladylike things—letting Jude and his guys know they could go ahead and bring on their hands. Me, I used the general whirlwind of hormones and excitement to snake my way out of the herd, locking eyes with Elle as I went, and together, we made a beeline for the doors. We'd almost made it there when we were impeded by a big-ass wall of shoulder-to-shoulder Jude and Piper... and corralled back into the fray.

I gave Jude my best *I really, really hate you* glare, the one he'd never seemed fazed by, just as he didn't now. Then I glanced at his big brother, Piper. Piper had shown up to my brother's wedding wearing his patched leather vest, the one that advertised his membership in the notoriously criminal West Coast Kings motorcycle club—which meant he was essentially wearing gang colors and didn't give one fuck what anyone thought about it. So the odds he'd give a fuck that I wanted out of this bouquet toss situation were not good.

He crossed his arms over his chest, both brothers smiling down at me with their identical evil dimples.

"Fine," I grumbled, giving in and heading back to the dance floor.

Stupid, sexy, badass men.

"That guy keeps taking pictures of you," Roni informed me as I edged up beside her in the crowd. I looked around in vain for Elle's platinum-blonde hair and wondered if she'd managed to escape. Lucky bitch.

"Huh? What guy?"

"Photographer with the sweaty little beard." Roni indicated one of the wedding photographers, who was currently angling to photograph the swarm of drunken single ladies jockeying for position to catch Katie's bouquet. "I'm telling you. Every time I see him. The bride's over there, you're over here, and he's shooting you. I'm pretty sure he's taken more pictures of you than her."

"Ignore him," I told her, distracted, as Amanda bounced into the crowd nearby. "I'll mention it to Maggie." I had more important things to worry about than some horny dude with a camera—for example, that this entire event was almost over and Brody still wasn't acknowledging the fact that I was alive, much less present.

At least I hadn't had to watch him dance with Amanda all night.

Well, Brody didn't dance. At least, he never had, back then. Though taking a woman in his arms and making her feel like the only woman in the world as he held her close and swayed to the rhythm of a song... that, he could do. He'd done it with me, once, on a night I'd never forget, for reasons both good and bad.

Strangely enough, he didn't do it with Amanda. While I'd spent every slow song tonight in the arms of the nearest available man, determined not to end up a sad wallflower, Brody didn't dance once, with anyone.

Maybe he wasn't in the mood.

Every time I caught a glimpse of him while I was dancing, he did look kind of... surly.

I didn't see him now, but then again, I wasn't looking. A bunch of the guys were crowded around, laughing and probably taking bets on who was about to get a black eye or a bloody nose, but I was too busy keeping an eye on Katie and her bouquet.

"Better get ready to jump, Maggs," Zane called out as Maggie was shoved in next to me, looking pretty surly herself.

I put an arm around my petite friend and told her, "We'll duck together." Because in my experience, there were two groups of single women at a wedding. Group A, who wanted to catch the bouquet, and group B, who totally didn't.

I just hoped we could get the hell out of the way in time.

Then Katie let fly—and the ladies of group A surged forth with the collective focus of a bunch of drunk and therefore slightly off-balance women in high heels, bent on a common goal. I tried to drop back, but instead got tossed forward in the wave, losing hold of Maggie. Then my feet went out from under me. I started to fall.

And I took Amanda—of all people—down with me.

Which I would've found suspicious myself, except that *I* knew I'd tripped. I tried to stop it, but in all the excitement I was definitely going down, right on top of Brody's date. My hands went up to shield my face from flying arms and elbows—and I caught the fucking bouquet.

Most of it, anyway. A few unfortunate flowers had popped off in the other girls' hands.

But, yeah. The bouquet was mine. I supposed that was one of the benefits—curses—of being tall.

Everyone cheered and yanked me up, shoving me forward for my moment of glory, as a sweaty-bearded photographer took my picture and I faked my very best *Yay! I can't wait to get married next!* smile... and a rather disgruntled-looking Amanda was peeled off the floor. Maybe she really wanted the bouquet.

Oh well.

Then Katie was dragged into the middle of the dance floor and deposited in a chair. Everyone gathered around to watch as my brother, to the wicked, bluesy groove of CCR's "I Put A Spell On You," took his sweet-ass time foraging under her dress, finally removing her garter... with his tongue. Which took some skill.

Even I had to applaud.

I stepped aside with Roni, who was still laughing her ass off—at my expense—as all the single guys gathered around, some strutting into place like peacocks, others shoved in or dragged in by friends. I couldn't help laughing myself; watching the garter toss at a wedding was always entertaining. Like the bouquet toss, it tended to bring out a certain side of some people you didn't expect.

For example, Zane, of all people, was right up front, cracking his neck and flexing his hands, like he was preparing to catch the winning kick at the Super Bowl. At least, that's how it looked to me. I knew shit all about football.

Still. Highly entertaining.

At least, it was until Brody caught the garter... and Zane and Jude tackled *me*, hauled me into the middle of the dance floor, put my ass in the chair... and the entire crowd started whistling, cheering, chanting, and from what I could discern basically ordering Brody to put the garter on *me*.

Fuck me.

Were we really doing this?

People still did this at weddings?

Yeah. Apparently they did.

The pervy photographer was on his knees in front of me taking pictures of us—me with the bride's mangled bouquet, Brody with the garter—as everyone and their dog gathered around. Then Brody was shoved in front of me and the song changed.

James Brown started belting out "It's A Man's Man's Man's World."

Brody, still wearing his suit pants, his crisp white shirt unbuttoned just enough to show off his neck tattoo, that sexy dip at the base of his throat and enough collarbone to seriously distract a girl, threw me a dark glance—like this was somehow my fault, when *he* caught the stupid garter!—and got down on his knees in front of me.

And all the breath went out of my lungs.

Oh. My. *God.*

This was happening.

While everyone watched.

Brody reached down, lifted my foot, and slipped off my shoe to a round of cheers, whistles and *ooh-la-la*'s... and the feel of his hand, his fingers warm and strong and sure on my bare ankle, made me quiver.

I *quivered.*

I'd never quivered at a man's touch before.

Other than Brody's.

Heat rose through me as my body went liquidy, all resistance melting away as I permitted him to do this incredibly intimate thing which had now become a group activity, a spectator sport, for the amusement of our friends.

As James Brown belted out the naked truth, that this world, a man's world, would be nothing—*nothing*—without the female of the species, Brody rested my foot on his lap and held my leg in his hand like it was precious, exotic, and utterly beautiful.

My nipples hardened and my toes involuntarily curled.

I held my breath as my heart rammed in my chest. A bead of sweat rolled down between my braless breasts.

It wasn't like I'd never had a man slide a piece of lingerie *onto* my body before. At photo shoots and fashion shows, I'd had all sorts of people, men and women, dress me in all kinds of things. But this... this was different.

This was Brody.

Sliding a delicate, frilly garter over my toes and up my leg... slowly. While everyone watched, whistled, and took pictures.

At least now he was acknowledging my existence. Didn't mean he was looking me in the eye.

"Higher!"

"HIGHER!"

It was just past midnight, most everyone was at least half on their way to shit-faced, and as Brody slid the garter up over my knee and stopped, the crowd, as one, urged him to slide it higher up my leg.

So he did.

He slipped it right on up my thigh, taking the hem of my dress with it... sending tingles all the way up to my clit.

I bit my lip.

More whistles.

More pictures.

Brody's warm fingers grazed my thigh... and I stirred restlessly as my pussy clenched. *Oh, damn.* He had the sexiest hands, ever. Manly and strong but not overly-large, a little rough from just the right amount of time spent doing manly things. All I could think about was that hand continuing up, up... and touching me between my legs... and my girl parts throbbed with longing.

I almost wanted him to do it. Right here, right now. With everyone watching. I didn't care.

But maybe that was the champagne.

Finally, his blue eyes lifted to mine. And I heard Roni's voice in my head.

Hey Brody, did you know my pussy's bare beneath this dress?

That was exactly what she'd said, in her best imitation of me, as she'd convinced me to go commando. I saw her now in the crowd, grinning at me like the Cheshire Cat, eating up every second of this torture... as Brody's hand and that frilly garter slid higher still...

Shit.

I tensed, leaned into his ear, and whispered, "I'm not wearing any underwear."

His hand froze on my thigh.

Like he gives one flying fuck what I do with my pussy.

That's what I'd said to Roni in response to her teasing. At the time, I'd believed it.

Except now that he was giving some sweaty-bearded photographer an eyeful of it, apparently, he did care. I knew this because he suddenly lunged, punched the guy straight in the face, seized the camera, took out the memory card and handed it to a stunned Katie.

Yeah, he cared. A lot.

Enough to draw blood, which was now dribbling down the photographer's face from his probably-broken nose.

Then a blur of giant men descended on the scene, including Jude and his brother Piper, the big-ass biker, and I got the hell out of the way.

Someone grabbed my hand and pulled me from the fray. "What the hell was that about?" Maggie asked as she drew me across the room.

"Um... I'm going commando?"

"Oh, Jesus."

"Also... you, uh, might need to fire one of your photographers. Before Brody kills him."

"You don't say." She released me and started back toward the fracas, but I grabbed her arm.

"I swear," I told her, "I am not trying to make a scene at my brother's wedding!"

Jesus, though. First my ass in the cake, now this?

"Word of advice, gorgeous," Maggie said sternly, but she was grinning at me. "Next time, wear panties."

CHAPTER EIGHT

Brody

"JESSA!"

I heard her name, exalted through the darkness between the trees... and at first, I almost thought I'd imagined it. A shiver ran up my spine as the breeze licked up the back of my shirt.

I zipped up my fly and headed through the trees, back to the fire.

"Omigod, come sit down!" That, from a very happy-sounding but slightly drunk Katie.

"We thought you'd bailed." That was Roni, and I heard the cap pop off a fresh beer. Just as I reached the edge of the patio, I saw her; Jessa, standing by the fire in her furry jacket, taking a pull off the beer she'd just been handed. I'd stepped away to take a piss, and now there she was.

I stopped short in the darkness between the trees.

"Nope," Jessa said, wiping beer off her mouth with the back of her hand as she sat down. Like most everyone around the fire pit, she'd changed into jeans and warm boots. So at least if she was still going commando, no one would be the wiser.

"To sit at the fire," Jesse told her, "you have to sing a song." Then he thrust a guitar into her hands.

There were about a dozen people gathered around; just the band and a few friends with cold beers and a bunch of instruments, sitting on benches around the fire on a stone patio overlooking the hot springs. It was near three in the morning and a fat moon was glowing through the break in the trees above. The wedding reception had dissolved about an hour ago, the last guests wandering off to their cabins, but those of us who couldn't yet sleep had come out here to do what we always did when we were in nature together: play music, or at least enjoy a few more drinks and the talents of those who *could* play.

The mere possibility of hearing Jessa sing a song, right here, right now... my pulse jacked up and I got goosebumps, all over my body—that internal radar for other people's musical gift that Zane called my "talent boner" going off in a big way.

I didn't even think I'd see her again tonight, and I'd had mixed feelings about that. On the one hand, seeing her was torture. On the other hand, not seeing her? Worse torture.

Amanda *had* bailed, heading off to bed, so at least there was that. Apparently, the fact that I'd punched a guy in the face didn't go over so well with her, especially when word got around about why I did it.

I flexed my sore hand and hung back, just beyond the firelight, listening; I didn't want my presence to ruin the moment. If Jessa saw me, maybe she wouldn't play. Maybe she wouldn't even stay. But she seemed to be stalling as she sipped her beer.

"Even Katie sang," Jesse encouraged her. "Badly."

"'Bohemian Rhapsody'!" Katie said. "It's my specialty. Especially in the shower, in my car, and at campfires."

"Ah, a campfire classic." I could see the side of Jessa's face, rimmed in firelight, her eyes shining. She looked a little drunk, but happy. "Jesse can never remember the words." She shot her brother a disparaging look and started tuning his guitar.

"Don't fuck with my guitar," he said, but he looked damn happy. Paulie handed him another acoustic but he didn't play, waiting instead for Jessa to start.

I leaned against a tree as Jessa started to strum, tentatively at first, almost shyly. Everyone fell quiet to listen as she cleared her throat. "I'm a little rusty."

"Don't think," Jesse prompted. "Just play."

I didn't recognize the song at first. Then Jessa opened her gorgeous mouth and let her soft voice out, and the words of Hozier's "Take Me To Church," carrying through the night, rose every hair on my body.

Jesus, the girl could sing.

Jesse joined in on guitar, but no one else sang. Zane's voice or even Jesse's would've overpowered hers, and no one wanted that. There was just *something* about Jessa Mayes' voice; sweet, delicate, both fragile and strong, and so emotive. She'd changed the lover in the song's lyrics from "she" to "he" and made it her own, and when she sang? You got pulled right in. Everyone seemed to lean in closer to hear her... all of her. Every little intake of breath, every catch, every little sigh between the words.

The spaces in-between the words; Jessa knew, like any great songwriter, that those spaces were everything.

She would've made an incredible solo artist, maybe headlined her own shows, if she'd ever had the desire. Just Jessa. That voice and that face and a guitar.

Epic.

As she finished the song, everyone just sat there staring at her, speechless.

"Damn." Katie's brother-in-law, Jack, finally broke the silence.

"Right?" Roni said. "You should hear her when she's singing Feist in her underwear and making me breakfast." Then she stood up, singing "I Feel It All" in an imitation of Jessa's sweet voice and twitching her ass in the air.

"Bitch," Jessa muttered, smiling.

"What? It's good to have you home." Roni sat back down, grinning.

"I'll fucking cheers to that," Zane said, and glasses and bottles were clinked all around the fire pit.

I took that as my cue to slip back in and rejoin the circle. I'd already sung my song, so at least Jessa didn't have to hear me croak my way through "Heart of Gold." My musical talents did not lie in performance—of any kind. Luckily Zane's harmonica kind of stole the show, plus almost everyone was kinda drunk, so there was that.

"I'm expecting you to make me those badass blueberry pancakes of yours, soon," Roni went on. "It's been years since you treated me to a breakfast concert."

"I can't remember the last time I ate a pancake," Jessa said almost wistfully, glancing at me as I sat down across the fire from her.

"Christ," Roni said. "You really need to quit the modeling biz, stat. Life without pancakes... next you're gonna tell me you've stopped giving head because of the calories."

"You only gotta count the calories if you swallow," Ash put in helpfully.

"Hey, hey." Jessa raised her beer. "To my brother and his new wife."

Beers were raised again and everyone cheered as the laughter died down. "And to my little sister," Jesse added. "May she live long and sing a lot of songs."

Jessa smiled, looking embarrassed by all the love.

Then the music continued. With all the rock stars jamming, it was a killer lineup for a private concert in the woods. The businessman in me wanted to pull out my phone, stream it live and watch the cash roll in. But this night wasn't about that.

As they started into what I personally considered one of the greatest songs The Beatles ever recorded, "Don't Let Me Down," Zane on lead vocals and Jesse, Dylan, Elle, Ash and Jessa belting out the chorus, sending it right on up to the stars, I sat back, just soaking up the vibe of it. Just like I had at so many jams around so many fires over the years, since we were just a bunch of kids. And it felt good.

No; it felt incredible.

It felt so totally fucking *right* to have Jessa here among us; like she'd never even left. Nothing could be more right than this.

Nothing could be more wrong than watching her leave us again.

I felt it, in my blood and in my bones, in my fucking soul, as she played with the band. Jessa Mayes belonged here. With us.

Why the fuck couldn't she see it?

Everyone else could.

I watched in utter fucking fascination as the music took her over, as she got all lit up in a way I hadn't seen her get lit up in a long fucking time... since around the time her mom died, maybe.

Since long before the band left on that first world tour, and we lost her.

Many songs later, the fire was dwindling and no one was bothering to build it up anymore. The newlyweds had long since disappeared. Those of us who were single—or avoiding going to bed—sat around talking shit, drinking, smoking weed and more or less trying to outlast each other. Like a bunch of eighteen-year-olds who weren't gonna pay for this tomorrow.

Zane, Maggie and I, as usual, were the only ones not getting trashed. Zane because he didn't drink, and Maggie and I because we'd made it our responsibility years ago to look out for these lunatics. Besides, I tended to make an even bigger dick of myself with Jessa when I was drunk, and I wasn't about to spend the brief time I had in her presence wasted.

I wasn't gonna spend it sleeping either, which meant I was pretty much waiting for her to get up and leave, because I sure as shit didn't have the balls to end this night. Not when she was still sitting across the fire from me. I glanced her way, but she wasn't looking at me; she was gazing into the flames, a beer clutched in her hand.

Then Maggie announced that she was about to go pass out—and Zane suddenly got the bright idea to go for a polar bear swim, which, big fucking surprise, turned into a naked polar bear swim.

Zane, Roni, Dylan and Ash headed for the nearest dock and into the water—not the little pools of hot springs among the rocks below;

the frigid waters of the cove beyond. Which left me with Maggie and Jessa by the fire.

"BRO-*d-d-deeeeee...!*" Zane sang from the water. He was in first; pretty sure his teeth were chattering.

Roni was next in, with a squeal.

"I'm good," I called out. "Be right here, making sure no one dies." I couldn't help snickering as Dylan and Ash jumped in the frigid water, hollering. "Idiots," I mumbled into my beer. I could see them, like the slick heads of seals bobbing on the water in the moonlight.

Then my eyes met Jessa's across the fire and my smile faded.

Maggie, sitting right next to me, was saying something, but I didn't hear a word as Jessa got to her feet. She wobbled a little, finished her beer, set it down, and turned to walk straight out the dock.

I really should've stopped her. She'd been drinking, and she didn't look all that steady on her feet. But since I was dead to her... I just sat there like an asshole watching her strip down, shedding her furry jacket and the sweater beneath, then her T-shirt—a worn black shirt. My shirt? I could've sworn it was, and that shit was messing with my head.

She skimmed it up over her head and tossed it aside. Her back was to me, her hair tied up in a high knot, the firelight skimming off her naked curves... which meant the assholes in the water had a frontal view. But she didn't take off her bra. She kicked off her boots, shimmied out of her jeans—flashing her perfect ass in a pair of nude-colored panties—and hopped in the water.

Maggie applauded next to me, laughing as Jessa emerged from underwater and shouted, "Jesus! Fuck, that's cold!" which just made Maggie laugh harder.

"Maggie!" Zane threw his arms around Jessa, pulling her close, which I didn't fucking love. At least I knew for sure it was too cold in that water to get a hard-on, even for Zane. "Get your ass in the water!"

"Don't let the old man cramp your style, Maggs," Ash put in.

Maggie glanced over at the "old man"—me, apparently—and rolled her eyes. Then Dylan joined in the ribbing, and Zane shouted, "Maggie May! Get your ass in the water before my dick falls off!"

"Jesus Christ," Maggie grumbled, getting up. "Doesn't he ever shut up?"

Obviously, it was a rhetorical question, because we both knew the answer. Maggie didn't usually let Zane's mouth get to her, but seconds later she'd stripped down to her underwear and was in the water, screaming.

Ash was then out, naked, running shivering up the boardwalk into the woods, followed closely by Roni, then Dylan. Jessa was out next, quaking, her shoulders drawn up around her ears... her nipples looking like they were about to slice through the pasted-on silk of her flesh-tone bra. She might as well have been naked.

I tried not to stare, but shit. I'd never seen Jessa this naked. Didn't love that I wasn't the only one seeing it, either.

Fortunately, Zane was too cold to care. I met her on the dock with a wool blanket someone had left by the fire and wrapped her in it, just as Maggie streaked by. The both of them could've been buck naked and making out and Zane probably wouldn't have stopped.

"Holy mother of fuck," he gasped as he dashed by, hot on Maggie's tail. "My balls are up behind my eyeballs." Then he caught Maggie and swung her up over his shoulder, caveman style.

Maggie smacked Zane's bare ass, hard, as he hauled her off into the trees. "Do not drop me," she ordered. "I'm freezing!" They disappeared into the dark, leaving Jessa and I alone.

She was wrapped up tight in the blanket, wavering on her feet, shivering so hard her teeth were chattering.

"You should go back to your cabin," I told her. "Get a fire going."

I didn't wait for a response.

I headed back to the fire pit to put the fire out. She needed to get warm—somewhere else—and I needed to get the hell away from her and her see-through panties. She didn't seem to get the memo on that, though, because she followed me.

When the fire was out I stood to leave, but she stood in my path.

"Yeah... a fire's a good idea," she said, blinking up at me, her big brown eyes all bleary and needy and soft. "Guess I'll just have to try and get it lit and whatever."

Seriously?

I was not fucking falling for this shit. What was I, a fucking lumberjack now? She want me to go out and haul down a tree for her, and those big brown eyes were supposed to get me to do it?

Fat fucking chance.

"It's a luxury resort," I said flatly. "I'm sure they've made it real easy for you. Probably stocked your cabin with everything you need and then some."

"Yeah, probably." She glanced up the path leading to the boardwalk and bit her lip.

"What's the problem?"

"Nothing." She started up the path, but stopped when she reached the start of the suspended boardwalk.

I came up behind her in the dark. "What's the fucking problem, princess?"

Jessa cringed at the old nickname. "Never mind."

I studied her dark silhouette, trying to figure out what the fuck she was up to.

I had no idea.

Used to think I knew her, could read her, knew all the shit she never told anyone, even me.

I was wrong. So totally fucking wrong.

"Have a nice night." I bypassed her, heading into the trees. "Try not to freeze to death."

"It's just..." she called out after me. "I'm kind of lost."

I turned back. "You're *lost*?"

She drew the blanket tighter around herself. "Yeah, okay? That's why I was late coming down to jam. I got lost. It was light out when I arrived, and I've had a lot to drink, and it's all dark, and this walkway is dangerous. There's no rail in some places, you know, and it's a fucking maze..."

It was dark. The twinkly lights along the boardwalk had gone out, probably on a timer. And she was right; it was kind of a maze.

And she did almost fall off it last night. Still made my stomach turn to think about it, about what might've happened if I wasn't there.

Wasn't really in the mood to agree with her, though.

Instead I muttered, "Jesus, Jessa," took her by the elbow, and led her into the dark.

CHAPTER NINE

Brody

"NUMBER FOURTEEN," I said, pointing at the carved wooden numbers in the middle of Jessa's cabin door as I shut it behind us. Luckily, she was too drunk to note or ponder the fact that I knew exactly which door was hers.

"Oh. Shit. I didn't know they had numbers. Guess I was kind of... distracted... when they showed me around..."

I wasn't listening.

I ditched my jacket and went straight to the fireplace, ignoring the suitcase that was tossed open on the bed, her lingerie spilling out of it. Silky, lacy, skimpy shit—

But yeah, I was ignoring that. Definitely wasn't picturing her wearing it or wondering why the fuck she'd *failed* to wear any of it when she showed up at the wedding without panties on and gave that photographer an eyeful.

I flexed my hand. My knuckles were bruised and one had split, but the blood had dried. At least I knew the guy whose face had taken the brunt of the damage wasn't gonna do shit about it. Not after Piper and Jude had a talk with him. I wasn't gonna deny that it was convenient as hell that our head of security was connected to a powerful outlaw motorcycle club, and when problems needed to disappear, they tended to do just that. I'd never asked Jude to ask his brother for anything on my account, but I wasn't naive about it occasionally happening. And in a case like this, I wasn't complaining.

I got the fire going with a wooden match and got it burning hot. Wouldn't take long to get the room warm. It was smaller than the one Amanda and I were given, just a single with a double bed instead of a king.

I was just turning to stand when I realized how thin the walls between the rooms were, as the unmistakable sounds of fucking started coming right through. No doubt Jessa's good old friend Roni was entertaining someone, or more specifically two someones, in an adjacent room. Loudly.

No secret that Dylan and Ash liked sharing women, and no secret that Roni liked taking it from more than one guy at a time, so no big surprise there. Didn't mean I was in any mood to listen to it.

"Wait. I got it," Jessa said, digging out her phone and turning on some music. It was Arctic Monkeys, "Why'd You Only Call Me When You're High?". She went to the bedside table, dumped a bunch of pine cones out of a decorative bowl that was sitting there, and lay the phone in the metal bowl, which worked pretty well as an amplifier. Then she turned it up, turned to me and smiled.

It was a big, dorky smile, just like she used to smile when we were kids. Which might've been cute as she stood there all damp and drunk, wrapped in that ugly wool blanket—if not for the fact that I was still oscillating wildly between wanting her and wanting like hell to hate her.

Then she moved to sit on the edge of the bed—and missed. She wasn't kidding that she'd had a lot to drink.

As I looked at her down on the floor, smiling her dorky smile and kind of giggling as she struggled to get up, all cocooned in the blanket, I realized she was definitely gonna need some help getting through this night.

Which meant I should rally one of the girls to look after her, and get the fuck out.

Instead, I went into the bathroom and got the water running warm in the bathtub. If Jessa Mayes died of hypothermia tonight and I was the last one to see her alive, pretty fucking sure her brother would never forgive me.

"Please, don't be angry with me."

I looked up into the big window over the tub and saw her reflected in the glass, leaning against the bathroom door, watching me.

"I can't take it," she said, "not on top of everything else."

I had no idea what "everything else" was, but it really wasn't my problem. Neither was her discomfort with me being angry.

"I'm fine," I said.

"You're not."

"It's the middle of the night, Jessa. I'm fucking tired."

"You are not fine."

"Neither the fuck are you."

She hugged herself and said, "How would you know?"

"You're right." I stood and faced her. "How would I know? How would I know a fucking thing other than what you told me? You refused to come on tour with the band because you said you didn't want to be famous. Then you became a fucking supermodel."

"I am not a supermodel."

"No? Well, the only place I get to see you is on the fucking internet, in your underwear, like all the other assholes with their dicks in their hands."

She gaped at me. "It's not *my* underwear," she objected, like that made a fucking difference. "And they pay me a lot of money to wear it."

"We would've paid you too. We did, tour or no."

"It wasn't about the money. It was about me finding out who I am. I just couldn't do that on tour with the band."

"How would you know? You never gave it a chance."

"I'm not having this same argument with you again."

And just like that, the wall went up.

I sucked back a breath and turned away—but there she was in the goddamn window. Moving closer to me. "You're angry because I didn't come with you guys when you left on that first world tour," she said softly, "and you've never forgiven me."

Well, *fuck me*.

I was kinda stunned that she would go there. Say it right out loud like that, when she'd run away from it for so long. But then again, alcohol could be one hell of a truth serum.

Had she actually started to comprehend what the fuck she'd done?

Was this heading toward a legit apology?

Fuck that. I wasn't accepting an apology from her. I wasn't accepting shit all from her.

Jessa Mayes could take her apologies and her too-little-too-fucking-late and go fuck herself.

I turned to look her right in her brown eyes—and I knew I was lying to myself. Fucking right, I wanted her to apologize. I wanted her to get down on her knees, suck my cock, and tell me, *I'm sorry, Brody. I never should've left. It was the worst mistake I've ever made. Please tell me what I can do to make it up to you...*

Yeah. Right.

"I was angry about that," I told her. "I'm not anymore."

"You've been angry with me for years," she whispered. Then she put her hand on me. Laid it right on my bare skin, on my bicep; just like she fucking owned me.

I froze, every muscle in my body going rigid. Yeah, even in my cock, since all my blood was pumping there post-haste.

What the fuck did she think she was doing?

Touching me, just like she used to touch me, like no time had passed at all... like she could walk out the door, never look back, not even speak to me for *years*... and then she's right here, in my face, her fucking hand on me, and nothing had changed.

Because nothing *had* changed.

I still wanted her. Whether I wanted to accept that or not, my cock was making it pretty fucking clear. And Jessa? She was still pushing the same old bullshit.

"Get your fucking hand off me." I said it as coldly as I could, even as my blood ran hot.

She didn't flinch. She didn't snatch her hand back and run away like I expected her to. She just stared at me with her big brown eyes. This close, I could see all the colors in them. Hazel, green, gold.

"Take your hand away, Jessa," I said, my voice dropping low, getting gravelly as the walls of my throat got thick; too thick to breathe right. I leaned in a bit but she didn't remove her hand, just tightened her fingers, her nails digging into my tattoos. "Is that what you want?" I stepped into her space and she backed up, but she didn't let go. "You want what you never got?" I backed her right up against the counter and slammed my hips against hers, my body working on autopilot. "Yeah," I said, searching her face. Her eyes were softening and she swallowed, hard. "I can give you that."

I could. If my dick was all she'd ever really wanted from me, she could have at it. If that was all this was ever about, maybe I should've thrown any gallant gestures bullshit out the window long ago and just given it to her.

I lifted her, shoving her up on the edge of the sink. She didn't fight me. Her arms went around me and the blanket fell open. I ripped it aside and shoved myself between her bare thighs. Then I pulled her to me, holding her on the edge of the counter in her underwear—still damp and clinging to her and totally fucking see-through.

I leaned in to kiss her, but I didn't. I pressed my forehead to hers and waited for her to come to me.

She did.

She smashed her mouth to mine. As I kissed her back she moaned, opening for me, and then I was inside her—my tongue stabbing deep into her mouth. Her nails dug into the back of my neck as she pulled me in. She sucked on my tongue and my brains pretty much fell out of my head. Her legs were tangled up around my waist and as we kissed, hot, frantic and messy, finding a wet, greedy rhythm, she started rubbing herself against the crotch of my jeans... and I lost it.

I grabbed her hips and ground the length of my throbbing cock against her clit, slowly, then started fucking it against her... like I could dry-hump her right into submission. She whimpered as her thighs fell open... as I rammed my cock against her again and again. She looked like she was on the brink of an Earth-shattering orgasm as her head fell back, her mouth open. A flush was creeping up her chest. Her tits were swollen in her bra, her nipples hard. And her pussy? Even through my jeans I could feel her, soft and swollen and needy; hungry for me.

"D'you... have a condom?" she rasped out, her gaze meeting mine... and the look in her glassy eyes was like an ice-cold vise on my dick.

What the fuck was I doing?

No, I didn't have a condom. And no, I wasn't gonna fuck her on the bathroom sink while she was wasted. Because then what? She'd be on a plane, and thanks for the fucking memories?

I stopped dry-humping her long enough to force out, "I can't. Jessa... it can't be like this."

"Okay," she panted back.

"It can't be like it was, either."

"I know."

Then she kissed me again and I dove right back in.

Harder than before, faster, deeper, my head spinning with hunger, because it was *Jessa* and I had no self-control left when it came to her. I'd burned it out over the last God-knew-how-many years, wanting her, chasing her, waiting for her, trying to hate her, trying like hell to get over her and failing... jerking myself raw just wishing I had her... going goddamn insane without her.

"Jesus, Jessa." I tore my mouth away from hers. "It's been seven years. You can't—"

"Six-and-a-half."

I shook my head as I fought to catch my breath. "You can't do this shit to me."

She chewed on her flushed bottom lip. She was still gripping my neck, her chest heaving against mine. "I'm not doing anything."

"Like hell, you're not."

"What am I doing?"

"I don't know, but it feels bloody familiar. You. Wasted. Wrapping yourself around me." I still had her by her hips, my fingers digging into her. Afraid to let her go even as my words pushed her away. "How many times did you climb into my bed after some party? You drove me fucking crazy." I pressed into her, grinding myself into her softness, unable to stop. "Let me guess. You're just waiting for my balls to turn blue before you put the brakes on."

She pulled back, releasing me. "I was young and immature, Brody."

"You were old enough to know what the fuck you were doing."

She struggled in my grasp, trying to break away, but I held her. I wasn't letting go. "You think that's who I am?" she asked, still struggling. "That's who I want to be? The girl who left? The girl who just up and leaves everybody hanging?"

"That's who you were," I said. "Who the hell else am I supposed to think you want to be?"

She stared at me, her glassy eyes getting glassier as they gleamed with tears. Then she whispered, "It's your shirt. Your Zeppelin shirt. You were right. I've been wearing it for years."

Jesus.

Not something I ever expected her to say. I didn't even know what to do with it. "Jessa—"

"Shit! I left it down on the dock. I have to get it!"

I caught her as she tried to eject herself from the counter and set her back down. "Yeah, not happening. You are not gonna ruin Jesse's wedding because you got swept out to sea over a fucking T-shirt."

She shook her head slowly. "You're still mad at me."

I pulled away, letting her go as the blood crept back into my brain. "Yes, I'm mad at you. You ran out on everyone, Jessa. You should've seen what that did to Jesse. To the band. What it did to Seth—"

"Don't."

She pushed past me, stumbling off the counter, and reached to shut off the bath water, which was about to overflow. "You can go now," she said as she started to step into the tub, still wearing her panties and bra. "I'll be fine."

"Fuck. That," I spat out. She stood there, blinking at me as I stalked over to the tub. "I waited for you for *years*. I gave you *everything* I had to give. I gave you all the space in the fucking universe, and all I wanted was for you to be *present*. In my life. And you refused to give me that."

She sank into the bath without a word.

"I was mad," I went on, "because you fucking *left*. Because every time I came home you were gone, and anytime we were in the same city you were too busy to see me. Because whenever I called you, you didn't answer, and you never returned my calls. I was mad because I had to have a relationship with your voicemail for six-and-a-half fucking years."

She looked up at me, her eyes pink-rimmed. "So you're just never going to forgive me, is that it?"

"You broke my heart!"

I shouted it at her, hurled it at her with all the anger and frustration I still felt, just raging beneath the surface.

She stared at me, looking kind of stunned. She shook her head. Then she laughed, a humorless laugh. She stood up in the tub and pointed at me. "What's it been, a decade?" she said, shoving her finger in my face. "Since you stood there, you stood right there in front of me and said you'd wait for me. And then *I saw you* with Christy Rempel."

"Right," I said. "You have a really fucking selective memory if that's the way you remember things going down. I told you I'd wait for you, Jessa, and I did. I didn't say I'd be a fucking monk while I did it."

"And *I* told you that waiting for someone forever is a bad, bad idea."

"Yeah, because you saw it in some bullshit movie. And that's where you live, in a fucking movie, between the lyrics of a fucking song, Jessa, because you sure as fuck don't live here with me."

"I told you not to wait for me!"

"And *I told you* I was in love with you."

She drew her head back, like I'd slapped her. Probably should've; I fucking wanted to. "You did not."

"I did. That day in my truck, in the rain. I told you." My voice got quiet as I remembered, but I kept looking her in the eye. I wasn't running from this shit anymore. "I told you I'd loved you forever."

She hugged herself. "I mean... you kind of said something about—"

"Kind of? How does someone 'kind of' pour their heart out to you? I begged you not to leave, and you left anyway."

"Because I had to!"

"Why?" I took a step closer, as close as I could get without falling in the tub. "Tell me why the fuck you had to."

Jessa slumped into the water with a splash and didn't look at me again. "I didn't know you were in love with me," she said, "and it's not my fault if you were."

I stared at her, but she didn't say another word. *For fuck's sake.* That's all she had to say?

"Yell if you're gonna drown or something," I bit out, slamming the door as I left the room... before I drowned us both.

CHAPTER TEN

Jessa

MY BROTHER DIDN'T MESS AROUND. AS soon as I told him I'd be staying in Vancouver after the wedding, I saw the musical gears turning in his head. Not that I'd decided to stay for musical reasons, but it was a little flattering how quickly he set out to woo me.

Yes, I'd planned to leave right after the wedding, but that was before Brody decided to dry-hump me within an inch of an orgasm.

I'd made my decision at brunch the morning after. When I'd walked into the lodge, hungover, just hoping to fade into the background and maybe force down some French toast without barfing, I instead found Brody and Amanda gone and everyone else staring at me as my brother raised a toast to me. He then announced, in front of everyone, that he and Katie had decided to postpone their honeymoon so he could stay in town and spend some time with his sister. "And just maybe," he'd added casually, "we'll write some music together."

To which everyone went nuts with excitement.

Yeah. No pressure.

I'd looked around at all those hopeful and expectant faces and told my brother, in front of everyone, that I could stay for ten days. After that, I had a photo shoot in L.A. I was committed to. And while I loved my brother, the truth was that I was only partly staying for him.

The other part was because I just couldn't leave things the way they were with Brody—which was all kinds of fucked up.

My memories of that night were... unclear. But I remembered enough. I remembered rubbing myself off on the stiff package in his jeans, ready to blow up like a load of fireworks dropped in a volcano. And I remembered what he said to me, too. About me breaking his heart.

I also remembered, more or less, how I'd handled that information, and it was pretty cringe-worthy.

Did I really throw Christy Rempel in his face?

What was I, fifteen years old?

So yes, I was staying, because I had to talk to him. I had no idea how I was going to do it, to work up the courage to start that conversation, though. The *I know that you know that I've fucked up, but here's what you don't know* conversation.

Hardest conversation I'd ever have to have.

Luckily I had ten days to figure it out, and by the looks of things I could easily fill those ten days with musical distraction. Because apparently my brother was planning to make full use of those ten days—and every available tool in his arsenal to persuade me to write some music with the band.

The night after the wedding, as I arrived back in Vancouver with Roni and got settled into the guest bedroom of her condo, Jesse sent an incredible acoustic guitar over for me to play on: a brand new Gibson Hummingbird Vintage, which was kind of a monster. A powerhouse of an acoustic, it was probably too much guitar for me—and not like my brother didn't know it. Clearly, it was something for me to grow into.

Something for me to write new music on.

The next morning, he sent Maggie over with a car to drive me out to Dirty's new rehearsal space for a little jam session with him and Zane.

Cool, right?

Especially when the new rehearsal space turned out to be an old church outside of town. When my brother mentioned "going to church," I just thought he was being cute, referring to the religious nature of his passion for music.

Apparently not.

The building was maybe a century old or so, smallish, originally built of gray stone that had seen better days. A lot of the exterior was in disrepair. Inside, beyond the entrance vestibule, there was the big main room, along with a small office, a washroom, and a tiny renovated kitchen. Most of the original wooden pews had been removed, but there were still three rows of them at the back. Some of the walls were partly deconstructed. There was exposed wood everywhere, a high arched ceiling, and a big, gorgeous stained glass window, which, like the rest of the place, had been hastily repaired over the decades but still held a kind of timeless, awe-inspiring beauty.

Where there would have been some sort of altar there was now just a large, low stage area blanketed with worn Persian rugs and lined with an intimidating wall of Marshall amps. Other music gear was strewn around, including several of my brother's guitars and one of Dylan's massive drum kits.

Best of all, the church sat on a corner lot butted up against an auto wrecker's lot and a stretch of farmland on the other side; no neighbors to complain about the noise.

"It's fantastic," I told my brother as he gave me the tour. "How did you get it?"

"Brody found it for us last summer," he said. "Apparently it hasn't been used as a church for about two decades. It's a bit of a drive, but I like it. I just make sure I go off rush hour and use the time to clear my head, work on writing and stuff."

"What happened to the other place?" The band's old rehearsal space was a studio right in the middle of town, not far from my brother's house.

"Gave it to Katie," he said with a grin. "She's using it as her art studio. But we moved out here before that happened anyway. Wanted a bigger space." Then he plugged in a black-on-black

Fender Strat and let his fingers fly—and raw, twisted, gorgeous music roared out of the amps behind him like some pissed-off beast awakening from its beauty sleep.

Holy hell.

My brother was a total rock god.

I plopped back on a stool to listen as warmth flooded my chest, like I'd just downed a shot of good whiskey. I had memories of Jesse rocking out when we were kids. He was good then; really good. He'd always been a gifted guitarist, but he was better now than he'd ever been.

I could hear it right away.

I could hear how his playing style had developed over the years, matured... his sound mellowing out around the edges and growing more substantial in the middle, fattening up... and it wasn't just the better, more expensive equipment. I didn't even know how to describe it, exactly. All I knew for sure was that when my brother took a stage and started working a guitar, my hair blew back and even I could see why girls threw themselves at him, half-naked, at his shows. Jesse had matured along with his music, and my once-annoying but cute big brother had grown into a rather beautiful, force-to-be-reckoned-with type of man.

I loved watching him play.

I'd seen him in concert over the years, here or there, but I'd always been careful to stay away from his shows unless I was one hundred percent sure Brody wouldn't be there. Which meant I missed out on many more shows than I ever attended. I'd also missed out on a lot of hang time with my brother, the time we might have spent together if I wasn't always so nervous about running into Brody. But today, treated to a private show and a front row seat, watching him play while his wedding ring gleamed on his finger, I really got to see and hear the man and the musician my brother had become.

There was also something fresh, new and alive in his playing, like I really hadn't heard since we were kids, and I was pretty sure that had a lot to do with Katie. My brother was crazy in love; I could feel a kind of unbridled bliss dripping from his fingertips as he played. And I couldn't stop smiling.

"Shit, brother." Jesse stopped playing as Zane walked in, a big grin on his face to match my own. "Is it okay that shit gave me a boner?"

"Since when do you care if anyone's okay with your dick being up?" my brother said, throwing him a look. "And if it is, don't sit next to my sister."

Zane didn't sit next to me. He sat in a pew, next to Maggie, who ignored him as she worked on her laptop. A short while later, when Zane joined Jesse and I onstage to jam and he promptly made the mic his bitch, belting out his sexy, angsty version of The Beatles' "I'm a Loser," Maggie put on coffee and settled in with a mug.

Jude was there too, but he was in and out of the church, on his phone a lot. If he wasn't directly working in his capacity as Dirty's head of security—which probably kept him busy enough, what with managing a security team to cover the asses of four mega-famous rock stars—he was working something else. I was pretty sure when he was in town he did work of some kind for his brother's motor-cycle club. And maybe when he was out of town, too. I didn't ask. I'd learned many years ago not to ask those kinds of questions. But I was used to having them all around—Jude, Piper, all the security. The constant entourage. And I loved that they all had my brother's back. That he was so loved. Jude had been a permanent fixture in our lives since my brother met him at age ten, and Zane since a couple of years before that.

This was my brother's tribe. *My* tribe.

I'd never realized how much that was true until I sat back in an old church and listened to Zane and Jesse jam on a bunch of old songs; just stuff they used to play together for fun in Dolly's garage when we were kids, or around a fire as we grew up. CCR's "Have You Ever Seen the Rain?," The Box Tops' "The Letter," Van Morri-son's "Gloria." I played along on my fancy new guitar, just keeping up wherever I could. Which wasn't really happening, but I had fun trying.

Where I was more useful was adding my backup vocals to the mix—and generally fangirling over my brother and Zane. Because seriously. These two got together to make music, it was like clash of the Titans. Just sit your ass down, try to keep up, and try not to get slaughtered by falling debris. The two of them together had always had crazy, off-the-hook energy, and chemistry through the roof.

Not only were they an extraordinary musical match, but their lifelong rivalry added an edge to everything they did. They were constantly competing, as far as I knew, for everything under the sun —other than women, which was probably a really, really good thing, and the only reason they'd managed to keep it together as a band— their friendship riding that delicate, serrated edge between soulmate and nemesis. It was kind of a love-hate-love thing.

They loved each other.

They hated each other.

They loved each other more.

By late afternoon, we were all caught up in the music, playing original stuff for each other, bits of whatever we'd each been working on since we last jammed together, which in my case, was a hell of a long time ago. They played me the few songs they'd already written for the new album, which were pretty killer, though I was eager to hear them played again when the whole band was here. For my part, I really hadn't been writing much these last few years, or at least I thought I hadn't been. But once I'd pulled out my phone and started sharing all the little bits of lyrics, poetry and general ramblings I'd been making notes of whenever the mood struck, there was a lot more of it than I'd thought.

"It's mostly a bunch of verbal vomit," I told them. "You know, shit I come up with in the shower to entertain myself." I'd just finished singing them some bits and pieces that I thought I might develop into a full song, but I hadn't yet. "I don't really write full songs anymore. Other than when Jesse held me in a room at gunpoint and ordered me to write them for his solo album."

"Right," Zane said, his expression thoughtful. "Same thing he did to get Katie to marry him, I guess."

Yeah. Childish burns like that... all day long. My brother just threw a drum stick at him.

"Seriously, little sis, that stuff is shit-hot."

"Yeah," my brother agreed. "You stick around a while, we'll make some of that into songs."

They stared at me expectantly. All of them. Jesse. Zane. Even Maggie looked up from her laptop, her face lit up in the glow of the screen, a pretty little blip in the dark at the back of the church. The sun had gone down a while ago and she'd lit candles for us; there was a whole mess of them burning all over the stage, sending shadows up the walls and giving the stained glass a moody, almost romantic look.

And not like I hadn't noticed the feast she'd brought in for dinner or the wine and cold beer that had been rolled out, or the joints that had been offered my way. Obviously, what Dirty had going on here was the perfect setting for writing their next kickass rock album—and yet they'd been struggling writing it, coming up with only three semi-finished songs in the last several months. So I knew what this little jam session was all about.

They were trying to seduce me.

Over the years, Dirty had tried about everything to get me to come back and write with them again. Every member of the band had hounded me about it. Not Elle, not as much as the others; she usually just opted to casually probe the subject whenever we saw each other, and let it drop when I brushed it off. But my brother? Dylan? Even Maggie? Relentless. And Zane? Obsessed. Every time we were both in L.A., he'd find out where I was, drag me back to his ubermansion and force me to listen to whatever they'd been working on most recently.

Please, Jessa, he'd beg, a big, charming grin on his face—the kind a Viking must've worn just before plundering some defenseless village. *Don't make me sing these shitty lyrics I wrote.*

And if I was any other girl—one who hadn't known him since I was four years old and would always see him as an obnoxious big brother—that grin probably would've worked. Because it wasn't like I wasn't at all tempted to write with the band again.

Far from it.

Writing with Dirty was the best thing I'd ever done. It was the only thing I'd ever really wanted to do.

But writing with Dirty meant working with Brody. And I just didn't know how that could ever work.

Consider me dead to you.

Well, clearly, he wasn't dead to me. Because Brody Mason would never be dead to me.

But after the other night, when we'd made out and then he'd stormed out, I really wasn't sure how much better or worse off we now were than when he'd uttered those five horrible words to me.

Maybe... one step forward, three steps back?

But of course, my brother had no idea about any of that.

"Let's do this again tomorrow," he said when I remained silent. It wasn't really a question.

"Definitely," Zane agreed. Also not a question. "First, though, we should throw some of those lyrics down on that track we were running through last week. You know the one." He and my brother exchanged a conspiratorial look. "I smell a tasty hook on that last line Jessa just sang. We've gotta twist that shit right into the chorus."

"Like this?"

And then my brother was off, fingers flying up and down his fretboard as he ripped into some new song I hadn't yet heard. When Zane kicked in with the vocals I didn't know the words. But sure enough, he threw in some of my new lyrics and what started to sound a hell of a lot like a song—a catchy, edgy Dirty song—took shape. It started out kind of dirty-bluesy... then Zane laid my words into the much heavier, raunchier chorus, indulging himself with a Robert Plant-esque scream that went straight to my girl parts and probably cracked a few sections of stained glass.

Jesus.

If I just closed my eyes and pretended it wasn't my family up there...

Wet panties. Guaranteed.

I kept my eyes open.

They played it again from the top, and again, until Jude slipped into the back of the church to listen and Maggie rose from her seat to stand next to me and watch; I'd cleared my ass off the stage when the guys started rocking out, because we were now deep in Dirty territory and I didn't belong up there.

When they finally finished, there was about a minute of silence as we all stood there, staring at each other. My ears were ringing. Then Zane threw his head back and laughed, his white teeth gleaming in the candlelight.

"What the hell was that?" Maggie demanded.

"That," Zane said into the mic, "was our next single, Maggie May." Then he did a dramatic mic-drop and jumped down off the stage to tussle my hair.

Next single... *no shit.*

Something had just happened on that stage, while Zane belted out my words to Dirty's music. Something I hadn't been a part of in far, far too long. I wasn't blind to it and I wasn't immune.

Magic had just happened. And it had me in tears.

The guys didn't judge. They just let me have my cry as they hugged me. Zane was first. "I said it once, I'll say it twice and as many times as you need to hear it," he told me. "It's good to have you home."

Then my brother wrapped me in his arms. For a moment, he didn't say a thing. Then he whispered, "Remember this."

Then the guys went outside to smoke a joint. Maggie went with them without a word, just a small smile in my direction... leaving me alone in the aftermath of that magic vibe.

I climbed up onstage and stared up at the gorgeous stained glass window for a while as the candlelight and shadow danced across it, hearing that new song in my head. The way Zane sang it... so different than I would've sung it, and yet... like it'd been written just for his voice.

Maybe it had.

When I finally turned around, Brody was there. He was leaning on the wall near the back of the church, watching me.

"Hey," I said, startled. "How long have you been here?"

"Since you left."

I let go a small sigh as my shoulders dropped. And just like that, all the joy, all the hope, all the warmth and the love and the kinship I'd felt here in this incredible old building, embraced by a few of my old friends—my *family*—making music with them again, making *magic*... it all evaporated in an instant.

Just like I'd always feared—no; like I'd always known it would.

I was left standing onstage alone, as if I were on trial, staring across a very empty room at a man I'd once abandoned, with no idea how to brave the chasm that lay between us.

It wasn't like I hadn't wanted to talk to him after our blow-out in the bathroom, but he hadn't exactly made it easy. By the time I'd gotten my drunk ass out of the bath he was gone, and Roni was waiting in my room instead, along with my Zeppelin shirt, rescued from the dock.

I hadn't seen Brody since.

I'd thought a lot about what I might say when I did see him, though. It was pretty much all I'd thought about. I'd even tried to write down everything that was in my head and somehow organize it. Simplify it. Get to the heart of the matter.

I'd thought about all the times I'd done this before, all the letters I'd written to him over the years but never sent.

I'd thought about what might happen when I finally told him what happened all those years ago. But the fact was I didn't know what would happen. That was the hardest part; the uncertainty.

I had no idea how he'd react.

Other than Brody, I'd only ever gotten involved with men I could predict. Men I felt like I could control. Brody I could never control, and that had always scared me. I still had no control over him, and I knew it. If he'd wanted me to, I would've come right there on that bathroom counter, in his arms; if he hadn't stopped it, I would've given him whatever he asked of me. At least, whatever he'd asked of my body.

I wasn't a screwed-up kid with a million reasons to say no anymore. But he had stopped it.

Because clearly, Brody was never going to let himself get carried away over me—even in my underwear, with my legs spread, wrapped around him and ready to go.

You drove me fucking crazy.

Brody had fallen for me once, but it was in his stance now, in his body language, in the look on his face and the way he looked at me: he was never going to make that mistake again.

I half-expected him to turn and walk out of the church, but he just stood there leaning on the wall, staring at me.

"You left," I said, carefully, "after the wedding. I didn't see you at brunch."

"Amanda had to be back in the city."

"Oh." I nodded, pretending like hell that the mention of his girl-friend didn't turn my stomach. "Right." I knelt down and got busy putting my new guitar away in its pink-lined case.

Brody walked up the aisle toward me. He stood in front of the stage and looked up at me, hands in his pockets... looking so much like that boy I'd first met on the playground it made my heart thud.

"Just don't fuck around, okay?"

I stared at him. "Excuse me?"

"Don't make them think you're coming back, that you're staying, when you aren't," he said, his voice flat. "Don't start writing songs with them you're not gonna finish and don't let them get attached to the idea of having you around."

Okay; that got my back up.

I wasn't one of his clients. I wasn't paying for his advice and I sure as hell didn't ask for it.

Brody could freeze me out, hate me if he needed to; that was his prerogative. But who was he to give me orders? Who was he to tell me what I could and couldn't do with the band? With my own brother? He was their manager, yes. But I didn't need his permission to hang out with them, to write a few songs.

They'd be my songs, too.

I stood and crossed my arms over my chest, giving back all the attitude he was giving me. "You telling me that as their friend, or as their manager? Or just out of the good of your heart?"

"I'm telling you that as a man who knows what it's like to be left by you."

With that, he turned and walked back up the aisle toward the exit.

Oh, *damn*.

Low blow.

I hopped down from the stage, going after him. "They told me you found this place for them?"

He turned back to me. "So?"

"So... it's amazing. Perfect." I met him partway up the aisle. "You always did know what was best for them. You've been a great manager to them, and a great friend. You should be proud of everything you've accomplished together. But... that doesn't mean you have a right to tell me where I fit in, just because you give a shit and you think that makes you boss. If the band wants to write with me... if I want to write with them... you've got no right."

"Actually," he said grimly, "I do. It's my fucking job. A job I've been doing every day while you've been gone. A job I'd do even if they never paid me. That's how much of a shit I give."

He got closer and looked me right in the eye, and I felt that magnetic pull between us, overwhelming. His eyes were dark and hooded and for a confused moment, I thought he might kiss me. And I wanted him to, even though I knew it was a bad idea; because if Brody kissed me again before I confessed all my fucking sins, things were only going to get more complicated. For both of us.

But he didn't kiss me.

"And for the record," he said instead, his voice low, "I've advised them against writing with you. I told them you're unreliable, you're unstable, and you're not committed. We've been down that road before, with Seth, and we all know how it ends."

Wow.

That was not flattering. At all. And being compared to Seth felt... unfair. And yet, somehow, exactly what I deserved.

But true or not, it hurt to hear all those unflattering things out of Brody's mouth. To know that he'd said those things about me to Jesse, Zane, Elle and Dylan.

I opened my mouth to respond, but he wasn't done.

"This isn't about you, Jessa. It's not about me, either. It's about Dirty. Things are raw with the band right now. With Jesse and Elle's break up, and their tenth anniversary album and tour around the corner, and now we're without a rhythm guitarist, again. They've got enough to deal with. They don't need any bullshit from you."

"Wait. What do you mean? What happened to Paulie?"

"Paulie's out." Brody rubbed his hand over his face, looking weary. Suddenly I recognized that dark look in his eyes, and it had little to do with wanting to kiss me. "His wife's been diagnosed with some shitty rare cancer. He's dropping everything to get her through treatment."

"OhmyGod." The words came out of my mouth in a blurred, pained breath.

"I just got the call. Came to tell the guys. Look," he said, sounding beyond tired, "this is gonna take the wind out of everyone's sails."

"Yeah." I hugged myself, suddenly cold. The church was drafty, and that warm and fuzzy adrenalin buzz of playing with the guys? Long gone. "I understand. Just let me know what I can do to help? Please."

"There's nothing you can do," he said, looking me in the eye again. "Except leave now if that's what you're gonna do."

Then he turned and walked out.

CHAPTER ELEVEN

Jessa

FOR THE NEXT few days I laid low.

I didn't go back to the church, even though my brother kept asking me to come; even though I knew the whole band was there and they wanted me to be. Because no matter how offended I wanted to try to be over what Brody had said to me, I couldn't deny that he was right.

If I was going to leave... the best thing to do would be to leave now.

But I'd promised my brother ten days. And he'd postponed his honeymoon for me. Which meant that I should suck it up and get my ass back down to the church to spend time with him. Jam with the band. Hang out.

Just be there, if nothing else.

But I couldn't bring myself to go back down there. For now, I'd told Jesse I needed a little time for other things. It wasn't a lie, but it was a bit of an excuse. And instead of visiting old friends like I told him I'd be doing with a good chunk of my time, I barely left Roni's place.

I did call my agent, to tell her I'd be staying in Vancouver until the day before the shoot, when I'd fly down to L.A..

But I barely spoke to anyone else, and I barely got out of my sweats.

I wasn't going to sit around and feel sorry for myself, though. I'd done enough of that for a lifetime as a teenager. So I got Paulie's address down in L.A. from Maggie and sent flowers. I called and spoke with his wife, and his nine-year-old daughter on the phone. Then I arranged to have two weeks' worth of healthy meals delivered to them by a concierge service, including some fun stuff for the kids, to try to help. I didn't know what else I could really do.

I'd never really believed God would answer my prayers. But I prayed for Paulie and his wife and their family.

Then I re-organized Roni's condo.

By the end of day two of my self-imposed sabbatical, I'd labeled and color-coded everything in her cupboards. When Roni came home that night, she took one look at what I'd done, raised her eyebrows, and walked straight into her bedroom without a word.

The next day, people started dropping by unannounced.

It started with Maggie, then Zane, then Elle. Dylan and Ash showed up with takeout. Everyone and their dog suddenly happened to find themselves in Roni's neighborhood with nothing better to do than check up on me.

Because rock stars weren't busy or anything.

And not that I didn't appreciate it, but it was also kind of annoying, since it was interrupting my funk.

It was also necessary, because by the morning of day four, I'd started to slip. I'd run out of shit to organize, I still hadn't figured out how to deal with Brody, and the inevitable brooding had set in.

I'd taken to sitting around in my sweats and Yankees cap, idly playing the guitar Jesse had given me but really playing nothing at all, listening to stuff like Lera Lynn's slow, sultry cover of "Ring of Fire," which was either a brilliant or totally horrendous song to listen to when you were deep in the throes of a screwed-up, lovelorn, scared-shitless sort of funk.

Then I binge-watched a bunch of heart-rending movies, making it through *The Notebook*, *The English Patient*, and half of *The Age of Innocence* before my new sister-in-law managed to drag me out of the house.

I was still wearing my sweats and ball cap, but I went with her when she asked me to come to her art studio—Dirty's old rehearsal space.

I had been here before. It was a clean, spacious studio with an open loft above and big skylight windows. Perfect for an art studio. As Katie and I stepped inside with her black lab, Max, I could see, though, why the band wanted something bigger, something a little more raw, with a few more stories to tell, for their rehearsal space.

"I've set up a little studio in the sunroom at Jesse's place, too," Katie said as she deactivated the alarm. "You know, facing the water?" I smiled at how she still called it *Jesse's place*. "I like to paint at weird times, sometimes. And I don't always want to have to haul my ass over here in the middle of the night." She looked around the room at her stuff as she turned up the lights, frowning. "Jesse's been really gracious. Making room for me, and, you know... everything that comes with me."

I just smiled, rubbing Max's head. "Well, that's what you do when you love someone, right?"

"Right." She sighed, squinting at her stuff, like the room was a mess. It totally wasn't. Her art supplies were all neatly arranged in shelving units along a side wall. There were canvases, both clean and painted, filed into a custom storage unit with tall, narrow compartments. But what caught my eye were the paintings that had been left out—leaned against the walls, there was a giant portrait on canvas of each member of Dirty. The one of Dylan stood on an easel; it was the only one that wasn't yet complete.

As I approached, I could make out the seemingly millions of brush strokes, the texture of the thick, layered paint, the hundreds of colors that seemed to have been used to capture the myriad shades of his auburn hair.

"Katie... these are freaking amazing."

"They're for the tenth anniversary album. For the tour and everything. And thank you." She smiled. "They want it to be kind of a retrospective as well as the beginning of a new era. All the new stuff, and the old stuff. They... um... really want you to be a part of that."

I looked over at her. *Damn...* now they had Katie doing their dirty work?

"So as you can see," she went on, her cheeks pinking a little, "this is a business visit as much as a pleasure visit." She indicated the blank canvas standing on a giant easel in the middle of the room. "Maybe you've figured out my agenda here?"

"Yeah. I'm kind of getting the picture."

She smiled even bigger. "Then you'll sit for me? While you're in town? I can sketch you out, it won't take too long. I'll take a few photos too, for reference, so I can get the details right."

"Sure," I said, because it was Katie. She'd put off her honeymoon for me; how could I refuse? And it was just my image. If Dirty wanted my picture on the album, as part of their tenth anniversary, I could give them that.

I took off my ball cap and shook out my hair. "Maybe... you could just let me brush my hair first?"

"Of course." Katie beamed at me. "There's a washroom in back..."

But I wasn't listening. My eyes had caught on a painting, partly tucked in behind one of Elle.

"You painted... Seth?"

It was him; no doubt in my mind. I recognized his eyes above all things, and my stomach turned over. A pale, grayish-green with a burst of gold around the pupils. She'd captured them perfectly. There were more lines to his face than I remembered, and his hair was longer. In the portrait, he had a beard.

But it *was* Seth.

"Oh. Yeah," Katie said, distracted, as she sorted through tubes of paint. "He came to sit for me the other day."

He came to...

Seth Brothers was in town?

At Katie's studio?

"The band wants him in the album artwork," she said. "They want him involved. At least, his image, since he co-wrote some of the most successful songs. The band wants to pay tribute to that history, to his contribution. Just like they're doing with you. Cool, right?" She smiled at me again. "For a bunch of people with such giant egos, they're pretty humble, huh?"

"Right," I said. "Cool." But there was a lump in my throat as I turned away from that painting, from those eyes that seemed to look right through me.

CHAPTER TWELVE

Jessa

AS IT TURNED OUT, posing for a painting was nothing like posing for photographs.

While Katie worked I could talk, drink wine, snuggle with Max and pretty much get up and walk around whenever I wanted to. I didn't even have to suck in my gut or arch my back. She was only doing a portrait of my face.

She even said I was free to go once she'd blocked in my face on her canvas and taken a few pics with her phone, but I was in no hurry. It was fun watching Katie work. She got all serious and her eyebrows pinched together, and I could feel how much passion she had for her art.

I could also see why my brother gave her the studio. There was something special here, in her work; in her need to do her work. It was the same thing I saw in my brother when he played: a true life's passion in action.

Made me wonder what the hell had happened to mine.

As a girl, all I ever wanted to do was write. I loved music, poetry, movies, fairy tales and love stories of any kind. I was such a little dreamer. When my brother's band started writing their own material instead of just playing cover songs, I started playing around with writing lyrics, and as it turned out, I found my passion in it. Not only that... I had a talent for it.

I'd co-written songs with Dirty that millions of people loved. Songs that had made them both famous and respected in the music industry—and made us all a lot of money, too.

And then I'd walked away.

I'd given up the thing I most loved, most wanted to do—and the man I'd most wanted to have—and pursued another life. One that I was good at, but at the end of the day really meant nothing to me.

An empty life.

A life that only felt emptier when my brother showed up to flirt, grope and generally adore Katie right in front of me.

By the time I got back to Roni's that night I was starting to wonder, seriously, if I should just leave town. Now. Before things got any worse.

Because where did I fit into all of this anymore? Did I fit in, at all?

Had I ever?

Right now I felt so lost, I didn't even know.

One thing I did know, for sure: the more times I came face-to-face with Brody Mason, the more impossible it became to think of leaving him again.

But I was going to leave; I knew that, too. This wasn't my home anymore. I couldn't mope around Roni's place forever. I had a career to get back to, and an apartment in New York.

But I also had to think about what my brother said.

Remember this...

After we'd jammed together at the church, Jesse had asked me to give some serious thought to writing a few songs with the band. Just for fun, he said. They didn't have to go on the album. But I knew that was lip service.

He wanted me to write with Dirty again.

I wanted that too, but I would never tell him so and risk him getting crushed when it didn't happen.

For the most part, Jesse and Zane wrote Dirty's music. It had always been that way, ever since I left the band and Seth was kicked out. And we all knew that was why the songs weren't ever as strong as the ones on the debut album—when we were all together. It wasn't that Jesse and Zane weren't great writers. They were. They'd managed to turn out hit after hit over the years.

But there was something different, something special about those first songs, that without Seth and I, the band had never been able to touch.

There was magic between the six of us.

A magic that my brother and I had tapped into while writing the songs for his solo album together. And feeling that magic again, just messing around, jamming and letting the music flow with Jesse and Zane at the church... I was sucked right into it again.

Nothing else in my life had ever felt like that. That sense of harmony. Like things just *fit*. Like they were meant to be. I'd only ever gotten that feeling writing music with my brother and Dirty.

And, years ago... there were times... times when I felt that rightness with Brody.

But now I just kept hearing his words, like tiny electrical shocks, rewriting the truth on my heart.

I've advised them against writing with you.

Now, Brody didn't want me around. He'd made that much clear. He thought I should leave, for the band's sake, if I had any doubts at all about working with them again. And I did have doubts. I had big, huge doubts that Brody would ever forgive me and *let* me work with them again. And if he thought I shouldn't work with them... he was probably right. Dirty and Brody were a package deal, and obviously, I'd hurt them all when I left.

You broke my heart!

I kept hearing those words, the way he'd yelled them at me, hurled them at me, like an indictment.

And maybe he was trying to protect the band... but maybe he was also trying to push me to leave so he wouldn't have to deal with me.

I just didn't know.

I didn't know if he really wanted me to go, or just wanted me to prove to them all how much I wanted to stay. To earn it.

And if so—did I take that chance? Throw the white flag at his feet and tell all, and hope he could somehow forgive me? Was there any chance that he could do that?

More... that he could ever be mine?

That I could have both Dirty *and* Brody back?

I lay on my bed in Roni's spare bedroom for hours, staring at the ceiling as I thought about him. It had been this way for years; no matter where I went or what I did, I thought about Brody. The shadow of him was always with me, keeping a running count of my failures.

Because I could never think about Brody without also thinking about the many, many chances I'd had to make him mine... and fucked it all up.

I could hear the thumping rhythm of The Doors' "Back Door Man" spilling out of the giant barn at the edge of the field. Even at nineteen, Zane could belt out that song, and the newly-formed Dirty—Zane, Jesse, Dylan and Elle—were beyond amazing. I was thrilled that Brody had discovered Dylan and Elle playing with their other band at some party and poached them for us. Everyone knew the four of them were magic together. We finally had our band, and we were going places.

As long as those places had me home, in bed, by eleven o'clock.

It was so fucking unfair I couldn't stand it. How was I ever going to be the next great songwriter if I wasn't even allowed to come to the show?

Yes, I was fifteen, but so what? I was old enough to party. I wasn't naive. I knew what went on at parties like this... more or less. I wasn't going to go all *Girls Gone Wild* or anything. I just wanted to hear the band and have a beer and be part of it.

Which was why I'd let Roni bring me here, to some biker party

outside of town where Dirty and a couple of other bands were playing. Me, just aching for a night of freedom and hoping to soak up
some of the musical vibe, and her, hoping to run into Jude's brother,
Piper.

Roni was new to my high school that year. She was a grade
above me, pretty, popular, and always up for anything. My brother
didn't particularly like her, since he probably figured she was a bad
influence on me. It wasn't her fault, though, that her entry into my
life happened to coincide with me growing a pair and deciding I
wanted a life.

Or maybe he just didn't like that half his friends wanted to
screw her. Fat chance, since Roni had her sights set a little... older.

As soon as Roni found out that my brother's best friend's older
brother was a member of the West Coast Kings—a real, badass
motorcycle club, which meant the seriously criminal kind—she was
all in. Apparently, my friend Roni not only liked older men, but if
they liked to live dangerously all the better. My other friends
thought Piper was scary, and not sexy-scary like Jude, just scary-
scary. I'd known Piper since I was a little girl, so I didn't think he
was all that scary, but I could see why other people found him intimidating, since he had all the muscles and the tattoos and he didn't
exactly walk around handing out lollipops.

Not Roni. For Roni, the scarier the better.

"You have to introduce me to him," she told me as we wound our
way through the crowd.

"You know the minute he sees my face, I'm getting kicked out of
here?"

"Whatever. Just wait 'til he sees your ass in those jeans."

Oh, Roni. She did not get it. It didn't matter how my ass looked
in my jeans. Correction: the better my ass looked in my jeans, the
faster I was getting kicked out. Especially with the way the guys—
men—in this place were looking at us as we made our way through
the crowd.

Well, looking at Roni, for sure. You couldn't really miss her in
her black velvet bustier and skin-tight jeans, a line of rhinestones up

the back of her butt that looked like a bejeweled g-string and made it really, really easy to picture her wearing nothing but one—which was probably the point.

I was a little more low-key in my brother's QOSA *Songs for the Deaf* T-shirt. It was red and had a black pitchfork across it. I'd cut both the neck and sleeves off so he'd never demand it back, and wore it hanging off one shoulder with my tight black jeans. I wasn't exactly Roni-hot, but I was feeling pretty cute, pretty good all around, until...

"What. The. *Fuck*."

Great.

I turned to face him.

"Hey, Brody," I said.

"The fuck are you doing here?"

Shit. He was *pissed*.

"You've got five minutes," Jude said, appearing next to him. No pre-amble, no "nice to see you, bratface."

"Five minutes until what?" I asked innocently.

"'Til I bounce your ass out of here," Jude said. "Say your hellos and goodbyes and let's get going."

Roni flipped her dark hair, looking bored. "I'm gone," she told me. "Call you later, 'kay?" Then she flashed Jude a smile. "Later, jailor."

"Keep an eye on that one," Brody told Jude as she sashayed off into the crowd.

"Why?"

"'Cause she's sixteen. She gets to drinking, bounce her ass home."

Jude snarled, throwing me a *why-the-fuck-has-this-become-my-problem* glare, and headed off in pursuit of Roni.

"Good luck with that!" I called after him, feeling all sorts of bitchy.

"You." Brody pointed his finger at me. "Outside."

He turned and stalked through the crowd toward the barn doors.

"What about my five minutes?" I called after him. Geez. He couldn't get rid of me fast enough.

I stood there with my arms crossed, huffing. I watched the band play for a few seconds.

But yeah, I went.

If I didn't, Brody would've just found me again. Even if he had to stop the band and announce over the mic that I was here, I was underage and it was past my bedtime—he'd done it before—and drag me out, which would've been hella embarrassing in front of all these people.

I followed him into the night, into the rain that had started to mist down, across the edge of the field and into the sprawling back-yard of whatever biker's house this was. We were alone in the yard, so I knew he was probably going to rip into me any second.

I went first.

"I can't just leave Roni! We came together!"

Brody turned on me so abruptly I slipped on the damp grass and skidded into him. I grabbed onto his leather jacket to steady myself.

"How did you get here?" he demanded.

"In her mom's car."

"Then she'll get home in her mom's car. You," he said, "are coming with me." Then he hooked his hand around my arm and hauled me across the lawn toward his Harley, which was parked in the deserted back lane alongside a couple of trucks, instead of out front where the Kings' bikes were. And not like I could stop him. He was twenty, I was fifteen, and he was way the hell bigger than me.

"Wait! I want to stay! Stop dragging me around!"

He released me in the middle of the yard, putting himself between me and the barn. "Get on the bike, Jessa. I'm taking you home."

"No, you're not!"

I resented that I wasn't allowed to be there; that my brother, Jude and Brody made all the rules and I had to follow them.

I resented that every time I came to a show without their permission, I was thrown out.

Most of all, I resented that Brody didn't want me there.

He swiped a hand over his face and swore into the dark; I could practically see the steam coming out his ears as he turned back to me. "Where the fuck is your jacket?"

I hugged myself against the misting rain. "I didn't wear one."

Brody scowled; his eyes had locked on my chest, where my shirt had slipped off my shoulder, baring part of my bra. He took a step closer, looming over me. "What the *fuck* do you think you're doing wearing that in there?" He jabbed a finger at my chest, into the *Sinners MC* pin that I wore on my bra strap, just over my left breast, grinding it into my skin.

"Ow!" I gasped.

"You know who those guys are in there?" He punctuated his words with more jabs. I backed away but he just followed, jabbing all the way. "You know *what* they are? You know what they'll *think* when they see this?"

"It's mine!" I said, slapping his hand away. "Stop jabbing me!"

"It says *Sinners* on it," he said icily. "That sound like a bunch of old ladies sitting around knitting scarves to you? It's a fucking motorcycle club, Jessa. That pin belongs to *them*, and so does any chick stupid enough to wear it to a party crawling with bikers."

"You gave it to me!"

"When you were fucking five! And I told you long ago to stop wearing it." With that, he ripped my beloved pin off my bra and whipped it into the wet grass.

"That's *my* pin!" I screamed at him. "You can't do that!"

"Like fuck I can't!"

My hand clutched at my bra where the pin had been. And yes, I knew what it was. Which was why I wore it *under* my shirt. I wasn't an idiot. "Why did you give it to me if you didn't want me to wear it?"

"Christ," he muttered, raking a hand through his rain-dampened hair. "Jesse is way too fucking soft on you."

"What does that mean!?"

"It *means* I thought you'd wear it for a couple of weeks, lose it, and forget about it. Or your brother would make you get rid of it. Or some teacher would get wise and tell you you couldn't wear it anymore. You weren't supposed to keep it forever. Now stop acting like a brat. You're not five years old anymore."

"I. Was. Eight!" I shouted. "And you shouldn't have given it to me if you didn't want me to wear it!" With that, I dropped to my knees in the grass, searching for my pin.

Brody grabbed my elbow and tried to pull me up, but I jerked from his grasp and scrambled through the grass on my hands and knees in the direction I thought the pin might've bounced. He stepped in front of me, stomping his boot down on a flash of silver—

My pin!

"Get OFF!" I cried, pushing and then pulling at his boot, but it was no use. The leather was damp and slick, and he weighed like five hundred pounds; the rocks in his head weren't helping. "You're so fucking BOSSY! You think you know EVERYTHING! LET. ME. GO!"

But he was already hauling me to my feet. "*Jesus*, Jessa." He shoved me back, all the way back, across the yard and up against the rough, scaly bark of a tree. I was so mad I could've spit. Maybe I should have. Probably would've been more effective.

When I struggled and tried to knee him in the groin, the way my brother had taught me to do, he shoved his knee between my legs, grabbed my wrists and pinned them on either side of my head. Then he pressed his hips against me, trapping me against the tree with his weight.

So much for my brother's self-defense lessons.

"Get your shit together, princess," he said in a low growl, "and calm the fuck down." It was oddly quiet; the throb of the music from the barn was muffled as the rain misted down around the tree, and Brody's breathing was all raspy and weirdly uneven. "You wanna bring the wrath of the Kings down on me over a junk pin?"

I looked up into his dark blue eyes. His body was hot and heavy against me. I'd never had a boy—a man—pressed against me, so I only had the stories of some of my girlfriends to go on, but he definitely felt... hard.

A flood of heat rushed through me as I swallowed.

"Piper's not even here," he said, still holding me pinned against the tree. "You want me to go head-to-head with a dozen pissed-off bikers, *armed* pissed-off bikers, 'cause you keep screaming like a banshee for me to get off you? You want someone in that party deciding you need to be relieved of me, just so he can take my place?"

Okay. That got through.

The guys in that party were kinda scary. Like scary in the way Piper was scary to other people—because I didn't know them, and yeah, they were probably armed. But mostly, scary because Brody seemed to think I should be scared of them.

No way I'd admit that to him, though. I didn't need him.

At that point in time, I was well on my way to convincing myself I didn't need anyone.

I bit my lip and sniffled, shaking my head.

"Hope you've got something nice to wear to my fucking funeral," he said, releasing me. He eased back an inch, but didn't step away.

"I wasn't going to get you in trouble," I whispered into the small space between us.

Brody was still breathing hard, and something in his eyes had changed as he stared at me. They looked kind of... dreamy, and darker than usual.

"You, at this party," he said, "is nothing but trouble."

"Why? Why can Roni be here but I can't?"

"Because I don't give a fuck about Roni."

"But what if something happens?"

"Like what? She falls on someone's dick?"

I sucked in a massive breath, preparing to blast him for that.

"She's not a virgin, you know," he added quickly. "Half the guys at your school have already—"

"Shut UP!" I shouted at him. "Don't talk about her like that. You don't know!"

"I know you like her and she's fun to have around, and she gets you in trouble, yeah?"

"So?"

"So, it's my job to bail your ass out of trouble when you get into it. And when I see you walk into a party like that, I know trouble's coming. I'd rather pre-empt that shit *before* it hits the fan." He got in my face again, forcing me back against the tree. "Get used to it and stop acting like a spoiled princess who can do whatever the fuck she wants without any consequences. I know and *you* know that you're still a snot-nosed little brat inside, but guess what, sweetheart? Those guys don't know shit about you. All they see is some hot teenage ass they wanna get up inside."

"That's disgusting!" I cried. "And I do *not* need you to bail my ass out of trouble! Who the hell made that your job?"

"YOU did," he said, "every time you called me crying in the middle of the night."

"I did NOT call you crying!" I protested, embarrassed, but that wasn't true. After the tampon incident, I'd just started going to him instead of Jesse whenever I needed something; I wasn't even sure why. Maybe because he kept coming around, checking up on me. He was just always *there*, even when my brother wasn't.

Maybe because I'd seen what my brother had gone through for years, how hard he worked to take care of me and our mom, and I didn't want to be the one to spoil all his fun when he'd rather be playing gigs or getting laid than looking out after his kid sister all the time.

Maybe because more and more I'd felt like a burden in my brother's life.

But Brody... Brody never made me feel like a burden.

Until now.

"No? You *don't* call me crying whenever you need something?" he accused. "Crying to me about your mom always sleeping and

Jesse pissing you off and every time some prick tries to get in your pants? Who's there to swoop in and save you, Jessa? It's *me*."

"Then stop doing it if you don't want to! And I'll stop calling!"

I stood there fuming, shuddering, just trying not to break down in sobs. I didn't need this. I didn't need a fucking babysitter. Where did he get off, thinking he was doing me some kind of favor by ruining my life?

He blinked at me.

"I don't want you to stop," he said, and then, suddenly, his mouth was on mine.

He kissed me, hard, forcing my mouth open... and as soon as I got over the shock of it, I succumbed to it. My bones went all liquidy as he shoved his tongue in my mouth, hot and strong. He pressed me against the tree and I clung to him, feeling lightheaded. Kind of like the whole world was spinning and somehow we were dancing and he was leading, and I was going with him, wherever he would take me... and then suddenly I lost track of the steps, of where his lead ended and mine began, and I was kissing him back... harder and faster, pushing back, tasting, sucking, wanting more. My body grew hot against his...

And then a little shiver prickled through me.

I got scared.

I pulled away, breaking the kiss. I stared at him as he panted, looming over me.

I could only guess how much more experienced he was than me, but I had a rough idea. I saw the girls my brother's friends hung out with, and I was pretty sure Brody wasn't exactly saving himself for the priesthood.

And yes, I was afraid. I was afraid of that burning look in his eyes, a look I'd so desperately wanted directed at me, yet now that it was... I did not know what to do with it. I was well aware that Brody was no longer a boy, that he was a man; that he had been a man for a long time, while I was still fumbling around in that awkward border-land between girlhood and what lay beyond. I had no idea how ready I was or totally wasn't for what would follow that look.

He ran his knuckles, softly, over my cheek. "Jessa—"

"I've seen you with Christy Rempel," I blurted. "Everyone knows she's the worst kind of slut."

Okay; that was maybe a slight exaggeration. In truth, all I knew for sure was that Christy, who was the older sister of one of my classmates, was nineteen, voluptuous, had her own car and an apartment, and a job. In other words she was a *woman.*

But throwing her reputation under the bus was the only thing I could think of to do in that moment to drive a wedge between us.

"I'm sorry," I said, mostly for the comment about Christy, but also because I had to get out of there.

I turned to run, but my stupid boots slipped on the wet grass again. Brody's hand closed on my arm, hauling me back around to face him. "Don't run from me," he said, his voice all low and husky, his blue eyes soft. "No matter what happens... I'll never hurt you, Jessa."

"I know," I said, hiccuping a little. I'd been doing so much yelling and trying so hard not to burst into tears, I was getting a headache.

"I know you're not ready for this," he said, sifting his fingers into my hair, gently gripping my neck, sending shivers down my spine and making me wonder what, exactly, *this* was... and really, really wanting to know. Wanting him to show me.

Then he drew me closer, until our lips touched again, gently this time... I breathed in his clean, manly smell, like leather and the wind off a green field on a warm summer day, and heat tore through my body like wildfire. He breathed softly against my face and whispered, "I'll wait for you. I'll wait for you 'til you're ready."

Maybe some girls would've been thrilled to hear that. Swept up in the romantic implications of it. Swoony.

I just felt sick.

"You can't wait for me," I protested, and he frowned.

"Why the fuck not?"

"Didn't you ever see *Legends of the Fall?*" I sniffled. "You know, when the girl tells Brad Pitt she'll wait for him forever?"

"So?"

"So... forever is too long, so she ends up marrying his brother and then blowing her head off."

"Jesus," he muttered, his thumb skimming over my cheek. "That sounds depressing as fuck, Jessa."

I shrugged and tried to smile. "Sorry for the spoiler."

"No worries. I'm never watching that shit. And I'm not blowing my head off either, you want me or not. I promise you that."

Then we both realized what he'd said; what *I'd* said. I knew it by the look on his face, at the same moment it hit me. My dad hadn't shot himself. But suicide wasn't exactly a vague romantic concept in my world.

"Jessa." Brody moved closer, pulling me against him so his body was flush against mine, big, strong, and warm against the night. "I'm not gonna do that shit and neither are you," he said softly, "no matter what happens in our lives. Stop brooding on that nasty shit or it's gonna eat up all the good and the sweet in you, and princess, there's a whole lot of good and sweet. So just *stop*. No one's gonna die here, yeah? People don't have to die just because they care about each other."

I gave up the fight and started crying, the tears flowing openly down my cheeks. "Either way," I told him, "I don't want you waiting on me. I can't handle that kind of pressure, Brody."

"Jesus, babe, get your shit together," he said, but the words were soft, almost a whisper, and he held me tight, kissing the tears from my cheeks. "Nothing's gonna happen to me just 'cause you love me."

I sucked in air and held my breath.

Because I *loved* him?

Brody *knew* I loved him?

I didn't know whether to be embarrassed or relieved.

He sighed, resting his forehead against mine. "How about I wait for you for a year, and then we'll see what happens."

I exhaled shakily and nodded a little, because I couldn't speak.

"Yeah?"

"Yeah," I said, not even fully understanding what exactly I was agreeing to, just knowing that I wanted it. I wanted him, so bad.

I always had.

"Good. Now get your ass on my bike."

He took off his leather jacket and put it on me. Then he pulled me through the misting rain and drove me home, and I thought I knew what was going to happen. I saw my whole life rolled out ahead of me as the pavement whipped past and the white lines blurred into each other on that highway, my arms wrapped tight around Brody's waist.

My brother and his band were going to be superstars. When I got brave enough, I'd show them the lyrics I'd been writing, and they'd put them in their songs.

When I got really brave, I'd kiss Brody again.

Then I'd marry him. We'd have kids, and everything would be perfect.

That was the fantasy.

Then my mom died.

Seth happened.

A whole lot of other shit happened.

And in the midst of my grieving and my awkward coming-of-age among my brother's friends, infatuated with a man I didn't yet know how to make mine and foolishly thinking I had all the time in the world to figure it out... it was the heartbreak I didn't even see coming that trampled my dreams.

CHAPTER THIRTEEN

Brody

"SO... HOW YOU BEEN, BRO?"

"Great," I said.

I was hammering on a punching bag and Jesse was looking at me like I wasn't fucking great at all. More like I'd grown horns out of my head. That cautious tone of voice really fucking irritated me.

Since the wedding, everyone had been talking to me like that.

Well, since I'd walked Jessa back to her cabin and told her she broke my heart, and she blew me the fuck off, and I started leaving a trail of broken shit in my wake.

I didn't know you were in love with me, and it's not my fault if you were.

Fuck.

Couldn't they all just get a fucking clue? I didn't wanna talk. Usually, Jesse was fine with that. Heart-to-hearts with his bros weren't exactly his forte. But he did have a gym in his house, and I definitely felt like punching things. A lot.

I hadn't counted on Jude being here, though.

Jude had little patience for other people's bullshit, just like I did, so usually that worked for me. But when he said, "He means what the fuck's up your ass?" I started to seriously regret dropping by.

"You've been wearing that ugly face all week. You know, you keep scowling like that, it might get stuck."

I threw an ugly look his way and kept punching.

"Think about it. How're you gonna get laid, that happens? Your sparkling personality isn't gonna do it."

I ignored him.

"He's right," Jesse put in. "Ladies like to laugh, and you've got shit for jokes. Good thing you've got money."

They were fucking with me. Trying to make me laugh, ease up a bit. Or piss me off enough that I snapped and maybe flipped out of this shit mood I was in.

I glanced over at them, where Jude was spotting Jesse on the bench press. "How about you girls worry about your own pretty faces, yeah?"

I caught Jude throwing a sideways glance at Jesse. "This wouldn't have anything to do with Jessa coming back to town, huh?"

I turned my focus back to the punching bag. "Broke up with Amanda."

Yeah, that sounded convincing. A convenient excuse for the rotten funk I'd been in. And it was true; I'd broken up with her as soon as we got back from the wedding. Which sucked, in a way, because there was a whole lot to like about Amanda. She was smart, compassionate, pretty, athletic, and seriously into me. Plus, she hadn't broken my heart, so she had that going for her.

If I'd never met Jessa Mayes, I probably could've seriously fallen for an Amanda.

But I did meet Jessa Mayes. I met her when I was young, angry and had shit all in the way of love in my life, and that lonely eight-year-old girl with the big brown eyes made me smile for the first time in a long time.

She made me smile a lot, back then.

Never mind that the woman she'd grown into had caused me more pain than anyone else I'd ever known. Any way I tried to get around it, there was no denying it. Jessa Mayes was in my mother-fucking bones.

She always had been.

Amanda wasn't the reason I'd been walking around slamming doors, rattling windows and breaking shit that got in my way.

And even Amanda knew it.

"It's her, right?" she'd asked me, just as I was about to walk out of her life. "Jessa," she said. "The rose on your hand."

It'd taken me kind of aback. I'd never told anyone the meaning behind that tattoo.

She'd just shrugged and said, "You stare at it a lot. And... you stare at her a lot."

I couldn't argue with that.

And yeah, the rose was for her.

I'd had it done nine years ago, at a time when things between us were getting really fucked up. It was on my right palm, at the base of my thumb. Just a small rose entangled in thorny vines, to mark the spot where, even though things between us were fucked up, she'd kissed me at my father's funeral.

It was the only way I could think of to somehow ink Jessa Mayes onto my body and not raise too many eyebrows. And I *had* to ink her onto my body. Had to have her with me, to remind myself that there was something between us, something real... or at least there had been, once, even if it was temporarily fucked up.

At the time, I'd really believed it was temporary.

"She okay, man?"

Jesse was still eying me across the gym, and all I could think was: *How the fuck would I know?*

Then I realized he wasn't asking about Jessa.

I took a break to guzzle some water before I sweat out my body weight and passed out. "Yeah," I said, but I had no idea if that was true.

I honestly hadn't thought about it.

Since I'd walked away from Amanda after telling her it was over, I'd felt nothing in that direction but a sense of relief, of finality, the likes of which I'd never come close to feeling toward Jessa.

I went back at the bag with a vengeance. Because what the fuck else was I gonna do to keep from losing my mind?

I hadn't seen her for days. Not since I'd confronted her at the church and basically told her to leave. She hadn't returned the phone call I'd made to her this morning and she wasn't responding to my texts.

Nothing fucking new, right?

And yet, it still gutted me.

I wouldn't have thought there was anything left for Jessa Mayes to take, since she'd already eviscerated my heart and soul so many years ago. But apparently there was still shit for her to carve out of me...

I could still feel her, damp and near-naked, her silky bra and panties clinging to her as she wrapped her goddess-like body around me, rubbing herself against me. Could still feel her heartbeat, her heat and her need.

Could still taste her as she kissed me, like she'd been starving for my kisses all her life.

Could still hear her, her helpless whimpers... gasping with antic-ipation... and singing by that fire in the night with a smile on her face.

I could still feel the long, smooth curve of her thigh as I slid that frilly garter up... up...

I'm not wearing any underwear.

Shit.

How the hell was I supposed to let her go again? When I'd glimpsed the pain and the regret in her eyes? When I'd held her, all drunk and vulnerable in my arms? Worse, I'd felt the hunger that was still there between us. A hunger that had never been sated.

Jessa wanted me. And still... she was running from me.

This time, maybe I was running too.

This morning, I'd driven past the church. I didn't stop. Not because she might be there. Because what if she wasn't? What if we were losing her again?

What if we were losing her because of what I'd said?

There's nothing you can do. Except leave now if that's what you're gonna do.

After I passed the church, I drove back into town and over to Roni's place, since it was nowhere near my route coming back from the church. Yeah, pretty much like a stalker would.

I didn't even know what the fuck I was planning to do or say if I saw her. If Jessa was even there. Even when I'd called her, I didn't know what I would say.

Apologize again?

Beg her to stay with the band again?

Fat fucking lot of good that ever did.

I was just making up my mind not to stop, to just drive on by, when I saw her. A few blocks from Roni's, standing at the curb, waiting for the light to change so she could cross the street. She was carrying a takeout coffee from JJ Bean and gazing off into nothing; not vacantly, but the way she used to when she was working out a song in her head. It was just about to rain but she had no umbrella, no jacket. Her hair was twirled up into a messy knot thing on top of her head. She was wearing Ray-Bans and pink Chucks and ripped jeans, and a T-shirt that said *Rock 'N' Roll Stole My Soul*. Looking just that little bit awkward, like she always did: like some angel fallen to Earth, trying to pass as a regular person.

She was right *there*, in the same city as me, right on the street across from me, and we weren't even talking.

I was nowhere near the neighborhood and just thought I'd swing by to stare at you and not say a damn thing. Cool?

I didn't stop. I kept right on driving. I drove to Jesse's house and headed for the gym. I didn't even have workout clothes with me. I just took off my shirt and started punching things.

At least I was working out like a fiend. If I could remember to eat once in a while, if I could get some sleep, I'd probably be feeling pretty damn good. Physically, at least.

As it was, I was just trying to beat the shit out of myself and in the process pummel the anger and frustration and impotence away, the powerlessness that overtook me whenever I got in the same room with Jessa. Whenever I was reminded of how she'd crushed me, all those years ago... over and over again. And the memories... all the fucking memories that were coming back to bite me completely in the ass.

Because in every single one of them, I'd fucked up.

At least maybe I'd eventually exhaust myself so I could sleep.

I caught Jesse's eyes on me again, and Jude's. They weren't even lifting anymore. Just watching me, and once in a while throwing each other a look, doing that annoying best-friends-forever mind-reading shit they did.

What the fuck was I doing here?

"Heading home," I said abruptly, yanking my shirt over my sweaty torso and heading for the door.

"Shit, Bro, you can take a shower if—"

I slammed the door behind me before I could hear the end of that sentence. What the fuck did I have to say to anyone anyway? I couldn't be around people like this.

I couldn't even stand myself.

At least tomorrow I was getting the fuck out of town.

CHAPTER FOURTEEN

Brody

THAT NIGHT, I lay in bed awake for hours. Again.

I kept thinking through the last night Jessa spent in my bed. And the next day, when I told her I loved her.

And all the things I could've—should've—done differently.

I stared at the tattoo on my forearm. The runes that spelled out *abstinence*. And that joke ran through my mind, the one that sometimes did when I looked at that tattoo.

Abstinence makes the heart grow fonder.

I'd had that tattoo marked on me like a brand at twenty-five, angry and righteous, like I could make her feel the pain of the needle etching the ink into my skin across the miles. A reminder to myself, that I'd see every fucking day; every day that I abstained from Jessa. From calling her, from messaging her, from thinking about her. From loving her.

And every day that I'd failed miserably at all of it. Because I would never stop loving her.

It was fucking chemically impossible.

I could pretend I didn't, but it was a fucking lie. I was drawn to that woman like a magnet. I always had been.

She was drawn to me, too. I knew she was.

We'd smashed together enough times, whether we liked it or not, that even as stubborn as she was, she couldn't deny it.

And every time we smashed together, I came away more damaged and disoriented, wondering why the fuck my world made just that little bit less sense.

Yeah. My world, without Jessa Mayes in it, was fucking nonsense. A total fucking sham I'd been working my ass off to make heads or tails of for years.

You might think, over time, that would get easier to do.

Time heals all wounds, and all that shit.

Wrong.

Time did not heal wounds. I was now thirty years old and I'd been aching for Jessa Mayes since we were kids. By the time I was twenty-one, she'd broken my heart. When I was twenty-four, she ripped it right the fuck out.

And what did I do?

I slapped a dirty bandage over that shit and left it to rot.

There were people crowded into every square inch of my house. The music was pumping, drinks were flowing, the sweet, slightly skunky smell of good pot clung in the air, and I really should've been fucking ecstatic. Dirty's debut album, *Love Struck*, had just dropped, and it was shooting up the charts with a fucking bullet. We felt poised to take over the world.

Yeah; I should've been over-fucking-joyed.

Instead, to distract myself from the fact that it was the night of Jessa's high school graduation—which meant she was going to her grad party with a bunch of horny teenage assholes—I threw a party for the band at my new house.

My father had died last year, leaving me a larger inheritance than I'd expected, since when he was alive he never gave me shit. So I'd taken his money, invested some in stocks, invested some in the band,

and invested the rest in a piece of real estate up the side of the mountain in North Vancouver, overlooking the city. A piece of real estate with a big-ass house on it; a house that my father would hate, especially if he saw the three-car garage where I stored my bikes, the music room filled with band equipment, and the party room filled with beer kegs.

Since my house was bigger than anyone else's at the time, it quickly became the party house. This was the biggest party I'd thrown yet—but then again, we had the most cause to celebrate—and all the usual suspects were there.

At least, most of the usual suspects.

Jessa was at a high school dance, probably getting groped. Or giving it up to some jock in the back of a car. Because that's what hot girls did when they graduated from high school, right?

Seth was God-knew-the-fuck-where, but that was nothing new. More and more, he'd been ghosting in and out, partying with a different crowd. As our newest member, he hadn't become quite as invested as the rest of the band, who were pretty much one big, happy, but slightly dysfunctional family—just the way we liked it.

Around one a.m., Jessa rolled in, alone.

Impossible to miss her, as usual, but especially so because the boys went up in a fit of chest-puffing pride for their number one girl when she appeared, wearing a silky little charcoal-gray top and black sequined tights with sparkly silver Chucks, a limp white corsage on her wrist, and looking kind of dazed, her eyes glassy from a night of whatever debauchery she'd been up to.

The guys flocked to wrap her up in a whirlwind of hugs, then Jude tossed her up on his shoulders and paraded her through the house, passing her off to Zane and Dylan to do the same. Eventually Dylan deposited her in front of me.

She stood there looking awkward as I looked her over.

"Hey, Brody."

"That what you wore to your grad?"

Her pretty mouth twitched downward at the corners. "What was I supposed to wear? Some fancy dress?"

I didn't give one fuck what she wore. What I gave a fuck about was why one of the skinny straps of her shirt was broken; she'd tied it in a knot to keep the whole thing from falling off.

"Oh, I dunno. How was your *date*?" I pretty much spat the word at her. Yeah; definitely knew I sounded like a crazy jealous freak. So be it. "You get laid?"

She cringed. "Don't be gross."

"Isn't that what high school kids do on their grad night?"

"You're drunk." She eyed the bottle of Canadian Club in my hand. "Just leave it alone, okay?"

I didn't leave it alone. I *was* drunk.

I didn't normally drink much at band parties since I'd taken it upon myself, early on, to be the businessman of the group. The level-headed one, the man behind the band; the one who kept everyone else's shit together. But that night was not a normal night, and I was drunker than I'd been in years. I was sloppy, messy, stupid drunk.

"I mean, I wouldn't know," I went on. "Never went to my grad. You'll have to correct me if I'm wrong."

"I didn't go with a date," she said, hugging herself. "You have a good night? *You* get laid?"

"Not yet." I took a swig from the bottle of rye, staring her down. "Who gave you that ugly fucking corsage?"

"My brother did!"

"Yeah? He rip your shirt getting at your tits too?"

She turned on her heel and disappeared into the crowd, and I let her go. I had nothing else to say to her anyway.

Jessa Mayes could go fuck every horny little prick in that high school for all I cared, and she could go fuck herself while she was at it.

I didn't even keep tabs on her for the rest of the night like I usually would. At least, after a while, I stopped. The last I saw her she was in the kitchen, doing shots with Jesse and Zane—a totally fucking rare sight, but maybe they were finally starting to accept the fact that she was a woman and not a little girl anymore. Though I could understand it was difficult to swallow that point when she acted like such a goddamn spoiled brat all the time.

God, I fucking missed her.

I missed hanging out with her, just getting up to shit. She used to be so fucking *fun*. And she used to like hanging out with me. Long ago, before we'd had that first kiss under the tree out at that party, and for a while afterward... we were friends. And she used to flirt with me like crazy.

And I fucking ate that shit up.

At first, I'd thought the way she went out of her way to touch me all the time was to irritate her brother. The two of them were always bickering and battling for control, Jesse still fighting the fact that she was growing up and getting a mind of her own, that she wasn't always gonna be that little girl who'd followed him around and did exactly what he said. And him seeing her sitting next to me, her leg draped across my lap or her arm slung around my neck, whispering in my ear, was sure to get her unceremoniously thrown out of whatever room we were in.

How long had it been since she'd done that shit?

Since Seth.

Or maybe earlier than that; maybe since her mom died, and she seemed to lose her sense of humor.

Somewhere near three a.m. and the bottom of my bottle, I decided I should find her to apologize.

Christy had left a while ago because she had to work in the morning. I was mildly disappointed I wouldn't get to fuck her while I was thinking about Jessa, which was also a relief, because even I knew the frequency with which I was doing that was getting really fucked up.

Christy and I had become official about half a year ago—when I'd told myself to stop waiting for Jessa. Which was right around the time I'd pretty much stopped talking to her.

But not talking to her didn't mean I didn't think about her, all the fucking time.

When I'd hooked back up with Christy, it had been over a year since Jessa's mom had died and shit had fallen apart for her; I knew it had. I'd tried to be there for her and somehow give her the space she needed. She'd turned sixteen before her mom died, and that year I'd given her to decide she was ready to be with me? It had run way the fuck out.

But I wasn't gonna pressure her to hook up with me; not in the midst of what she was going through.

For a while, I'd lost track of her. She was modeling a lot, she was in school, she had more friends her own age. I was busy managing the band and she was spending more time alone, writing.

And then suddenly all the evidence started adding up to the fact that she was spending more time with Dirty's new rhythm guitarist and co-songwriter than she was with me.

I never saw that shit coming.

But I saw it happening right in front of me like a slow, slow, slow-fucking-motion train wreck with the force of a locomotive that I could not stop.

Since then, everything had been messed up and fucking inside out.

I searched for her all over the house, in a bit of a frenzy... pretty much resigning myself to the fact that I was a total piece of shit because she'd left the party and I hadn't gotten my drunken shit together to apologize for being an asshole—when I stumbled out the back door and right into her.

She was on her way inside and we got kind of tangled up, mostly because I was drunk and she was trying to keep me from falling on my face, and I was holding on to her, not because I didn't want to fall on my face but because I didn't want her to leave. I was just so fucking relieved she was still there.

"Jessa," I said, my voice all slurry and pathetic, "you're here."

"Dance with me," she said. She was still holding onto me. I was holding onto her.

Then she burrowed her face in my shirt.

The Black Keys were playing on the sound system in the party room, the music pouring out the windows into the dark around us, but I just stood there like an idiot, wavering and drunk. "What?"

"It's my grad night," she said. She peered up at me, her face still buried in my shirt. "I should get to dance."

"You didn't get to dance?"

She started to pull away. "Can you for once just not turn this into an argument, and dance with me?"

I pulled her to me before she could get away, and I danced with her, really fucking slowly. We were barely moving at all, just sort of swaying to the music a bit and holding onto each other. Mostly because if I did anything more I might lose my balance and take her down with me.

I just held her tight and nuzzled my face into her hair, smelling her.

Jessa.

This was happening?

Why was this happening?

Why didn't she get to dance?

As her heart beat against me, her breaths warming my chest through my shirt, her hands clasped tight around the back of my neck, all I could really feel in my sorry-ass state was jealousy.

Blistering, fucking festering jealousy.

Because I could see Seth through the windows into the party room.

He'd turned up about an hour ago. Looked like he'd been having a rough night, but I knew for fucking sure he'd never gone near Jessa, because I'd kept an eye on him since he arrived. More and more I'd had an eye on Seth, for various reasons; some to do with drugs, and even more to do with Jessa.

She never said she was dating him, or dating anyone. And not like I expected her to. Jesse probably would've had a shit fit if she started openly dating Seth Brothers. For one thing, he was three years older than her, which was three years too many in Jesse's books. For another, Seth liked his drugs—pretty much more than he liked anything else. But the girl had definitely learned over the last few years how to keep her brother off the "people in the know" list. If she was partying, drinking, or smoking up, chances were, Jesse was blissfully ignorant about it. I didn't much care about that—until it seemed that I, too, was getting excluded from her go-to list.

Seth clearly wasn't.

Why she'd decided to let him, of all people, into her very secretive—and apparently, exclusive—inner circle was beyond me. Why she was hanging out with him so much, or dating him, or screwing him, or whatever the fuck she was doing, was totally fucking beyond me.

I liked Seth. Everyone did.

I did not like him with Jessa.

But how could I begrudge her the one thing she had in her life that seemed to be giving her some kind of comfort? Comfort that, apparently, I'd totally fucking failed to provide?

Because Jessa sure as shit didn't come to *me* when she needed something anymore. She'd stopped coming to me around the time Seth came on the scene, and I wasn't fucking stupid. But no matter how I tried to wrap my head around it, I couldn't allow myself to believe that Jessa was giving it up to Seth.

Not her.

Jessa Mayes was, and would always be, in my mind—until the day I had sex with her—a virgin. How could she possibly be anything else?

I couldn't stand it.

And yeah, that was my bullshit male pride talking. Because I couldn't fucking stand that Seth, or anyone else, had gotten a taste of her first.

No. More bullshit.

I couldn't stand that he'd gotten a taste of her *at all*.

And according to one incredibly ill-advised comment he'd dropped in my face when I'd confronted him on the subject late last year, he had.

Which was how he'd ended up with a fractured eye socket and a chipped tooth, and I'd stopped talking to him for all of December.

But that was a short-sighted plan since he was not only my friend but my client, and "Dirty forever" and all that shit.

So instead, I stopped talking to Jessa.

I told myself I'd let her choose.

Three long years ago, I told her I'd wait for her, and if she wanted me, I told myself she'd come.

I'd told her I'd wait a year, but I was still fucking waiting.

And it was eating me up, bit by bloody bit.

The next morning, I'd parked my truck on the street in front of Dolly's house, where Jessa had lived since her mom died. It was raining and gray, and I was hungover as fuck.

Jessa sat silently in the passenger seat, slowly taking off her seatbelt. She was wearing my Led Zeppelin T-shirt and her sequined tights. Last night, after we'd danced together in the dark, she'd slept in my bed, fully dressed. And even though she'd slept in my bed, holding me through the night, I couldn't say that was a good thing.

It wasn't the first time it'd happened, either. But it'd been a long, long time.

Mostly I used to find her there in the middle of the night, after some party, and more often than not she was drunk. But she'd hold me tight when I slid in next to her, and if she was awake enough, she'd kiss me.

I'd kiss her back.

But if I ever tried to put my hands on her—and I did—she'd stop me.

I didn't pressure her. I didn't push her boundaries. I left them intact, telling myself when she was ready, she'd be mine.

Last night, she'd kissed me just like she used to. I'd kissed her back, sloppily and drunk, grateful, desperate, frantic for her. Then I tasted the salty taste on her lips.

She was crying.

She wasn't making a sound, but the tears were running down

her cheeks. So I tucked her head under my chin and held her close until she fell asleep.

I knew she was sad about Dirty leaving on their first world tour, but she'd already told us she wasn't coming with us. Jesse threw a fit at first, but he'd gotten over it. I still hadn't.

But what the fuck could I do? I couldn't make her come.

I looked at her, sitting there, staring out the passenger window of my truck.

"I think you should come on tour with us," I told her.

"I can't," she said, just like every other time I'd brought it up. "I've got school."

"We can work it out. Maybe you can take a distance course or put college off a year. This is a once-in-a-lifetime opportunity, Jessa. You can't just pass it up."

"I've committed to Europe," she said. "I'm going for the summer."

"I think that's a mistake."

"So you've told me."

Shit. I was always saying the wrong thing when it came to her.

"What I mean is, modeling isn't your only option. I know they've offered you a contract to do the Europe thing, but we can get you a better deal. With the band—"

"I know my options."

But she didn't. She didn't know *all* her options.

"If you want to do something else, Jessa, I'll manage you," I told her. I'd never brought it up before, but I was getting fucking desperate. It was pretty much the last card I had to play. The only thing I had left to offer her. "If you want to do a solo thing. If you really don't want to be a part of Dirty, we can do something else. You've got the talent—"

"I'm going to Europe," she said. "And then I've got college. I'm not going on tour."

"But we could cut a demo for you. The kinds of contacts we're making... the world is opening right up for us. You have no idea. I know we can make it happen for you."

"I don't want it to happen," she said.

Jesus, the girl was stubborn.

Every way I'd tried to come at it, she just shot it down. She shot *me* down.

I stared at her, still staring out the window. "You know, I never would've kissed you if I knew you wouldn't be able to stand me afterward."

She looked over for the first time, blinking at me. "What?"

"Last night. I never would've kissed you back, if it meant you weren't gonna be able to look at me now."

"I am looking at you now," she said, holding my gaze.

Yeah, she was. Fucking finally.

How long were we gonna keep doing this fucking dance? Play this stupid childish game?

We weren't children anymore. And I sure as fuck wasn't playing.

"Why the fuck aren't you mine?"

"Isn't Christy yours?" she said, her voice light, but it was a fake kind of light, with a whole lot of heavy behind it.

"Christy is Christy."

"What does that mean?"

"It means I'm not in love with Christy."

She just stared at me. She didn't say a thing, but her eyes were starting to shine.

"You remember that weekend we went surfing up in Tofino a few years ago? When Dylan's van broke down?"

"I remember," she whispered.

"We all got drunk around the campfire, yeah? And you and Jesse got in an argument over who knew more classic rock. He said he did because he could play the songs on guitar and you said you did because you knew all the words. And someone dared you to sing 'Bohemian Rhapsody' and you did all the parts, and I laughed so fucking hard I almost fell in the fire. But you dove in and saved me, somehow, and you burned that hole in the ass of your jeans. I thought I was gonna break a rib laughing. I was sore the next day."

She just blinked at me, her eyes shining with tears.

"I have about two hundred thousand memories of you like that," I told her, "and I loved you in every single one of them."

It was raining harder, and the rivulets streaming down the windows made shadows on her face that almost disguised the tears rolling down her cheeks. "Why didn't you tell me?"

"Because you were fifteen and I was twenty and it just... it wasn't right."

"I'm eighteen now," she said, and she took a deep, shuddering breath. "When is it ever going to be right, Brody?"

I reached over, drew her face close to mine, and I kissed her.

The feel of her, warm and wet as I sucked on her tongue and she bit softly on my bottom lip... the taste of her and the soft slide of her lips as she entwined her hands in my hair... This was fucking everything.

I dragged her closer until she was wrapped around me, until she was sitting in my lap while the windows fogged up and the rain beat down, her heart thumping against my chest.

"I won't share you, Jessa," I managed to utter between kisses.

"Share me..." she breathed. "What do you mean?"

"Seth," I said, and I regretted it the second it was out of my mouth.

Her body went rigid.

Her face fell.

"I don't know what's going on, between the two of you—"

She pulled away, out of my grasp. "I have to go." She didn't even look at me when she said it.

"Jessa—"

"I have a modeling gig. I'll be late."

"I can give you a ride."

"I don't need one."

She was already opening the door, so I gave in. Anxiety was firing off her like sparks, raising the hairs on my skin. It totally fucking unnerved me.

It always did when she turned tail and took the fuck off—which she did a lot.

But I caught her hand, stopping her. "Okay, sweetheart," I told her. "We'll talk later, yeah?"

"Yeah," she said.

"Call me if you need a ride."

Her brown eyes met mine. She nodded. Then I let her go. I watched her climb out of my truck and dash off through the rain.

We didn't talk later.

Instead, she pretty much avoided me until she left for Europe. She was away for two long months. Then she started college. I left with Dirty on our first world tour.

I saw her one more time on a break in that tour.

And then... six-and-a-half years would pass.

If I'd known, I never would've let her go that day.

But hindsight was twenty-twenty, and when it came to Jessa Mayes, I'd always been so fucking blind.

CHAPTER FIFTEEN

Jessa

RONI HAD GONE OUT for the night with some dude or another she was sleeping with, so I put on *Dead Crazy*, Dirty's second album, cranked it up, and made myself some dinner. I'd had a mild hangover the last three mornings in a row, thanks to the concerted efforts of Katie and Maggie to drag me back out into the land of the living, and while I'd appreciated their efforts, I really needed a booze-free night in.

I was dancing around in the kitchen in my woolen knee socks, worn old Brody T-shirt and panties, making my patented low-fat zucchini-and-eggplant lasagna—which tasted a lot better than it sounded—when Roni walked in, scaring the shit out of me.

With a couple of dudes.

Biker dudes, on second glance. Big, serious bikers, wearing the telltale leather vests; vests with patches on the chest that said *Sinners MC*.

The scary, shaved-headed one was looking me over, slowly, his eyes lingering on my panties. The blond one was grinning ear-to-ear.

"Uh... hi," I choked out, trying to discreetly cover myself with a tea towel. "I thought you said you were gone for the night."

Roni grinned, cocking an eyebrow at my outfit. "Couldn't leave you all alone, now could I?"

Guess not.

After I'd put on some pants, I ended up sharing my veggie lasagna with them, sort of; Roni's "friends" opted to snort some lines and didn't seem to have an appetite for much else. I politely declined when they offered to share, as did Roni, though I got the distinct feeling she was doing so for my benefit—that if I wasn't here, they would've been snorting the coke off her boobs while they fucked her on the breakfast bar.

Since I had no interest in witnessing or taking part in such activities, I figured I should probably make myself scarce—like before they got impatient with me cockblocking them. The party had moved into the living room, but I was cleaning up and more or less hiding in the kitchen when Roni walked in.

"You wanna hook up or what?" she asked, sashaying over to me and grabbing my hips, dancing with me. "Usually I'd just go ahead and enjoy them both myself, but for you, to get you out of this rut you're in... I'm willing to share."

"That's what I love about you, Roni," I said. "Your generosity."

"Come on, it'll be fun. Like old times."

"In what old times did we tag-team a couple of bikers? Because if we did, I sure as hell don't remember it."

She huffed and pulled away from me, heading to the fridge for more beers. "You're so unimaginative. What are you saving yourself for anyway?" She slammed the fridge door shut. "Let me guess. Brody." She rolled her eyes.

"It's not like that."

"The hell it isn't. At least be honest with yourself while you're pining away. Which one of you are you trying to bullshit anyway?"

I didn't answer that.

"I've seen the way you lick him with your eyes. It is so like that."

Maybe it was. But if I'd never talked to anyone else about it—and I hadn't—I wasn't about to talk to Roni.

"Even if it was," I said lightly, busying myself wiping down the counter, "I don't think he wants to go down that road with me, you know?"

"Oh, Jessa," she said. "All roads lead to fucking."

She walked past, beers in hand, and flashed me a parting smile. "Door's always open if you change your mind."

I ended up in my room and put some music on, just in case the festivities down the hall got loud. I locked the door and wedged a chair against it for good measure, in case either of Roni's guests decided to get "lost" on his way to the bathroom.

Then I flopped on the bed and thought about what Roni'd said.

Which one of you are you trying to bullshit anyway?

Him. I was definitely bullshitting Brody if I'd somehow convinced him I didn't want him.

Because I sure as hell knew I did. No way I could lie to myself *that* well. Even if my brain wanted to believe it, my body knew differently. My heart knew it, too. Which was why every time I was around him I lost the ability to think straight.

Just like when we were kids.

Worse, because now I was a grown-up. I was supposed to have my shit together and all that.

I picked up my phone and held it a while, working up the nerve to send him a text. But what to say?

I knew I still needed to have a talk with him; there was no way I was going to skip doing that before I left town. I needed him to know why I ran all those years ago; that it wasn't because I didn't want him. Even if it meant he'd never be able to forgive me. Even if he couldn't stand me after what I had to tell him. Even if it meant he was finally going to realize that I was never the girl he thought I was... that girl he thought he loved.

I had to do it.

Even if I was never, ever going to be his princess again.

And I really should've done it by now. Except that I hadn't. I hadn't answered his call two days ago, and I hadn't replied to his texts.

I was leaving town in three days for my shoot in L.A., but somehow the really chickenshit part of me had convinced the rest of me to leave it until the last minute. Just talk to him right before I left town, so I could disappear afterward.

Yeah. Mature.

All I was accomplishing by putting it off was torturing myself anyway. I *wanted* to talk to him. I wanted to see him, too, but seeing him was a slippery slope. There were only so many times I could see him without kissing him again, drunk or not. There were only so many times he could get in my face without me throwing myself at him and rubbing my pussy on him again, and there were only so many times I could do that without suffering a major blow to my self-esteem when he refused to fuck me.

But maybe, eventually, he would fuck me?

All roads lead to fucking.

And that was a bad thing, right?

Why, again?

Oh, right. Because I'd been lying to him for years. Well... lying by omission.

Same thing.

So no seeing him, then, until I was prepared to suck it up and come clean.

In the meantime, the phone was a safe option, right? No possibility of accidental fucking.

So I texted him; I said the only thing I could think of to say to him right now if I wasn't bullshitting. The same thing he'd said to me many, many times over text.

Thinking about you.

I sent the message and tossed the phone down on the bed. He wasn't going to respond. I knew he wasn't.

Even if it wasn't for all the times I'd recently pissed him off, or failed to respond to *his* texts, or the fact that he thought I was trouble for the band, those six-and-a-half years of radio silence, which he'd shoved in my face ad nauseam, made it pretty clear where he stood.

He'd said it himself, right to my face.

Brody Mason thought I was "unstable" and "unreliable." Translation: fucking crazy and a big fat load of pain-in-the-ass.

Oh, and judging from our make out session on that bathroom counter, during which he'd pretty much accused me of intentionally giving him blue balls, it seemed he also thought I was a cock tease—never mind that he was the one who'd put a stop to things and left *me* hanging.

What the hell would he want with a cock tease when he had the lovely Amanda?

I ditched my jeans and panties for some well-worn sweats and took off my bra, but I left his shirt on. I thought briefly about masturbating, but that seemed too depressing. So I got comfy with my laptop and watched some junk on YouTube instead.

Then I put on *Romeo + Juliet* so I could watch Leonardo DiCaprio and Claire Danes kill themselves over each other, because at least I still had a sense of humor. Just barely.

The night wore on.

Brody didn't text.

I'd almost fallen asleep when a burst of laughter from Roni's room jolted me awake.

Okay, maybe I was asleep.

Slow, sexy music was still playing faintly from my laptop. Pink Floyd's "Hey You." The words jarred me from my daze. Something about being naked... and sitting by a phone...

I wasn't naked, but... I groped for my phone to check it.

There was a new message.

Brody: Thinking about you too.

I blinked as the light from the screen stung my eyes, making sure I'd read the words right.

He'd texted me back.

And he was thinking about me.

Instantly, I was wide awake. I turned the phone to vibrate so I wouldn't miss any more messages, and texted him again.

Me: I got your messages. Just wanted to think about some things before I got back to you.

Then I chewed on my lip and waited, but I didn't have to wait long before he texted back.

Brody: Up to you.

Well, he sounded pissed. Still.
But at least he was texting me back.

Me: Is it lame if I apologize over text message?

Brody: Yes. But I'll take it.

Hmm. Progress.
If only it were that easy.
I took a breath and took a leap.

Me: What r u doing?

Brody: Eating take out in my underwear.

Okay. Maybe it *was* that easy?

Because I got a definite visual on that. A visual he wanted me to get?

Brody lounging back on his bed, long legs crossed at the ankles, all naked and tattooed except for a pair of... briefs? Black briefs? Really, really small ones that barely covered his big dick.

Yeah, I was a pervert like that.

I pictured him with a take-out container in his lap, next to his big dick, and maybe some chopsticks? Slurping on noodles...

I could really go for some noodles right now.

I snorted to myself. But I decided to roll with it. He's the one who mentioned his underwear, right?

Me: Are we sexting now?

Brody: Depends. What are you wearing?

Damn. Was Brody flirting with me?

Was I flirting with Brody?

Yes. Yes, I totally was.

All those years I'd avoided him, ignoring his messages... was this what would've happened if I'd answered back?

Flirting?

Sexting?

Yes. You know this is what would've happened. Which was why you didn't answer.

Okay. That was the hard truth.

But was it wrong that I liked it when he flirted with me? That I'd liked it a hell of a lot better when I thought he had me on some pedestal, even though I told myself all those years that it was wrong? Because at least then, he didn't hate me.

Brody: ??

Shit. I was leaving him hanging.

Again.

Only this time... he'd accepted my apology. A lame one, but still. A door had cracked open, and I wasn't about to let it slam in my face.

Me: The comfiest sweat pants ever invented. And your shirt.

Brody: Sounds sexy.

I had no idea if that was sarcasm or not.
I decided to rid myself of any doubt.

Me: No underwear though.

Shit.
Shit.
He wasn't answering.
Why wasn't he answering?

Brody: Commando again? Do I need to come over and take care
of any photographers?

Me: Nope. I'm all alone.

Brody: One sec.

One sec?
Okay. I was sweating. Blatant, *blatant* flirting.
If he didn't say something one hundred percent flirtatious right
back, after his "one sec," I was going to backpedal the hell out of
here and call it a night.
The minutes. Ticked. By.
One sec, my ass.
I put the phone down and tried to get into a video about how to
cut an onion without crying. Because that was a handy thing to
know. I was planning to make Roni nachos and margaritas tomorrow
night, to thank her for letting me stay with her longer than expected,
saving me from booking myself into a lonely hotel room or crashing
with the horny honeymooners over at my brother's place.
After that, I pulled up a vid on how to make a killer strawberry
margarita.
After that, I started thinking about Brody in his skimpy black

briefs—not that I'd really stopped—and my hand found its way between my legs. Just kind of rubbing the crotch of my sweatpants, but still. If he was going to leave me hanging, again, I was prepared to take matters into my own hand.

Things were just starting to get good when finally, fucking *finally* my phone buzzed.

Brody: Sorry had to take a call.

Me: Cool

Brody: Zane says there's a party at my place tomorrow night.

Me: Sounds like Zane.

Brody: Yeah have to prepare. Stock the bar. Make sure smoke alarms are working. You know.

Stock the bar? A little shiver of horror ran through me.
Zane was a recovered alcoholic. He didn't mean...?

Me: Zane's not drinking???

Brody: He's not drinking. Everyone else will be.

Oh. Right.
Of course. Even if Zane was drinking, Brody wouldn't be stocking booze for him. He'd be checking him into rehab, like *stat.*
But *Jesus.* Scare a girl much?
My hand was nowhere near my crotch anymore.
The whole idea of Zane falling off the wagon, or even the mention of Zane himself, a dude who was like a brother to me, was enough to kill the buzz.

Brody: You coming?

Um, no. I definitely wasn't coming anytime soon.

Me: ?

Brody: To the party.

Did I want to go to the party?
Yeah, I kinda did.
Especially if Brody was inviting me.

Me: Should I?

Brody: Yes.

Me: Ok

Brody: Why? You wanna come now?

Come?
Like over to his place??
Now?

Me: ?

Brody: Take off the pants.

I stared at the message. Four little words, impossible to misin-
terpret.
   Still...

Brody: Commando, yeah?

Me: Yeah...

Brody: You should take off the pants.

Brody: So you're wearing nothing but my shirt.

Holy shit.

Me: I guess that would be sexier

Brody: Sexy as fuck.

Okay, then.
This was... happening.
A shiver of excitement rippled through me, even as a weird, floaty unreality made me blink and look around, just to make sure I wasn't dreaming.
But if I was dreaming, Brody would be *here*, right?
So I decided to follow orders. Not like he could see me. What harm could it do?
I was about to do it anyway, whether he told me to or not.
I slipped the sweats off and kicked them on the floor. Then I lay back on the bed in the glow of the screen of my phone wearing nothing but his shirt. Pretty much like I had many, many times before. I'd slept in the thing for years. Probably why it was falling apart.

Brody: Are they off?

Me: Yes, sir.

No response. But I was reasonably confident that you didn't get to be as bossy as Brody was and not like someone following your orders, and calling you boss or sir or high commander or whatever. Especially if that someone was a chick you'd just ordered to take off her pants.
I reached down and touched my clit, because I couldn't help it.
Brody just told me to take off my pants...
Just the thought of it was getting me hot. And *damn*, that felt

good. All warm and melty... I sighed into the bed. Might as well enjoy this while I could. It probably wouldn't take very long; I'd only been hot for him all week.

Well, all my life...

And if Brody was into this... yeah, it wasn't going to take long.

The pleasure spooled, hot and tight in my core, aching for release...

Brody: U touching yourself?

I struggled to balance the phone on my stomach and type with my left hand. My right hand was much too busy.

Me: Ys

Brody: Do you ever get off thinking about me?

God, yes.
All. The. Time.

Me: Yse

I closed my eyes as the image of him in his bed washed over me, and my pussy clenched. I was tensing up, just trying to relax as the pleasure built. He wasn't eating take out anymore, I decided. Nope. He'd tossed the noodles on the floor and shoved his skimpy underwear down and grabbed hold of his long, hard dick—

My phone rang and I almost screamed.

Brody.

I fumbled with my incompetent left hand and answered on the third ring.

"*Hello,*" I gushed, breathless. My fingers were driving me right to the edge. I could go off any moment. One too-deep breath, the sound of his voice...

"Do it, now," he said, his voice all husky and thick.

"Do... what...?" I bit my lip.

"Get off," he said. "I wanna hear you."

"You should... maybe you should come over?" I gasped out, because really, if we were doing this... maybe we should just *do* this.

"I'm in Chicago," he said.

"What?" I paused what I was doing down below. I blinked, took a few breaths, got my bearings.

He was *where?*

"I'm in Chicago," he repeated. "My mom needed help moving into her new place."

My head spun a little, trying to keep up. "Your mom lives in Chicago?"

"Yeah, for about three years now. She's on her second divorce since my dad died."

"Oh." My hand dropped away. *Back away from the pussy. This is not the time.* "You're at your mom's house?" Nothing to make a girl feel like a perv like the mention of a guy's mom.

"I'm at a hotel. Are you touching yourself?"

"Uh... no."

"Focus, Jessa," he said, his husky tone laced with amusement. "I know you want to come. I can hear it in your voice."

I bit my lip again.

Really?

What did he know about the sound of my voice when I was about to come?

Of course, there was the other night, in the bathroom... or maybe he was just speaking from general experience.

Which reminded me—*Shit!*

"What about Amanda?"

"What about her?"

"You know what." Jesus. I'd totally forgotten about Amanda. "Shouldn't you be doing this with her?"

"She didn't text."

My mouth dropped open.

"I'm joking, sweetheart," he said softly. He laughed a bit, very Brody-like, and tingles ran through me. "We broke up."

"Oh." I sighed my relief and relaxed back into the bed; didn't even realize how much I'd tensed up. I didn't know what else to say. The wires in my head were crossed. My body was throbbing. All I could hear was my pussy screaming at me to keep doing what I was doing, just listen to Brody's voice and forget about everything else.

"Have I killed the mood?"

"Uh... no..." I slipped my hand back down and picked up where I'd left off. "Just... talk about something else."

"Like what? Like how I'm gonna slide my tongue between your legs the first chance I get?"

"You are?"

"Yeah. Definitely. You gonna let me?"

"Um... okay..."

"I'll be home around eight tomorrow. You should be at the party."

"I... I will be..." I was panting now, softly, trying not to do it into the phone for some reason.

"Good," he said. "Then maybe you can show me what you're doing right now. It's not fair you're doing that shit for me and I don't even get to see." He sounded frustrated; a little anguished, even.

And maybe I was a terrible person, but it was turning me on.

Maybe I was a cock tease?

"Yeah," I breathed, my brain completely disconnecting from reason. He could say about anything right now and I'd agree.

"Or touch," he said.

"Yeah..."

"Or taste."

I came then—I couldn't stop it if I tried. The thought of Brody tasting me, of him wanting to taste me... and I just blew up. I cried out softly, kind of into my pillow, remembering Roni and her guests. Likely they couldn't hear me. I still had music on, and they were probably too busy anyway.

Brody could hear me, though. For sure, he could.

He heard me all the way in Chicago.

"*Fuck... Jessa...*" I heard him murmur, and he was breathing heavy.

"You should touch yourself," I managed to say. "Take your cock out."

Geez. I'd never said anything like that to a man.

Felt good.

"It's already out," he said, his voice thick with arousal.

"What are you doing?"

"What I always do when I think about you getting yourself off."

"Oh," I sighed, still touching myself as I came down. "You think about that?"

"Yeah," he said. "A lot. *Jessa...*" His voice got huskier and all breathy as he jerked himself off, which I was pretty sure he was doing by now. "You asked me to come over..."

"Yeah," I said.

"You want me to?"

"Yeah. I want you to." I swallowed, but I'd been this brave already; I could be braver. "I wish you were here."

"Why? You want this, sweetheart...?"

"Yeah. Yeah, I want it. I want you... deep inside me."

Oh, shit. *Did I say that?*

Truth. It was nothing but truth. But... wow.

Brody liked it; his breathing got faster, heavier still.

"Tell me what you're doing right now," I said.

And he told me.

He told me how hard he was for me, how much he wanted me. He told me about what his hand was doing, and how much better it would've felt if it was me; how hot it was when I came, and how he was going to come too, soon, but he didn't want it to happen too fast, because this was all just way too fucking good, and he could barely believe it was real...

"It's real, Brody," I whispered.

And for some reason that I now could not fathom, I realized that the thought of a guy jerking himself off had never seemed all that incredibly appealing to me, yet the thought of Brody with his dick in his hand, all hard and throbbing and wanting into my body... oh, God, yeah... I was all over that.

And he was really, really good at phone sex.

I'd never had phone sex before. I'd never had a long distance relationship. I'd never had any relationship where I needed to get off, like *now*, so bad that I had to do it over the phone while just listening to him breathe and coax me along.

It was new. Hot. And familiar, somehow. Because my eyes were closed as I pictured him, and *that* I'd done plenty of times.

Hundreds of millions of times.

Really, when had I *ever* had sex, with myself or anyone else, when I wasn't thinking of Brody?

Never.

Never, ever.

"I'm gonna come, Jessa..."

"Yeah," I whispered. "Come." And as I listened to his tight breaths, the low grown as he lost control of himself—picturing him coming, his cock in his fist—I came again, losing myself in the sounds of his ecstasy, in the image of it in my head. All the while just kind of blown away that this was happening.

And wondering how we'd gotten here.

Lasagna. I'd been making lasagna.

Then Roni came home and turned my night inside out with her *Which one of you are you trying to bullshit anyway?* Because that's what a wild card did.

For once, I'd have to thank her for it.

"Sweetheart...? Are you crying?"

"No," I sniffled, realizing I was. "Shit. I'm sorry."

"Babe. What's wrong? You okay?" His voice had softened and filled with worry.

I took a few shaky breaths, my mind gone all to mush in the

wake of that last orgasm. But one thought stood out, prickling at me like a burr.

"Why did you go to Chicago, Brody?"

"I told you, sweetheart. My mom."

"Yeah. But... you were getting away from me, right? You wanted to get away."

There was some rustling around as he changed position. "Babe. I had some shit to take care of. That's all. Don't read anything into it. I'll be back tomorrow night, okay?"

"Okay."

"You good with what we just did?"

"Yeah. Yeah, I'm good."

I was. It was a total rush.

A rush that had let loose a whole flood of shit I didn't even know how to process. A whole flood of shit that was sweeping over me now, threatening to take me under.

"I just... I wish I could hold you now," I whispered.

Brody swore under his breath. "We shouldn't have done that over the phone. What the fuck was I thinking."

"No... seriously. It's okay. It was good. Great. I just... I miss you."

I did. I so fucking missed him.

Not just today, or the last few days.

I'd been missing Brody my whole fucking life, and these few moments of intimacy we'd just shared, over a phone, had brought that to light.

I wanted him home. In my arms. *Now.*

He was silent a long moment.

Then he sighed and said, "I miss you too, Jessa," his voice rough with emotion.

This.

This was exactly what would've happened if I'd ever texted him back, if I'd ever returned any of his calls over the years. We would've ended up right *here*... only without all the wasted years between us.

I cried harder, cradling the phone, trying to hold my sobs in so

Brody wouldn't hear. I just sobbed and sobbed as I listened to his voice, muffled, from far away.

Jessa?

Sweetheart... don't cry.

I'll be home soon.

CHAPTER SIXTEEN

Brody

I ARRIVED home to find a smallish party getting underway in the party room at the back of my house. Just the band and some close friends having a jam and a few drinks. They were pretty settled in and things were starting to get loud. They'd probably go all night.

I made the rounds, quickly, but my head wasn't in it. The only person I really wanted to talk to was nowhere to be seen, so I went looking.

I ran into Maggie in the hall. "Jessa here?"

"Yeah," she said, narrowing her eyes at me a little. No idea what that look meant. Didn't wanna know. "Not sure where. Haven't seen her in a while."

"Thanks." I walked past her, ignoring the look she was still giving me. "Good job, yeah? Keep... uh... holding down the fort." Then I grabbed my travel bag from the foyer and disappeared upstairs.

I poked my head into the other rooms—two guest bedrooms that friends sometimes crashed in, and one that I'd meant to make into some kind of proper gym but never had—then headed to my room at the end of the hall.

No sign of Jessa.

Maybe she'd left?

I dropped my bag and sat down on the edge of the bed, pulling out my phone—but then I saw her. Through the glass door, out on the rooftop patio. She was lying on the outdoor couch in front of the fireplace, where a fire was burning steady.

I couldn't see her face, but I could see her long legs stretched out and her long hair spilling over the cushion. She was wearing some kind of knit leggings and furry slippers, like something out of a Victoria's Secret catalogue—winter edition.

I tossed my phone on the bed and went to the door, watching her. I paused there, my hand on the doorknob and my chest tightening, as I suddenly remembered, vividly, the last time I saw her before she left, six-and-a-half years ago.

Right here, in my bedroom.

She was almost finished her first year of college and I was home with the band on a break, part way through the tour. It was the night before we went back out on the road and there was a huge party. It'd been a great night for everyone but me... and maybe Jessa. She'd shown up with a date, for one thing. Some greasy piece of shit who got kicked out by Jude when I caught him dealing, which, at any Dirty party, was un-fucking-welcome; party favors at a Dirty party came courtesy of Piper and the Kings, and anyone with half a brain cell knew as much.

Jessa knew as much, but she wasn't happy when her little friend got thrown out.

Still, she stayed.

Christy and I had broken up long before I'd gone on tour and I wasn't with anyone that night. Didn't want to be. Spent the entire night trying to get Jessa alone, while she just kept trying to get me to talk to this cute little Maggie girl she'd met in college. I couldn't help grinning a little at that memory. Looking back, it was clear she was trying to get Maggie a foot in the door with the band, and good thing; Maggie had proved ten times her weight in gold over the years. At the time, though, I thought Jessa was trying to hook us up, and I was the least bit interested. She could've been trying to introduce me to the entire Victoria's Secret runway lineup and I wouldn't have been interested. I just wanted to get Jessa alone.

I'd spent the last hour or so before she left arguing with her in my room. It was the only place we could be alone and I'd dragged her up here when we started fighting. It was the same fight we'd had for months before the tour. I was still angry about it; I just tried to pretend not to be. Because clearly, no matter how I felt about it, it didn't change a fucking thing.

But that night, when she'd shown up with that piece of shit, it rubbed me the wrong way and then some. I'd had a few drinks and my defenses had slipped. I could no longer pretend it didn't bother me that we were leaving, again, and she wasn't coming with us. I knew she was sick of the same fight, and maybe nothing I could ever say or do would make her change her mind, just for the fact that she was sick of the same damn fight. But I wasn't gonna give it up. I couldn't.

And that fight ended like they almost always did—with Jessa walking out. But that time... it was the first time it really got through to me. That this wasn't a temporary thing. That Jessa wanted out—for good.

Out of the band... and out of any kind of possibility of a life with me.

I still couldn't accept it.

The next day, before we left town, I had a bunch of roses delivered to her. White ones, with a card that said, *Call me when you change your mind.*

She never did.

The thing was, I always thought she would.

I'd never stopped waiting for that call.

And maybe that was what scared me most of all. That I could lay everything I had at her feet and she could just walk away—and now, I could do it all again. Open the door to her, offer everything I had to give... and she could still walk away and leave me hanging.

Break my heart all over again.

Because of course, she fucking could.

When I joined Jessa on the patio, she seemed to be in a good mood. Kind of contemplative and relaxed. And she was definitely happy to see me; she got up and threw herself into my arms and gave me a long, tight hug, before settling back onto the couch with a sort of self-conscious smile.

So that was different.

Better.

Then we talked. Actually talked, without fighting, like we used to do for hours on end when we were kids. And for once, it wasn't about all the shit that had gone wrong and the distance between us. It was just talk, and it felt so fucking good.

At first, I sat on one of the chairs that faced the couch, leaning forward on my knees to be close to her where she lay. I loved watching her, that sparkle in her eyes when she was happy; that sparkle I hadn't seen in way too fucking long. The way her lips moved... that beautiful sweet curve of her upper lip and the fullness of the bottom lip, the way the corners twitched when she was amused... the way she showed all her teeth when she laughed.

Gradually we got closer until I was sitting, then lying on the couch right next to her. Both of us on our backs, sides pressed together, just shooting the shit like there was no one else in the world whose two cents mattered.

We lay like that for a long time, just talking.

I hadn't forgotten about my promise to get my tongue between her legs, but maybe we'd work up to that. I really wasn't up for anything that was gonna make her cry again.

This peace between us was just too good.

Eventually, she said, "I'm sorry, Brody."

I took a deep breath.

I'd been waiting to hear those words from her for years, but hearing her say them, so sincerely, I just wanted to let her off the hook. When it came down to it, I didn't really want her apology; I just wanted her.

"I know," I said.

"I mean... I've screwed up. I keep torturing myself, you know? With all the bad memories... all the times I've messed things up."

"I guess that's how we're different," I said, watching the firelight and shadow play over her features. "Mostly, I keep torturing myself with the good."

She stared at me for a long time.

"I just... I hope you can forgive me," she whispered.

"There's nothing to forgive. I've been an asshole myself, Jessa. You know that. You don't owe me any apology." I stared back at her in the firelight; so fucking beautiful. The kind of beautiful wars were waged over. "Not if you're here. With me."

She didn't say anything, just nodded.

"I meant what I said, though. At the wedding. You know... in your cabin." And I said it again, the hardest thing I'd ever had to say to her, really. "It can't be like it was before."

Yeah, I wanted her back, more than I'd ever wanted anything in my life. But if having her back meant more of the same, more of the past... I totally couldn't fucking do it.

Not even for her.

I could not have Jessa in my life and not be *with* her.

"I don't need it to be like it was before," she replied softly. "But I do need my friend back." Then her hand slipped over mine, soft and strong.

"You never lost me," I told her.

We lay in silence a while, holding hands, my heart drumming in my chest, and then we got talking again.

"Fill me in on what I've missed," she said. "You know, with the band."

"What do you want to know?"

"Everything," she said, that sparkle in her eyes. "I want to know everything."

So I filled her in, the best I could, on the highs and lows of six-and-a-half years working, traveling and living with a bunch of talented, egotistical, moody, unpredictable and definitely somewhat insane rock stars. Mostly, the many highs. The biggest parties, the most epic concerts, the amazing places we'd been.

I also told her about all the messes that Maggie, Jude and I had mopped up over the years. Which, in the early days, meant tantrums and trashed hotel rooms (Zane), random disappearances minutes before concerts were scheduled to start (Dylan), trails of broken hearts and death threats from discarded women (Zane and Jesse), ridiculous pranks and practical jokes that ended in nights spent in jail or the hospital (Zane and Dylan), and blow-out fights ending in either tears and a whole lot of broken shit, or laughter (Elle and just about everyone).

Nowadays, the dramas surrounding the band were a little less... full-throttle. Everyone was on the brink of their thirties; Dylan and I were already there, Jesse, Zane and Jude were next, and Elle would soon follow. Ten years working together as a band, longer for Jesse, Zane, Jude and I, and everyone was mellowing out. Thinking about what was next. For the band; for themselves. The days of partying all night long, sleeping all day, banging an endless line of willing groupies and drinking everything alcoholic in sight had lost at least some of its appeal.

I'd seen the way everyone in the band—not just Elle—looked at Jesse with Katie. Katie had changed him, in a good way; Jesse had always been a happy guy, but something had happened this last year.

"She's brought out the best in him," I said. "Without even trying, she showed him there was more to life than the one he'd been living, epic as it was."

"Yeah. I see that."

"I think the guys are jealous, actually." I meant Zane and Dylan, but I was jealous of what Jesse and Katie had too. For sure I was.

I kept talking, and Jessa kept listening. She begged for more details when the stories got good. Smacked me on the arm when they got too crazy to believe. Best of all she laughed, that soft, bubbly little giggle, and even better, that big, throaty laugh like she just might choke—the one she'd laughed when we were kids.

Jesus, I'd missed that laugh.

When it was her turn to talk, to share what life had been like for her these past six-and-a-half years, she held back. I knew she did. But I took what she gave me.

Mostly she told me about her travels, some of the most incredible photo shoots she'd done, the places she'd been. And I was glad to hear she'd been happy. At least, she'd definitely had some good times over the years. Maybe I was eighty percent happy and twenty percent jealous... but really, I never wanted her to be unhappy.

I just wished she'd been happy with me.

"Turks and Caicos," she mused. "That was the most fun ever. They have the bluest water, and it's just so beautiful."

"Near the Bahamas, right? I've never been."

"You should go," she said, but I left that alone.

If Jessa was there in a bikini, not a problem. I'd book my flight this minute.

"Night swimming there is pretty epic... it's a little warmer than it was up at the wedding." She grinned at me. "I don't think I've ever been that cold. When I jumped in the water, I thought my heart was going to stop. If Zane didn't put his arms around me, I think it might've. You were smart not to come in. But then again... you always were the smart one." Her smile faded, replaced by something else... a certain wistfulness. Admiration, maybe. It was the way she often looked at me when we were really young.

Like I could do no wrong.

"The amount of alcohol you drank," I said, "you're lucky you didn't get hypothermia." That much was true; jumping in that frigid water, drunk, in the dark, was a fairly risky move, and I didn't like her taking those kinds of risks.

"Lucky me, then, that I had you to make me a fire."

"I see you got this one started just fine without me."

"Actually," she confessed, "Jesse did it." She bit her plump bottom lip. "Brody... I was drunk that night, but I don't want you to think... That wasn't all bullshit just to get you back to my room. I hope you know that. I mean, I knew you were there with Amanda. Even if I wanted to—"

"Uh... hi."

We looked up to find Maggie standing over us.

She looked carefully from Jessa to me and back. "Am I interrupting anything?" Clearly, she knew she was.

Great fucking timing, Maggs.

"I brought you some bevvies," she added quickly. She was double-fisting a couple of drinks in round brandy snifters, something that looked and smelled of coffee, with whipped cream on top. "Mexican coffee," she said. "Kind of. Dylan brought a shit-ton of tequila and Katie was feeling nostalgic for her barista days, so we improvised. It's got Kahlúa, dark chocolate liqueur, cinnamon and espresso. And, you know, I thought you guys might be a little chilly."

Which meant she knew we were out here. Which meant she'd snooped in my room and saw us out the window.

Jessa looked happy to accept the coffee, though, so I let it slide.

A bit.

"Jessa," I asked, my eyes never leaving Maggie as she handed me a coffee, "you cold, sweetheart?"

"I'm good," Jessa said. "The fire is nice."

Maggie was staring me down, giving me another one of those narrow-eyed looks, but I stared right back. I knew she was pretty tight with Jessa, and it was cool of her to have her girl's back. I'd always appreciated Maggie's attention to detail, when it came to business. As long as it wasn't *my* business.

I drew a line at her butting her nose into my personal shit, and she knew it.

"Alright, well... I'll be down in the party room, making sure Zane doesn't burn the place down, if you need me," she told us. Or rather, she told Jessa. "And I'll make sure no one bothers you guys."

Then she threw me another narrow look and left.

After she was gone, Jessa and I looked at each other. She smiled. "You better be nice to me," she said. "Or you're on Maggie's shit list. Just saying."

"Yeah. Well. Hers wouldn't be the only one."

"That's true," she said, maybe a little too pleased at the thought, and sipped her drink. "Mmm!"

I took a sip of mine. "Jesus, that's good."

"Is there anything Maggie can't do?" she mused.

Yeah. Keep her nose out of my shit.

I set my coffee down on the low table in front of the fire and got serious. "You have a lot of people here who care about you, Jessa."

She didn't say anything, just nodded and sipped at her drink, licking whipped cream from the corner of her mouth. There was the tiniest dabb of it on her nose.

"What?" she whispered.

I swiped it off with my fingertip. I showed it to her and she gave a little giggle. She took my hand and pulled my finger closer, and licked it off with a little flick of her tongue. Then her eyes met mine.

When she let my hand go, I laid it on the side of her face, running my thumb over her flushed lip, her cheek. Then I took her coffee and reached to set it on the table. When I turned back to her, she was nibbling on her lip.

"I spoke with Dolly," she said. "I have a photo shoot in a few days, down in L.A., but I was thinking... maybe I'd come back up afterward for a bit. I don't want to outstay my welcome at Roni's, but Dolly says I can stay with her for a while. Zane's there too, but she has room."

"That's nice of her."

It was. But no fucking way I was letting Jessa go stay with Dolly. She had a nice place, a really fucking nice place that Zane bought for her, but it was even farther from here than Roni's. I knew Jessa had a shoot; if she was actually considering coming back afterward, though, I was gonna go ahead and hope like fuck it was at least partly because of me. And whatever happened between us on the phone last night.

And whatever was happening right now.

"But you should stay here." My heartbeat throbbed in my throat and I swallowed thickly. "I've got plenty of room, Jessa. And... I want you here."

She parted her lips to say something, but I leaned over and kissed her instead. Softly. I brushed my lips against hers and stayed there, feeling her breathe. Her breath caught, then deepened. I felt the exact moment when she yielded to me, and I nudged her lips open to stroke my tongue against hers.

She kissed me back, so I went in for more. I kissed her deeper and deeper until I was half on top of her and our bodies were fused together.

"This can be your safe place," I told her. "I want this to be your safe place. I want to be that for you." But I was kissing her when I said it.

Yeah, I wanted her to feel safe. I wanted her not to run away.

But I also wanted my dick up inside her. So fucking sue me.

I wanted my tongue in her mouth, my hands on her tits, her long legs wrapped around my back, and I wanted her screaming, sweating, panting my name as she came on my cock, over and again.

I'd settle, though, for a kiss.

It was a fucking start, right?

But then her hand strayed over my chest and caught my nipple through my shirt, her fingernails scratching as she squeezed at me... and pure sex coursed through me, all other thought fleeing my head.

Within seconds I'd peeled off her sweater, yanked her tank top up and bared her tits. She wasn't wearing a bra.

I looked into her eyes, big and dark, beautiful... aroused.

"Brody..." she breathed.

I ran my hand down her curves. I kissed her neck... the swell of her full, round breasts. Took her hard nipples in my mouth, licking, sucking at the flushed pink tips as she panted softly. I went slowly at first, my heartbeat throbbing through me, urging me to hurry the fuck up as my dick throbbed along, but I went slow. Feeling her heat up under my touch... listening to her breaths quicken, soften, grow more desperate. She had to want this.

Had to.

If she didn't... I was finally gonna go ahead and just die. Put myself out of my fucking misery.

If she turned my ass down one more time... walked away from me again... I could not fucking take it.

Her furry slippers went next, then her leggings. Gone. She was in her tank top, kind of, and lace panties, and as much as I wanted to paw her like some rabid dog in heat, I was mindful of the cold and covered her with my body.

She didn't complain.

She wrapped her arms around me, pulling me down to her. I kissed her again, deep, rocking my hips against hers because I couldn't fucking help it. I tried to keep still, to calm the fuck down and just let her lead a bit, let her come to me so I'd be sure of what she wanted. But what she wanted was pretty fucking clear as she spread her legs and ground her pussy against my dick.

I stirred, restless, fighting the urge to take her, just fuck her right through those lace panties. I was sweating... almost shaking as I held myself back. I'd never been so crazed with desire.

At least... not since she'd been in my bed.

Yeah. We kept this up, I was about thirty seconds from coming in my pants like a fucking kid. Like I'd come for her when I was twenty-two and she was seventeen, rolling around in my bed, in secret, in the middle of the night. Just from kissing her, I'd come; barely even any tongue.

Only that time I was fully dressed, and I didn't tell her I'd blown my load; I was too fucking afraid I'd scare her off. Lame, right?

And here I was, thirty, messing around with her again, in secret, and she had me ready to explode... although this time, she was starting to undo my jeans.

"Brody," she gasped against my mouth. "I want to make you come..."

I drew back, away from her seeking hands. If she took my dick out, it was all over.

"Yeah, sweetheart. You first." I kissed her bare stomach, moving down her body. "I wanna taste you."

I looked up at her face as I reached her panties. She looked at me like she'd never wanted anything more; like she was seconds from going off in an explosion of lust whether I touched her or not.

She looked like I felt.

My balls pulled up tight as I smoothed her lace panties down over her hips and I saw her for the first time. Her pussy... beautiful, just like the rest of her. She wriggled in anticipation as I breathed on her. My tongue found her sweetness, slick and wet, delicate, and I groaned involuntarily as I swiped up, taking my first taste of her pink flesh.

"You go off," I told her, my eyes finding hers again, "I'm right behind you."

"Brody... yeah..." she sighed, and I dove in deeper, finding her opening, hot and wet and waiting for me. I tasted her, inside, out, and as I licked my way up to her clit, nudging at the firmness under her softness, she went off. She cried out, grabbing at my hair in fistfuls, holding me there as I took her in my mouth.

I sucked on her, hard, then caressed her gently, watching her reactions... and as she came—arching her back and gasping... then came crashing down, relaxing onto the couch—I could feel the walls falling down, shattering around us. Something opened in her as she looked at me.

She bucked a little as I licked her again, and I felt her soften... her big brown eyes watching me.

"Come here," she said, breathing soft and fast.

I crawled up over her; her head was thrown back on the cushion, her long hair fanned out around her, and she was looking at me that way she did; the way she used to long ago. The way no other woman had ever looked at me... like I was the only man who'd ever mattered.

Her man.

She reached down, grabbing the length of my cock in my jeans and she squeezed, hard, rubbing up and down.

"Jessa... fuck, I'm too close," I managed to say as we kissed in a desperate, clumsy frenzy. She fumbled with me, with my fly, which just made my dick jerk, tightening... "*Fuck*... I can't even..." But she got my jeans open and clawed my underwear aside.

I blew on her stomach as she caressed me, gently, driving me fucking insane, and she writhed beneath me as I did it like she couldn't get enough.

"Ah... shit." The breath hissed out between my teeth as she kept stroking me. I leaned down over her on my elbows, wanting to collapse, but not knowing how she'd feel about me smushing my spunk between us. Then she caught my mouth with hers, slipped her tongue between my lips, and we were making out like a couple of kids in the dark, again, while everyone else partied.

Like we'd picked up right where we left off.

I ran my hand down and rubbed my come into her belly. She moaned into our kiss like she liked it, so I smeared it down between her legs... letting my wet fingers slip right up inside her as she lifted her hips to meet me. I didn't plan to do it and I didn't think about what I was doing. It just happened as my body responded to her sweet softness, drawn in by her heat and need.

"Give it to me," she whispered, riding my fingers. "All of it." She squeezed my cock in her hand and whispered, "I want all of you."

I was still half-hard, so I gave it to her as she spread her thighs around me. *Jesus*... so fucking tight.

Hot. Sweet. *Wet*.

My pulse pounded in my brain and somewhere in the back of my mind the thought of a condom flitted by. Then Jessa grabbed my ass, pulling me deeper, and the thought was gone—and I did not care. I kissed her... rocking into her a few times until she'd taken me; all of me. Then I lay still, my cock throbbing, squeezed inside her tight, slick flesh, catching my breath.

"Brody... that was...."

"Don't say it, princess," I told her, holding her hips down and grinding into her. "Don't say it like it's over..." I ground into her a few more times, just savoring the feel of her as my cock perked back up, and then I got serious, fucking her like I'd always wanted to do.

Jesus Christ... I was *fucking* Jessa.

When she started undulating beneath me, wanting more, I blew out a breath.

"Sweetheart... Jessa... *fuck me*..."

I'd never felt anything like this before. Not even close to this. Wanting her... wanting more of her, faster and harder and just plain *more* than my body could keep up.

Her body could, though, her urgency building beneath me as she moved.

"I know you just came and you're probably kind of... um... sensitive," she panted beneath me, her hips swiveling against me as she rode me from beneath, "but is it wrong... if I just use your super-hot... hard body... to get off again?"

"Please," I said, "use me."

She laughed her beautiful laugh and I kissed her, deep, claiming her mouth with my tongue as we fucked, slow and wet. At some point I noticed it was starting to rain, just a misting drizzle, typical for this time of year. It was fucking cold actually, but the fire was still warm, almost hot on my back, and the heat between us... we were both sweating.

Wasn't long before I was so lost in her that I had no idea which way was up. Literally. Somehow, she'd gotten me on my back. She was riding me like she couldn't get enough, fast and hard... then slow, grinding against me and wiggling around, savoring the feel of our bodies connected for the first time.

Then there was no more slow. It was all fast, hungry thrusts as her body claimed mine, over and over, and I just held on for the ride, watching her, the pleasure building fast—my chest burning in a way it never had when I'd been with any other woman.

For once, I didn't close my eyes, imagining I was with someone else.

Her.

It was always her.

"Brody..." Jessa's hands gripped my neck as she rode me, her nails digging into me. "Brody... God, I missed you..." Tears shone in her brown eyes.

"You don't have to miss me anymore." I held her face in my hands, our eyes locked together. "I'm here," I told her, fucking breathless. "Just take it, sweetheart... "

I was stiff by now, every muscle in my body locked up tight, every nerve tuned into her movements as her body slid against mine. That strange burning in my chest coiling tight, squeezing out all the air.

I was vaguely aware that the band had stopped jamming. Zeppelin was cranked through the surround sound system, and as "Babe, I'm Gonna Leave You" climaxed, pumping through the roof beneath us, Jessa fucked the living hell right out of me.

And yeah, I wanted her to take what she needed, but Christ... I was only fucking human. And I'd wanted this, wanted her like this, for an inhumanly long time.

I grabbed her neck and pulled her down to me. "You've got about five seconds," I panted into her ear, gripping her hip with my other hand, "to tell me to pull out."

"Don't pull out," she panted back.

Her eyes met mine, and the thought came into my head: What if I knocked her up?

And it *turned me on.*

I was gonna shoot. Immediately.

She reached around behind herself and rubbed me off, her hand and her pussy strangling me as my orgasm hit, hot and fast... mind-blowing. I grabbed her tits, squeezing as I blew into her, molten heat jetting from my body as waves of pure ecstasy rocked through me. I pretty much left the planet for a few seconds...

It was Jessa's soft scream that brought me back to Earth.

She was coming on my cock, and all I could do was watch in breathless awe as tears rolled down her face.

"Oh, God," she gasped, "I've never..." She was still riding me, milking out every last drop with her tight pussy as I groaned beneath her, utterly fucking useless. Her hair was all damp with misting rain and sweat and sticking to her neck, her chest.

Then she collapsed on top of me, her warm, wet body slick

against mine. I locked my arms around her, panting, but I wasn't coming down.

I may never come down again.

Instead, my heart was gonna explode, because I had Jessa in my arms, my cock was still inside her, and I was never letting her go. She was *mine*.

At least, according to me. And my cock.

I'd finally fucked her. *She'd* fucked *me*, and there was no coming back from that. And yeah, in that moment, I knew it.

I was fucking done for.

CHAPTER SEVENTEEN

Jessa

I SPENT THE NEXT DAY, after spending the night in Brody's bed, at the church, making music with the band—the whole band. Elle and Dylan were there this time, and it was awesome.

But I also spent a lot of that time—whenever I thought I could get away with it—daydreaming about my night with Brody... and fantasizing about the night ahead.

And I couldn't stop smiling.

Zane even asked me, joking, if I was high. At least I was pretty sure he was joking.

I was also pretty sure they all knew I'd spent the night with Brody in his room; for one thing, we'd both disappeared upstairs pretty early, and for another, I was wearing yesterday's clothes. But other than a few sly glances, no one bugged me about it. Not even my brother.

Late in the morning, I texted Brody to ask him if I could make him dinner at his place. I was planning to tell him I'd think about his invitation to stay with him. The truth was, I wasn't feeling all that comfortable at Roni's anymore, what with all the coke-snorting bikers coming around for gang bangs. But I wasn't about to move my stuff into Brody's and get comfortable, when we still had to talk.

Since I was leaving for L.A. tomorrow, I wasn't going to rush that talk. Not when we could spend tonight enjoying each other instead. The kind of talk we needed to have wasn't the sort to be rushed anyway, I told myself.

I was planning to make Brody fajitas, because I rocked at making fajitas, and tell him over dinner. I thought that might soften things, so he didn't take it as a rejection. More of a "let's wait and see." Because when I thought about having that talk, the one we'd have to have when I got back from the shoot, I couldn't imagine him still wanting me to stay with him after we'd had it.

So mostly, I tried not to think about that.

Brody: I have a meeting at my place. U can join, though. Fajitas sound awesome if u don't mind cooking for 3.

Me: Sounds good

I was disappointed we wouldn't be alone, but it didn't really change anything. We'd still have time to talk after his guest left, maybe while we undressed each other, before all the sex.

I knew it was wrong that I was putting off all the shit I needed to tell him. That this was cowardly of me. That I'd kinda promised myself I was going to tell him *before* we ended up naked.

Oops.

But the thing was, it was *Brody*. And I'd gotten carried away with how incredibly good it felt to get along with him for once. After all the years we'd been apart... and the years of turmoil before that... didn't we deserve just a day or two to get along?

He'd given me his truck for the day, so on the way back from church I stopped off at Roni's to shower and change, and picked up the ingredients I needed. When I got back to Brody's place, I got caught up telling him about the day's writing session and the new song we were working on as I unpacked the groceries.

"It was something Jesse said," I told him, "about Katie. And something she said about him. We had this conversation the other day, about the studio he gave her; about making room for someone

when you love them. And I got thinking about that. Making room...
you know, physically and mentally; making space in your home,
your heart. Then Jesse told me that sometimes she comes to bed in
the middle of the night with paint all under her nails and smeared
on her face, her hair all tangled up in a bandana, all sweaty and
mumbling she's so exhausted from painting all day. He said it's like
sleeping with a street urchin." I grinned, kind of rolling my eyes.
"I've never seen him talk about a woman like that. With that *light* in
his eyes. I told him Katie literally lights him up, you know? The way
music always has. And he just said, 'She makes it easy.'"

Through all of this, Brody just smiled at me. He was sitting on a
bar stool with me trapped between his thighs as I unpacked the
groceries around him. He played with the ends of my hair, listening
to me babble in such an excited rush I barely remembered to
breathe.

"Anyway, that's the name of the song."

"What is?"

"'She Makes It Easy.' It's kind of a play on words, 'easy' being a
slide-into-home reference."

Brody raised an eyebrow and I rolled my eyes.

"That was Zane's contribution. Apparently a wet pussy is his
version of a happy home."

Brody laughed.

"Whatever. It's got this really fucking sexy vibe. Jesse had this
melody he'd come up with and I started playing around with some
lyrics to lay down on top of it, and the whole thing just started to
flow... the chorus came fast... and the song just came together. It was
like old times. When we used to just write without worrying about
how it would fit on the album. But they liked it so much that they
said it's definitely going on the album. They even said it's going to
help shape the direction of things. We played it for Jude and he
liked it too, and you know how picky he is—like it really has to rock."

"Can't wait to hear it," Brody said. "Maybe you can sing it for
me tonight." Then he started kissing my neck, and the doorbell rang.

Damn.

"You never told me who's coming over," I said, melting into his kisses.

He slipped his arms around my waist, holding me close. "I didn't know how you'd feel about him coming over. It's Seth."

I felt my face freeze in a weird half-smile. Then I found myself saying the last thing I'd ever have imagined I would say at hearing those words.

"Great. Hope he's hungry. There's plenty."

"You're okay with this?" Brody searched my face. "Because I can have him leave, reschedule if you don't want to see him."

Shit. Was he testing me on this or something? What the hell was Seth doing here anyway? First the painting... now this?

I'd thought Seth Brothers was a thing of the past. Wasn't Dirty done with him, like years ago?

"Why wouldn't I want to see him?"

"I don't know," Brody said evenly. "You tell me."

I shrugged. "Haven't seen him in years. Might be nice to catch up." My guts roiled even as I said the words, but I'd always had a hell of a poker face. "How's he doing, anyway?"

"Guess we're about to find out. We've spoken a few times, but this is the first time I've met with him. Think he's sniffing around about the guitarist position. I hear he's doing well, though." He was watching me, gauging my reaction.

"Cool. I'll make dinner, and you guys can talk shop." I turned back to my dinner preparations.

Guitarist position?

Seth was here about the guitarist position?

And Brody was meeting with him?

I knew Dirty was on the lookout for a rhythm guitarist, yet again, since losing Paulie, but I had no idea they were casting such a wide net. Really wide, if they were actually considering opening the door to Seth again after throwing him out.

"You sure?"

"Yeah. Bring him in."

Brody stood there watching me for a long moment. "Okay."

Then he went to get Seth as the doorbell rang again, and I got ahold of myself the best I could.

When they came in, I spared Seth a glance, careful to look him in the eye but not show a thing on my face.

He looked mostly the same, and yet, like a different man than the Seth I'd known. The few lines on his face had deepened, the angles sharpened, and cute had turned to beautiful in a manly, rough-edged way. And he had more hair. Light brown and slightly wavy, it used to just dust his chin but now it was long enough that it was pulled into a man-bun on the back of his head, and he had a short beard. He no longer had that ever-present pothead softness to his eyes, though. They were clear and sharp, and when he met my gaze he smiled, dimple and all.

"Hey, Jessa," he said softly, rocking back on his heels, just like he had as a teen when something floored him.

I said hi and gave him a hug, quickly; a hug that ended before he seemed to want it to. Then I made myself very, very busy. Fajitas were simple enough, but mine had a lot of different steps to get all the seasonings and the sauce right, and there were a lot of ingredients.

"A model who cooks," Seth mused. "Multi-talented woman."

"She writes music, too," Brody said, watching me.

"Right," Seth said. "How could I forget."

"Okay, out of this kitchen," I said, waving them away, and finally they got scarce, heading down to the party room to talk while I got busy making fajitas. I tried not to overhear what they were saying; I couldn't quite make it out from where I was, even if I tried.

After a while I turned on some music and tried to forget that Brody and Seth were chatting in the other room. It was just too fucking strange. And too much like no time had passed at all. Like I was right back there, smack in the middle of those difficult years, not knowing which way to run.

Soon, I was lost in the memory.

It was far too fresh, as if it happened not long ago... which was maybe what happened when wounds weren't fully healed, no matter how long ago they were actually inflicted.

I was hurting. And I could still feel that hurt, hot and fresh.

I was high.

I was in a club I shouldn't be in, with people I wasn't supposed to be with. My brother was playing a gig across town. He thought I was home in bed. It was one in the morning and I was sixteen, but I was not home in bed.

I was dancing.

And I'd just popped some pills.

I felt the vibe of the room around me as other people got high, too. The music was loud, pumping, and it felt like the entire crowd was starting to rush, everyone caught up in the electronic vibe as it built in that way it did when the DJ was really, really good.

I was dancing with my girls. Most of them were also underage and shouldn't be here. I didn't care. I was thinking of nothing but the music, and my body, moving with the music. I didn't want to think about anything else. Just the music.

Then I felt his hands on my waist.

Big, warm, possessive hands.

I turned around. Seth stood there, moving slowly, and my movements slowed to meet his. His eyes were hooded in the rippling lights as he gazed down at me. He got closer, gradually closer, until his hands had tightened on my waist, gripping me, and his hips were pressed against me. We moved as one, slowly, as his face got closer.

"Still the dreamer," a familiar voice said behind me and I turned so fast the spoon flew out of my hand and clattered against Brody's fridge.

Seth picked it up and took it to the sink, watching me. "You used to zone out like that all the time. Never quite knew what you were thinking, but you were an incredible writer when you put it on the page."

"Where's Brody?"

He looked away from me, washing the spoon in the sink. "On the phone." He dried the spoon and turned back to me, took a couple of steps across the kitchen and held it out to me. I took it and got back to cooking.

"You and him... you're together now?"

"It's none of your business, Seth."

He didn't respond, and I hoped he'd left. I didn't want to look up to check.

"Look..." he said, "I just want to apologize, Jessa. The last time I saw you, you were pretty upset. You know... at the party, here at the house—"

"What do you want, Seth?"

"I just want to say I'm sorry. For all the shit I pulled back then. To be honest, I don't remember a lot of it. I was pretty messed up—"

"I know you were." I turned to face him, still gripping the spoon.

Brody walked in, and I went back to stirring my fajita sauce. If he picked up on the tension in the room, he didn't show it. He just put his hand on my arm and kissed me on the temple, gave me a lingering look, and he and Seth disappeared again.

When the meal was ready, I set out two plates on the bar with all the fixings for fajitas.

Then I ran out the door.

CHAPTER EIGHTEEN

Jessa

ADMITTEDLY, it was not the smartest move I'd ever made.

I realized that in retrospect. But when I'd called Roni up, I thought she'd take me to the latest hot little bar where we'd drink martinis, and then maybe we'd find a gay bar with hot music where we could dance the rest of the night away and I could forget my troubles for a while. Or at least pretend they weren't there.

That was really more my speed these days, and more of what I was accustomed to when I went out with my girlfriends.

Instead, she'd brought me here. To a house with barred windows, hidden in the trees up a dead-end road on the mountainside in North Vancouver; a road that was lined with Harleys, and a house that was packed full of bikers, the friends and associates of bikers, and women who were looking to screw bikers. Or who *were* screwing bikers, like right out on the dining room table, which one particularly ambitious young woman was doing, right now.

I supposed when I said I wanted to party, Roni and I had a really different idea of what that meant.

I knew she was into bikers when we were teenagers. I knew she'd dated one of the Kings back then, a friend of Piper's, on and off.

I knew she'd had a couple of guys in Sinners jackets back to her place the other night for a three-way.

Still.

I did not expect *this*.

While she got cozy with the blond guy I'd met at her place the other night, I excused myself to find a ladies' room. Which ended up being a bathroom no one was currently fucking in, where there was vomit in the toilet and a sink clogged with a wad of bloody toilet paper.

"Shit, Roni, seriously," I muttered as I locked myself inside.

Then I called Jude.

"Hey," I said, relieved when I got him on the second ring. "Tell me something. If I was at a party with a bunch of guys in motorcycle leathers that say Sinners on their vests, should I be worried?"

I got silence. For about ten seconds.

Then, "Say that again?"

"Um... I'm at a house party with a bunch of bikers. Most of them are wearing Sinners stuff. Is that bad?"

"How many guys?" he asked. "How many bikes?"

"Maybe... eight bikes or so. About twenty, twenty-five guys. I counted six of them wearing Sinners stuff. And... there's a guy with a Bastards jacket, too."

He didn't even have to tell me that wasn't good. The Bloody Bastards were yet another motorcycle club, of the outlaw variety, who'd been all over the news the last few years down in L.A., making all kinds of grief for law enforcement.

Why there would be one at a Sinners party I didn't know, didn't care, and didn't want to stick around to find out. I just wanted to leave. And preferably not on my own, wandering the mountainous roads in my high heels, waiting on a cab to find me.

"Let me guess," he said after another silence. "Roni."

"I don't want to be here, Jude."

"Where are you? Give me the address."

"I don't know the address. I'm in North Van. I can use the GPS on my phone to send directions."

I did that. Then I lingered in the bathroom, wondering how the fuck I'd gotten myself into this—and pondering the irony that if I'd been sixteen I probably would've been thrilled for Roni to bring me to a party this crazy—until a couple of girls started pounding the door down and I had to move on.

I hung out in the vicinity of the front door, more uncomfortable with the idea of heading outside into the dark, alone, or maybe not so alone, than staying right where I was. Roni was nowhere to be seen. But it wasn't like I didn't have company.

A particularly friendly guy with a tattoo on his arm of what appeared to be a rabid wolf eating the Easter bunny alive made conversation with me while I waited. I had no idea if he was one of the Sinners or what, and I didn't care to know. I told him I was just waiting for my friends, but he didn't seem interested in that detail. Thankfully, I had good friends, and it didn't take long for them to show up.

I saw Piper first. He was standing just inside the back door talking to a couple of other bikers. He was wearing his Kings vest and seemed to know these guys, thank God. Though their conversation didn't look all that friendly.

All the more reason to get the hell out of here.

Then I saw Jude. He was coming out of a back hallway... followed closely by Brody. They must've been looking for me.

"Oh, there're my friends," I said casually to the guy standing over me. "I should go. Nice talking to you."

I didn't wait to find out what he thought of that. I beelined for Jude and Brody, past the dining room table where yet another young woman was sharing her talents with a couple of guys. Jude just gave me a steady look and a nod, and I walked right on past him, taking the hand Brody offered and following him straight out the back door. My heart was thudding. I didn't like the feeling of not really knowing if I was in danger, or not knowing if that guy would've taken no for an answer if he decided I needed a go on the dining room table.

I didn't like it at all.

I held tight to Brody's hand as he led me around the house without a word, down the driveway and onto the street... past the line of Harleys and toward where I saw his bike parked, next to a couple of others I could only assume belonged to Jude and Piper.

As we left the property, Brody let go of my hand.

I'd had a few drinks, just a few, but I couldn't keep up in my high-heeled boots and was afraid I'd slip on the slanted street.

Brody paused and turned, waiting for me to catch up. He looked past me, back up at the house between the trees, where the thump of music emanated into the night.

He stared at me a minute, then scanned the lineup of bikes along the road. And I knew. I knew how it looked. I also knew how fast Brody and the others had dropped what they were doing to race up here to get me.

"It's just a party, Brody," I said lamely.

"Yeah? You know what kind of party that was?"

I shrugged, hugging myself. "Roni had friends there."

"Friends. Yeah."

"It's not like that. I just came with her."

"Yeah? And where was she when that guy was breathing down your neck? Because she sure as fuck wasn't there between the two of you. In case you didn't know, she was in a bedroom in the middle of her latest fuck-for-all. With the door open for any-fucking-one to see."

"That's Roni's business," I said.

"Not when she leaves the door wide open, it's fucking not."

"Nothing was going on, Brody. I just needed to blow off some steam."

"Yeah?" He got in my face. "Blow off some steam on the first guy you happened to stumble across? Or were you gonna let him blow off on you, like you let me do last night?"

I blinked at him, appalled. "Don't turn what we did into something dirty when you don't even—"

"I know what kind of party that was, and what a girl goes to that kind of party for."

"So that's it? Last night I'm a princess because I spread my legs for you, and tonight I'm a whore because I talked to another guy at a party?"

"Hey, princess." A young guy in a Sinners vest materialized out of the shadows between a couple of the Harleys, smoking a cigarette. "When you two're finished having your little domestic out here, come on back to the party. We'll take care of ya." He smirked at me. Then he looked Brody up and down, sizing him up. Then he made a kissy face. At Brody. And smirked some more.

Brody took me by the arm and hauled me down the street to his bike. I didn't fight him.

"Get on the bike, Jessa. We can talk about this when we get home." He was using his *I'm not fucking around* voice, which I knew well.

I didn't care.

Anger was rising through me, hot and fast, fueled by the combined humiliation and hurt—that he actually thought I came here to hook up with some random guy less than twenty-four hours after having sex with him.

Intimate, intense, *incredible* sex.

At least, it was for me.

"Why? You've already made up your mind about the way it is," I said. "You've always been the bloody judge, jury, and executioner. But you don't know shit, Brody. You said so yourself. You don't know me anymore. I am not your princess. *I never was.*"

"Yeah," he said. "I'm pretty fucking aware of that."

"I never asked you to put me on a pedestal. No one can live up to that. Do you know how much fucking pressure that is?"

"What the fuck are you talking about?"

"You said it yourself. You saw me on the internet in my underwear when you had your dick in your hand. If that's what you want from me, for me to be that girl, that fucking fantasy you've had since you were fifteen and you saw my boobs for the first time, you can go screw yourself. I am not that girl."

He stood there, grinding his jaw, and for a horrible moment I thought he might get on his bike and just leave me there.

"First of all," he said slowly, "you were ten years old, and I did not see you that way. You were a fucking *kid*. You were sweet and you were a funny little shit, but I did not have a hard-on for you when you were ten, so don't make me into *that* guy. I had a crush on you when you were thirteen and I was eighteen, and fuck me if that makes me a pervert or something in your books, but I never acted on it, Jessa. You looked older than you were, and sue me if I thought you were beautiful. You fucking *were*. I only kissed you when you were fifteen because you were going to parties a lot like this one and I knew someone was gonna get their hands on you first, and it was killing me. I told you I'd wait for you and I fucking meant it. I didn't want you getting hurt, by me or anyone else. So fuck me if I cared about you. As for having you on a pedestal, sweetheart, I am more than fully fucking aware of how perfect you are not."

I blinked back the hot sting of tears brought on by his words.

Shit. Just *shit*.

Why the hell was I always doing this? Why was I always getting into fights with him that neither of us could possibly win?

"I just want to go home. Can you take me home now, please?"

He swung a leg over his bike and settled on the seat.

"Get on," he said, when I just stood there, hugging myself.

"I mean, home to my brother's," I told him. "I think... I want to stay there a while."

I wrapped my arms tight around Brody's waist, spreading my thighs wide to accommodate his big body. And as we tore down the street, it was like we'd driven right back in time.

I'd always felt so safe at Brody's back.

I savored the feeling of being there again, the wind in my face, moving as one, leaning with him when he leaned, holding on tighter when he accelerated, not even letting go when he stopped at a light. Just trusting him. My life, literally in his hands.

I'd never been on the back of anyone else's bike, and that was fine with me.

As we got closer to my brother's place, I held on tighter. Brody had grown stronger, more solid than when he was younger. I was all wrapped up in the woodsy smell of him, his leather jacket, his hair... and the warmth of him between my legs. The familiar growl of the machine, the power of it, the vibrations...

Too soon, we pulled into my brother's driveway. The front of the house lit up as we set off the motion sensor lights. Reluctantly I let go and climbed off, knowing I had to apologize. He'd said some hurtful things too, but I'd had the entire ride here to stew in my regret over the way I'd behaved—after he'd come to my rescue, no less.

I owed him an apology, and I owed him a thank you.

He turned off the bike and got off, and when he turned to me he looked just as pissed as when he got on half an hour ago. "You running again?" he said. "Tell me if you are, so I can cancel that 'Welcome Home, Jessa' banner I ordered for the party."

And that warm, safe, regretful feeling dropped away, leaving me cold.

God, he could be such an asshole.

"I don't know how long I'm going to stay," I said. "I'm just taking it day by day."

He stared at me. "Day by day," he repeated.

"Yes."

"Any chance you wanna give me a little more than that? Call me fucking crazy, but 'give me all of you, Brody' gave *me* the idea that maybe you'd want all of me again sometime before you vanish. Or is that just what you say to every guy when his dick is in your hand?"

I turned on my heel and walked away.

"Perfect. Walk away. What you're best at."

I whirled on him. "Why would I stay? What is there here for me, besides one guilt trip after another?"

We stared at each other and when I couldn't take the anger, the accusation in his blue eyes anymore, I turned away again. I heard him coming, his boots pounding, scraping on the concrete. He grabbed me and spun me around.

"Are you fucking kidding me?"

Then he kissed me.

He walked me back into the wall of my brother's house and kissed me like he wanted to tear me apart.

When he stopped to get air, he said, "How many times do I have to do that to get through that thick, bullheaded skull of yours?"

"Brody—"

He kissed me again, roughly and thoroughly.

Then he put his forehead to mine, panting softly. "Do you need me to say it? Because I fucking will. *Do not leave me again.* If you go across the fucking world again and I can't see you... touch you... and you're gonna freeze me out and pretend I don't exist, I will not be able to handle it, Jessa." He cupped my face in his hands. "Promise me you aren't gonna do that again."

I breathed into the silence. I didn't speak. I couldn't. I couldn't promise him something I didn't know how to do.

All I knew how to do was run.

He pulled back and stared at me. My mouth was open. I was trying to speak, I was, but no words were coming.

His hands dropped away. "Is it Seth?"

"No." I shook my head. "No."

"Jesus." Brody stepped back, way back, and clawed his hands through his hair. "You always chose him, didn't you? It was always him."

"I *didn't*—"

"Like hell you didn't."

Panicking, I hurled back at him, "When did you ever choose *me*? We both know you hooked up with Christy again after you said you'd wait for me."

"When weren't you sneaking around with Seth?" he fired back.

I shut my mouth.

"I was never gonna force you to be with me, Jessa. You were sixteen, and you were *reeling* after your mom died. I felt you slipping away, and yeah, I fucking saw you with Seth, and it gutted me. I wasn't gonna be the asshole who gave you an ultimatum and made you choose. If you loved me, you would've been mine. But you weren't *ever* mine. If you were mine, you would've given a shit about what I wanted. You did not give one shit, Jessa."

"That's not true—"

"I didn't give a shit if you were a model or driving a fucking garbage truck for a living. Whatever made you happy. But you were not happy, and I begged you to stay with the band. I fucking *begged* you. I was not gonna beg you to love me."

Tears were forming in my eyes, fast. "I did love you, Brody."

He stared at me for a long moment as that sunk in.

Then he shook his head and took a step toward me. "Fuck this. Fuck waiting, and fuck being the good guy. You've got one choice to make and you need to make it now. Once and for all. Him or me."

"Brody—"

"*Him* or *me*."

I was speechless. I had no idea how to right all the wrongs between us that I had caused. He really thought I chose Seth?

Over him?

When I didn't speak, he drew back. His face was hardening in that way it did just before he shut down.

I really wasn't the only one who knew how to walk away.

"Tell me one thing," he said tightly, as lights started coming on in my brother's house. "Were you fucking him? All that time, behind my back? Right under my nose?"

I was stunned. Still speechless.

"You think he didn't tell me? Because that's sure as fuck what he said about it. And since you never say a goddamn thing, I'm starting to wonder what else you're fucking hiding."

I said nothing.

It wouldn't have mattered. Brody had already made up his mind.

Judge, jury, and executioner.

He took another step back and seemed to resolve himself to some unspoken truth as he looked at me.

"I'm done," he said. "I'm so fucking done with you."

Then he got on his bike and roared away, just as the front door opened and my brother stuck his head out.

"What the fuck?" He was shirtless, doing up his pants, his hair all mussed up. He took one look at me and came out to gather me up. "Was that Brody?"

I didn't answer. I couldn't.

I dissolved into tears in my brother's arms.

CHAPTER NINETEEN

Jessa

"YOU STAYING?"

Maggie stepped back into the church after walking the band out and called over to me.

It was one in the morning and I was still sitting onstage, on my ass, my guitar cradled on my knees, practicing. As if I didn't know this song, and every other song I'd ever written with Dirty, inside out.

When the band found out I was planning to return to Vancouver after my shoot in L.A., they'd gotten all excited and asked me to come to that secret show they were playing in town tomorrow night—and come up onstage to play a song with them. I'd said yes. And while I'd considered not coming back at all after Brody and I had our blow-out fight in my brother's driveway, I'd spent every moment while I was in L.A. wishing I was here instead.

Because I'd rather be making music with Dirty than modeling, any day of the week. I had to keep my word to come back and play. But I also had to talk to Brody—that much hadn't changed, no matter how pissed at me he was.

That didn't mean I wasn't a wreck about all of it.

"I'm in no hurry," I told Maggie. "But if you need to leave, I can lock up."

She disappeared for a moment, into the kitchen, re-emerging with a bottle of wine and a couple of coffee mugs. She hopped up onstage and took a seat on a big equipment case across from me.

"Don't you think you've practiced enough?" she prodded gently. "There is such a thing as over-rehearsing, you know."

"I know," I said, setting my guitar aside.

She was right. But I was honored that the band had asked me to play, and I figured I owed it to them—not to mention to her and Brody, since they worked so hard behind the scenes to make this show happen—not to make an ass of myself.

I leaned back against an amp, sighing. "I don't think I've ever been this nervous," I told her. "Like puke-my-guts-out-and-then-some nervous." It was true. Usually the nervous energy surrounding any kind of performance, strangely, gave me a sense of calm; it was like I instinctively knew how to convert that energy into a kind of numbness, an imperviousness against such things as stage fright.

Or maybe it was just years of practice.

"You gonna hurl?" Maggie's lips quirked as she poured a mug of red wine for each of us and passed one over to me. "Because I can get you a waste basket or something."

"No," I said. "I think that pizza you brought in for dinner is saving me."

"Right," she said, knowing full well that I hadn't eaten more than a couple of bites of pizza. Eating pizza and getting hired for swimsuit shoots didn't exactly go together, at least not in my body type. She eyed me in that Maggie way of hers, like she could see right through to all the crap I wasn't saying. "You really that nervous about the show? Or is something else going on you wanna talk about?"

"Yeah. I'm that nervous about the show," I said. And I was.

My guts were also tying themselves in knots, though, over Brody.

I'm so fucking done with you.

Five long days had passed since he said those words to me.

And for five long days, he'd proven a man of his word.

I'd been out of town most of that time, but I'd tried calling him more than once to ask if we could talk. He didn't answer. I didn't even know if he was getting my messages.

Of course... he totally was. He just didn't want to talk to me.

I'd seen him only once, this evening; he'd dropped by the church, shortly after I arrived. I'd come straight from the airport, eager to get in some practice time with the band before tomorrow's show. Brody stayed for all of two seconds, long enough to have a few words with the band while ignoring me completely, then left.

These past five days, I'd gone over and over every word he'd said to me in my brother's driveway—and every word I'd failed to say. It was killing me, that he'd wanted me to talk to him, had practically begged me to, and I'd choked.

I was still choking on the fact that he seemed to think I rejected him. That I chose Seth instead of him. That he seemed to think I never actually loved him.

I had to tell him otherwise. He had to know the truth.

How had he never known the truth?

Was it really possible that Brody thought I never even cared about him at all?

No. I couldn't live with that. We'd both be at the show tomorrow night, so I knew that would be my chance. I'd sit on him if I had to, to get him to hear me out. Or get Jude to.

Whatever it took.

But first, I had to get through the show.

"It's a lot to absorb," I told Maggie. "The band... wanting me to play with them. It's flattering, but..."

"But it's a lot to get your head around," she said.

I sighed. "I'm not a rock star, Maggie. Musicians like Zane and my brother... Dylan and Elle... they're not just rock stars. They're *rock stars*. I'm just kind of a geek, you know? I like words and sitting in a quiet space and daydreaming, writing things down on paper with pretty-colored pens. I know I work as a model, but I'm really an introvert. I get my juice here, in a small group, or on my own, with room to think. The guys in the band, they think on the fly. They're reactive and combustible—"

"And you're more of a slow burn," Maggie said with a grin.

I sighed again and smiled; Maggie knew me pretty well. "They feed off that crazy energy onstage. I've never been like them that way. Never really wanted to be," I confessed. It sounded like a betrayal or something, in the dark of the church... the band's sacred space. "Does that sound crazy?"

"Fuck, no," Maggie said. "You think I wanna be a star? My dad was a rock star. Well, still kind of is, if you ask him. And I've worked six years with these crazies, and I know it's not all glitter and fairy-tales. Don't get me wrong. They live a charmed life, and they live it to the hilt. But it's not for everyone."

She held up the wine bottle, and when I nodded, she reached over and topped up my mug.

"Do you know what's going on with Seth?" I asked her casually. If anyone had the scoop, it would be Maggie. "Like... what's your opinion on him coming back into the picture? You know he met with Brody." It wasn't a question; Brody would never keep something like that from Maggie.

She sipped her wine and gave it some thought. "Hard to say. Brody hired me on after Seth was already gone. But Zane was still drinking, you know? The band was probably at the height of all the craziness that surrounded the first album, and yet they were still really coming together in a way, after you left, and then Seth... It felt like this epic seismic shift was going on and I kind of landed in the middle of it. Growing pains? But I really couldn't say how Seth leaving changed them. I only know what I hear."

"What do you hear?"

She shrugged. "Everyone seems cautiously optimistic about him... resurfacing. I think they're uneasy, though, about trusting him again in any way. It's almost like he's an old lover who broke all their hearts. They'd like to give him another chance, but once bitten, twice shy, right?" Her pretty lips curled into a slight smile. "There's a thrill in the air, though. You can feel it. That potential, like embers smoldering. The fire on that relationship never really went out, I guess."

"Right." I sipped my wine uneasily and kind of regretted asking. It wasn't exactly what I wanted to hear. But it didn't really mean anything; it didn't mean they were going to decide to trust Seth again. Not when there were so many talented guitarists out there who *hadn't* broken their hearts.

Though I understood what Maggie meant. There'd always been fire between Seth and the rest of the band. Me included.

It's hard to put out that kind of fire once it catches.

"Though it is pretty fucking clear they miss you like hell," she added.

I smiled at her, softening at her words. Maybe it was the wine, or Maggie, or the church and the candlelight... sitting here, surrounded by the band's stuff, like I really was part of it again... but it felt really fucking good. "Thanks for that, Maggie."

"Don't thank me. They love you. We all do."

And then it came; the discomfort. Geez. Was I ever going to stop feeling guilty about hearing that?

"Look," I told her, "I feel like I owe you an apology. Or at least, an explanation. For why I've been... avoiding you."

She cocked an eyebrow at me. "I didn't know you had been."

"Yeah. Well..." I picked at the rip in the knee of my jeans. "I haven't exactly been making myself available. But I want you to know that the reason I've stayed more in touch with Roni than with you over the years, for example, is because... well, my relationship with Roni is just... kinda frivolous. She doesn't expect much from me or hold me to a higher standard. Whereas you'd never let me get away with the shit I try to pull."

Maggie just brushed that off. "I just figured you're going through some shit. That's your business. I'm here for you, whatever happens, you know?"

"I know." I gazed at my old friend, feeling worse for her understanding. It was intense, how much I'd missed her; just talking to her, like we used to talk. Back in college... before I left. "Everything's falling apart, Maggie," I confessed, my voice small in the dark of the church.

"What is?"

"Me and Brody." I whispered it into the shadows, like the walls had ears, though there was no one to hear it but me and Maggie.

"Oh?"

"Before you came on the scene, you know, years ago... we had a thing. Kind of. It's... complicated. I mean, I had a thing, for him."

Her eyebrows went up. "And?"

"And... I guess he's always wanted me, too. You know... from afar."

"Uh-huh," she said, taking that in. "Afar."

"Yeah."

She eyed me skeptically. "Okay. Excuse me if I'm missing something here, but have you looked in a mirror lately?"

"Um... sure?"

"So... you're telling me he likes that from afar? What the fuck's wrong with up close? What does he have, an aversion to beauty or something?"

I smiled a little. "No. That part's kind of on me."

"You've got an aversion to beauty? I know he's my boss and all, but Brody's *hawt*, Jessa. I can say that because he's not my type, so I've never been tempted to go there."

I grinned, curious. "What's your type?"

"Ugh," she said, waving a dismissive hand in the air. "Walking disasters. Brody's got his shit together. Apparently that doesn't do it for me." She frowned. "But we're getting off topic here, and I'm still confused. What's the problem with you and Brody?"

"Maybe the problem is that he's got his shit together." I sipped my wine, a bit of a lump in my throat; I really wasn't used to this level of candor. I'd spent most of my life avoiding it. But I took a deep breath and plunged. "I've always been afraid that if I let him get close, he'll decide he doesn't want me anymore. You know... when he sees how not-together my shit is."

Maggie frowned, clearly unimpressed with that line of thought.

Not that I expected her to be anything else. "Look, you know I love you, hon," she said, "but if you're gonna sit here and sell me bullshit, I'm not really buying."

Okay. That was about the last thing I expected her to say.

"What do you mean, bullshit?"

"Oh, Jessa." She sipped her wine. "You and I have always clicked, right?"

"We have," I agreed.

"But you never really let me in, and sometimes that gets... old."

"Sure I do," I protested.

"No, you don't. You keep me at a distance, just like you do everyone else. You tell me what you want me to know, let me see what you want me to see, and that is never the full picture. We're all entitled to our privacy and our secrets, but Jessa, you hold yours in front of you like a shield and that is the bullshit I speak of."

I shook my head slowly, processing that. "I never knew I did that. Only let you see certain stuff... that I used it like a wall. I mean, I know I've done that, at times, with people in the past. I didn't know I was doing it now. With you." I bit my lip. "I'm sorry for that."

"Well, isn't honesty refreshing?" She shrugged. "I'm not much for bullshit. I get enough of that from Zane."

"Maggie. You give nothing but honesty. I'd expect no less, and I love you for it. Please don't stop now, even if I give you bullshit."

"Okay. Why don't you tell me what you've been doing with yourself since the wedding. Before you went down to L.A. for your shoot."

"Hanging at Roni's. And, you know, we've had a few girls' nights."

"Uh-huh."

"And I guess I'll be seeing more of my brother. And Katie. I'm staying at their place now."

"I heard."

"And making music, a bit, as you know." I took a swig of wine, fortifying myself, getting a feeling where this was going. "Spending a little time with Brody."

"Uh-huh. And you've been dying to get back to modeling the whole time, right? Dying to leave?"

"Well... no."

She threw her hands up, in the direction of the stained glass window. "Hallelujah, Jesus."

I couldn't help laughing. "What?"

"It's about time, is all." She leaned over and handed me the bottle of wine so I could top up my own mug this time, which I did. Generously. "Look, Jessa. I've got no issue with your career of choice. You know that. While these other guys bitch and moan about you coming back to us, I figure you might as well rock the modeling thing while you can. I mean, you'll have to choose a different path at some point, obviously, because no one wants to see a bikini model with crow's-feet and sagging breasts, and that is the sad truth."

I laughed again. "Yeah, I'm kind of aware that's the way it works. Maybe I could be the first, though?"

"The first what?"

"Bikini model with sagging breasts and crow's-feet. Set a new standard for beauty."

"Not gonna happen in this life, but good luck with that in the next one," she said. "Seriously. You ever think about why you were drawn to modeling?"

"I wasn't really drawn. It was just an opportunity that presented itself when I was too young to think about it and I went with it. I was lucky."

"More bullshit." She shook her head at me. "Jessa, you were drawn to modeling. You can't tell me any girl gets as far as you have and she doesn't want it, and want it bad. You've got to compete against all those other gorgeous bitches for every job you get, and you know that isn't easy. Looking hot in a photo or on a runway is one bit of work, but I'm gonna tell you, after mopping up Dirty's shit for the past six years, it's not the hard work they'd have you believe. Competing for those jobs where you get to look hot in a bikini? That's hard work. Living on a diet fit for a very small rabbit, dealing with other bitches' problems in your face whether you want them there or not, getting rejected over and over again for things that are beyond your control, *that* is hard work. And you've done it. You don't fight that fight, and win, unless you want it. So why don't you tell me again, and no bullshit this time, why you were drawn to modeling."

Damn. Maggie was *good*.

"I don't know," I said, genuinely at a loss. "Because I got to travel and make money?"

"You were gonna get to travel and make money with the band. You serve up one more heap of bullshit and you're out of here on that hot ass of yours. I mean it."

"Damn."

"I can tell you why you became a model. Because you were super fucking good at it. You were beautiful, you *are* beautiful, and when you rock that into a photo or down a catwalk, no one can touch you. Modeling, for you, is skin deep. I get that. I've met a *lot* of beautiful girls, and a lot of models over the years, at our video shoots, backstage, at parties, and some of them just aren't *there*, you know? That's the way it is for some girls. That beauty is a way to keep people out."

"Yeah. It's that," I admitted.

"And not just men," she said. "Everyone."

I digested that.

Then I took a breath, took a sip of wine, and asked, "Did I ever tell you about the drugs?"

She cocked an eyebrow at me. "Drugs?"

"It started before I met you," I said, kind of embarrassed. "And it's not like I came to class wasted, so maybe you never knew."

She looked at me with compassion and not one ounce of judgment. "Jessa, you never told me. But it's not like I didn't know."

I stared at her, a little shocked. "What?"

"I saw you, at that party out at Brody's... remember? That first party you took me to, when you introduced me to Brody and the band. You'd come with that guy, and Brody caught him dealing coke, and there was a bit of a kerfuffle when Jude bounced him out. You weren't too happy... I wasn't sure exactly what happened there. But I saw you, later in the night, arguing with Seth outside. You were upset."

Shit. Maggie saw that?

How much had she *heard*?

"I wasn't eavesdropping or anything," she added quickly. "I went out to smoke a joint with some of the guys, in the backyard. Zane dropped a comment, something about Seth and you and 'too much speed.' I don't know, at the time I didn't think much of it. Just figured you guys were high, and there were a lot of drugs going around back then, but... I guess maybe Zane knew more?"

Zane knew?

Oh, God... I'd been so stupid. So naive.

If Zane knew, maybe my brother knew.

Maybe everyone knew.

Maggie sighed at the look on my face. "Would you please do me one sweet favor and stop being so hard on yourself?"

I chewed on my lip, just kind of stewing in this uncomfortable mix of relief and shame.

Why did I think I had to hide from Maggie? Sure, I knew she was kind of a straight arrow; a little booze, a little pot... but it's not like she hadn't seen it all and then some working in the Dirty universe. Her dad had lived that life, too; so in a way, she was born right into the craziness. And it's not like I was being served up heroin on a silver platter; I'd heard stories about her dad's parties back in the day, and whatever I'd heard, she'd heard more. Maybe even witnessed. If anyone would understand the things I'd been through, it was Maggie.

"Jessa, please listen to me," she said softly, before I could say anything else. "I know you lost your parents, young, and I know there was pain. A lot of it. We all saw it. You think you hide that stuff and you are good at hiding, hon, I'll give you that. Behind that pretty face of yours, it's hard to know what's really going on. But believe me, I've seen the worst there is, and it is not pretty. It might've once been pretty, but that pretty goes fast. My dad was more or less an addict, you know? I mean, I never really thought of him as one, but he put his party life over me and my mom, so what else would you call it? He's pushing sixty and he's still high every time I see him. God only knows how he's made it this long with whatever shit is in his veins. But that's the glamorous life, you know? He's rich, he's got a new young babe on his arm every other month, and he likes his drugs. Whatever. It's ridiculous the shit he gets away with. I've seen what drugs can *really* do. You know I volunteer at a women's shelter? I have for years."

"Yeah. I know."

"Well, those are the ones who've fallen through the cracks. They didn't end up with the glamorous life. I've met women who've lost teeth to meth addictions and men's fists, who've lost everything, and worst of all their self-esteem, their self-worth, their self-preservation. They've lost *themselves*. Believe me when I say, I've known lost women. What I see when I look at you is not a lost woman. I see a woman who found a way back to herself, long before it was too late. Don't give up on that."

"Thanks, Maggie," I managed, tearing up. "But would you understand what I mean if I say that sometimes I think I'm not hard enough on myself?"

"Fuck that," Maggie said. "As your friend, I'm here to tell you it's okay to let yourself off the hook for whatever's happened in the past. And I'll tell you something else that may be a revelation to someone like you. I know it is to a lot of women who walk into the shelter." She leaned in and said, "It's okay to ask for help."

"Yeah," I said, starting to really get that concept. Especially when I saw all the strength and compassion in Maggie's pretty gray eyes. "I know we're the same age, but you know, I've always kind of looked up to you?"

"Shit. What kind of drugs did you say you did again?" She grinned and sipped her wine.

"I didn't say. And I'm serious. I've always admired you. You're tough as shit, but you've always kept your sweetness, you know?

Like you come strutting into a room in your high heels, all five-foot-nothing of you, and start kicking butt and taking names, and all the guys just melt. They're useless globs of putty in your manicured hands. Even Zane, and that's saying something, believe me. You just always seem to have it all figured out. You have this amazing, perfect life you've built for yourself that's just so *you*, and I envy that."

Maggie just stared at me, her eyebrows going up... way up. "Perfect life?"

"Yeah. You know. You've got the band. You kick ass at your job, and you've got the work you do at the shelter, too. You rock all of it. You help people. You help me. And, you know, you've always been an incredible friend to me, and shared with me, let me in, and I haven't even—"

"I married Zane in Vegas," she blurted.

I froze, stunned.

"You... *what?*"

"Oh, for the love of Christ," she gushed. "That felt so fucking good to just say it out loud to someone. Pass me that wine?"

I passed her the bottle and stared at her in disbelief, my mouth gaping open as she took a swig.

"You... How? When? *Why?*" I stammered.

"Exactly." She sighed. "You see, Jessa, we all do stupid shit we're not proud of. Perfection is an illusion. Even beauty is kind of an illusion. And that's what you are when you model. An illusion. But here's the thing: you're a real person. You deserve a real life. So go out there and live it already, and stop worrying what everyone else thinks. You don't need to be perfect or even beautiful all the time. Just love yourself and the rest of it will figure itself out."

Yeah, that was some kick-ass Maggie advice, but I was kinda stuck on that other thing she said...

"You... *married* Zane?"

"Yeah."

"Zane."

She rolled her eyes and took another swig of wine. "Yeah."

"*Zane.*"

"Yes."

"And then... you got a divorce?"

"Nope."

"No?"

"No."

"As in... you *are* married to him? *Right now?*"

"Technically... yes."

"What does that *mean?*"

"You know. 'It's complicated.'"

"Oh, no. Do not throw my words back at me," I said. "You are not getting out of this that easy."

She grinned a little, kind of painfully.

"When did this *happen?*"

"Last April."

"April! That was almost a year ago!"

"I'm aware."

"And you're living together?" I couldn't quite wrap my head around it. Zane lived in L.A., and she lived here.

"No. We are not."

Oh.

"So you're just... married."

"Technically."

"But not really... married?"

"That's about it."

"Because... Zane..." I floundered, unsure how to put it. "He isn't really..."

"He's not husband material," she said flatly. "You can say it. We both know it's true. And yet, I'm the idiot who married him on a stupid fucking whim in Vegas."

"Right. And you aren't... like... secretly an item, then?"

"Well, every other time I see him he has some random woman wrapped around him, so no."

"And yet... still married?"

"Yup."

I gaped at her. I couldn't help it. This was *huge*. "Does anyone else know about this?"

"No one. Well, my dad and his latest arm ornament. They were there, at the fucking ceremony. Other than that... no. And we made them promise not to tell. But Jesse saw us, apparently. Coming back to the hotel in the middle of the night, me with my bouquet and all, and he put two and two together... He asked me about it about a month afterward but I just denied it like hell. Laughed in his face, actually. Told him we were just partying, that I was wasted and Zane was looking out for me, that the bouquet and the ring he saw me wearing were just gags, party favors given to Zane by some bachelorette party we ran into while we were bar-hopping. Guess he figured the whole notion of me marrying Zane was so ridiculous, when I laughed it off, he bought it... ended up apologizing to me for even asking." She shook her head, her shoulders dropping. "God, I'm such an asshole."

"You are *not* an asshole. It's your private business. If you don't want anyone to know, that's your choice."

We sat there for a few minutes, drinking wine, me from my mug and Maggie straight from the bottle.

"It is pretty ridiculous, though," I ventured, cautiously. "You. And Zane. In Vegas." I cast her a sideways glance. "Married."

"Uh-huh."

"*Mrs. Zane Traynor,*" I mused.

Our eyes locked. I snorted a little as I tried not to laugh—which made Maggie lose it. Apparently, we were both in need of some tension relief, because once we got going, we totally fell apart.

"*Hey, babe,*" I said, in my best impression of Zane, "*can you fetch my slippers?*"

"Oh my God." Maggie mopped the tears from her cheeks with her sleeve. "Stop making me laugh or I'm gonna piss myself."

"Shit," I said, getting a hold of myself. "I really don't mean to make light of your troubles."

"Yeah, you do."

"No. Seriously," I told her. "I really appreciate you telling me this. It means a lot that you trust me enough. I have very few real female friends, and I need to start valuing the ones I have more."

"Well, you're doing better than me, anyway. I've got pretty much none. Except you. And maybe Elle on a good day. And now of course there's Katie. You might say... I'm married to my work."

We fell apart again.

Yeah, we needed tension relief. Big time.

Ah, shit. Speaking of tension relief... I sobered again.

"Have you had sex with him?"

"It's Zane," she said, mopping her tears away again. "What do you think?"

"Uh-oh."

"Just don't ask. You really don't wanna know."

I wrinkled my nose. Zane was hot and all—like way hot, objectively—but there was still the brother thing, as in he felt like one to me. "No, actually, I don't."

"Good. It's too depressing."

Ouch. That sounded bad.

Like really bad.

"So I take it... things aren't good between you two?"

Maggie took another swig of her wine and gave me a look. "It's complicated."

Right... "So... are you planning to stay married, then? I mean, I'm assuming not, if you're still keeping it a secret."

"If I knew the answers to such questions, Jessa Mayes, I wouldn't be drinking wine straight from the bottle."

Ouch again.

I chewed on my lip, considering. "Have the two of you... talked things through, though? Together?"

"Come on, Jessa. You know there's no talking to that man."

"Damn."

"You could say that."

"So... what are you going to *do*?"

She wasn't laughing anymore, and suddenly the tears she was wiping away were real.

Oh, shit.

Shit.

"I don't know," she whispered. "What would you do, if you were me?"

I stared at Maggie, stunned. I'd never seen her cry before. And I felt so much compassion for her in that moment. So fucking *much.* Because she had feelings for him. *Real* feelings. That much was obvious.

If she didn't, there'd be no problem at all. Just divorce his ass, or get an annulment or whatever, and be done with it.

But she hadn't done that.

"I guess that would depend," I told her honestly, "on how much I loved him."

CHAPTER TWENTY

Jessa

THE BACK DOOR was exactly that; a bar with its main entrance off a narrow, skeezy alley in back. Maggie and I arrived together for the Dirty show, walking in at the tail end of sound check, a giant bouncer who seemed to know Maggie letting us in. The first thing that struck me was how much smaller and danker it felt than it used to. The second thing was the smell; it smelled exactly the same. It was the sweet, slightly rank smell of decades' worth of spilled beers seeping into softening wood and carpets that never fully dried, mixed with sweat and cologne.

It was a dive bar, really, and that's what I'd always loved about it. A rotting old monument to the past, the Back Door was one of a very few bars in town where local, up-and-coming rock bands could still play. Dirty had gotten their start here; the owners had let them play and drink when they were still underage. Plus, they were affiliated with the Kings motorcycle club, so there was that connection. The owners also owned Misty's, the strip club downstairs. As far as I knew, there was never any Misty; there was however a Bear and a Snake. Father and son, they were built like tanks and about as friendly to strangers, but as long as you had no problem with them— or the Kings—they had no problem with you.

Both Bear and Snake were longtime Dirty fans, and Bear's wife, who was roughly the same size and build as Bear, had a long-standing crush on Zane. I was also pretty sure Snake was in love with Elle, since I never saw him as warm and fuzzy as when she walked in a room and started giving him shit. I had memories of Elle at age twenty, all pretty and badass in her leather miniskirt and sneakers, her platinum hair in braids, her electric bass slung over her shoulder, sneaking me—then age seventeen—into the Back Door by telling Snake I was her twin sister. I knew he didn't believe it, since I was taller than her, even back then, and we really didn't look alike. But I still remembered him letting me in, never taking his eyes off Elle, and never cracking so much as a hint of a smile as he told her, "So long as you play 'Love Me Two Times' for me tonight, Elle."

And they did. Dirty had made it a practice to come back here to play at least once every couple of years, and over the years, it had become tradition to close out every show at the Back Door with that song.

Now, as Maggie and I made our way into the bar, Aerosmith's "Dude (Looks Like a Lady)" was cranked and my brother's guitar tech, Jimmy, was center stage, doing his infamous Steven Tyler impression with the mic stand, lip-syncing the song for the amusement of the other stage crew.

I saw my guitar behind him, on a stand next to several others that belonged to my brother, and I got tinglies—and that nervous-sick feeling in my gut. The crew was working out the light show and as more lights came up, I saw the banners; big prints made from Katie's portraits of the band members, even bigger than the paintings themselves, hanging along the back and sides of the stage. There was Jesse, and me, then Elle, Dylan, Seth and Zane.

So fucking surreal.

I took a deep, deep breath as Maggie pulled me up in front of the stage, where we found Snake. He gave me a giant hug and cracked a rare smile as he told me the band was backstage, and whatever I needed, just let him know. I thanked him and we applauded Jimmy's performance. When Jimmy saw me, he flew down off the stage, spinning his ball cap backwards to give me a kiss. When he hugged me, he lifted me right up off the floor. "I've got you all set up," he said in my ear as he put me back down on my feet, still wrapped around me. "Can't wait to see you play tonight." He held onto me for as long as Maggie put up with it, letting go when she peeled him off.

I just smiled. Jimmy had always had a bit of a thing for me, which he wasn't shy about. He was sweet. I didn't mind.

"How's it coming?" Maggie asked him.

"No worries, Maggs," he said, hopping back up onstage. "We'll make this shit look good." I had no doubt that was true.

Myself, I wasn't quite sure how an entire Dirty show, typically destined for stadiums and giant arenas, was going to fit on that tiny stage, amps, egos and all, but I trusted that the crew had it covered.

"Just make it *sound* good," Maggie said to him. Then she looped her arm through mine and said, for my ears only, "Pretty sure Jessa can make it look good."

"Oh, God."

"Still nervous?"

"Yes."

"Don't be," she said, grinning. "Secret show... very little in the way of expectations."

I rolled my eyes, not buying that for a second. "Right."

Tonight's show, like the others Dirty had played here—since signing their record deal—had only been announced a couple of hours before doors would open at nine o'clock, which meant it had just been posted on the old-school marquee that hung over the entrance. Already, people were accumulating outside; Jude had a bunch of security guys stationed in the alley, and they'd had to fish us through the crowd to get us in. And of course, word would get out fast.

Bear, Snake and their staff would keep all the money from liquor sales and tips, money collected at the door would go to charity, and everyone was happy. That palpable electricity that always charged the air before a Dirty show could be felt, but it was definitely under-scored by an unspoken sadness—at this show, Dirty was supposed to announce that Paulie was joining the band. Brody had booked the show while the band was in town, especially for that reason.

Since that was no longer happening, they were donating the proceeds from ticket sales to the hospital where Paulie's wife was receiving treatment instead.

I just hoped I could do my part and do honor to Paulie, since he couldn't be here, without doing something ridiculous like fainting onstage. Though maybe that would hold a certain entertainment value of its own—make people feel like they'd gotten their money's worth, and then some.

The show sold out in twenty minutes—basically, as fast as the door staff could process people in. Within half an hour of the Back Door opening, the bar was at capacity. And I heard there were still a few hundred people hanging around on the block outside, hopeful they might squeeze in later, if enough people left early.

Unlikely.

Once everything was ready for the show and the doors opened, the band and the crew, along with Bear, Snake, Maggie and me, and some friends of the band who'd started showing up, headed downstairs for the private VIP treatment. Apparently, Bear and Snake were keeping Misty's closed tonight, for us, but they had a bartender, a few waitresses and several strippers on hand to take care of our group.

Clearly, Misty's was where the money was. Even though it was in the basement of the old building that shared the dive upstairs, the strip club had been renovated over the years and both felt and smelled clean. Literally, it smelled of bleach. Which I supposed was a good thing. Everything was shiny, glittery, mirrored and/or pink—including the girls.

Everyone, especially the scantily-clad female staff, flocked to take care of the guys in the band, treating them like—well, like rock stars.

Maggie was right. My brother—and his friends—did live a charmed life.

Okay; the modeling biz was pretty sweet too, what with being paid to look pretty and all. But I'd also spent the last ten years of my life dieting, exercising my ass off and, once I'd outgrown my rebellious phase, going to bed early, while my brother partied the night away, drinking, eating and generally doing whatever the fuck he wanted. He worked out a lot, too—he definitely wasn't born with those washboard abs the girls liked so much—but shit.

It was moments like these that reminded me my brother and his band weren't just rock stars... they were rock royalty.

Elle was treated just the same, Snake setting her up with her entourage of girlfriends at a big table in the corner with their own waitress.

Maggie sat me at a table with Jimmy and some other people I sort of knew and told me to chill the fuck out, and while she did the rounds, doing whatever Maggie did to keep things organized while everyone else had a good time, Jimmy talked my ear off. I had to admit it was flattering that he never took his eyes off me, all the while a very curvaceous blonde got naked about six feet from his face.

I wasn't quite sure if I was glad that Brody hadn't shown up yet, since the strippers were doing their thing, but it did make me more nervous. Because where the hell was he? And yes, I was a lingerie model. But yes, it still made me uncomfortable to think of Brody in a room full of strippers. Especially when my nerves were already so raw—and getting rawer with every minute that passed without him showing up.

There was no way he'd skip out on a Dirty show just because I was here, right?

No. No fucking way.

After a while, Roni showed up and joined our table. Katie showed up, as did Ash, along with more friends of the band, gradually filling the seats around us, and I could almost forget we were playing a show tonight; it just felt like we were having a party. Even the strippers became just part of the scene, kind of like sparkly curtains.

For her part, Katie took the entertainment in stride. Though she'd barely been with my brother for six months—hard to imagine when you saw them together, so seemingly in sync all the time—she seemed pretty accustomed to all of this by now. She sat on his lap with a smile on her face, laughing and covering her eyes when the stripper working the pole in front of their table—to a classic Dirty song, "Get Made"—got too close. She sipped her drink and periodically made out with my brother, and not for the first time, I admired her ability to just be herself no matter what was going on around her.

It helped my nerves. A bit.

When Brody finally walked in, right before show time, he stopped by the bar to talk to Bear and his wife. He saw me staring; at least, I thought he did, but he looked kind of through me. Maybe he was looking past me, at the naked blonde hanging off the stage, the one Roni was currently misting with a spray bottle.

He definitely looked at Jimmy, who had his arm slung around my shoulders. I was wearing my stage clothes, which meant cute, high-heeled ankle boots, tight jeans and a silver halter top with a low back, and Jimmy was running his thumb back and forth across my bare shoulder. I let him because it was Jimmy and Jimmy was a flirt, but he was harmless.

Brody didn't seem to find him harmless, though, which just made me more nervous—because now what? He was *more* mad at me? For hanging out with my friends? For letting another guy put his arm around me?

When he was "done" with me?

He was full of shit, that's what he was.

At least he didn't seem all that interested in the entertainment. Maybe because he'd seen it all before. Maybe because I was in the room? But mostly because he was too busy shooting Jimmy death looks.

By the time everyone headed back upstairs for Dirty to start their set—the band and key crew heading backstage, the rest out into the bar to watch the show—I was a wreck of nerves and adrenalin. As the band prepared to take the stage, my anxiety grew; this was definitely not the way I felt backstage at a fashion show. Modeling had never really freaked me out; maybe because I'd started doing it so young?

Or maybe because Brody was never there when I did it.

Truth be told, I was most nervous about playing—and fucking up—in front of him.

But it was only one song, right? I was only joining Dirty onstage near the end of the set. Until then, I'd be watching the show from side stage, with Maggie and Katie and Jude. And Brody.

Fuck.

I knew I could walk out there and strap on my guitar without falling on my face, even in my high heels. I knew I could smile and look like I had my shit together, even if I felt like a hot mess. But what if my fingers shook?

What if I fucked up the song?

"Just keep playing," Elle said, when I voiced my concern to her. "Don't overthink it. Jesse will cover for you if you fuck up and no one will really notice. Whatever you do, just keep playing."

"Uh-huh." That wasn't making me feel any better. "What if I forget the words?"

"You won't," she said. "They're your words."

Then she handed me a shot of bourbon, which my brother always had on hand before a show, and we all did a shot together, and that was that.

Zane didn't do a shot. He smoked up with Snake at the side of the stage and watched the room from behind a wall of amps. Zeppelin's "Heartbreaker" was rocking the place as the crowd's excitement built. Backstage, though, everyone seemed so *relaxed.* Well, kind of relaxed-excited. Dylan sat with one foot thrown up on his opposite knee, in his kilt, idly drumming on his boot as he talked with Brody.

Brody, who hadn't yet said a word to me or even looked me in the eye, even though I was still staring at him.

Yeah. I couldn't do this.

I turned to Jimmy and gave him a smile he couldn't refuse. "Can I borrow your hat?"

It smelled of Jimmy's guy shampoo as I pulled it low over my eyes. Then I pulled on my leather jacket and slipped past Jude. If I left without telling him, though, he'd be pissed. Plus, he'd come looking for me. So I leaned into Maggie's ear.

"Give me two minutes to get out there, then you can tell Jude where I've gone."

"Oh, Jesus." She gave me a sharp look of disapproval.

But she let me go.

I snaked my way out through the throng of security guys; they were too focused on keeping people from entering backstage to care about me exiting. And within seconds, I was in another world: the frantic beating heart of the crowd, pumping with blood; roaring like it was hungering for blood. I melted into it and managed to slither my way up close to the front of the stage.

People were packed in tight, bodies pressed together and facing forward, waiting for the show to begin, screaming and shoving and laughing and wrangling for position, for the best vantage point. For the best spot to see Zane's face, or to be seen by Zane. But if you knew how to wait for the small openings, to shift when the crowd shifted, to make your gains foot by foot...

A guy stood back to let me in, and as I settled into the little notch of space in front of him, I heard him say to his friend, "Soon as the show starts, that ass'll be wiggling all over my dick..."

He was talking about my ass, but I didn't care. I wasn't staying long anyway. Just long enough to see... to *feel* the show the way it was meant to be felt.

From the midst of the crowd packed in so tight they could barely breathe, so ravenous for Dirty, they'd let themselves bleed if they had to.

I stayed out there, willing to bleed, a lot longer than I meant to.

Once Dirty took the stage, I just couldn't find the will to go. Zane was all gorgeous and spun of gold, like a sun god under the lights, or maybe a sex god, in his skin-tight white shirt with the sleeves cut off and his nipple piercing showing through, his smoldering, powerful voice ramming into every dark crevasse at the back of the bar. My brother was quite the god himself in his leather pants, wailing on his guitar. Ash, who'd joined the band just for the night to cover rhythm guitar, fit right in with his sexy tats and edgy vibe. Dylan, as usual, was a total powerhouse on drums, like an octopus with his arms flying around. And Elle, in her extremely short skirt and embroidered tights, her platinum-blonde hair in a killer fauxhawk, slamming on her bass, was a freakin' idol to every girl who'd ever dreamed of rocking out.

I was blown over by the sheer force of it. Not just the volume or the energy but the giant, pumping fist of it, battering at the crowd, pulling us up by our hair and slapping us all silly.

I couldn't walk away.

I kept telling myself, *Just one more song...* but I was a liar.

The power of the show, like I'd predicted, could barely be contained on that tiny stage. I kept wondering, as the floor shook beneath my feet, if we were all going to die in a massive cave-in.

But what a way to go...

I just tried to be careful not to blow my voice by screaming too much.

I kept my jacket zipped and my elbows at my sides so I wouldn't get groped. I felt the guy behind me put his hands on my hips, but he let go when I glanced back at him and shook my head.

I saw three different girls get topless in the crowd and wondered at their bravery... or stupidity.

I saw someone throw up, right in the middle of the crowd.

I saw people making out.

I almost got kicked in the head, five different times, once by a stiletto heel, as people crowd-surfed.

Halfway through the show, the guy next to me took out his dick. I was too shocked to believe what I was seeing; I couldn't have gotten out of the way fast enough if I'd tried. For a split second I thought he was jerking off. Then I realized he was pissing in his beer cup.

He saw me looking and gave me a drunken, prideful grin. "Don't wanna miss the fuckin' show," he shouted at me over the music. Then he raised the cup over his head, roared like some crazed barbarian—and threw the cup, piss and all, into the crowd.

Thank God he tossed it *away* from me. But I took that as my cue to get out of there.

My heart was pounding, blood thrumming through my body; I felt all weirdly disoriented as the floor I could never see through the tight crowd came up to meet my feet, everything around me at once off-kilter and hyper-vivid.

I'd once stepped onto a city street without looking. The noise of a jackhammer on concrete from a nearby construction site had blocked out the sound of an approaching bus, and the bus had whipped past me so close that it literally spun me around. I had never felt so uncomfortably alive as I felt in those first few seconds after near-death. Squished into that mad throng, as Dirty's music beat the shit out of that crowd, I felt that same feeling.

So frighteningly, gratefully *alive*.

By the time I clawed my way out of the crowd and security let me backstage, and Jude looked down at me with a hooked smile and said, "Satisfied?" I was laughing hysterically.

As it turned out, I didn't fuck up.

Once I was poised to strut onstage, I'd realized that all I really had to do was go out there and play a fucking song. Dirty would take care of the rest. Anyway, their fans were ravenous, insatiable and loyal, and in truth, there really wasn't much I could do to fuck things up. A Dirty concert was a thing unto itself, and it was way the hell bigger than me. It was bigger than any one of us.

That was a freeing thought.

Zane said some beautiful things about me, about who I was and the work I'd done writing songs with the band, only some of which I registered; I just kept going over the song in my head, like if I didn't it might suddenly vanish—the chords, the words, all of it. But at some point, I definitely heard Zane refer to me as both a "genius" and a "goddess."

No pressure.

Dylan and Elle had just come offstage, following a killer performance of a Dirty classic, "Runaround," which I'd co-written with the band. Elle hugged me and Dylan kissed my cheek. Jimmy handed me my guitar, I heard my brother say my name, and Maggie actually had to give me a little shove to get my feet moving.

I strapped on the guitar as I walked onstage, smiling. It wasn't a fake smile. I saw Jesse and Zane beaming at me and took my place between them. I was aware of the screaming of the crowd, the vibrations of the applause in the old wooden stage beneath my feet. There were lights in my eyes, but I could see the sea of faces on the dance floor in front of the stage, beyond the shoulders of the security guys. I was still stunned by how loud it was out here, how many people they could jam into such a small place.

I thought of that guy tossing his cup of piss into the crowd, and just hoped no one threw piss at me. I figured we were taking a risk slowing things down for an acoustic song at this point in the show, but I trusted Dirty knew their audience. Really, we could probably piss in a cup onstage right now and the fans would eat it up. Zane would probably do it, too, if he thought the fans wanted it.

But we didn't do that.

Instead, we played one of my favorite Dirty songs from *Love Struck*, "Road Back Home." I knew people probably expected me to play "Dirty Like Me" with the guys, since it was our most famous song, but when they'd asked me which song I wanted to play, I chose this one. I'd written it with my brother after our mom died, and it was one of my favorites; I'd always thought it was a song she would've liked.

One of the most painful things about losing her, for me, was that she'd died before she got to hear our songs.

I thought about her now as I played, and a calm overcame me. Not a numbing calm or a pretend calm, but a deep, genuine calm. The music flowed. I was pretty sure I sounded better than I did in practice at the church, but maybe it was the sound system or the acoustics in the place, or maybe it was just that I was so happy.

For just those three-and-a-half minutes, up there onstage with my brother and Zane, singing our song, I felt truly at home. I could pretend we were just playing for our friends, around a fire, and it felt *right*.

As the song ended, I exhaled in the silent pause. I saw the sparkle in my brother's eyes, maybe because he was getting sweaty and sparkly all over under the lights, but maybe it was the emotion of the song. Then the crowd went ballistic, the guys hugged me, and Zane shouted "Jessa Fucking Mayes!" into the mic as I walked offstage, giving the crowd a final dorky wave in answer to their whistles and screams.

Elle and Dylan hugged me tight, then they headed back onstage as Zane started telling the crowd some story. Maggie, with a giant smile on her face, wrapped me in a hug and said, "You're amazing. You know that, right?" Katie jumped up and down and kissed me. Jimmy kissed me, too.

Brody met my eyes, but he didn't say a thing or move to touch me.

And I just felt relieved that it was all over.

I got in position to watch the rest of the show from side stage; I knew they only had a few more songs to go, so I could just enjoy this part of the show and try to get my heart rate back to normal, now that my part was done.

Except that it wasn't really done. I still had Brody to deal with.

"So, as you all know, my favorite guitar player in the world cut a solo album last year, and then he went on tour," Zane was saying onstage, obviously talking about Jesse, "without me." There were *boo*'s from the crowd at this. "I know. It was brutal. And he had a great time. Sold a fuckload of albums and blah-ditty-blah, oh, and he fell in love, with this totally cool chick."

He paused as the crowd's applause and hoots and whistles drowned him out for a good minute or so. Katie was next to me, grinning, and I put my arm around her.

"And meanwhile," Zane went on, "while I was bumming around down in L.A. just kinda feeling sorry for myself," —pause for sympathetic *aww*'s from the crowd— "I was walking down the beach one day and I heard this guy playing guitar, and it was really good." Now the crowd gave up some *boo*'s on Jesse's behalf. "Naw, guys, it was good," Zane said. "So good, my heart kinda stopped." The crowd quieted down to listen, something in Zane's voice holding everyone captivated. "I went over and I told him, you gotta come play with me sometime. So he did. And we had a great time." I had no idea where Zane was going with this, but tingles were creeping down my spine when he took a breath and said, "So great, we asked him to come tonight and play a song with us. Come on up here, brother."

I peeked out over the crowd as people started shuffling around, craning to see. A couple of security guys were moving through; they were escorting someone to the stage. He had on a trucker hat, pulled low over his wavy brown hair and freshly-shaven face, but the crowd started recognizing him just as I did.

"*Seth!*" I heard a girl up front scream, and a wave of female gasps and shrieks went up—like it was 1964 and the Beatles had just walked in.

My brother reached down a hand to help him up onstage. Ash handed his guitar off to Seth and bowed to him, like he was some kind of legend. Which maybe he was. Then Ash came offstage and the band tore into "Dirty Like Me." The crowd went apeshit. My heart drummed along in a rapid-fire rhythm with the song, knowing every beat.

I felt kind of shell-shocked, and it was over fast. When the song ended, the band surrounded Seth for a bunch of back-slapping hugs. Elle threw herself into his arms and kissed him on the cheek—twice. Then the lights went down, and they all came offstage.

I got the hell out of the way. They were swarmed anyway, all of them; Seth included. By the time Dirty went back onstage to rip into an encore performance of one of their greatest hits, "Down With You," Seth was gone. Vanished, as mysteriously as he'd material-ized... just like he'd always been so good at doing.

By the time Dirty hit the stage again for their final encore of the night, treating the crowd to their classic cover of The Doors' "Love Me Two Times," I was in tears.

CHAPTER TWENTY-ONE

Jessa

"SO, WHAT DO YOU THINK?" Zane's ice-blue eyes met mine as he mopped sweat off his face with the T-shirt he'd just peeled off, and clawed his now-limp mohawk back. "Wanna do that again sometime?" He tossed the shirt aside and grinned at me in a way-too-happy, carnivorous sort of way that I knew from experience was probably a bad thing.

We were backstage, Dirty had just come offstage for the final time, and we were all gathered around in a tiny dressing room—just Zane, Jesse, Elle, Dylan and I, sweaty and spent, flung across the furniture—and they were all looking at me.

Staring, actually.

"Um... sure? Maybe." I didn't actually know if I *ever* wanted to do that again, but this didn't seem like the time to put that out there. Clearly, they were all in their afterglow phase. Why ruin it?

"Yeah?" Dylan asked. "How'd it feel?" He'd also stripped off his drenched T-shirt and his kilt, and was now sitting next to me on the couch in nothing but his incredibly revealing white underwear, his booted feet thrown up on a broken end table and his arm slung behind me. The overwhelming—and alluring—aromas of sweaty men, whiskey, beer and pot assailed me. I met Elle's eyes as I avoided the sight of Dylan's prominent package, and she smirked knowingly. I wasn't sure I'd ever understand how she got used to this.

"Terrifying," I said, straight-faced.

Elle snickered and Zane laughed. "That's how it's supposed to feel." He shot my brother a look, which was when I noticed the serious expression on Jesse's face. He sat quietly in a corner, his dark eyes on mine.

"What?" I demanded.

"What would you say if we told you we want you to join the band?" Jesse asked me, and everyone got really quiet.

"Join...?" I repeated stupidly, the connections in my brain not quite working right. My head was still pounding from the adrenalin and the thunder of the crowd; from being completely blind-sided by Seth's appearance, and disappearance. "What do you mean... join?"

"Join Dirty," Elle said. She cocked her head at me in that cute way she did, smiling. "As our new rhythm guitarist."

"And lyricist, of course," my brother said.

"And we know you can sing," Dylan added with a grin. "You know, decently."

"A fuck of a lot better than Dylan," Zane said, grinning lazily. "You've got a lot to offer, little sis."

"Good-looking, too," Dylan added.

"A fuck of a lot better-looking than Dylan," Zane agreed.

I just stared at them all, blinking, like maybe this was a hallucination. I'd breathed in too many moldering-old-beer-carpet fumes in this place and it was getting to me.

Seriously?

Were they *serious*?

Gathering from the looks on their faces—Jesse's, Elle's and Dylan's *dead* serious, and Zane's with a maniac grin—they were.

I also noticed that Ash had suspiciously disappeared.

"What about Ash?" I asked.

"Ash already has a band," Dylan said. "He's not gonna quit as the Pusher's lead singer to play rhythm guitar with us."

I wasn't so sure about that. Dirty was only about ten times more famous than the Penny Pushers.

"And we didn't ask Ash," Elle said.

Which was crazy. Why not ask Ash? He was way the hell better than me on guitar.

I looked around the room, struggling to understand, which was when it struck me that Brody wasn't here, and he should really be here for this conversation. Where the hell was he?

And where was Maggie?

"What does Brody have to say about this?"

The expression on my brother's face got a shade darker. "Brody will say whatever we want him to say."

Okay?

I knew my brother was a little... put off... by what went down between me and Brody in his driveway the other night, though he didn't even know *what* happened. I wasn't about to get into it with him; all he really knew, as far as I knew, was that Brody and I weren't talking.

I watched as Zane kicked my brother's boot. Dylan just shook his head a little, tussling his sweaty auburn hair. Elle shrugged and smiled at me, sipping her bottled water.

"Just think about it," Zane ordered. Then he pulled out a couple of joints and handed one to me. "This might help."

It was the middle of the night and the Back Door had closed, but in true rock 'n' roll fashion, we were still partying—down at Misty's. The band and the crew, the bar staff and a few dozen VIPs. I'd made it a point not to get drunk—I didn't want to be wasted when I talked to Brody. But I'd smoked up with Zane to take the edge off, and I was glad I did. Because the pot had slowed down my anxious mind enough that I could truly absorb my surroundings.

For the first time, the shiny, glossy, pink-and-sparkly room really came into focus.

Maggie had just left. I couldn't really blame her, though she'd appeared unfazed by the sight of a pair of strippers leeching onto Zane like sparkly bookends in their skimpy stage clothes. When I asked if she was okay, all she said was, *Zane isn't into chicks who expect more attention than they're willing to give.*

And maybe she was right about that.

Those girls were definitely vying for his attention, but Zane just sat back in his chair, legs spread and relaxed. It was Dylan who had one of the girls—a cocktail waitress—right up in his lap. And while I perused the club with my slightly fuzzy eyes, watching the strippers work the room... and that cute girl flirting with Dylan, her cleavage in his face... and Katie in her miniskirt, with my brother all wrapped up in it... something occurred to my slightly doped-up mind that hadn't quite occurred to me before.

Why?

Because I was an idiot, apparently.

Because it should've occurred to me long before this moment that if Brody wouldn't look me in the eye and listen to what I had to say, I still had a whole arsenal of weapons at my disposal which I hadn't really put to use. I, too, had boobs and a butt. Among other things.

And it wasn't like it had never occurred to me that I possessed such assets. It just hadn't occurred to me, until now, to use them on Brody, so to speak.

Yeah. *Idiot.*

Since Maggie had made her exit, I figured I could slip away without seeming entirely ungrateful for the offer the band had just made me. The truth was, I didn't know whether to be more stunned by the offer or by the fact that Brody wasn't there when they'd made it. And I really needed to face that bullshit down. The silent treatment had gone on long enough.

Maybe this was payback for my years of avoiding him, but it's not like Brody had hunted me down and *made* me talk to him; not like I was about to do to him, right now.

I knew he was probably wherever Jude was, since Jude was also conspicuously missing from the party, so I went looking. I headed upstairs through the staff stairwell, into the backstage area, where I ran into Zane. He'd magically vanished in Maggie's wake, and now I knew why; he'd either walked her out, or followed her out.

"Hey, sis." He started to smile his charming, Viking-on-a-pillage grin when he saw me, but I shut that right down.

"You better be good to Maggie," I told him, because for the moment, I was over men and their bullshit. And Maggie being secretly married to—and possibly in love with—Zane, while he let sparkly strippers drool all over him in front of her, was bullshit.

His smile faltered. At the suggestion that he wasn't being good to Maggie, or because he was caught off guard that I *knew* he wasn't being good to Maggie? I couldn't tell. Wasn't really in the mood to explore it, either. But I figured I was within bounds.

Maggie had made me promise not to say anything about what was going on between them—what little of it I knew—but I assumed that didn't mean I couldn't say anything to *him*, since he already knew.

"Always am, little sis," he said, a bit of an edge to his voice. Then he burrowed his hands in his jeans pockets and drew up his shoulders, like a kid caught stealing. His eyes looked a little glassy and pink from smoking up, but there was something else there too.

Oh, Jesus.

Did he have feelings for her, too?

What a fucking disaster.

Had he even thought about her job while he was sticking his dick in her? How important it was to her? Because the reality was, Zane held the cards. If it was Maggie or Zane, she'd have to be the one to go. Zane was the face and the voice of Dirty, and as valued as Maggie was, the band was never going to fire their lead singer, a founding member, so they could keep her.

I wasn't exactly in a position to give relationship advice, though, and even if I was, Zane wouldn't hear it from me. Little sisters weren't really qualified to give that kind of advice. Jesse had never taken my advice over the years, even when I warned him not to go there with Elle because he'd break her heart. I'd seen that one coming from miles away, but did he listen to me?

Nope.

"How's Brody?" Zane asked, his cool blue eyes still on mine.

I planted my hands on my hips. "None of your business."

His pierced eyebrow arched and I didn't love the smirk twitching on his lips.

"Whatever. Get out of my way." The Viking grin was back as I brushed past him.

I hit up the ladies' room and checked myself out in the cracked mirror. I looked a little buzzed, since I was—a few beers and a couple of Zane's joints had taken care of that—but not in a bad way. And the silver halter was doing my figure some major favors.

Surely Brody had noticed that, even if he'd barely given me a glance?

Pretty much every guy who'd talked to me tonight—or even brushed past me—had put his hand on my bare back, which meant this top was doing its job.

How could Brody ignore me if I cornered him, wearing this?

Let him try.

In my slightly buzzed state, I couldn't imagine any other outcome to that maneuver other than Brody and me promptly making up, then making out.

All I had to do was get him cornered.

I peeled off my bra, dumped it in my purse, and went braless. The slippery fabric of the halter against my bare breasts felt like the promise of sex.

On second thought, I took off my panties too, then put my jeans back on.

Then I smoothed my hair, took a breath, and went to find Brody —and sex him into submission.

CHAPTER TWENTY-TWO

Jessa

WHEN I STEPPED out into the bar, I found big gates locked over the public entrance and Faith No More's cover of the Commodores' "Easy" playing from the speakers all around the bar—to an almost-empty room. But I did find Jude, at a high table in the corner with Piper and a couple of other guys in Kings leathers. They were the only ones left in the bar.

I didn't see Brody anywhere, and I stopped in my tracks.

Would he seriously have left? Already? It wouldn't be like him to leave a gig he'd organized *before* the band did, but maybe he was really that mad at me?

How the hell was I going to sex him into submission if he wasn't even here?

I started across the room toward Jude—but then he *was* here, out of nowhere. Right in my face... taking hold of my arm and steering me back into the ladies' room, as Jude met my eyes and kind of snickered.

Once we were inside, he shut the door and shoved the garbage can up against it.

"You're here," I said.

"Yeah," Brody said flatly. "So are you."

"Um... good. Maybe we can talk?"

He glared at me, but at least he was looking me in the eye. "What's to talk about? You think I'm gonna sit around with my dick in my hand watching you hook up with someone else, you're wrong. Been there, done that. Not interested. So if you're trolling for cock, you can do it somewhere the fuck else."

"Trolling for...?"

"Just do me a favor," he said, his voice dead-cold, "and do it somewhere other than in my fucking face, with my fucking friends."

"What the hell are you talking about?"

"Jimmy," he said. "Or Snake. Or any of the other guys you've been flirting with all night, or whoever the fuck else you want. Take your fucking pick."

"*Snake?*" I shook my head in disbelief. He actually thought I was trying to hook up, again—with anyone and everyone—to make him jealous? What kind of uberslut did he think I was? "You're such an asshole, you know that?"

"Get fucked, Jessa."

I took a step back.

With that sweet little sign-off, I expected him to walk out, but he just stood there staring me down.

"Would you please stop telling me off?"

He crossed his arms over his chest, making his muscular biceps and forearms bulge. He was wearing a thin, distressed T-shirt, and I could see everything through it. His hard nipples, his distracting pecs, his trim waist.

Maybe I wasn't the only one who'd figured out how to use their assets.

"Stop telling me you're gonna leave," he said.

"I *didn't.*"

"It was implied."

Oh my God. Had there ever been a more frustrating ass of a man on the face of the planet?

And I had to have the crazies over this one?

"Don't you have any faith in me? Like at all?"

"Depends if you're telling me you're gonna leave or not," he said.

"You made it pretty clear you want me to leave."

His glare turned from icy to arctic. "Is that what I said?"

"You said you're done with me, and honestly?" I threw up my hands in surrender. "I can't really blame you for that." So much for sexing him into submission. Maybe on this one I'd just have to admit defeat.

"The band made you an offer," he said. "You gonna take it?"

I blinked at him, jolted by his switch into business mode. "No," I said. "I'm not."

"That because of me?"

"It's because it's not the right fit for me, or for the band. And you, of all people, must know that."

He took a few steps toward me, closing the space between us. "If you and I work our shit out, you gonna change your mind about that?"

"About being Dirty's rhythm guitarist?"

"Yeah."

"No."

"Why?"

"Because it's *crazy*. You know that, right?"

"What's crazy about it? The band wants you."

"And you're okay with that? With me being a member of Dirty?" I just couldn't see how that could ever work. Even if I wanted to join the band... I wasn't good enough. Even if Brody and I could "work our shit out." "You know I'm not strong enough," I added. "On guitar, I mean. I'm not that good. You told them that, right?"

"You are good. And for the record, you're the only one who doesn't recognize it. With some work and devotion, you could be great."

"I don't think—"

"If you could see what we all see when you're up there onstage, with the band... You can learn to be better on guitar, Jessa. But that chemistry? That vibe? You can't learn that or manufacture it. You've been running from it for so long you don't even know it anymore, but you have it. That thing Jesse has? You've got it too, in fucking spades. Why not embrace it instead of hiding from it? Just live the fuck out of it like your brother does."

"I'm confused. Are you telling me to get fucked, or are you telling me to join the band?"

"I'm telling you if you were to commit, if you were to take it seriously and we could actually count on you for fucking once, you'd be amazing with Dirty."

I shook my head, because it was ridiculous.

I was never meant to be *in* Dirty, like playing with them on tour and stuff. I was just a part of the bigger picture... a songwriter. A lyricist. I never wanted to be a rock star. That was an entirely different beast and it definitely wasn't me.

"I mean... not that I don't appreciate the offer, but—"

"You belong in the band, Jessa. You always have." He shook his head, studying me. "I guess it's just a fucking shame you've never wanted it."

"I did want it," I admitted, cautiously. "I always wanted to be a part of it. I mean, the music... the music is everything. I've always known that. And I know there's a part of me that loves playing with them. It's amazing when we get together. But performing? I can't get onstage and do what they do. This show tonight was one thing. One acoustic song. Just a small bar in front of an unsuspecting crowd with zero expectations of me. But the shows Dirty plays on tour, arenas and stadiums filled with tens of thousands of people... that's not my speed, Brody. I'm no rock star."

He laughed in my face. "Not a rock star? You're the walking *definition* of a rock star, Jessa. Talented as hell. Sexy as fuck. Mysterious. Gorgeous. Charismatic..." His eyes raked over me. "Did I mention sexy as fuck?"

"A couple of times."

"Good. If it doesn't bear repeating, you're not a fucking rock star. And sweetheart, it bears repeating."

I swallowed, but stood my ground as he got close.

"The fans will *love* you," he said, and I wasn't sure if he knew it or not, but he was getting in my face; I resisted the urge to take another step back. "Jesse's beautiful sister... the gifted, elusive song-writer who quits her modeling career to follow her true passion... what's not to love?"

Then I did take a step back. "Is that what this is? You're looking for a chance to spin some hot new angle for the band's anniversary tour?"

He moved into me, and the air charged between us; I felt that crackle of electricity, that overwhelming, frenetic thing that turned my stomach to a swarm of butterflies, and up close, felt like a magnetic pull. I literally wanted to slam right into him.

"Sweetheart, don't tell me you can't handle a stage. I've seen you conquer a catwalk with those mile-long legs of yours. I've seen you get lost in the music." His gaze dropped to my mouth and his tongue swiped his bottom lip. "It's inside you, Jessa. It's *steaming* off you when you play. You want this."

Yeah... I was definitely starting to steam. Brody's proximity was pretty much making the world evaporate around us.

"I'm not comfortable with it, Brody," I managed. My back was to the bathroom wall—when did that happen? He had me cornered, instead of the other way around. "Standing up there on stage with a guitar," I said, "while Zane sings my words... it makes me feel... naked."

For some reason, that pissed him off. A lot. He sucked in an agitated breath. "You modeled practically naked," he bit out. "What's the fucking difference?"

"The *difference* is that was my body," I said. "You're asking me to bare my soul."

He stared at me for what had to be a full minute.

"Yeah. God forbid I ask you for anything." He drew back, snapping the charge between us, leaving me cold.

"You're wrong, you know."

"Wrong about what?" he said, like he really didn't give one fuck.

I took a breath and forced it out. "I never chose Seth over you."

Brody shook his head and turned away. "Have a nice life on your pedestal, princess." He kicked the garbage can out of his way, which sent it crashing across the room, and went for the door.

"It was you!" I called after him. "It was you, Brody, please, just stop... Don't you fucking walk out on me!"

He stopped dead and turned back to me. We'd both stopped dead in the wake of my voice, pretty much screaming those words at him. I couldn't help it. I just snapped.

How dare he walk out on me when all he did was punish me for leaving, over and over again?

"It was always you I wanted," I told him. "Don't you think that if I could go back to that first time you kissed me outside that party when I was fifteen and do everything from that moment on differently, I would? But I can't! I can't change the past, Brody. You'll never know how much I wish I could, but I can't. All I can do is stand here in front of you right now and ask you to see me, *me*, and not that girl who ran away! I'm. Right. *Here*." By this point, I was really losing it, so I just let it all come gushing out. Because maybe this was my last chance? How many times was he going to walk away from me, or let me walk away from him, before he really *was* done with me? "A world where I don't have you in my life... I lived that way for the last six-and-a-half years," I said, my voice reaching near-hysterical level, "and these last couple of weeks have just proven to me that I don't ever want to do that again! I can't! To be honest, I have no idea how I did it for so long and kept on living!"

I was panting by the end of it, my chest rising and falling in shuddering breaths, and his gaze dropped, his expression darkening.

"Where the hell is your bra?"

"Wh—what?"

"You were wearing a bra at the show and you sure as fuck aren't wearing one now." He was staring so hard at me, my nipples were getting hard in my slinky shirt. "What happened to it?"

"I took it off."

His blue eyes, cold and dark, met mine. "You took it off," he repeated.

I threw up my hands. "What the hell do you think? I had a quickie with Jimmy backstage? I took it off for *you*."

He stared at me. "For me?"

"Yeah. So I could do this." I shoved myself up against him, standing on my tiptoes, so we were almost nose-to-nose. Then I gripped his hand and ran it up my bare waist under my top, all the way up... to cup my naked breast.

Brody's eyes flared as his breathing changed, deepening and slowing right down.

"This?" he murmured, squeezing my breast.

"Yeah," I breathed. I dropped back down on my heels and brought him with me, my hand wrapped around the back of his neck. He ran the tip of his nose slowly down mine, and I shivered in anticipation. And I said, "You better fucking kiss me. You better not walk out on me, because I am not letting you go. If I have to make a giant fucking scene and make Jude hold you here at gunpoint, I am not letting you go..."

Then he nipped my lips with his and my pussy clenched, empty and aching for him. "Like this?"

"Yeah." I entwined my fingers deep in his soft hair. "And by the way... I took my panties off, too."

That got a groan of approval and the next thing I knew, his mouth was on mine, his tongue down my throat, and we were making out.

"I need you," I told him between kisses, clinging to him. "And before you accuse me... I do *not* say that to every guy. I have never said that to a man in my life."

"Jessa..."

"I've wanted you, wanted this, for as long as I can remember." I rubbed up against him like a cat in heat as I said it. "Since I can remember wanting this at all, I've wanted it with you."

To show him how much I meant that, I undid my jeans and shimmied them down over my hips, feeling bold.

He stood back, swiping a hand over his face as he drank me in. "You sure you want *this*, babe?"

I stood there, awkwardly, with my jeans around my knees. "Don't you?"

"I meant... it's pretty fucking dirty in here, princess. If you hadn't noticed." He slid his hands around my bare ass and pulled me against him, showing me that yes, he definitely wanted this. "And you, in my mind," he added, squeezing my butt, his voice dropping low, "are the furthest thing from dirty."

I glanced around. It *was* gross. It appeared to have been cleaned, hastily, the garbage emptied and everything kind of mopped off, poorly. But it didn't smell bad, just kind of mildewy.

I could live with that.

"I wasn't planning on touching anything in here but you," I said, as I slipped my hand down the front of his jeans and grasped his dick. It was rock-hard and standing at attention, eager to be grasped. "And anyway..." I bit my lip a little. "Maybe I like it a little dirty."

He groaned, his cock straining in my hand as he kissed me again. Then he spun me around by my hips. He caught me as I stumbled in my jeans, holding me up with a strong arm around my waist. I felt him fumbling to open his jeans with the other hand and he took his cock from my grip. The smooth skin of the head was silky and warm against my pussy, and a flush of excitement rushed through me.

"Last chance to change your mind." He was teasing me, probably; I was so wet, the head of his cock had already slipped inside me and his voice had gotten low and tight, the way it did when his brain had left the building.

"Fuck me, Brody," I urged him. If he didn't, he was going to have to make me come some other way—soon. I'd never been into sex in public places... had never even come close to trying it before, had never really had sex anywhere but in a bed or maybe on the floor next to a bed. But I was way too turned on by the thought of Brody fucking me in this dirty bathroom.

Then he was inside me, in one fast, possessive thrust. I cried out because it shocked me a little; it hurt a bit, but he didn't stop and I didn't tell him to. I bent forward a bit more to accommodate him, arching my back, and as he pumped into me, his thrusts got deeper, fit better.

I rubbed my clit as his cockhead did magical things inside me; it felt so plump and smooth from this angle. He seemed to know it, too, because he gripped my hips and gave it to me with short, fast strokes, digging into my front wall, and then shoving in deeper... short and hard, then deep... in an erotic rhythm that drove me insane.

I paused a little in touching myself, distracted by the over-whelming pleasure that was building in a rush from the inside out... different from the rush of a clitoral orgasm. Freer, somehow, wilder... like I couldn't control it, because really, I couldn't.

Brody had control.

"Come, Jessa," he rasped, between thrusts. "I wanna hear you scream."

"They'll hear me..." I gasped, my body riding the force of his thrusts, driving me back and forth against my hand.

"They won't hear," he said. "Scream for me the way you always wanted to... all those times you thought about fucking me..."

But I was distracted, weirdly conscious of the people out in the bar, and it was keeping me from letting go. Brody seemed to sense it. He reached around my front, underneath my hand, pressing his warm fingers over my clit—and wrapped his other hand over my mouth.

"You want it dirty, babe?" he whispered in my ear.

Then he fucked me, hard and fast, lifting me on my tiptoes until he made me scream, his thrusts and my orgasm tearing me apart.

Brody shuddered against me. He growled as he bit my neck, and I felt him shoot. But he didn't stop; he fucked his come into me, gravity and his slowing thrusts making it messy. I felt some dripping out, running down my thigh as I took him the way I'd always wanted to take him—hard, wild, and free... and just that little bit dirty.

Later, we showered off the dirty back at Brody's place. We were pressed together under the hot water and I was sucking on his neck. I kind of wanted to leave a hickey, just because I could, the way I had when I was seventeen; because I wanted to see it on him afterward.

The bathroom lights were on a dimmer and we'd put them low, so it was kind of like we were in another world; suspended in time, nothing else that mattered beyond this dim, steamy space and this private moment between us. I had him naked and wet and all mine, his body slippery against me, and I couldn't get enough. I'd kissed him everywhere at least a dozen times, in a slow exploration of his body.

I'd licked his tattoo; the tribal pattern that ran down the left side of his body. I bit his nipples just to see what would happen (he liked it). I bit his ass (he liked that too, but he laughed because it tickled). I nibbled his neck and sucked on his fingers and kissed his feet (he liked everything).

"Are we just gonna keep doing this?" he whispered, as he slicked the head of his cock against my pussy, getting ready to fuck me again.

"Yeah," I panted.

"I meant, without a condom."

I peered up into his deep blue eyes. They were hooded and hazy. It was almost dawn and we hadn't slept or even laid down yet. I felt kind of dazed from lack of sleep, but I refused to close my eyes on this. He grabbed my wet hair and tugged my head back, then leaned in to bite my bottom lip.

"Have you ever done it without a condom?" I asked him, shuddering as he shoved his cock between my legs and the hard shaft brushed my clit.

"Only with you."

Right answer.

"Me too." I kissed my way down his chest, kneeling on the tile floor of the shower as I made my way down his lean abs and the sexy V of his groin. "I don't want anything between us."

Then I took his cock in my mouth for the first time ever. I'd kissed it moments ago, but that was just a tease. This time I enveloped the smooth head with my lips, lightly stroking the rigid shaft with my hand. His cock jerked at my touch and he groaned, relaxing back against the tile wall. Water sluiced over him, running down over my tongue, and I kept licking, the warmth of the water and my tongue caressing him.

"You have no idea," I told him, "how long I've wanted to do this."

"Not as long as I've wanted you to do this," he groaned.

I smiled, tracing the lines of his cock with my tongue, taking my time, learning what made his breath catch, what made him groan, what made him stir or clench or spasm. Just savoring the feel and the taste of him.

In my somewhat limited experience, penises were all pretty much the same. Or so I'd thought. But I'd never actually had a boyfriend, and the men I'd slept with I hadn't exactly taken my time with. I'd only given head a few times, pretty much because a guy asked me to, I'd never swallowed, and I'd definitely never done it like this.

As it turned out, penises were not all the same.

Brody's was thick and long and beautiful, and I'd never really thought of a cock as a thing of beauty before.

Maybe because I'd never been in love with the man attached to it?

Everything about Brody was beautiful, and strong, and yet... there was something about his vulnerability that fascinated me. That he was making himself vulnerable to me, now... he wasn't grabbing my hair in his fists and forcing his way into the back of my throat, or driving the rhythm or generally fucking my mouth. I'd been mouth-fucked before. It definitely wasn't my favorite.

Though if Brody wanted to do it, I'd let him.

But he didn't. He just leaned back and took what I gave. It kind of felt like I was worshipping him, here on my knees, caressing his strong body... and yet, like I had all the power. I was setting the pace, gradually coaxing him to the edge, and when I got him there, I held back, slowing down, making him wait for it.

I savored the feeling of Brody, a man known for his decisiveness, his bossiness, his managerial prowess, giving up control to me.

I savored his responses, every twitch or involuntary shudder, the flex of muscle beneath my hand, the tightening of his skin, the changes in his breathing... the way he started squirming around, his back squeaking against the wet tile wall as he got closer to totally losing it.

"Jessa... *babe*..." was all he managed to say, and maybe that was my warning to get out of the way if I didn't want to swallow, but no way was I doing that.

It was like I'd already told him: I wanted all of him. Nothing between us, ever again.

He arched off the wall as he came in my mouth, hot and thick, the taste of him salty and musky and *him*. He groaned and kind of panted as I took it, everything he had to give, and when he fell back against the wall, I gentled my touch. But I still had him in my mouth, sucking, caressing, easing him back down.

He shuddered and bucked, sensitive to every touch.

When I finally slid away, I said, "Tell me..." I was still down on my knees in front of him, peering up at his face, the both of us all blissed out and sated. "Tell me you're not done with me." And I did not just mean now.

I did not just mean sex.

He knew that, right?

He hauled me up against him and delved his hands into my hair, kissing my face with dazed, sex-drunk kisses as he held me close, his pupils large in the dim light.

"I will never be done with you," he said.

CHAPTER TWENTY-THREE

Jessa

BRODY MASON WAS TAKING me on a date.

I'd never been on a real date with Brody, ever, and I was so, *so* excited I thought I might pee myself.

I didn't tell him that, though. I just sat in the passenger seat of his truck, gazing out into the night, grinning like a lunatic and intermittently holding his hand, whenever he didn't need it to drive.

After the show last night, we'd barely slept; we'd had sex so many times over the past eighteen hours we'd almost forgotten to eat, and I was sore and exhausted and giddy in a really, really good way.

In a way that only made me want more.

Wherever Brody was taking me, I just hoped he was planning to do me again when we got there. The feel of him inside me, pressed against me, wrapped around me, his hands all over me, seeking, wanting... I was officially addicted to it.

Besides, I figured we had years to make up for. Every time I opened myself to him, my body was an apology, a plea and a promise, telling him everything that I hadn't yet found the courage to say... when we were alone, naked and fused together, all that was true in my heart could no longer be ignored or denied.

I was in love with Brody. And really, what else was new?

Maybe he knew, but I hadn't exactly said it out loud yet. I was going to, though. Whether I planned it or not, it was going to come falling out of me, sooner or later, in a moment of uncensored bliss.

He squeezed my hand and I squeezed back.

We were an hour outside the city and I still didn't know where we were going. We'd turned off the highway onto some kind of service road that seemed to be heading nowhere; there were street lights, but I couldn't see anything in the dark fields on either side of the road except a bunch of trees. A few minutes after I'd lost sight of the highway in my rearview mirror, we turned off onto a creepy gravel road—creepy because there were no more street lights; nothing but snarls of bush lined the side of the road. The field on the other side might have been farmland, but it was too dark to tell.

"Wow. Nice place to bring a girl," I commented, as we turned off the creepy gravel road onto an even creepier dirt path, barely discernible in a field of weeds, running alongside a rickety barbed wire fence. But I was still grinning. "This where you bury all your dates?"

Brody shook his head, but smiled back. "Anyone ever tell you you've got an incredibly twisted mind?"

"Yes." I beamed at him. "You. Many times."

The truth was, I was loving every second of this. Not only had I never been on a date with Brody, but I had no idea what kind of date he'd take me on. All I knew was what he told me, which was, "Don't bother with high heels" and "Dress warm."

I kept expecting something to magically appear just over the horizon in all this darkness. Then suddenly Brody turned us off the "road" into what amounted to a little gravel driveway... leading to absolutely nothing. Well, there was that barbed wire fence.

We pulled up to it and parked. "Hop out," he said. I grinned, hopping out as he shut down the truck, and we met outside. "Look up," he ordered.

I looked up, but there was nothing to see.

The sky?

It was dark, overcast, a deep blue-black with mottled spots that I could tell were clouds. I could barely even see the moon glowing through.

"What am I looking at?"

He put his arms around me, drawing me against him. "Nothing," he said. "Because the weather app on my phone fucking lied."

I looked at him, giggling a bit. "What?"

"Just picture the biggest, darkest sky you've ever seen, pricked with a million stars."

"Ah." I wrapped my arms around his neck. "I'm picturing."

"It was supposed to clear up. See that glow over there, near the horizon?" I followed the way he pointed, back in the direction we'd come from. "That's the city. And those dark shapes over there? The mountains. On a clear night, it's gorgeous out here. Like magical gorgeous." He kissed my cheek, his lips lingering as his breath warmed me. "Jessa Mayes gorgeous."

I grinned and gave him a lingering kiss for that.

"Might still clear up," he whispered as he kissed his way along my jaw, and I sighed happily. "We can wait a while and see. The clouds seem to be moving."

They were. As I watched, I could see them shifting around in front of the moon. "How do you know about this place?"

"Because I've seen it. With all the other girls I bring here, right before I kill them."

"Ew." I wrinkled my nose. "Not funny when you say it."

"It's Piper's," he said, giving my butt a squeeze, then letting me go and heading back toward the truck. "He's got a place, other end of this field. Moved out here about a year ago."

"Oh. I didn't know." I looked out across the field but all I saw was blackness. The house must've been pretty far. "Must be nice. Quiet." I watched him pull a backpack from the back of the truck. "Can I help?"

"Nope." He hooked his arm through mine and we hopped over the barbed wire, which about thigh-height, more to keep animals out than humans. Brody started pulling things from his bag. He laid out a big, thick blanket on the grass and ordered, "Sit."

I sat. I watched him arrange a bunch of candles in jars all around the blanket and light them. Then he pulled out a big travel canteen and two mugs. He poured us each a drink and tossed in some mini marshmallows he'd brought in a bag.

"Marshmallows," I mused as he handed me a mug, and his eyes caught mine.

"Yeah. You like them in your hot chocolate, right?"

"Sure." I blew on my mug; it was steaming hot.

As the candlelight danced over Brody's handsome face, he looked so young, and I was reminded of the many times he'd handed me a mug of hot chocolate with marshmallows by a fire, when everyone else was drinking booze and I wasn't allowed. At the time, I was annoyed. Now, I couldn't stop grinning if I tried.

How sweet was he?

I could get used to sweet Brody. A lot less annoying than asshole Brody—though asshole Brody was also annoyingly hot.

"So, what happens on this date if the stars don't come out?" I asked.

He settled back on the blanket facing me. "Then we find some other way to entertain ourselves," he said, in a tone that went straight to my girl parts.

"Isn't it a little cold for that?"

He sipped his drink, eying me over the rim of his mug. "The candles will keep us warm."

"Right. They're a regular blazing campfire."

"We could pretend they're a campfire. Know any ghost stories?"

"No scary stories." I set my mug aside and settled back on my elbows. "You start telling me scary stories, the odds of you getting laid on this date get slim."

"So the odds are looking good, otherwise?"

"I'd say they're decent. Don't get ahead of yourself."

The odds were looking better every minute.

We'd finished our hot chocolates and Brody was making me laugh, which was more of an aphrodisiac than I'd ever realized. Yeah; laughing with a guy was a definite turn-on. Maybe this was why I'd been so hot for him when we were young. Because back then, he'd made me laugh a lot.

Well... there was that, and there was his broad chest. His deep blue eyes. The way he'd looked at me... and how hot he'd looked in his leather jacket.

Still did.

This was the Brody I remembered from way back. The Brody I'd always wanted... the Brody I'd left behind.

The Brody I was so deathly afraid to disappoint.

And here he was, looking at me again just like he used to.

I smiled at him. "Don't look at me like that."

"Like what?" He wasn't smiling, exactly, but he was definitely undressing me with those blue eyes of his. They were aglow in the candlelight, and he'd laid a hand casually on my thigh. Except his touch wasn't casual at all as his fingers traced a little pattern back and forth over my jeans, mere inches from my clit... sending signals right up through my core and short-circuiting my brain.

"Like I'm made of sugar," I said.

He cocked an eyebrow at me. "What, like I want to lick you all over until you dissolve in a sweet puddle?"

"Exactly."

"Why the hell not?" His voice got lower as his fingers migrated closer to my happy spot.

"Because. You still owe me stars. I demand stars before I melt." Of course, I was all for Brody licking me all over, but I definitely didn't mind the foreplay of flirting first. Not to mention making him work for it a little.

He glanced up at the sky, which wasn't looking any clearer than when we'd arrived. "That may be a tall order."

"And you still have to get me home at a decent hour, you know," I reminded him.

His expression clouded over and I bit my lip. *Oops.*

Wrong thing to say.

Brody had only found out today about the photo shoot I was doing tomorrow, and he wasn't happy about it. I also knew he wasn't happy I'd done that shoot in L.A.; he'd told me in an intimate moment in his bed last night that he thought I wasn't coming back afterward like I'd said I would. I'd told him, half-teasing, that if I didn't come back it would've been his fault, since he told me he was done with me. But that didn't go over so well. I'd also explained that this was only a one-day shoot, here in town. My agent had set it up when she found out I was coming back to Vancouver; it was kind of a last-minute thing because one of the models they'd booked had gotten sick, and I wasn't even all that psyched to be doing it. But that didn't go over so well, either.

And I knew why. I knew Brody felt threatened. That he thought it would take me away from him again; that as soon as I got back to modeling, I'd disappear from his life, stop taking his calls, and we'd be right back where we were. Which was nowhere.

I wanted to reassure him that wasn't the case, but I was uncomfortably aware that we still needed to have a serious talk, about serious things—which might change his opinion on whether he wanted me to disappear from his life. And I'd done the math: I had to get up for the shoot in less than eight hours. I wanted to spend every one of those hours with Brody, and I didn't want to waste them fighting. Granted, we'd need to sleep. I couldn't show up at a shoot, even one I was less than excited to do, on no sleep. But other than sleep, we were flirting, having fun, and having sex tonight. I refused to do anything else.

After the shoot, when Brody saw that I was still here, we'd have time for the other talk.

"You know," I said brightly, trying to keep the mood upbeat, "usually when we're around a campfire, we sing."

"No, you sing. I croak like a bull frog. We're not doing that."

"Okay... then how about a campfire game? Do you know any games?"

"I dunno. I Spy?"

I laughed. "In the dark?"

"Truth or Dare?"

"Right... I can only imagine what kind of dare you'd come up with. I'd be naked in seconds, no doubt."

"Scared?"

I kind of was; it was cold. "No."

He smiled a slow, wicked smile. "So you go first, then. You want truth or dare?"

"I thought you were kidding."

"I was kidding. Now I'm not. Truth or dare?"

"Okay. Fine." If he wasn't afraid, I wasn't backing down. And to prove it, I'd go all in. "I pick truth."

"You sure about that, princess? You've gotta be one hundred percent honest here, or I'm pretty sure you're in violation of the rules of the game. Bad things might happen."

"Well, I wouldn't want bad things to happen. Ask me. Whatever you want to know." I said it, and I kind of meant it, but I was a little nervous about what he might ask.

How serious did he intend to turn this little game?

"Do you really like marshmallows in your hot chocolate?"

Okay. Not so serious, then.

"No."

"I knew it. Why do you always put them in?"

"I don't. You put them in, and I just never wanted to hurt your feelings."

He shook his head in disbelief. "Who doesn't like marshmallows in their hot chocolate?"

"I don't. Too sugary."

"Is that a modeling thing, or you really don't like them?"

"Don't like them. Never have. If you ask me, the only thing that belongs in hot chocolate, besides chocolate, is booze."

"Well." He lay back on the blanket, tucking an arm behind his head like a pillow. "Guess I just learned something new about you."

"About time." I grinned down at him, hugging my knees.

"You kidding? I learn something new about you all the time."

"Really?"

"Sweetheart, it'd take centuries to unravel all the mysteries of Jessa Mayes."

"Really," I said, now doubting his sincerity. "Tell me something you've learned about me lately, Mr. Kiss-Ass."

"How about the way you wiggle your feet around when you write."

"What? I do not."

"You rub your feet back and forth on the floor when you're thinking."

"I do?"

"Yup."

"That's weird."

"When you read," he went on, "like out of a magazine, your lips move and you repeat the words you like."

"That's not even true."

"You repeat them three times," he said. Then he mouthed, *inevitability... inevitability... inevitability*, in an imitation of me, apparently.

"So? Inevitability is a great word. Here, I'll use it in a sentence. 'Brody being a smart-ass is a definite inevitability.'"

He smirked.

"Seriously? I seriously do that?"

"Yup."

"Jesus. What a dork."

"It's cute."

"It's lame. And stop trying to butt-kiss your way out of this. It's your turn. Truth or dare."

"Okay. Truth."

"What does the tattoo on your forearm say?"

His smile faltered a little. "Abstinence," he said.

Huh. Definitely never would've guessed. "Why do you have that tattooed on your arm?"

"Nope. You only get one question per turn."

"That is one question. It's a two-parter."

"No two-parters. Your turn. Truth or dare."

"You asked me like five questions in a row about stupid marsh-mallows!"

"Because you let me. I'm gonna go ahead and enforce the one-question rule, though."

"That's not fair."

He just shrugged, all smug and sexy. "Never said I'd play fair, sweetheart."

I rolled my eyes. "Fine. I can be the bigger person here. Truth."

He eyed me for a moment... like he was weighing whether or not I'd be honest on this one. "Who got all that birthday cake in my Donkey Kong arcade at Elle's twenty-first? Was that really you?"

Oh. That.

He narrowed his eyes at me. "Truth, princess."

"It was Zane."

"I fucking knew it. You know I've asked him like ten times over the years? He bought me a new one because it couldn't be fixed and he *still* wouldn't cop to it."

"That was nice of him."

"Right," he muttered. "Because the price was worth having it over me, that I'd bought his lies."

"He just wants you to love him."

Brody scowled.

"You'd already threatened to ban him for lighting the dining room table on fire at Christmas, so I offered to take the fall. We both kind of knew you wouldn't be mad if it was me." I shrugged, because it was true. "Besides... you weren't really talking to me at the time anyway."

He stared at me a moment. Then he sat up and kissed me, gently.

"Your turn," I whispered against his lips.

"We're still playing?" He kissed me again, nudging my mouth open and lapping his tongue against mine in a slow, hot, totally X-rated move meant to distract the hell out of me. But I held him off, my hand on his hard chest.

"I did two truths. It's your turn."

"Fine." He sat back. "Dare."

"What! I want to know what that tattoo means. And I am not screwing you again until you tell me, Brody Mason."

He just smiled, a slow, cocky smile, like he didn't believe that for a second. "My pick. I pick dare."

"Ugh. Fine. You'll be sorry you picked dare, though."

"Bring it on, babe."

"Yeah? You're not gonna wuss out when you hear what it is?"

"Nope."

"How can you be so sure?"

"Because," he said, "there's nothing I wouldn't do for you, sweetheart." But he said it way too sweetly, which meant he was full of shit.

He was definitely scared of what I was going to make him do—me and my twisted mind.

"Okay, then. I dare you to sing me a song—of my choice."

"No problem," he said, like it was no big thing, when I knew it was. Brody hated singing. Mainly because he was no good at it. And the guys—Zane especially—never let him forget it.

It was kind of his Achilles' heel.

"Oh, and before you do? You're gonna strip down." I smiled at him, nice and pretty.

In return he gave me a filthy, nasty look. "You want me to sing a song for you, naked, right here?"

"I do," I said, cuddling cozily into my furry jacket. "Right now."

That filthy glare stayed on me another minute, but I wasn't backing down. Finally, he stood up and started taking off his clothes.

I lay back on the blanket and enjoyed the show.

Leather jacket... gone.

Scarf.

Sweater.

T-shirt.

Belt.

Boots.

Brody's eyes stayed locked on my grinning face the entire time. I was pretty sure he was waiting for me to say, *Just kidding!* and let him off the hook.

I didn't say that.

He had his jeans undone when he stopped and sighed. "You really gonna make me do this, princess?"

"Yup," I said, distracted by the way his loosened jeans hung low on his hips.

He didn't miss it. "How about instead I give you a peek, and then we go back to the truck and warm up?" He flashed me a charming smile that made my heart skitter, but I stuck to my guns.

"Nope. I want the full monty. Right now. It's a dare. If you don't do it, 'bad things might happen.'"

The charm crumbled off as he threw me another dirty look. Then he shed his jeans and stopped again. "Come on, Jessa. This is a stupid dare. It's fucking February."

He stood there, shivering, in his skimpy blue briefs and striped socks and I just kept smiling. "Poor baby. Take it off."

"Merciless," he grumbled. Then he lost the undies, drop-kicking them off his foot.

I clapped and whistled for that maneuver, slick as it was, but he just glared at me, covering up the good stuff with his hands.

"It *is* pretty cold out," I said, taking my time with a long, lingering perusal of his naked form, the candlelight dancing over the curves of his lean, sculpted muscles. The light and dark patterns of his swirling tattoos. The sexy V of his torso, the slight rippling of his abs... that sexy-as-all-hell indent between his hipbone and his crotch. "So I'll let you keep the socks on."

"What's the damn song?" he prompted, impatient, starting to bounce up and down to keep warm.

"Hmm." I considered. "On second thought, put your boots back on."

I watched as he pulled them on, grumbling all the way.

"Now back up so I can get a good look at you, and I'll tell you the song."

He turned and walked away a few paces, standing with his back to me. I didn't mind, since it gave me a perfect view of his firm, muscular butt and his long, strong thighs. Geez. Brody Mason had the best butt, ever. He could've been a butt model, or a butt double for movie stars, or something. I'd told him that once, and I was dead serious.

He'd just laughed.

"You know what?" I mused, inspired by the view. "I'm feeling some Bad Company coming on..."

"Great."

"Yeah. I definitely want to hear 'Feel Like Makin' Love,' don't you? Such a classic."

"This is bullshit."

"Come on. The vocal range in that song isn't even difficult. Anyone can sing it."

"Whatever." Then, his back still to me, he started singing.

"Hey! Turn around!" His butt was sexy and all, but I wanted to see the rest of him.

"Fuck that."

He kept singing. I laughed as he mumbled his way through the first few lines. I prompted him with a few lyrics when he didn't know them.

Then he started flexing his butt cheeks to the rhythm of the song and I almost died laughing.

He stopped. "Come on, Jessa."

"Turn around and I'll think about letting you stop."

"Don't be a bitch. It's cold. I've got shrinkage."

"*Tuuurn arou-ound,*" I sang.

He turned, still cupping himself. His nipples could've cut glass, and his muscles were jittering under his skin.

From where I was sitting, though, it was plenty hot.

"You're a terrible human being," he said.

"Just get to the chorus. I want to hear the chorus."

So he sung the chorus. By the end of it, he was getting into it, grudgingly. He even did a little dance. I was laughing so hard by now I was afraid I really might pee my pants.

"You happy?" He stalked over, grabbed the blanket and yanked it out from under me so hard I went tumbling off, still laughing. He wrapped himself in it and ran for the truck.

I got the hell up and went after him, in case he got any ideas about locking me out and leaving me here as punishment. He climbed into the very back seat and I followed, shutting the door behind us.

I was still laughing.

"Shut up and make yourself useful," he said, pulling me on top of him. The blanket fell open and I almost felt bad about how cold his skin was. Then we were making out, both of us struggling to get my boots and tight jeans off. My lace Hanky Panky thong went next. Brody tore it off, as in ripped it to shreds.

"You're going to have to start buying me new panties," I said, gasping as he slicked his fingers between my legs and up inside me.

"Uh-uh..." he mumbled against my lips, licking and biting as he kissed me, "... just tear them all off until you've got none left... you can go commando all the time."

"I don't think that's—"

He covered my mouth with his, so the conversation was pretty much over. Then his fingers were gone and his cock was in me, filling me in one forceful thrust. He groaned and dropped his head back on the seat as I rode him slow, then fast... slow, then fast... letting him warm up beneath me. It didn't take long before we were both hot and I was peeling off my furry jacket.

He pulled me down for a kiss, but every time he tried to slip his tongue in my mouth I giggled again, the vision of him dancing around in his boots, serenading me with his croaky, off-key voice, lodged in my brain. And every time I laughed, he smacked my ass, hard, the sharp sting bringing me right back to what we were doing... and sending all sorts of wicked signals to my clit.

"*Ohhh...*" I moaned the third time he did it. I rode him faster as the pleasure built in my core in a sudden rush, my mind and body singularly focused on that sweet pinnacle... just out of reach...

I loved getting off on Brody.

Loved it.

I'd never, ever felt anything like this. This chemistry with a lover. Total physical and mental harmony, no matter what our bodies were doing.

Not even close.

I was totally lost in it when he gripped me by the back of my neck.

"You," he said, nibbling on my bottom lip, "are a very bad girl, Jessa Mayes." Then he smacked my ass again, hard, and I started to come.

"*Brody...*"

"No, you don't," he growled. "Not without me."

He held my hips and pumped up into me, and together we crashed over the edge... slamming together and collapsing back on the seat, entangled and convulsing.

In the sweaty, tingling aftermath, I buried my face in the warmth of his neck, inhaling his manly smell; clean leather and the woods after a rain... fresh air and everything good.

Once I'd regained use of my brain, I whispered, "We never saw the stars."

Brody tightened his arms around me and murmured, "Just did."

CHAPTER TWENTY-FOUR

Jessa

BRODY PEELED off my shirt and my bra and lay me back on the leather seat of his truck, spreading my legs—and I loved it. I loved that after we'd had sex, he wanted more. That he was never in a hurry to get up and leave... and more, that I never felt the need to get up and leave.

This was new for me. Very new.

I wondered if it was new for him.

I also loved that look in his eyes. The way his gaze worshipped my body just the way his hands did... his mouth. That he knew when to give it to me fast and hard, to take over and use his strength to give me pleasure... and when to take his time, letting me catch up to him. He took his time now, rubbing his cock between my legs, slowly, just savoring the fact that he could. That we could finally, *finally* touch this way. Naked... Nothing at all between us.

He kissed my neck while he nudged my clit, just teasing me, warming me up all over again as that rush that only he could stimulate flooded my body.

And soon, he'd fill me with his body. His tongue. His fingers. His cock, hard and thick, straining... finally easing into place.

He liked to watch my face as he took me. Liked to watch himself entering me, again and again.

Liked to watch as he made me his.

Except this time, he didn't do that.

He just kissed me, everywhere... eventually landing between my legs, exploring... learning every sensitive place on my body, inside and out.

"Aren't you... tired?" I asked, playing with his hair, feeling like I should give him an out if he just wanted to lay back with me and catch his breath.

But he didn't stop. He just fluttered his tongue in a way that made my eyes roll back in my head. "Don't you wanna come again?"

I just watched him in awe, his gorgeous face between my legs, unable to even gather my thoughts to answer; he was blowing them all over the place with his patient tongue.

"No?" he teased. "You really look like a woman who could come again."

"I do?"

"Oh, yeah."

Oh, yeah...

He nibbled my clit and I went spinning over the edge, helpless... bucking against him as he wrapped his warm lips around me and I went into free-fall, shocks of pleasure ripping through my body.

When I could speak again, I whispered, "My God. Brody... I've never done this before... "

"Done what?" he mumbled, still kissing between my legs.

"With a guy... you know... I don't know how you... " I lost my train of thought as he went at my clit again, no chance of resisting or keeping up a conversation. I came, again, falling apart on the seat of his truck, clawing at the leather.

"Oh... *God*..."

"You've never had multiples with a guy?" he asked, sounding slightly amused as he kissed the inside of my thigh.

"Uh... no. I've never come at all with a guy."

"You've never...?" He looked up at me, stunned. "You've never had an orgasm during sex?"

"Not with a guy."

He considered that, and his eyebrow slowly raised. "Are you telling me you've slept with women?"

I rolled my eyes. "Don't get your hopes up." I relaxed into the seat with a sigh. "I meant other than by myself... you're the only person I've ever..." I bit my lip.

"Shit." Now he looked almost pissed off. "What kind of losers have you been sleeping with?"

"Well, I—" I didn't get a chance to answer that since he pretty much killed my ability to think, again, when he stuffed two fingers inside me and started fluttering them around—at the same time he flicked his tongue over my clit with determination, and I came again... a quick, sharp ascent to a pinwheel burst of color and light. I shut my eyes tight as the bliss ripped through me.

Holy... shit.

What the hell were we talking about?

Oh, yeah. Orgasms.

When I could retrace my line of thought, I managed to say, "It wasn't really their fault. I mean... I never really, you know, stuck around long enough to—"

This time, he rose up over me and shut me up by kissing me, his tongue plundering my mouth, musky-sweet with the taste of my sex.

"Don't tell me," he growled. "I don't wanna know. Don't ever tell me about anyone you slept with before me."

"Okay, but I just wanted to explain—"

"Yeah, no. Don't wanna hear it, princess. And neither of us wants me spending the rest of my life in prison for murder, so let's just rewind and pretend no one's ever kissed you but me, yeah?"

He grinned at me a little, but there was a softness in his blue eyes. A vulnerability that made my breath catch.

"Yeah," I whispered.

Then he kissed me again, sinking against me and drawing the blanket over us.

We lay intertwined for a while, my back to Brody's front, my body cocooned in his, his heavy arm slung around me. My eyes were closed and I was playing with his hands, my fingers winding through his, just enjoying the pleasurable tickle of his skin against mine.

I opened my eyes and examined his fingers, noticing how smooth his nails felt. "You don't chew your nails anymore."

"Guess not."

"When did you stop?"

He was silent a moment, maybe thinking about that. "Sometime after my dad died, I guess."

There was a connection there; I knew there was. Brody had never liked talking about his parents, especially his dad. He'd never said much to me about him at all, other than to tell me, when I was seventeen, that he'd died.

"I remember the funeral," I said softly. I'd never forget; there had been too many funerals in my young life. But what struck me most about that funeral was how grand it was, how many flowers there were, how fancy everything was compared to the tiny, humble services for my parents... and how many people turned up to the funeral of a man whose son never had a word to say about him. "You didn't cry."

"No," he said. "You did." He entwined his fingers with mine. "You held my hand the whole time."

I ran my thumb over his tattoo, the one on his palm, of the rose and vines.

"This hand," he whispered.

I kissed his palm, right on the tattoo.

"You did that, too," he said.

Yeah. I remembered that, too. "That's what the tattoo's for?"

"That's what the tattoo's for."

Wow. I'd always wondered... but never been sure.

I'd been there when he got that tattoo. Jesse and I both were. We'd gone to a tattoo parlor to get the tattoos that he'd promised me we'd get together when our mom died, and while we had the abstract angels with the tall, proud wings inked on—Jesse's, large, on his inner arm, and me, small, on my ankle—Brody had the rose and vines inked on his hand.

That was right after his father's funeral.

"I think you were a bit drunk," I said, remembering back.

"Maybe," he said. "A bit. But I knew what I was doing."

I brought his hand to my lips and kissed the rose again. Then my eye caught the tattoo on his forearm. "You ever going to tell me what this one means?" I ran my fingertips along the runes. "*Abstinence*... I mean, I know I said I wouldn't fuck you before you told me, so I've kind of lost my leverage here."

"It means self-restraint," he said. "Resisting something. Like something you're hungry for and dependent on."

"Thank you, Mr. Dictionary," I replied. "But that's not what I was asking."

"No?"

"No. Why do you have it tattooed on your arm?"

There was a silent pause. "Promise you won't get upset?"

"I make no such promise."

Brody kissed my shoulder. "Then I'm not telling you."

I considered that.

"Okay. How about I promise I won't totally freak out and start throwing shit? But I can't promise you how I'm going to feel when I don't even know what you're going to say."

His arms tightened around me. "It's supposed to remind me why I should stay away from you."

My hand stilled where I was caressing a trail back and forth along the tattoo. "And why should you stay away from me?"

His arms tightened even more and he said, "Because I can't."

Oh.

Wow.

Had anyone ever said anything like that to me before? That bravely honest? That filled with love and pain and humility?

"I love you, Brody."

It was the only thing I could think of to say in reply to a comment like that. And I meant it. With every part of me.

He sighed against me and held me tight, and I just let him; let the rhythm of his breaths and his heartbeat become familiar. I never wanted to forget this moment.

"I want you to know why I acted the way I did the other night," he said after a while. "When we came to get you from that party, with the Sinners. It's just like I told you, years ago. I won't share you, Jessa."

I looped my arms around his and held him tight. "I know. I'd never ask you to."

"It's just..." He cleared his throat, and I could've sworn he sounded nervous—and Brody didn't really do nervous. I felt his heart in his chest, beating against my back. "I know Roni's into that... scene. But—"

"Brody..."

"I just want you to know I don't think you're a whore." He nuzzled into my neck, resting his head against mine. "You said that, that I thought you were a whore because you went to that party. I don't think that, Jessa. But I think it's dangerous for you to go to parties like that." He was silent for a moment. "I know you know Piper," he went on carefully, "and maybe that makes it seem harmless... but you do not want to get caught up in that world, Jessa, for one of those guys to take a liking to you that you can't shake."

"I know."

"I don't think you really do." His hold on me tightened again, like he was afraid I might pull away. "When I was young... I fell in with some of those guys, for a while. It was not a good scene."

Well... that explained some things. I turned my head toward him, so I could see his eyes.

"That pin you gave me?" He'd never told me where he'd gotten that Sinners pin when we were kids, but I'd always wondered.

"Yeah," he said. "That pin."

"Well, I loved that thing," I told him. "I'm still mad at you for losing it, you know."

"I didn't lose it."

"What?"

He sighed, silently. "That night, when I went back to that party after driving you home, I found it in the grass and threw it in the garbage. Just to be sure it didn't somehow find its way back to you."

My mouth dropped open. I twisted around in his arms to look him straight in the eye. "Then I'm even more mad at you."

He pulled me on top of him and I squirmed in protest, the full contact of our naked bodies revealing that he wasn't at all put off by me being mad. Nope; he was turned on.

"Let me make it up to you," he said with hooded eyes.

"No," I said, but when he pulled me in for a kiss, I didn't resist. Much.

"C'mon, princess," he taunted me, his hand sliding down around my ass to caress my swollen pussy—dripping wet from the sex we'd already had... and the sex we were clearly about to have. "Give it up, baby."

"Shut up."

"Make me," he said, shoving his tongue in my mouth.

So I made him. I wrestled his tongue in a fight for dominance, which I only won because he let me. I plundered his mouth like I owned it, sucking on him until his cock jerked beneath me, jabbing into my stomach, and I knew he was as insatiable for me as I was for him.

He slipped a finger into me from behind and started fucking me with it, slow and wet, and I rode it shamelessly.

"So we're just staying here?" I asked between kisses, trying not to sound happy. "Like, forever?"

"For as long as we need to," he mumbled against my mouth.

"Mmm... How do we know when we're done needing to?"

"When I'm done fucking you." He fumbled around down below and I lifted up a bit, straddling him, so he could maneuver. I swiped my hair out of my face to get a good look at him. His eyes were heavy-lidded the way they got when he was thinking with his dick. He was stroking himself, looking at me as he did it.

I bit my lip. "Are you ever going to be done fucking me?"

His eyes caught mine as he found my entrance.

"Fuck, no."

Then he slid into me, gripping my hips with his hands and rocking me against him. I was so wet, so swollen and accustomed to his hard length, I took him easily. But I squeezed him tight, giving back as good as I got as he kissed his way down my chest.

He gripped my ass, catching my swollen nipple in his mouth, and as I rode the edge, he touched my opening—the one behind my pussy. It didn't bother me. I was way too turned on to dislike anything he might try. Actually, it felt good. Tingly and exciting as he pressed against me. That touch, so intimate, drove me closer... and as I rode him harder, more insistently, seeking my release, he shoved a finger inside me.

Whoa.

That felt too, *too* good. Like a rush of sweet and salt... tingles spreading up and out, through my core, along my spine... I gasped his name as I came, flying apart in a sudden burst, as strange, unexpected pulses of pleasure rippled around his finger, deep inside me. He had me impaled with his finger and his cock, his other hand wrapped around my breast, my hard nipple in his teeth, and the pleasure... it was everywhere. All-consuming.

Cosmic.

As I slid back down from that ecstatic peak, Brody seemed to catch me. He kissed his way up my throat and I dropped my face to meet his.

"Fuck... you're good at sex..." I grinned at how stupid that sounded, even if it was true.

"I love you, Jessa," he said, his voice gruff, and I got lost in his hands, his thrusts, as he kept at me. "Fuck... I love you..." I melted into him, kissing him, sliding my tongue deep in his mouth as he drove up into me and let loose, filling me with his heat. I reveled in his spasms, the feeling of this strong man falling to pieces beneath me, even as he squeezed me and kissed me and rocked into me again and again, groaning.

Afterward, once we'd had a chance to catch our breath and

regain use of our limbs, he stumbled out into the night to collect his clothes and his phone.

I hopped out after him, wiggling into my jeans, and pulled on my furry boots and jacket. I'd left my purse out there too, and I really wanted to grab the little tube of hand sanitizer I carried in my makeup bag. It probably wouldn't even cross Brody's mind, since he was a guy, but the thought of him walking around touching everything with a finger that was just up my butt was grossing me out... as epic as it might've felt in the moment.

"Yeah, sorry I missed you. How'd it go?"

As I walked past him, he was dressed and already on a call. The man never stopped working.

Well... except for when he was fucking me. Hmm. I'd have to make note of that.

If you want Brody's undivided attention, just spread your legs.

I giggled a little to myself, smiling at him as his eyes met mine.

"Seth show up?" he asked into the phone, and I froze in place. My breath choked in my throat. "Alright, brother. Fill me in tomorrow. I'll come by in the afternoon."

When he hung up, he was still looking at me. "What?"

"Clean your hands," I said, whipping the sanitizer at him. I didn't mean to throw it so hard—but he ducked a bit to avoid the missile, catching it with one hand just before it hit his face.

"What's wrong?"

"Nothing," I said, striding back toward the truck, but I was already getting that tunnel vision thing that I got when I couldn't deal and I just wanted to go.

Go anywhere.

Go the fuck *away.*

"Jesus," he said, still standing there, watching me, "are we back here again?"

I snapped then. I threw my purse at his truck. Yeah; not one of my finer moments. I saw it bounce off the door and splat to the ground before I pivoted and started walking in the other direction. Away from the road.

Straight off into the dark of some field in the middle of God-knew-where.

In the tunnel of my thoughts, I was already trying to figure out how to get out of this. My phone was in my purse. So I couldn't exactly call Piper. But if I kept walking, I'd have to hit some other road, or eventually I'd find his house, or—

"Jessa." Brody's voice, sharp and freaked the fuck out, cut through my thoughts. "What're you doing?"

"Nothing," I said. Which, of course, was all sorts of ridiculous. But I was already in full-on flight mode, which was pretty much akin to a panic attack; kind of overrode logic and rationality.

"Where the fuck are you going?" He was closer now, his voice in my ear, and I had to resist the urge to run like hell with everything I had. I stopped short as his hand closed on my arm. Then his other arm went around my waist. He held me from behind, his grip like steel, so I couldn't run if I tried. "Jessa," he said, his voice dropping, low and soft. "Just stop, okay? Tell me what's wrong."

"Nothing's wrong," I said, but my breathing was all choked up and I was sniffling a bit. The feel of him, warm and strong and unyielding, wrapped around me, had jolted me out of flight mode and into something else.

Fall-the-fuck-apart mode.

"I'm taking you to my place," he said, his voice still soft, but firm. "You're staying with me."

I didn't answer, but I also didn't argue.

I let him guide me back to the truck as tears slid down my face. I didn't even breathe as he picked up my purse. He opened the door and I got inside. Then he did up my seatbelt and put my purse in my lap.

"Thank you," I managed to whisper.

Brody's eyes met mine. He nodded and shut the door, but I'd seen it clearly on his face—how much my falling apart bothered him.

No; it didn't bother him. It *hurt* him. It pained him and it worried him.

It scared the shit out of him.

It scared the shit out of me, too.

CHAPTER TWENTY-FIVE

Brody

JESSA GOT BACK from her shoot late. Really late. I'd told her she didn't even have to come back to my place that night if she didn't want to, if she was too tired, but that was just bullshit to see what she'd say. At least she'd texted to tell me she was going for drinks with the client afterward; a good-looking dude, as it turned out.

Yeah. I'd done a Google search on him. Because I was jealous like that. According to the web he was also gay, but somehow that didn't help.

I'd never felt so insecure with a woman as I did with Jessa. Like I had no fucking clue where I stood with her—unless we were fused together, my dick deep inside her as she purred my name.

When she got back to my place, smelling of booze, she showered and went straight to bed before me, even though I'd waited up for her. She barely paused long enough to give me a kiss. It wasn't like she'd had time to fall in love with someone else in the hours she'd been away from me, but still.

It was pretty clear to me by now what she'd been up to, in terms of men, all those years we'd been apart. I'd done my best to keep tabs on her in any way I could; I wasn't gonna put Jude up to spying on her—whether he'd even do it for me or not was debatable—so that meant piecing together scraps of info gleaned from other people talking about her, mainly her brother or Maggie, and no one had ever mentioned any kind of serious relationship in her life. You only had to look at Jessa once to know she must've had a hell of a lot of offers, though, and obviously, she'd had lovers. She'd told me herself, more or less, about the guys she'd slept with... and what it was like.

When she was with me, she came like a fucking rocket. Over and over... But she'd never come before, ever, with a man? Not once?

So maybe, just maybe this was a woman who'd become accustomed to using sex, and men, when it suited her—and not to get off. And when she was done with those men, with taking whatever it was she got from that kind of sex, no doubt she tossed them aside just as fast.

No fucking way I was gonna be one of those guys. If I had to keep making her come until she got that through her head, I'd do it.

When I slipped into bed with her she was still awake, but she didn't say anything. I reached out to her. She wasn't naked under the sheet; she had on my Zeppelin T, which she liked to sleep in, and her panties. I got close, spooning her, gently kissing her neck, and she stirred, breathing softly. I slid my hand down the curve of her waist. I slipped my fingers inside the edge of her panties, pulling them down over her hip.

Her hand found mine and stopped me.

"I'm so tired," she said sleepily. Then she rolled slightly away, so we weren't even touching.

So fucking much for spooning.

I let it go. But I wasn't gonna kid myself this was just about being tired.

After the Dirty show, we'd fucked all night and pretty much all the next day. Since her little freak-out on our date? She'd barely touched me. Ever since that phone call. Ever since she'd found out Seth had gotten together with the band to jam... she'd barely looked me in the eye.

Obviously, something was bothering her.

Seth coming back on the scene, apparently.

I flopped back on my pillow and tried to relax, but what the fuck? Was she upset he was playing with the band?

She said she didn't want the guitarist gig. Was pretty vehement about it, actually.

The other possibility swirled in my brain like it had all fucking day, as much as I tried to ignore it and just chill the fuck out, not jump to conclusions.

Maybe she still has feelings for him.

Yeah. Fucking maybe.

Who the fuck knew?

I never really knew for sure what was going on between her and Seth in the first place. Whatever it was, maybe she'd never gotten past it.

Maybe that's what this was about? But how the hell would I know.

Not like she was saying shit all to me about it.

I woke up with my guts all tied in knots, feeling like I was a hundred years old, so bent out of shape and brittle, and ready to snap. Over breakfast Jessa was foggy and distant, which was maybe due to her late night, but I wasn't gonna risk it.

"So what's the problem?" I asked her. "Are we ever gonna talk about it?"

She looked up at me, all distracted, over her tea. "Talk about what?"

"You tell me. Seth's back on the scene and you're walking around like the sky's about to fall."

She blinked at me, slowly shaking her head. "No, I'm not."

I tossed my fork down on my plate, the eggs she'd made for me only partly eaten, whatever appetite I'd had gone. I sat there fuming as she stared at me, resisting the urge to upend the entire table, which seemed like it'd be pretty fucking satisfying right about now.

So yeah, maybe I had some anger management issues to deal

with. I'd file that away for later introspection. But it's not like I went around all my life wanting to flip dining room tables.

It was just *this*. This bullshit. With *her*.

Never-fucking-ending.

"No?" I said.

She shook her head slowly, her big brown eyes watching me—kinda like a skittish deer about to bolt into the woods, never to be seen again.

And yeah, I realized that coming at her like this was probably the last way I should go about it if all I really wanted was to get her to open up and talk to me, but fuck it. I was pissed, and fuck, no—I didn't want to hear about it. I didn't want to hear about how uncomfortable she felt because her old boyfriend was back and how that'd brought up old feelings or whatever.

I thought we were done with this shit.

She'd said it was *me*—always me; not him. That I was the one she'd always wanted. So what was the fucking problem?

"Seth's not after you anymore, is that it?" Her eyes got bigger and I could tell I'd struck a nerve. "You know, he used to follow you around like a fucking puppy. Maybe you miss that."

"I miss a lot of things, Brody," she said. "I don't miss that." Tears had started to gleam in her eyes, but fuck that. She wasn't getting out of this by crying.

"If you want me to come crawling after you," I told her, "that's never gonna happen. I'm never gonna be your lapdog. So you can cry all you want. It's not gonna change a thing."

She didn't even respond to that, just looked away. She sniffed like she was trying really hard *not* to cry, but I was getting really sick of her crying... crying and not letting me in so I could just help fix whatever the fuck was wrong.

"You know why I kept messaging you?" I asked her. "All those years... even when you never responded?" She looked at me through her tears, which had started to fall. "After a while... I pretty much did it to torture myself."

"Don't," she said. "Don't say that."

"I did it to remind myself why I should *stop*. Because every time I messaged you to tell you I was thinking about you, or I wanted to talk to you, or I was sorry for how things went down, and you didn't answer, it was another stab to my fucking heart. But I'm *done* being a masochist, Jessa. You want to leave me hanging again, I'm not gonna be waiting around when you get back. You want to go out and party with your friends and fuck your way around the globe, never letting anyone in, including the guys you fuck, you do what you've gotta do but I am not chasing after you."

Jessa got up and left the room. I didn't follow, though everything in me kicked and screamed at my ass to go after her.

Because what if I didn't and she walked out?

Fuck it. If all she was ever gonna do was run away, I was in for a world of hurt anyway. Might as well get it over with.

So I cleaned up our breakfast plates like everything was normal, when it totally fucking wasn't. Then I just stood there in the kitchen staring at the wall.

Then I broke. It didn't take long.

I went around the house, checking every room, panicking that I'd let her go—and what if I found her packing? What if she was getting the fuck out, for good?

I didn't find her until I walked into my office. She was sitting back in the chair behind my desk, staring at the wall in front of it, where her portrait hung. The giant one Katie had painted... the one I'd had delivered to my house while she was at her shoot yesterday.

"You have my painting," she said softly. She'd stopped crying, and looked from the painting to me in wet-eyed wonder.

"I thought you were leaving," I said flatly.

"You have my painting," she repeated.

"Yeah. Well... we're kind of done with them now. They've been scanned for all the stuff we need to make. The album and shirts and whatever. I figured Katie didn't need to store them all at her studio. You know, she probably needs the space..."

Yeah, right. That was the reason I took it. To help Katie with her storage issues.

Jessa stood and came around the desk, stopping a couple of feet from me.

"I'm not leaving," she said, her voice soft but certain. "You can try to drive me away, if you need to. If you need to test me on it. I understand why you would. You can try. But I'm not going. Not without saying goodbye. I'd never leave again without saying goodbye. And I don't want to say goodbye." She took another step toward me, tentatively. "If that's okay with you."

Was she serious?

She seriously didn't know if I wanted her to stay?

I closed the space between us, sliding my hand under her hair to cup her head, and pulled her to me. "Jessa," I said, my lips brushing hers. "It's more than okay."

My other hand found her hip and I pulled her against me as I kissed her, slow and deep. Her arms went around my neck as she arched against me.

Within seconds, I had her on the desk. Her legs were around my waist, her hands in my hair, and she was shoving down my sweats. We were clawing at each other, grabbing and clutching and desperate to get closer. She grabbed my cock, squeezing, and pumped me a few times, tight and fast. I yanked the crotch of her panties aside. When she whimpered, biting down on my bottom lip, I filled her.

A few more deep, hard thrusts and I was all the way in... smothered in all her hot, tight, and wet. My heart was racing, my breathing ragged. I wanted to fuck her to pieces, just slam all my anger and frustration into her as she begged me for more.

Instead, I put my forehead against hers and breathed her in. I breathed with Jessa until everything slowed right down.

Then I fucked her, deep and slow, saying a whole lot of stupid, fucking risky things.

Don't ever leave me...

I can't fucking breathe without you...

And when she came, gasping and clawing at my back, she whispered in my ear, "I love you, Brody. I love you so much... sometimes... it scares me."

CHAPTER TWENTY-SIX

Brody

I SPENT the next few days, on and off, popping into the church. Jessa hadn't been back to jam with the band since the show at the Back Door. Basically, since Seth started coming down to play. And I didn't love it. I definitely wanted her to be here. The band did, too. But I was willing to give her some space on this.

Some.

Not the kind of space I'd given her back then—miles of it, until I totally fucking lost her.

But I could give her some.

She'd told me she loved me. Repeatedly. So yeah, in truth, I'd tear down the fucking moon and give it to her if I thought that was what she needed.

Eventually, maybe whatever was bothering her would fade. Maybe she'd feel comfortable enough to talk to me about it. Maybe with my support she could deal with it, or let it go, or whatever she needed to do to walk back in here again.

Seth wasn't here every day anyway, but he'd been to a few sessions. I'd sat in so I could gauge the vibe, and it was good. Really good. I could tell everyone had their guard up, but the fact was, Seth fit into the mix just like he always had. Like he did from the very first day Zane dragged him home to jam at nineteen... to the day we had to kick him out because he'd gone so far off the rails with his drug addiction.

By that time, he was shooting heroin, and lots of it, acting totally erratically and completely falling the fuck apart.

But that was then.

Right now, he showed no signs of that fucked-up junkie. He was just Seth Brothers, brilliant guitarist... cool, somewhat mysterious, and likable as all hell. A man born to be a rock star.

We'd just had a particularly incredible day. Maggie had brought food by and the band had been here for ten hours. Seth had just left, and just the band and Jude and I remained. Jude locked the doors and I headed up to the stage where everyone was sitting around. I could feel the excitement, the exhaustion and giddiness, dampened only slightly by that ever-present caution.

I knew what they were thinking. It wasn't like we hadn't all been thinking it for a while now.

"I think we should bring him in, formally," Zane said, straight-up. "So he knows we're all taking this shit seriously. We're taking him seriously, and we give him a real chance. Do up a couple of songs for the album, see how it feels."

"He's clean?" Dylan asked. "For real?"

"So he says," Zane said. "Sure looks that way to me."

"When I had dinner with him, he seemed clean," I told them. "And he definitely wants to come back."

They all looked to me. I knew my opinion held a lot of weight, and I took that shit seriously. I wanted to be honest but fair. To Seth. But mostly, to the band.

I knew they were worried about trusting him again. We all were.

"You think we should do it?" Jesse asked me. "Ask him to come back?"

"Seth never had a talent problem. And he's as good now as he ever was. Better, I'd say."

"Yeah, he's way the fuck better," Jesse agreed. "Which is saying a lot. Can't say I wouldn't love a really strong guitarist to join the lineup. And what he brings in writing... damn, that'd be sweet."

"You sure you wanna share the spotlight?" Zane asked with a grin. "Got room onstage for two of you cocky guitarist pricks?"

"There's room for your inflated ego, we'll fucking manage," Jesse replied.

"I'll admit," I told them, "I would've loved to see Jessa in the role. I think she's a great fit. She's family, and she's got this thing... would've been killer to see where we could take it. But second to that, if we can work with Seth, it would make for a hell of a tenth anniversary. If we can keep Jessa in the mix too, writing, we've got it fucking made."

"Yeah," Elle said, "we don't want to lose Jessa." She gave me a loaded look. "So whatever we can do to keep her around, we should be doing it."

Message received.

"I'll work on it," I said, sounding confident. "She's not going anywhere." I hoped like fuck I could deliver on those words.

"We're not losing Jessa," her brother said, also giving me a look.

"So what happens if we invite Seth back, and he goes off the rails?" Dylan asked.

"We front-load all that shit into his contract," I said. "He's off the wagon, he's out. We've been down that road with him, not doing it again. But you've all gotta agree this is what you want. Maybe give him a few more sessions, feel it out."

"I'm good with Seth," Zane said. "He was a huge asset to this band, and it was fucking beautiful for a while, before it went south. It fucking sucked when he left. Personally, I've missed the guy."

"We all know no one's ever been able to take his place," Elle said. "And to be honest, I don't know if Jessa would. It would've been great, but it would've been different. Seth's a better guitarist by miles. We all know that, too. He has an edge Jessa doesn't have, and it would be cool to see what happens. With both of them. And we all know Seth's a good guy, without the drugs."

"We've never known him without the drugs," Dylan said, and that was a cold, harsh reality that we all had to swallow.

He was right.

We never really did.

"You didn't know me without the booze until I sobered my ass up almost seven years ago now," Zane put in, "and that turned out pretty fucking fine."

"Actually," Jesse said, considering Zane with a sidelong glance, "kinda liked you better when you were a drunk."

In response, Zane walked over, punched Jesse in the gut, hauled him off his stool, and a brawl broke out, the kind where they laughed as much as they beat the shit out of each other, and maybe a few things got broken along the way.

Fucking teenagers.

At that point, I left it up to Jude to referee. I had Jessa waiting for me.

Meeting adjourned.

It was five days later that I came home to Jessa with the news.

"We've asked Seth to come back to the band," I told her, standing in the bathroom off my bedroom, watching her brush her hair. She was getting ready to go to bed, with me, and I couldn't get enough of her like that. In her panties and my old T-shirt, in my home. I just leaned against the door frame and watched her, drinking it in. "They've asked him to play on the album. Go on tour, if that works out. The full deal." I watched her face reflected in the mirror, gauging her reaction. "He said yes."

She stopped brushing and laid her hairbrush carefully on the counter. Her eyes met mine in the mirror. "Of course he did."

"You're not happy?"

She turned to me and shrugged. "I have no right not to be."

"That's not what I asked."

I went over to her and slid my hands around her waist, meaning to hold her close, so we could talk without her trying to run away. But she pulled me to her and started kissing me, deep.

Next thing I knew she was steering me toward the bed, and then my clothes were off and she was on top of me, forcing herself onto my cock so fast it almost hurt. I grabbed her hips and held her still so I could get the angle right; then I drove into her. She tumbled, taking me with her, pulling me on top, and I got totally lost in fucking her, in her ragged, desperate cries.

Harder, Brody...

Fuck me harder...

I came when she did, hard. There was no stopping it. She fucked that orgasm right out of me, rubbing herself on me even after I was spent, like she couldn't get enough.

Panting, I eased off her. I looked at her, lying there in my shirt, limp on the bed, staring at the ceiling in a haze, her shredded panties halfway down one thigh. One of us had ripped them getting them off. I wasn't even sure who.

"What the fuck was that about?" I asked her, still panting. "Because it sure as fuck wasn't about you and me."

She drew away, curling into a little ball on her side. "What does that mean?"

"It means I'd like to know whether we're fighting or fucking or falling apart. With you, I never know. It's kinda one in the same."

"It's not," she protested.

"You use sex as a weapon, Jessa. You use it as a wall, you use it as a shield, you use it as a goddamn knife."

"That's not true."

"No? Then why don't you try telling me, for once, what's really going on in your head? Because you never tell me shit. You just fuck me to turn my attention where you want it. Just like when we were kids and you'd do shit to get my attention, yeah? Good attention, bad attention, it didn't matter. Always mouthing off, arguing, running away and expecting me to give chase. Well, you have my attention, okay?"

"Fuck you," she said weakly, and rolled further away, looking crushed.

"Talk to me," I said, softening my voice. "You really don't have to fuck me to get me to listen."

"Fine. I'll talk." She turned to face me. "I feel blindsided by Seth being asked back into the band. It makes me feel like everything's out of my control and it scares me."

"Why?"

"I should have a say," she said. "The band wants me writing songs with them, don't I get a say on the new lineup?"

"Frankly, no," I told her, getting out of bed and pulling on my underwear. "You've disappeared on them again, haven't been to a session in over a week. You can't have it both ways, Jessa."

She got out of bed, discarding her ripped panties, and pulled on some new ones from the drawer she'd been using in my dresser. Officially, she was still staying at Jesse's, wouldn't bring all her things over here, but she'd slept here every night.

She threw me a hurt look. "So you're choosing Seth over me, is that it?"

"Are you giving me an ultimatum?"

She crossed her arms over her chest. "Maybe."

"Why does it have to be one or the other?" I stared at her a long, long moment, waiting for her reply.

She stared back.

And in that loaded silence, I felt the rage rising up, jagged and hot. Wasn't gonna unleash it on her, so I turned, picked up the first thing I saw—a glass of water on the bedside table—and smashed it against the wall behind me. She jumped, startled. "What the *hell* is going on between you and him?"

"*Nothing*," she said.

"Then what *went* on between you and him? I thought the two of you were tight, and then you up and disappeared."

"That's not what happened."

"For fuck's sake, Jessa—"

"It wasn't my fault!"

"How was it not your fault? You left us."

"Stop saying that!"

"Then tell me what happened!"

"You're going to keep throwing that in my face forever, aren't you? I. Left. I know! It was the biggest mistake I ever made, and you're never going to let it go."

"No," I said, calming myself the fuck down. "I just want to understand." I took a few steps toward her, softening. "Why the fuck are you fighting this? You say the word, and you've got your shot with the band. You're in. They wanted you first. They're only giving Seth a shot now because you turned them down, and because I asked them to."

She blinked at me. "You did?"

I sighed. "The rhythm guitarist position has been a revolving fucking door for the past six years and we're all tired of it. We need someone permanent, someone who can really bring something special to the band. Seth could be the one, but it should be you."

"Brody." She shook her head. "Just... don't start that again, okay?"

"Why the fuck not? I can't believe you can't fucking see it when everyone else can."

"It, it, it. What the fuck is *it*?"

"*It*, Jessa. You have *it*. That indescribable, intangible, heart-stopping thing that makes the world stop fucking turning when you walk in a room. When you open your mouth and you sing, and your heart pours out, and your words... Jesus, Jessa, your lyrics, the things you write... the way you write... you know how many people can write like that? How many musicians wish they could write like that? How many wannabe stars wish they could sound like you, or look like you? Or had half the connections you have?"

"So what? So fucking *what*? So I'm supposed to follow some path you and my brother have decided for me, just so you can live out your dream of managing me?"

"I don't care who you get to manage you. This is not about me. This is about you, throwing all that shit away. It kills me that you're fucking wasting it all—"

"Wasting it? How am I wasting it?"

"Modeling, Jessa. What the fuck are you doing modeling, when you have all this talent—"

"Are you kidding me? Do you have any idea how hard it is to get to where I have? You think I don't work my ass off? That it's not of any worth at all?"

Shit. This was going way the fuck in the wrong direction.

I took a breath. "I know you've been successful—"

"Yeah, I have. And I've done it without you. Without the band. Just *me*."

"I know that. You've done well for yourself. I'm not saying you haven't."

"Then why do you keep attacking it, like what I've done is such a mistake?"

"Because it is a mistake when you're throwing everything else away in pursuit of it and you're running away from your life, from the people who love you. You know what that's usually called? It's called an addiction, Jessa. And it's not fucking healthy."

"Really. You think I'm addicted to modeling, you really don't know me."

"No," I said. "I think you're addicted to the high you get from the validation of it. The distraction of not having to deal with your life, your regrets, and your feelings."

"You're so wrong," she said, hugging herself, but I knew that was bullshit.

"What happened to your big dreams?" I pressed. "Your notebooks all crammed with your ideas? You used to have something to *say*. You had so fucking much to say, you were overflowing with words. And now I have to pry them out of you with a crowbar."

"What do you want from me? You want me to stand here and talk about my feelings? Like what? How shitty I feel because I ran away? Is that what you want to hear me say?"

No. I didn't want to hear that. I wasn't trying to punish her. All I really wanted was for her to let it all go. Whatever was keeping her from being here, with me.

"I remember sitting with you, talking for hours," I told her. "Writing songs with the band, and going on tour, that's all you ever talked about. I couldn't shut you up about it if I tried."

"I was a kid. What the fuck did I know?"

"You knew what you wanted."

"I'm not going onstage, Brody. I don't want to be onstage and I don't want to perform anymore."

"Then you don't have to."

"Did you know my agent calls me *every day* asking when I'm coming back, telling me about all the jobs I'm missing out on? I could go. I could go right now."

"Then why don't you? If that's what you want? If that's where you belong?"

"Because I don't want to do it anymore!" she cried. Then she closed the distance between us, getting so close I could see all the colors in her eyes as she looked up at me. "Do you have any idea how wrong that feels? I've worked so hard, sacrificed so much, to just walk away... Don't you get that? I *had* to succeed at it because I chose it and everything I ever did from that point on was wrong. If I didn't make it work, then the whole thing would just crumble like a house of cards or a bunch of dominoes or some other stupid metaphor I can't even think of right now!" She swiped her hands through her hair, frustrated. "But I'm so tired of it, Brody. I'm tired of working so hard to be what other people want me to be." She took a shaky breath. "That shoot last week was beautiful. We shot at the Crystal, you know, the hotel? In the ballroom and on that big, sweeping staircase in the lobby, and I got to wear the most epically gorgeous dresses—"

"I know."

She frowned. "You know?"

"I saw you." Kinda felt like an idiot telling her this way, but since it came up... "I was downtown anyway, for a meeting, and Jude texted. He'd seen you. And I might've... swung by to look." I shrugged, feeling weird about it. "I couldn't resist."

She was still frowning. "Why didn't you say hi?"

"You were working. I didn't want to bother you." That was true, but now it sounded lame. "Shit. Do I sound like a stalker?"

"Kind of." She sounded a little amused, but she didn't smile.

"Well, you looked like a princess. For real." That was true, too. More than true. She was wearing a wedding gown with a long train when I saw her on that staircase, with all the lights and a big team of people flocking around her. I'd never had a fantasy of watching a woman walk up the aisle toward me until that moment. She looked like a goddess, but Jessa always looked that way to me.

"Yeah," she said, but she didn't look happy about it. "They treated me like one, and I didn't even want to be there." She shook her head. "I felt so fucking ungrateful, thinking about all the girls who'd love to be in my place, and I didn't even want it. When I'm modeling, I'm not me, Brody. And that used to feel good to me. Safe. It doesn't feel good anymore. I just... I want to write. I want to write songs and jam with the band and then I want to hang out in the recording studio and help them tweak the songs and fight over them and laugh like crazy, just like I did on the first album, you know? I want to be *happy*. I want to go watch them play live. I want to watch Zane sing my songs and I want to get excited and scream and dance until my throat is sore and my ears are ringing. That's all I want. I want to feel like I'm where I belong. I just want to be a part of it again, but I want it to be *my* part. Not rhythm guitar. Not backup singer. Not what you or anyone else envisions for me. I just want to write songs. That's all I've ever, ever wanted."

Well halle-fucking-lujah.

"Then why did you leave?" I asked her softly.

Her shoulders dropped and she exhaled a deep breath. "Are you ever going to forget about the past? Just let it go?"

"Are you?" I stared her down, letting her absorb that. "When are you ever gonna let me in? I'm not the enemy, Jessa."

She nodded a little, but looked away. When she looked back, there was pain in her brown eyes. "You said you'd never hurt me."

I reached for her, slipping my hands around the back of her head and drawing her in close. "When did I hurt you?" I asked her, holding her in my hands like she was precious, because she was. "Tell me when, so I can fix it."

She sniffed a bit, resisting the tears that were coming, fast. "You said you were done with me."

"Yeah," I said, stroking my thumb back and forth across her cheek. "Obviously I was wrong." I held her gaze for a long moment, letting her feel those words. Wanting to erase whatever hurt I'd caused. Then I leaned in to kiss her.

"You let me go," she blurted, just as my lips touched hers.

I drew back and looked at her.

"Back then..." She sniffed again. "I ran. I know. But you let me." She closed her eyes and the tears spilled down her face. "You let me go," she repeated. "You didn't fight for me."

"What?"

"I know you asked me to stay. Many times. And I know it's totally irrational of me... but there's some small, stubborn part of me that still hurts because you didn't come after me. You didn't tear apart heaven and Earth to get me back. And I need to know... I need to know that there isn't some small part of you that won't fight for me in the future, if things get tough."

I pulled her against me, holding her tight. She buried her face in my chest.

"Jessa..." I whispered, my voice hoarse. "I never wanted you to go. I wanted you to stay. I just... I thought I was doing the right thing by letting you... *fuck*... I don't even know anymore. It just seemed like every time I tried to fight, I just pushed you further away. And I didn't want to lose you." My voice broke and I nuzzled into her hair as I held her tighter. "I lost you anyway."

"You didn't lose me, Brody," she whispered. "I was always yours."

CHAPTER TWENTY-SEVEN

Jessa

WE SPENT the night making love, until we couldn't anymore. Until we were too tired, too sore, too spent, and we passed out in each other's arms.

In the morning, I woke to Brody moving between my legs. I wrapped myself around him and we made love again, slowly, as the sun came up.

He went to take a shower while I lazed in bed, and eventually I got up. I stretched, leisurely, sore in all the best ways.

I'd wanted to bind myself to Brody last night and never let go. I'd felt warm and safe and loved in his arms, his body pinning mine, possessing me; his hands, his weight, his tongue... his cock... all of him. His body told me without words that I was his, that we were together, that he loved me, wanted me, cherished me. That he would always protect me.

That he would never even think of leaving me.

In the cold morning light, without his arms around me, I felt... awful. His words from last night kept replaying in my head, and I knew he was right.

I was the one who couldn't let go.

I'd been blaming myself, for years, for everything that happened. *Everything.*

With him.

With Seth.

Even with my dad.

I'd blamed myself, when I'd forgiven all of them. I'd forgiven Brody for letting me go when I ran away, even though it wasn't easy. I'd forgiven Seth. I'd even forgiven my dad for leaving, for doing that awful thing to himself that he did and leaving me behind to deal with it. That definitely wasn't easy, but I did it.

Yet I'd never forgiven myself. Because if I did that... it would be like giving myself permission to breathe. To just be. To be *me*, not just the model who looked flawless in pictures but was a royal mess inside.

But I *was* a mess.

Still.

As much as I'd been able to forgive him, I'd always felt dirty and conflicted over what happened between me and Seth. I'd cared about him, and if I'd been a better person, I thought, a stronger person, I would've been able to help him. Things wouldn't have spiraled out of control. He wouldn't have gotten so deep into drugs and he wouldn't have been kicked out of the band.

As Brody's words went around in my head, I realized how completely and mercilessly I'd blamed myself for Seth's life falling apart, for the brutality of his addiction, for everything.

Why?

I asked myself that question as I cleaned up the glass Brody had broken against the wall. And the answer came to me, so clear.

Because it was easier for me to believe that everything was all my fault, that I had screwed everything up, than to accept that Seth had done bad things, made bad choices, that were beyond my control.

Just like my dad did.

The hard truth was that I'd wanted to help Seth. I'd wanted to save him and I'd failed, epically—and this struck right to the heart of my pain over what happened with my dad. I couldn't save my dad, either. How could I? I was five years old when he killed himself.

But I had never gotten over it.

I was still paying for his mistakes. And now Brody was paying for them, too.

He was right about another thing: I was the one still holding the past between us, like a weapon. So maybe it was time I laid my weapons down.

For good.

Except I couldn't really do that unless I faced the mess I'd made and, once and for all, cleaned it the fuck up.

But I still hadn't done it. I still hadn't talked to Brody. I'd kept putting it off, with one excuse or another. I'd been scared to face it head-on; to talk to him, and risk losing him. And now here I was, tiptoeing around him, terrified that everything between us would inevitably fall apart when he found out. I saw it coming. And I did feel powerless, like it was out of my control, when that wasn't even true.

I'd asked Brody to fight for me. And I loved him. No; more than that.

Brody Mason was the love of my life.

So when was I going to fight for him?

Now. Right fucking now.

I found his phone, and I used it to text Seth while he was still in the shower.

Brody: Need to talk. Meet for coffee?

By the time I'd finished getting dressed, Seth had replied.

Seth: Yup-when & where?

I texted him where to meet, my fingers shaking just a little, then deleted the thread.

I left Brody a note to let him know I'd be back in a while, that I was going to pick up groceries. I told him I'd make us dinner tonight. I realized how it might seem when he got out of the shower to find

me gone, so I drew some girlie little hearts on the note so he'd know I
wasn't running away.

Then I took his truck and headed downtown before I lost my
nerve.

Seth was already there when I walked in. I saw him right away, and
it struck me how odd it was to see him sitting there, in the middle of
a busy cafe, by himself, with no one bothering him at all.

If any current member of Dirty tried to pull that, they'd be
mobbed.

But Seth had been out of the band for six years. He was wearing
a hat, and the stubble of his beard had grown back in, helping
disguise the Seth Brothers the world used to know.

Since getting kicked out of Dirty, he hadn't really done anything
else, at least musically; I'd heard about him playing with some band
here or there, but nothing that ever amounted to anything close to
the fame he'd had a taste of with Dirty.

It was a tragedy, really.

A waste.

Those familiar green eyes locked on me as I crossed the room,
and Seth sat up as I approached his table. His gaze moved between
me and the door as I pulled out a chair, his expression guarded.
"Brody coming?"

"No." I sat down across from him, setting my purse on the table
between us. "It's just me."

He nodded, absorbing that. "Can I buy you a coffee?"

I shook my head, then blurted out, "Why do you have to do this?
Can't you find another band?" He stared at me, and I knew I'd
struck below the belt, but I didn't come here to mince words.
"Didn't you already ruin enough?"

Okay. That was a low blow, too. Very low. But on the drive here,
in the process of working up my nerve to confront him, I'd gotten a
little angry.

"Me?" He looked honest-to-God confused. "I got kicked out of the band, Jessa. Or did you not notice that?"

"You got kicked out because you were a drug addict. That has nothing to do with me. For a long time, I thought it did. I was a kid. I was wrong."

I waited for him to defend himself. To deny. To do whatever drug addicts did when they felt ashamed of their behavior.

He just nodded.

"You're right. I was an addict. I'll always be an addict. That isn't your fault. But you chose to leave the band. I didn't. I got kicked out. Now I'm clean, and it's my chance to play with them again." Seth held my eyes, his gaze steady, so different than it used to be. "I lost everything once and maybe you don't think that has anything to do with you, but you never really did believe that I loved you."

My gaze was steady, too. No matter what he said to me, I had words I needed to get out, and I wasn't holding them back. "I believed you," I said. "But I was in love with Brody. You knew that, too. I told you I was."

He looked away, like he still didn't want to hear it.

"You think you lost everything?" I leaned in over the table so he couldn't possibly mishear me. "I loved Brody since the day I met him, Seth. I always have, and I always will. He didn't have to do anything to deserve that love, and he sure as hell didn't manipulate it out of me. You wanted me to love you but I couldn't and you just couldn't accept that. You were my friend, Seth, and you took advantage of how messed up I was."

He was shaking his head as I spoke. "I didn't mean—"

"No? Well, that whole experience fucked up everything for me. Worst of all, because of what happened, I ran away from everything that mattered. I hurt Brody, and now he's defending you to me, fighting for you to have a chance with the band. He has no idea what happened between us, and if he knew, you know he'd never support your position with the band."

"What the fuck do you want me to say, Jessa?" Anger flashed

across Seth's face, along with what looked like hurt. He looked scared, actually, and it made me kind of nauseous.

I'd never wanted to hurt him. It still made me feel like shit to do it.

I sat back in my chair and took a breath. I really didn't come here to argue.

"You've already got everything," he said. "You've got Brody, you've got your royalties from the songs, you've got your modeling career. You don't need this. I do." He was desperate. I could see that now. He wanted this, bad.

And as I calmed down off the adrenaline kick brought on by facing him, by saying a lot of hurtful, spiteful, arguably unfair things I'd never had the chance to say before, I didn't want to be the one to take it away from him. I really, really didn't.

But I also wanted this. My home. My family. My band.

Most of all, Brody.

And I just didn't know how I could have them at the same time Seth did. I didn't know if I could share them with someone who'd been such a huge part of all that pain I'd been through.

"I remember the day I met you, too, Seth," I told him quietly. "You were a really nice boy. Quiet, kind of shy. So cool... even Zane wanted to be like you. Everyone liked you. They loved you, actually. I think they still do, despite all you've done to them, and to yourself, or they wouldn't want you back in the band." Then I gathered my nerve one last time and said the thing I'd really wanted to tell him all these years. "I'm just sorry that whatever it was inside you that hurt so bad turned you into what you became."

He said nothing in response.

As I got up to leave, I told him, "You need to come clean with the band, Seth. Tell them everything. I'll give you a few hours, but you need to do it today. I'm not going to sleep one more night without getting things out in the open. If they still want you after that, so be it. I'll just have to accept it."

He looked up at me. "And if I don't tell them shit?"

I softened a little, looking down at him. "I don't think you understand. I'm telling them, too. I'm just giving you a chance to give them your side of it."

When I pulled into Maggie's driveway, she came outside to meet me, her face scrunched with concern. Maybe I'd scared her with my call for help.

"I fucked up, Maggie," I'd told her, as soon as I got her on the phone.

"What do you mean?"

"I mean... I'm in love with Brody."

"In love?"

"Yeah. Like... hard. And for a long, long time."

I'd left the cafe with a killer urge to run. I could easily envision myself driving straight to the airport, getting on a plane, and never coming back. It was itching under my skin, twitching at the back of my brain. Like I was jonesing for it. *Escape*.

Easy. So fucking easy.

And so fucking wrong.

I resisted that urge, because I knew it was wrong. My time for running was done. If I kept running, I was going to die running one day. It might not be tomorrow, but some day... I would die alone, still running.

So instead, I practically fell into Maggie's arms. For someone so petite, Maggie gave a great hug.

When she drew back, she looked up into my eyes, my watery, tear-pricked eyes, and asked, "Are you okay?" Then she frowned before I could answer and added, "Do I need to kick his ass?"

"No." I laughed and wiped the tears away before they fell. "But I love you for asking. I know you and Brody are tight. Thank you for not taking his side."

"His side?" she said. "Oh, no. No, no. We girls stick together. And Brody and I are not that tight. Yes, we work together. And yes, perhaps he's slightly more in touch with his emotions and has his bullshit slightly more under wraps than *some* men I know," she said, no doubt thinking of her "husband" as she said it, "but he's still a guy. And you're you." She made a sweeping gesture to indicate my entire being. "I've known you for years, Jessa Mayes, and you are lovely, inside and out. Brody may be hot and smart and generally level-headed, but he's still a dude. And since he put that look on your face, I'm thinking he probably fucked up his share too."

Then she pulled me inside her cozy little condo and put on a kettle for tea.

"What happened?" she asked as she looked over at me, cuddled into her beanbag chair with my knees pulled up under my chin.

"Nothing, really. That's the problem. Brody told me he loved me when we were kids, and I couldn't handle it. I didn't really feel worthy of his love. So I ran away."

"And then what?"

"And then I just kept running."

She came to sit next to me, on the floor. "And now? What's going on?"

I sighed. "I feel like my heart is going to explode every time we get naked together." Maggie's eyebrows went up. "Other times... it's like we want to tear each other apart."

Now her lips quirked as she fought off a smile. "Well, shit."

I tried to smile a little too. "So maybe there's hope?"

Maggie shook her head, considering. "I'll be honest, hon... I'm not sure that means there's hope, but it sure as hell isn't a bad thing. I mean... if things are that intense between you, there's a reason, right?"

"Yeah." I hugged my knees tight as she went to pour the tea. "He says I broke his heart, Maggie. He thinks I didn't want him, back then. That I ran away from him. But I totally didn't."

Maggie took that in. She came back over, handing me a mug and settling on the floor, cross-legged. "Well, it's obvious you're over the moon for him now. He'd have to be blind to miss it. Like hearts and rainbows shoot out of your eyes every time you say his name. It's sickening, actually."

"You're just saying that because you're all married and bored," I teased.

"Oh, Christ. Don't remind me of that bullshit. I haven't had anything to drink yet today."

"Sorry," I said, blowing on my tea. "I don't think being over the moon has ever been our problem, though."

"Then what the hell is?"

I hesitated. "Just... stuff. Stuff we never talked about but we need to. And I don't know how it'll change things when we do." I knew it would change things, but somewhere along the way I'd gone from believing he'd want nothing to do with me once I told him the truth, to thinking that maybe if I just fucked him enough he'd overlook it.

Stupid. Brody had never been that guy—the one who let his dick make his decisions. But I was getting desperate.

I sipped my mint tea, breathing in the fragrant steam, letting it calm my nerves. "Frankly, Maggie... I'm scared to fucking death."

"Yeah," she said. "I see that." She looked momentarily contemplative, even sad. Then she said, "Fuck it. Life's too short. You need to talk to him. Talk to him about everything, even the shit you're most scared to. *Especially* that shit. You talk to him and he's not cool with it, nothing changes. You go about your separate lives and he still holds a grudge or whatever the fuck he feels he needs to do in that man-brain of his. On the other hand, you talk to him and he's understanding, maybe you talk it through. Either way you win, because you faced your demons head on, and that takes the kind of courage you can't turn back from."

"Yeah. You're right," I said. "I know it. I just haven't found the courage. That's all it is. I'm a huge coward."

Maggie sipped her tea in silence for a minute.

"You know, Jessa... Brody's been acting like a grumpy-ass, grunting bear since you came back," she said. "I've never seen him like this. I've also never seen him serious about anyone else. He's kind of a serial monogamist; always has some girlfriend around, but they never last long, and he never seems that into them. Like he smiles more when he's with the guys, you know? It's like he's the kind of guy who wants to be in love, but he never finds anyone to feel that way about. That's gotta be by choice. It's not like he hasn't met a crapload of available women since you've been gone. On the road, they're like horny bees swarming on honey, on all the guys—Brody included."

"Maybe you just don't know?" I said, not loving that image; really, it was unlikely that Maggie knew everything about Brody's love life, right?

Maggie fixed her no-bullshit gray eyes on me when she said, "Maybe he's waiting for you, Jessa."

CHAPTER TWENTY-EIGHT

Jessa

IN THE END, I took Maggie's advice.

It had been hours, anyway, since I left Seth in that cafe. The sun had gone down. And I hadn't heard a word from anyone.

If Seth had told the band right away, like I advised him to, I would've heard something by now.

"Nothing?" I asked Maggie for like the dozenth time as we both checked our phones.

She shook her head. "Sorry, hon."

Moments later, Brody knocked on the door. I'd messaged to let him know where I was. I'd also apologized for getting caught up and missing dinner. He'd come straight over like I'd asked him to, and when Maggie let him in his eyes cut straight to me where I was sitting on the couch.

"Were you leaving?" he demanded as he came thundering over. His face looked slightly windburned from racing here on his bike, and he looked off-put... frazzled. I'd worried him again.

Guess my little note with all the hearts didn't cut it.

"I wasn't—"

"You're not leaving."

"No," I said calmly. "I wasn't leaving."

"You want me to fight for you?" His voice was rising, like I hadn't even spoken. "This is me, fighting. *You are not fucking leaving.*"

Shit. He was really wound up, and that stupid inability to get my thoughts out of my mouth whenever he was around, and pissed at me, kicked in, and I started struggling to find the words to defend myself—when Maggie cut right in.

"Just shut up and listen," she said. "I'll put her in my car and drive her to the airport myself if you wanna keep acting like a crazy deranged bear with a firecracker up its ass."

That got Brody's attention. I kind of doubted Maggie laid into him like that very often. Or ever.

He stood back, clawed a hand through his hair and took a breath. Then he shot Maggie, who was still hovering between us, a dark look.

"I'll just... head out for a while. Take your time." She threw me a look and pointed at her phone, which I took to mean, *Message me if you need that ride to the airport.*

Then she vanished.

Brody shed his jacket, rubbed a hand over his face and sat next to me on the couch.

"We need to talk," I said softly.

"Yeah," he said, blue eyes locking onto mine. He took hold of my hand and held it tight against his thigh. "So, talk."

I talked.

I told him everything.

And I started at the beginning.

I told him about how it felt after my mom died. I told him about the crushing weight of the loss of her, after already losing my dad. The dark despair and powerlessness I'd felt.

I told him how it felt to be the kid sister, the good girl, always following everyone else's rules, doing my best to keep everyone smiling while I felt like I was dying inside.

I told him how it felt to be cared for and protected by my brother, and Jude, and Zane, and by all my brother's friends growing up. By him; Brody.

And by Seth.

How it felt to be guarded and policed and so protected, so loved, so cherished that I was treated like a princess. That I thought I had to act like one, pretty and happy and shiny and perfect, to deserve that love.

And the toll it had taken on me to act that way when inside, I felt anything but perfect.

How it felt to be told I couldn't stay out late, couldn't date, couldn't drink, when everyone around me was doing just that. How it felt to be left out of the party, when all I really wanted was a grand distraction from all my ugly feelings. A distraction from myself.

I told him about the first time I did drugs to find that distraction. About the first time Seth gave me pot, when no one else would.

I told him about the next time, and the next. About the times I'd sneak out of Dolly's house in the middle of the night to hang out with Seth and smoke up. About the parties Seth took me to when Jesse and Dolly thought I was home in bed.

I told him about the first time pot turned into pills. How the highs got higher, more frequent, and then the lows got lower in-between.

I told him about how the need for a distraction turned into a desire to get high. How my guilt over lying to Jesse and Jude and Zane and Dolly and *him* about where I was and what I was doing and who I was doing it with just fed the darkness inside me.

I told him about the other lies I'd told. How I'd told my brother I was at modeling jobs when I was getting high. How I told him I was sleeping over at a girlfriend's house when I was out all night with Seth.

And I told him. I told him what happened when I got scared Seth might stop giving me drugs. Because he'd never asked me for money to pay for them. He liked me, and he gave them to me freely. Except they weren't really free, because Seth had feelings for me.

I knew that, and I used it.

I told him how, when I saw him with Christy, in my messed-up state, I'd turned to Seth for comfort, and I'd crossed that line I never should've crossed with him, because I didn't love Seth.

Then I told him about Seth introducing me to MDMA.

"You did ecstasy with Seth?"

Those were the first words out of his mouth.

I could see the conclusion he was drawing in his head, and he wasn't wrong.

"Yes. I did ecstasy with Seth."

Then I told him the rest of it.

I told him about the first time I slept with Seth so he'd keep giving me pills.

"Please understand. At that point, I would've done pretty much anything if I thought it would make me feel good. I just wanted to feel better. But having sex with Seth didn't make me feel better. In the end, it made me feel worse. I saw what it was doing to him... and I was so hurt over what was happening—or, what wasn't happening —with you, and whenever I felt worse... I wanted to get high."

I told him, and I didn't cry. I'd shed more than enough tears over all of it over the years, and I wasn't going to cry about it now. The time for crying, and lying, and running from the truth was done.

So I kept talking.

I told him about the next time I had sex with Seth when we got high, and the time after that. I told him how Seth told me he loved me. I told him how I loved *him*, Brody, but he was with Christy, and I was so sure I'd fucked everything up, and I wasn't strong enough to give up the drugs, or ask anyone for help, and how all my secrets and lies and pain twisted me up inside until I couldn't stand myself.

I told him, for the first time, why I ran away that last night I saw him, during that break in the tour.

"I saw Seth that night, too. He cornered me and he was all fucked up. I knew he was doing a lot of coke then; I didn't even know what else, but I knew he was in bad shape. He said he wanted to be with me. He wanted me. He wanted... what we had before. I told him I couldn't do it anymore. When he pressed me on it... I told him. I told him I was in love with you." I could barely look at Brody as I said it. The shame of it was crushing, the regret, that I'd never told him how much I loved him. I'd only told Seth. "I told him I loved you and he called me a whore. And I *felt* like a whore, Brody. I'd let him fuck me for drugs when I was sixteen. It went on, off and on, for almost two years. I never told anyone what was happening. I just let it happen. I didn't care. I didn't care about myself anymore. I just wanted the pain to stop. The thing was, I just got more pain."

I looked at Brody, feeling shaky. Through it all he'd sat next to me, his thigh pressed to mine, holding my hand, barely breathing. When I saw his face now, his blue eyes dark and storming, I could see the force of his anger, barely restrained. I could see it rising in him, like a tidal wave about to crash and smash everything in its path. And for once I saw it for what it was. It was not anger aimed at me.

"He was struggling," I said softly. "He said he was in love with me, and—"

"He raped you," he said quietly; deadly quiet.

"*No.* It wasn't like that—"

Brody stood abruptly. "You're telling me you had sex with Seth so he'd give you drugs. For two fucking years. Behind all our backs."

I stood to face him. "He didn't force me. I wanted—"

"Like hell he didn't. He took advantage of you."

Then he turned away, like he couldn't even look at me anymore.

I got up close behind him, wanting to wrap my arms around him, but I didn't.

What if he pushed me away?

I didn't know what else to say to him. I didn't want to make it worse. I just wanted him to understand.

"I didn't run away from you, Brody. I didn't run away from Seth, either. I was running from what I'd done to myself. I wasn't that girl. That twisted girl who'd made so many mistakes, who felt dirty all the time and so completely lost. I wasn't your princess either. Do you understand? I just needed to find *me*."

He turned back to me, his eyes shining with tears. "And did you find that? Did you find what you were looking for when you left?"

"No." I shook my head, hugging myself. "I got clean. Things got worse before they got better, but I got clean. It took a few years to totally stop with the pills, to stop thinking I needed uppers or painkillers to deal with my life. But it was what I had to do. I'll never regret that part." I sighed. "I was terrified of going on tour with the band, Brody. I'm not going to say there weren't temptations everywhere I went. There was plenty of partying in the life I chose; but going on tour.... I just couldn't go on tour with Seth. I needed to distance myself from him. Not because he was awful to me. Because he was tied up in my drug use, and I knew it would be one party after another. I don't know where I would've ended up if I kept on like I was. It wasn't even the drugs... I wasn't using every day or anything; I can't even say for sure if I was an addict. I can still drink or smoke a joint without going over to the dark place. But the pills were different. Maybe it was the timing of it all, or my age, but I was losing myself. And I was so fucking depressed. It would've been the depression that killed me, just like it killed my dad. And the pills... they fueled that." I moved a little closer to him, looking up into his face. "But no, I didn't find what I was looking for until now. When I came back to you."

Brody looked down at me for a moment, his eyes gleaming. Then he drew me into his arms... and the relief I felt at his acceptance was so intense, so overwhelming, I did start to cry.

"Jessa. Don't cry." He kissed the tears from my face. "You never did anything wrong. Please tell me you know that by now."

I shook my head. How could he say that to me after everything I'd just confessed?

"I did everything wrong, Brody."

"No. We did wrong. We didn't protect you." He held me tighter. "I didn't protect you. I thought I was doing the right thing, giving you space. You were young, and..." He trailed off, shaking his head. "*Fuck me.* How could I not've seen what was going on? All that time?"

"Don't do that," I told him. "Don't blame yourself for my mistakes, Brody. I lied to you. I hid what I was doing from you and from everyone else. You guys had a lot on your plates and you were away a lot. It really wasn't that hard to keep it a secret; I had excuses for everything back then." I shook my head at the memories. "But no more excuses, and no more lies. I just want it to be over. And I don't want to blame myself anymore. I'm working on forgiving myself. But with you, there's nothing to forgive. You tried to love me and I ran away. That wasn't your fault."

I sighed and dropped my head against his chest, emotionally exhausted. I clung to his solid comfort, to the fact that he wasn't walking away. That he was holding me, despite everything I'd just said.

"I just need it to be done," I told him. "Once and for all. I need it to die, where it belongs. In the past."

CHAPTER TWENTY-NINE

Brody

I FOUND him at the church.

He was onstage, with the band, and they were in the middle of playing one of the new songs—one of the songs Jessa had co-written; the one about Katie and Jesse... "She Makes It Easy."

I didn't know he'd be here, or so I told myself. Really, I figured I'd held myself remarkably together to make it out here. To convince Jessa I was just gonna head to the gym to blow off some steam after I took her back to my place and tucked her into bed. She was all tender and exhausted and I'd left her there, when I probably should've just stayed.

I barreled straight up onstage, past a curious Zane, a slightly shocked Elle, and right over to Seth, who barely had time to register what the fuck was happening before I punched him in the face.

I'd only done that twice in my life.

I'd been in a lot of scraps when I was an angry kid with a chip on my shoulder and shit to prove. Had been in a few tussles at some bar or crazy party or another with the band over the years. Mostly in the early years, when we were still young and still had shit to prove.

But only twice in my life had I been pissed off enough to sucker punch a guy right in the fucking nose. Once, when that photographer had his lens up Jessa's skirt.

And right the fuck now.

"You fucking raped Jessa?!" I bellowed in his face.

"*What?*" That was Jesse, somewhere behind me, and there was a bunch of ugly feedback as someone's guitar—maybe all of them— went flying.

"No! Fuck, no!" Seth said, as I slammed him up against the wall of amps, but I wasn't fucking listening as I drove my fist into his face, again and again.

"No? What the fuck do you call it when you make a sixteen-year-old girl suck your cock for drugs?"

I was gone by that point. I felt the hands on me, even as Seth and I grappled for control. He was trying to fight me off and we went down, him half on top of me, and not because he was on the attack— because I was holding onto him. I wasn't fucking letting him go. But I hit something on the way down and then he was gone as someone tore him off.

I was vaguely aware of someone holding my head as a shit storm went off around me.

"I would've killed him," I said, panting. "I really would've killed him."

I wasn't sure if I meant just now or years ago.

"You're not killing anyone." It was Elle. She stroked my hair back from my face. "Just breathe." She was dabbing something against my cheek.

Blood. She was mopping blood off my face.

"Jesus Christ, Maggie, call an ambulance!" I heard her shout over the other voices, but I was fading fast.

Maggie was here? Hadn't even seen her when I walked in.

Tunnel vision.

"Motherfuckerhitme," I said, words slurring together. "Gonnabesick..."

Then I was sick. And seconds after that, I was gone.

CHAPTER THIRTY

Brody

THE NEXT TIME I walked into the church, the setting sun was turning the stained glass window to liquid gold, amber, and scarlet. Candles by the dozens were lit all across the stage on candelabras caked in months' worth of dripped wax.

Jessa and Jesse were there, right where they should be: sitting cross-legged on the edge of the stage, facing each other, bent over their guitars, their heads bowed together as they scribbled in their notebooks.

It'd been days since I'd broken Seth's nose. The rug where we'd both bled—and I'd puked—had been removed, and you'd never know what went down here. And Jessa didn't, exactly. She knew I'd gotten into it with Seth, but I'd spared her the details. Pretty sure everyone else did, too. The truth was, if Jude and Zane and Dylan hadn't been here to tear us apart, and I hadn't hit my head on that amp and gotten a mild concussion, I didn't really know what would've happened.

I'd had no plan when I walked in here other than talking to the band, then confronting Seth. But as soon as I saw him, that plan changed to making Seth Brothers hurt. And once Jesse realized why, he was on board with that line of thought. Not that Jude and the others weren't, but everyone was so shocked by the sudden blood-shed, the situation was diffused pretty fast.

Jessa had spent the last few days telling me, over and again, that Seth never raped her. He'd never forced her, never threatened to stop feeding her drugs if she didn't put out. But her words of reassur-ance did fuck all to calm the ugly black rage festering inside me every time I thought about it.

Yeah; I'd have to get on that anger management thing. Soon.

I headed over to where Maggie was slumped back in a pew, feet up, half-listening to Jessa and Jesse as she worked on her laptop.

"No, no, no, you've got it all wrong," Jesse was saying. "It's 'If you could only be...' and then it's 'dirty like me...' and then the chorus."

"No," Jessa said. "No fucking way. You should've dropped the chorus *after* that first hook, then it's 'If you could see.' You're fucking up the song. It's a *progression* of emotion. You can't have the 'If you could see' before the 'If you could be.' How can you see that you are something if you haven't even been it yet?"

"It's about the other person seeing it in *me*, though."

"No, it's about the singer of the words seeing it in himself."

"So it's not about you, the listener, anyway, it's about me."

"No. You're not getting it."

"What the fuck, Jessa," Jesse grumbled, playing a couple of lines from the chorus. He hummed along irately as Jessa grinned to herself.

"This been going on a while?" I asked Maggie.

"Uh-huh."

"I thought they already wrote 'Dirty Like Me,'" I said, amused. "Ten years ago."

"Uh-huh. They're rearranging it. You know, for shits and giggles." She rolled her eyes. "Artists."

"Perfectionists." I headed up toward the stage. "Quit kicking that horse," I told them as I approached. "It's dead, yeah?"

Jessa looked up at me, smiling. "We're just messing around."

"Yeah. Because my sister informs me that I played it, quote, 'all wrong' on the solo tour."

"You did," she said.

"How was it wrong?"

"I just told you."

"Lyricists," Jesse bitched. "Think you know everything. Learn to tune your guitar properly and we'll talk."

"I know how to tune my guitar."

"Not well enough to hear how that song is supposed to sound."

"I *wrote* that song, jackass."

"You wrote the words, baby. Not the same thing."

"Without which, you all would have no song. No *hit* song, which made you rich and famous."

"She's right," I said. "Hate to tell ya."

"Don't take her side just because she's cute and she knows how to rhyme."

"Ugh. You're such a dick."

Jesse grinned a shit-eating grin.

"Can I have a word?" I asked him.

He untangled himself from his guitar and set it aside. I kissed Jessa on the head and she gave me a sweet smile as Jesse hopped down from the stage. As we headed up the aisle, I could hear her twiddling on her guitar, tuning it.

"We good?" I asked him when we stopped just inside the entrance.

"Yeah," he said. "We're good."

Great. Because the other day, while I was on bullshit post-concussion bedrest and he'd come to my place, ranting and raving about leaving the band if I didn't get rid of Seth, like yesterday, it was definitely *not* good.

"Then we don't need to be looking for *two* new guitar players?"

"Nope."

I stared him down. "You know you own part of Dirty, right? You go, the name probably goes with you." It was true. Jesse left the band, we had all kinds of legal bullshit to deal with, and the other band members would have to fight for the right to use the name... and possibly lose it. If he wanted to be a dick about it, they probably would. He owned a fourth of it, on paper. They split the royalties on everything, but he also wrote a fuck of a lot of the music and could fight for more if he ever wanted to. "Not to mention you write most of the killer shit. So basically, the band is fucked without you."

"I know that."

"Plus, you know, the chicks dig you something fierce. You and all your fucking leather pants."

Jesse grinned that dazzling grin of his, so like his sister's. "Know that, too."

"Good. Don't forget it."

"I'm here, Bro," he said, getting serious. Then he pulled me in for a quick hug.

"Glad to hear it." I slapped his back and released him. "Maggie'll take care of the press. I'll deal with the record company. Zane's gonna do a couple of interviews, deliver a statement we're preparing, and you all can vet it before the lawyers do. Jude's got us covered with everything else. I'm hashing out some ideas with Maggs on how we're gonna find our new rhythm guitarist. You don't need to worry about that. Just keep your focus where it should be—writing a kick-ass album of number one shit with that sister of yours."

"Yeah, boss."

"I mean it. If I don't feel the need to fight, fuck or party 'til I black out, like immediately, when I hear these new songs, you go back at it until I do."

"I can take care of that," Jesse said. Then he gave me a pointed look, complete with raised eyebrow. "If you can take care of my sister."

Well, shit.

I really didn't expect *that* out of his mouth.

"Yeah," I said, tentatively. "Yeah, I can do that. Intend to. She'll let me, that's another story."

Then he did something else I didn't expect. He clapped me on the shoulder and looked at me like he hoped she *would* let me. Actually, he looked a little sorry for me. "She's back, right? Let's keep it that way."

I sighed. "Just tell her to come outside when she's done in here."

Jesse nodded, but he didn't let me go. "I'm gonna give you a little advice you gave me, not so long ago," he said. "You care about her, give her everything you've got."

Fuck me. What an asshole. Using my words against me.

That was exactly what I'd said to him, when Katie almost walked away and he had a panic attack.

He grinned. "Sucks being right all the time, huh, Bro?"

"Don't be a prick."

I went outside and my ass found the stoop around back of the church, where I could be alone until Jessa came. I just hoped I didn't have to wait long. I'd been wanting to have this conversation for days, but this was the first day I'd managed to keep it together enough to get out of bed. I was fucking tired and groggy all the time, and still on painkillers.

Note to self: never hit your head on a fucking amp while a two-hundred-pound dude is on top of you.

How the hell I'd gotten in as many punches as I did before they tore him away? Pure adrenaline. And he didn't fight back. They all told me as much.

Seth didn't hit me. Once.

I hadn't seen him, but I'd heard he was doing fine. Broken nose, and he definitely wasn't looking as pretty as usual, but he'd heal.

The worst of the damage would be the shit no one could see.

Jude had gone to have that talk with him. He'd bring Piper in if he thought it was necessary, but apparently Seth had no interest in pressing charges. He'd asked to speak with me, but I'd denied him.

No interest in talking to him again. Ever.

Dirty had just made him a formal offer and he'd accepted, but it wasn't irreversible. There was a whole lot of shit in that contract that, for the band's protection, stated in plain fucking English that Seth could and would be terminated for any drug-related issues. What "drug-related issues" meant was open for interpretation, and we'd purposely left it wide-the-fuck-open.

I'd say getting our underage lyricist hooked on pills at sixteen, behind all our backs, totally fucking qualified as a breach of that contract. I was also pretty fucking sure our lawyers could argue that point if Seth decided to have a problem with it.

My guess was he wouldn't fight it. If Dirty didn't want him, he really had no legs to stand on to mount any kind of battle. He had no rights in the music like the rest of them did, thank Christ, and like the first time he was dismissed, he'd just crawl away and disappear.

And good fucking riddance.

Now I could get back to doing my job, and doing it right this time. Because it was my job to take care of everyone, look out for them, and I'd totally fucking failed.

I just couldn't believe I hadn't seen it. Had a lot of time in bed these last few days, just laying there, to think it over. And over.

It definitely wasn't overnight, what happened with Jessa after her mom died. It was a gradual change, and everyone saw it. Elle had tried to talk to her about it back then, but got nowhere. Jesse tried too. A lot. He and I had almost come to blows over it, one dark night, a long time ago.

"What the fuck did you do to her?"

"Nothing. I loved her." It was the first and only time I'd admitted that to him, and he didn't look happy about it.

"What happened between you two?"

"Nothing happened."

"Then why won't she talk to you? Why won't she talk to me?"

"I don't fucking know. Don't you think if I knew I'd be doing everything in my power to fix it?"

And I would be. From this day on. Doing every fucking thing in my power.

I opened my eyes to find Jessa's soft shadow melting over the grass toward me. She sat down next to me in the dusk.

"Hi," she said.

"Hey."

She looked at me with that concerned expression she'd been wearing since I came home from the hospital. She brushed my hair gently from my face, fussing over me. I just stared at her—her slim eyebrows pinched together, her full lips slightly puckered, the worry in her brown eyes—as the last rays of the setting sun spun golden light across her face, and I felt that thing I'd always felt when I was close to her.

Wonder.

"How's your head?"

"Better," I said. "Was just resting my eyes."

She frowned.

"I've been thinking—"

"Maybe you shouldn't," she said. "Give that big brain of yours a rest."

I grinned a little, then sighed. "I've been thinking, Jessa, about how all the tactics I've used to be successful in my life... none of them ever worked on you. You know, in business, I get the biggest bone for being a bulldog."

She smiled.

"With you, I had to take a different approach, but I was always fucking it up. I want you to know I'm sorry for that. And I want to be crystal fucking clear that I never wanted you to leave. If I'd known what to do to make you stay, whatever it was, I would've done it. I would've done anything."

"I know that, Brody."

"The other night, when I said I don't care who you get to manage you? That was a lie."

She smiled again.

"Figured I should come clean about that. I don't want anyone else managing you because I'd be jealous of them. I've always been jealous of anyone who gets to be what I want to be in your life.

That's why I've always hated your modeling work. Why I always tried to butt my nose in where it didn't belong when it came to your career. I just wanted that part of you, if I couldn't have anything else."

"I know," she said softly.

"And while I'm being honest, the reason I wanted it was because I thought if I had that part of you, maybe eventually, I'd get the rest."

"I know that, too," she said.

A comfortable silence fell between us for a while, and she rested her head on my shoulder. But I wasn't done yet.

"I've been struggling, Jessa," I confessed. "Maybe you can help me, with figuring out how to see it the way you do. Without... hating him. I'll never be able to forgive what he did to you—"

"He didn't really do anything to me, Brody. I just—"

"I *can't*," I said, cutting her off. She looked up at me, but she didn't argue. "But... I can't regret everything, either, and it's fucking with my head. It's hard to look back and wish it all away. Wish Seth had never come along. If he didn't... maybe Dirty would never have become what they are. Maybe Jesse never would've met Katie, they wouldn't have gotten married, and you never would've come back to me."

"Maybe I never would've run in the first place."

"Yeah. That's the part that's really killing me."

We were silent again, this time a little less comfortably.

"You know we wrote 'Dirty Like Me' together," Jessa said. "Seth and Jesse and me. But you probably didn't know that me and Seth were barely speaking when we wrote it."

"I didn't know that."

"Yeah." She sighed softly. "I'd jam with Jesse and we'd write, then Seth would come up with the melodies, better melodies. All that beautiful, haunting, killer shit that hooks you, sucks you in and doesn't let go... that's all Seth. I didn't come up with the best of the lyrics until I heard the music he wrote. You know, it was usually that way. I wanted him off that song, at first, but even I couldn't deny he made it magic. He made everything magic back then." She glanced away, then her brown eyes found mine again. "Musically, I mean. So, no, I can't regret that either."

"Your lyrics make it magic, Jessa."

I meant that. The song worked for many reasons, but she was right. Without her words, it wouldn't be what it was.

Then something occurred to me...

"That song's about him? About... how you felt after what happened between the two of you?"

"No," she said. "It's about you. How I felt about you."

Oh.

Shit.

I tried to digest that. To think through the words of the song and what that meant... and I was overcome.

"You felt... dirty? For wanting to be with me?"

"No. And yes." She sighed again, nibbling on her lip. "The best I can describe it is like this. The more I wanted you, all the guilt over what was happening with Seth, with the drugs, all the lies... the secrets and the hiding... it ate me up. That's when I started really distancing myself from you. And spending more time with him. And later, when I started distancing myself from him, too, that's when we wrote the song. But I never should've gone down that road with him, even though it gave us that song. I've known that all along. I knew it then. I still did it."

"You loved him," I managed to say, looking at the concrete between my feet. "There's no guilt in that, Jessa." I meant that, too.

"Yeah," she breathed. "I loved him. As a friend."

She fell silent and I looked at her.

"I used to think about you. When he and I..." She trailed off, looking away. "But then... it just made me feel dirtier than I already did. Like I was betraying him, too. And most of all, I knew I was betraying myself." She glanced at me. "I thought if you saw the real me... what I'd become... everything I'd done... you wouldn't like me anymore. You wouldn't keep me on that damn pedestal you had me on. You wouldn't even be able to stand me. And I couldn't stand that. So..." She swallowed. "I ran. I ran from everything that hurt, and in turn, I just got... numb. I couldn't feel much of anything without you there to remind me I was still alive." She looked right in my eyes, hers shining with tears in the dusk. "That's why I couldn't just block your number and completely lose you. Those messages you sent kept me alive, Brody."

I took her hand in mine, but she looked down at the grass and her hair fell over her face. I knew this was a lot for her to open up about. And even if she was finally ready, it had to be really fucking hard.

"Did I ever tell you about my dad?" I asked her, knowing fully fucking well I hadn't. I'd never told anyone that shit. "About how he hit me?"

"No." She looked up at me and shifted closer, letting her leg press against mine like she instinctively wanted to comfort me. "You never told me that."

"Yeah. It started before I met you. When I was small, and it went on for years. Until I was big enough to hit back." I cracked my knuckles, remembering. "He would hit me in the chest, or the back, or the stomach. Places no one would know but me, places they wouldn't see at school. And I never told anyone. So it became this humiliating secret. He told me if I told anyone, I was a pussy. He told me that when I was seven years old, and I believed him. I believed him for a long time, Jessa. The thing is, I don't believe him anymore." I squeezed her hand. "We all have shit we're not proud of. I never would've judged you for what you went through."

"Brody..." she said softly. "I never knew."

"You remember that pin I gave you?" No stopping now; just tear that rotten bandage off, for good. "The one from the Sinners?"

She nodded.

"They recruited me. When I was twelve."

"Oh, Brody..."

"Yeah. There was this guy I'd see at the 7-Eleven by my school—the private school I went to before your school. He rode a Harley and he was all kinds of cool. At least, he seemed to be, to me. He was so tough, you could see how people just stepped the hell out of his way when he walked into the store. I wanted that. I wanted to not be scared anymore. He could see that, I guess. Or he saw something. I don't know." I looked at her; made sure she was really listening to this shit.

She was hanging on my every word, her big brown eyes locked on mine.

"He got me dealing drugs on the playground. I was just a kid, you know, twelve, thirteen. And he'd have me hand out freebies to the other kids. Try to lure them in so they'd want more, spend their parents' money. I did it for about a year before I got caught. I was lucky my dad's lawyers saved me on that one. But I have to carry that shit, every day. That because of my stupidity, some poor kid might've ended up a junkie."

Jessa squeezed my hand, tight. "You were just a kid, Brody. He took advantage of you. He used your vulnerability. That doesn't make you bad."

"Yeah. Well. If you feel dirty for what you've been through, sweetheart, believe me, I feel fucking filthy. And you should know by now that I never expected you to be perfect. I loved you, Jessa. You. Not what you thought you were supposed to be."

She sniffed a little, fighting back tears. "You should've told me. About your dad. About all of it."

"You should've told me about the drugs. About what was going on with Seth. Or told Jesse. Or Elle. Somebody. We would've helped you. We're your team. Don't you know that by now?"

"Yes," she said. "I do. I know it now. But I was so afraid back then... I would've rather you love that girl I really wasn't than never love me at all." She shook her head sadly. "Why didn't you tell us about your dad? Didn't you think we'd believe you?"

I took her face in my hands and looked her right in the eye. "We would've believed you, Jessa."

"I didn't know. I just didn't know which way it would go."

"With you," I told her, letting my thumb caress her cheek. "We would've had your back. And things would've been so different if we'd known. A lot of things would've been different..."

She closed her eyes for a moment as I caressed her cheek.

"Do you remember that day we first met?" she asked softly. "On the playground, when you saved me from those bullies?"

I snorted. "Way I remember it, you would've been just fine without me, princess. For a snot-nosed five-year-old, you sure had all the answers."

She narrowed her eyes at me. "I was eight. And maybe that was the problem, that I thought I had the answers. Sometimes I still feel like that lonely little girl, you know? Trying to carry the weight of the world on my skinny shoulders, not even realizing I don't have to, just trying so hard to save myself and drowning. And I know it's taken me too many years, but I've finally realized I can't do it alone."

"You don't have to," I said. I let my hands drop from her face and put my arm around her. "Come here," I said, tucking her into my side. She snuggled into me, wrapping her arms around my waist.

"You know," she whispered into the growing dark, her voice small, like she was sharing some terrible secret, "I've always been afraid of people leaving me? That's why I leave them first."

There was a silence as I took a breath.

"Because your dad left you."

"Yeah," she whispered. "Twice. He left when Mom was pregnant with me. That's why she let Jesse name me. Then he came back to us. And then... he left again. Forever."

Yeah. I knew that. And it'd definitely never been lost on me how much her dad leaving—twice—had fucked Jessa up.

"You know, Jessa, you told me the other night that you thought you had to be perfect to deserve love, when you were a kid. But maybe you've never stopped thinking that; that if you could just be good enough, perfect enough, no one else would ever leave you, hurt you like that, like your dad did, again."

Jessa peered up at me. "How is it that you know me better than I know myself?"

"Because I love you." I kissed her forehead. "Except it doesn't work like that, does it? Trying to be perfect doesn't make people stay."

"No," she said.

"Because then your mom died."

"Yes."

"It doesn't work like that because no one's perfect, Jessa. And no matter how flawless you try to be, you can't stop people from leaving you. Isn't it fucking freeing to finally accept that?"

"I guess I'll let you know, when I get to accepting it."

"Babe, when you love someone, when you really love them... you already have."

She took that in and I could see her trying to swallow it. I knew she had to, because I knew, about this, I was right.

She couldn't truly love me, or anyone else, if she was terrified the whole time they were gonna walk out the door. Which was why I had to stop being afraid she was gonna run away again. Because I did love her.

I loved her with everything I had.

"And by the way, there is no fucking way I'm gonna let you sit here and even try to tell me you don't see my flaws, because that's some straight-up bullshit, babe. And if you can still stand me with all my scars, maybe you can cut yourself some slack."

She smiled at me, and I knew I was right on this point, too. Because I was far from perfect, and she had never expected me to be. It was probably all the weird little idiosyncrasies that made me *me* that she liked about me anyway.

I knew I loved all those things about her. Stubborn, dorky, scared as shit, I didn't care. I loved her.

"You are ridiculously bossy," she conceded. "And crazy over-protective. And I still tolerate you. Putting me on the pill, for example, while embarrassing and perhaps a tad premature, probably did me a real solid. So I guess I owe you a thanks for that."

"I didn't put you on the pill," I said. "Your brother did."

"Right. And that had nothing at all to do with you and your giant black eye."

I grinned. "You remember that night? You told me I should stop smoking. You can be bossy yourself, you know that?"

"I remember. A girl never forgets the night the man of her dreams brings her tampons." She looked up at me, and I looked right back at her. And yeah, she'd just said that. *The man of her dreams.*

"I never had another cigarette after that one," I confessed. "Bet you didn't know that."

"Never?"

"Never." I took her chin and drew her face close to mine. "I have loved you forever, Jessa Mayes. Pretty sure I was fucking born to love you. I know you didn't really believe me when I said so, or maybe you just didn't want to... but I *would've* waited for you forever."

"Say it," I murmured into her sweet-smelling skin, kissing her neck as I held her down. And yes, I was being bossy. I did not give one fuck. "I want to hear you say it, princess."

"Say what?" she mumbled sleepily. "What is it you want from me now? Didn't I already meet all your demands?" Her hand crept down to my bare ass and squeezed.

"I want you," I said, kissing my way up her throat as I maneuvered between her thighs. "To stay. Here."

"Right here?" she asked, wiggling beneath me.

"Here," I said, thrusting slowly inside her. "In my home... in my bed... where you belong."

"Sounds very... caveman," she said as she took me, her breaths slowing, deepening.

I did my best cavemen grunt as I moved, sliding out, then in again. "Give me... more... pussy."

Jessa laughed and slapped my ass. "Stop it!"

"Mmm." I ground into her and her laughter melted away, replaced with a groan.

"*Brody...*"

"I'm serious." I slowed my thrusts and pressed my forehead to hers. "I don't go on the road much anymore, and when I do, you can come with me. Or you can stay right here, in my bed, waiting for me."

"Sounds fun."

"You can write, and you can still model, if you decide you want to..." I almost lost my train of thought as she moved her hips against me, urging me on. "You can do... whatever you wanna do."

"Well, thank you for your permission."

"You don't need my permission. And don't be a smart-ass." I kissed her, whispering, "I'm not telling you to change your life for me, Jessa. I'm asking you to finally share it with me."

CHAPTER THIRTY-ONE

Jessa

"YOU'RE OUT OF BOURBON!" I called up the stairs. "That shit will not fly with my brother, you know!"

"On it!" Brody called back to me from the kitchen.

I grinned to myself as he no doubt texted Maggie to pick some up; she was out getting booze and extra food for the party.

I turned to take a good look around Brody's party room, like I had so many times in my life. Nothing had really changed. The same couches, the same ottomans and cushions on the floor. Maybe some updated equipment—the small amps against the wall, the guitars on stands and strewn on the couches. The vintage arcades lining the far wall—the Ms. Pac-Man was definitely new. But the pool table and the big, mounted posters on the walls—Led Zeppelin, Pink Floyd, The Doors—were all the same. The wall of glass doors that opened right onto the backyard. Beyond, the killer view of Vancouver spread out below, sparkling in the dark, and the deeper dark of the water that surrounded it.

I *loved* this place.

Brody'd said he wanted this to be my safe place... and it totally was. It always had been.

I picked up the big bouquet of flowers he'd bought me while we walked around Granville Island Market this afternoon; we could have a rock 'n' roll party with beautiful flowers, right? We were grown-ups. And if Zane somehow destroyed them—a definite possibility—he'd just have to buy me new ones.

As I was arranging the lilies into a vase, Elle showed up. She scanned me, head-to-toe, with a slight grin. "Nice shirt."

"Thanks." I beamed at her. "You might say I'm a fan." It was a Dirty T-shirt with the sleeves cut off. It had a picture of the band on it, and though it was from only five years ago, they looked so much younger; the guys all with longer hair, and Elle with her sweet face.

"You look... happy," she said, cocking her head as she examined me.

"Yeah." I was trying not to smile so much, but I couldn't seem to come down off this high I was on. Me and Brody. Everything out in the open... and me and Brody.

Together.

Then I noticed she *didn't* look happy. "Listen... I wanted to talk to you, Jessa."

This sounded serious, so I left the flowers and gave her my full attention, letting her draw me over to a couch.

"I just... I feel somehow... responsible," she said as we sat down. "For what happened. You know... you and Seth." Her steel-gray eyes held mine. "I just can't stop thinking that I should've seen what was going on. You know, I was the girl in the group. I should've looked out for you."

I squeezed her hand, moved that she felt so much, and sorry that she felt like what happened was in any way her fault. "You did look out for me," I said, smiling reassuringly. "Remember, you used to tell everyone at shows I was your sister so they'd give me beer?"

"That's true."

"Believe me, back then, all I really wanted was a beer and to be treated like a grown-up. And to be one of you. To be just like you, really. To have the kind of respect you had from the guys. You were this kick-ass bass player; their peer. And I was... the kid." I shrugged. "You were pretty much my hero back then. You and Stevie Nicks. You're still one of my heroes."

"Thanks, Jessa." Elle sighed. "Seriously, though. I'm sad. I'm just so sad about all of it."

"I know."

I pulled her in for a hug, amazed that it was me who'd be comforting her at the end of all this—and truly humbled that I had the opportunity. That I could be here for her. That my friends cared so much, and that for once, I could be the strong one. Because as Elle wrapped her arms around me, I could feel the sadness in her.

Elle had cared about Seth, once upon a time. A lot of people had. Seth was special; we all knew it, from that very first day Zane brought him home to jam with us.

I wasn't the only reason everyone was sad about everything that had gone down. I knew that. And I understood it, deeply.

I was sad about losing Seth, too. I always had been.

It wasn't my choice that he go, either. I'd given him his chance to speak up for himself. He hadn't. He didn't say a word to anyone in his own defense. From what I knew, Jude had told him he was in breach of his contract—which I still didn't quite understand—and he just left.

That kind of made me saddest of all. That he didn't even fight.

But Maggie had told me that just proved he wasn't right for the band. And maybe everyone else agreed with that.

"Well... if it isn't two of my favorite girls."

I heard my brother's voice and looked up to find him standing at the bottom of the stairs, watching us.

Elle drew away, discreetly wiping a tear from her eye. Then she put on a smile, turned to my brother, and said, "Jessa and I were just discussing Stevie Nicks."

"Yep," I said, smiling.

"She thinks you and I should do a duet, a cover of 'Leather and Lace,' on the new album," she told Jesse as she walked past him.

"Uh..."

Elle grinned at me over his shoulder, then disappeared up the stairs. My brother looked at me and his eyebrow went up. "'Leather and Lace'?"

"It's a great song."

"Sure. Not Dirty's style, though, so I'm gonna assume you're full of shit." He crossed the room and dropped down on the couch next to me. "What were you two really talking about?"

"Just girl stuff."

"Uh-huh." He studied me a moment.

"Where's Katie?"

"Upstairs," he said, sprawling back on the couch. "Helping Brody out. He's prepping like a thousand burgers for the barbecue."

I just grinned. My man was good like that. He'd always loved playing host, having all his friends, everyone he cared about, together under one roof; under his wing. Looking out for everyone. Keeping us fed and happy.

I lay back on the couch next to my brother, tossing my feet up on the ottoman.

"I saw you, at the wedding," he said. "Talking to Elle. You were worried about her, about how she was doing. You've always had such compassion for everyone else's feelings, instead of dealing with your own, you know that?"

It was my turn to raise an eyebrow at him. "You saw that? While you were having your first dance with your bride?"

"Hey, I see things. I care. I care about Elle. You know I do. But anyway... I wasn't watching her. I was watching you."

"Afraid I was going to dive off the deck and swim away?"

"Possibly."

"I know it may be hard for you to trust me on this," I told him, "but I'm done with running away. I've had a bit of a revelation, thanks to Maggie and Brody. You know, talking things out with friends."

"Yeah?"

"Yeah. Turns out... I'm a bit of a perfectionist."

"You don't say." He didn't sound surprised at all. Not that I really expected him to be.

"I do say. And it's been kind of... damaging. I've been hard on myself, I guess. That's what everyone seems to think."

"What do you think?"

"That I'm tired of trying to be perfect. I'm going to try just wallowing about in mediocrity a while, see how that feels."

He laughed. "Good luck with that. Nothing mediocre about you, sis."

I shrugged, not really sure if he was serious or putting me on. "Thanks, I guess."

"You want," he said, "I'd be happy to dispel any notion you might have in your head that you're perfect, right now. For example, you have that weird thing about lids. Like you never put them on properly before you put stuff back in the fridge."

I rolled my eyes. "That does sound imperfect of me."

"And you're always putting the milk back with a teeny tiny dribble left. Just drink it, for fuck's sake."

"It's the perfect amount for tea!"

"I don't drink tea."

"Well, some of us do."

"And you leave your used tea bags all over the fucking counter."

"Because I like to reuse them."

"And you leave your dirty mugs all over the place without a coaster."

I laughed. "Shit. The big bad rock star wants me to use a coaster? Geez, I'm so sorry."

"When you leave ring stains on my furniture, I do."

"That was *once*, because *you* knocked into it and it spilled over. Totally your fault."

"*And* you tend to blame me for shit I didn't do. That was Max, not me."

"So blame the dog!"

"And you don't take criticism well."

"Are you done yet?"

"Nope." He grinned his big, dazzling grin, the one that made women—who weren't related to him—swoon. "Could go on like this for days."

"That grin doesn't work on me, so let's just skip to the end. I get your point."

"And you're always changing the subject when people tell you things you don't want to hear."

"Okay. You can stop now."

"What? I skipped to the end. That was the last one." I didn't believe that for a second, but he just nudged my left ankle with his foot; the one where I had the angel tattoo. "Remember when we got those?"

"Yeah." How could I ever forget? "After Mom died." I frowned at him a little. "Took us like two years to do it, though, since you were chicken."

"Since I wanted to make sure we got something cool and you didn't make us get matching pink unicorns or some shit."

I rolled my eyes. The tattoos *were* cool, and yes, they were my idea, but luckily he'd agreed to them.

"It was his shirt, wasn't it?" he asked. "That Zeppelin shirt of Brody's you always wear. That's where you got the idea to do the angels."

I just blinked at him, a little surprised he'd figured that out. The angel on our tattoos looked nothing like the image on the shirt.

He shrugged. "I told you, I see things. I care."

"I know you do."

He was silent a moment, just looking at me. Then he said, "It's always been Brody for you, huh?"

I swallowed. This wasn't something Jesse and I had ever discussed. I knew he had some idea back then, and maybe all along the way, that there was something between us. I was pretty sure he figured maybe I had some hopeless crush on Brody. But he'd never asked and I'd never told.

"Yes," I said.

He seemed to process that.

"It's you for him, too," he said, and it wasn't a question.

I just nodded.

"Well, for me it's Katie. And knowing she's mine... I can't tell you how that feels. How... right it is."

"I know," I said. "I see that."

"Then, if he's the one for you... what the hell are you waiting for? Mom and Dad are long gone, and I'm officially giving you permission to be happy, little sister."

I could feel my eyes tearing up, the little prickle inside, but I blinked the wetness back. "Oh, well. If you're giving me permission..."

He grinned, but we were interrupted then, as Zane, Dylan and Ash burst into the room with some friends, carrying enough booze to entertain a small army on leave, followed by Maggie and Elle. Zane immediately appointed himself DJ, cranking Thin Lizzy through the sound system, and the party officially got underway.

Dylan introduced me to his buddies, then I got caught up talking with Elle and Ash, and gradually the party room filled around us.

It was just like old times, but better—because I wasn't suffering in silent guilt, longing for Brody from afar... watching him across the room throwing me angry, hurt looks... wanting so badly to talk to him and just not knowing *how*.

This... this was so much better.

While I chatted with Katie and her friend Devi, I did watch Brody across the room. Mingling, talking and laughing, looking happy. Maggie was right. He did smile around the guys. A lot. But when he looked over at me, which he also did a lot, he didn't stop. He just smiled bigger.

And eventually, once everyone had drinks and burgers, then more drinks, and he was satisfied that his job had been done, he came over to me and took my hand.

"Come with me," he said, leaning in close to kiss my neck. "I want to show you something."

CHAPTER THIRTY-TWO

Jessa

BRODY LED ME UPSTAIRS, to the second floor. To the room at the very end of the hall—and when we stepped inside, I had to do a double-take.

Unlike the rest of Brody's house, which was clean and modern, but with woodsy, manly touches—big, solid slabs of wood and stone, interspersed with glass and clean white walls—this room was soft, warm, cozy, and undeniably feminine. But what really caught my eye was the music gear.

There was a Fender Stratocaster in a light coral color on a stand, next to my acoustic guitar. There was a small amp, a mic on a stand, and other equipment stacked in a couple of hard travel cases—also coral, with metal studs on them.

Then I noticed the big window seats along the bay windows, cushioned in velvety coral pillows... and the sofa and a couple of cushy ottomans clustered in one corner—also coral. My favorite color.

The walls were painted a soft cream. A very girlie chandelier sparkled in the center of the room.

On the antique desk, my laptop sat on a stand next to a bouquet of roses in a crystal vase—movie star roses; big, beautiful roses in a coral color... my absolute favorite flower.

There was a beautiful silver tea tray with a matching tea pot and a couple of antique tea cups on saucers, with an assortment of teas. There were colorful spiral-bound notebooks stacked alongside the computer. A rainbow of gel pens were arranged in a ridiculous mug my brother had made for me at school, when he was a little boy and I was probably still in diapers, that said *#1 Sister* on it.

There were other mementos around the room, too. Framed photos on the walls of my family; my mom and my dad and my grandparents, me and Jesse as kids, Grandma Dolly, and me and the band jamming when we were young.

Seth was in none of them, which I was both relieved and a little sad to see.

I perused the small library, a bookshelf on one wall filled with books about music—writing reference books and biographies of great songwriters, from David Bowie to Bob Dylan to Billie Holiday.

I spun around, just taking it all in.

"What is this?" I asked, my voice choked up with wonder. I knew what it was. It was a songwriting room, filled with lovely things, chosen with care, just for me. Things that I would love, and everything I could ever need to find solace and let my creativity flow.

"It's a place of your own, to do the thing you've always wanted to do," Brody said. He took my hands in his. "Maybe I'm taking the lyrics of that song you wrote about Katie and Jesse too literally, you know, about sliding into home?" His lips quirked. "And making space for someone when you love them. But I wanted you to know I'd make room for you."

"You did all of this? For me? Because of that song?" I was kind of in shock. I knew Brody could be sweet... but this?

"Maggie and Jesse might've helped out with some of it," he confessed. "But yes. It's for you, princess." He pulled me to him, wrapping his arms around my waist. "You like it?"

"Brody... *yes*," I breathed. "But... I mean... what if I fuck it up?"

He frowned.

"I know it sounds stupid," I said. "But I promised you I'd be honest." I put my hands on his arms and held on tight. I was holding on now with everything I had; I had to, to resist the urge to pull away. To run. Because I wasn't fucking doing that anymore, no matter how scared I felt. "And honestly, Brody, I'm scared. I'm scared to put everything into this and fail."

"Of course you're scared to fail." He smoothed a lock of hair out of my face, gently. "Because you want it so much. But failure is impossible, Jessa."

"How do you know that?" I asked, incredulous. "I wrote those lyrics for *Love Struck* when I was just a kid. I mean, literally a kid. The band, they were kind of kids too, barely twenty-two, twenty-three when they made it big. But I was *sixteen* when I wrote those words. I had no idea what I was doing. The beauty of that was there were no expectations of me, and I wasn't worried about what anyone would think. I just wrote. And you might not think so, but I paid attention to what went on after I left the band, Brody. I've seen the balance on my trust account; all the royalties I make from the songs. I know *Love Struck* is sitting up there on the list of top debut albums *ever*, right alongside albums I grew up listening to. That is *fucked up*." I took a steadying breath. "What if I commit to writing with the band now, on the new album, and everyone has these expectations that we're going to do another *Love Struck*, and it flops?"

"Shit. Is Jessa Mayes talking shop with me?"

I rolled my eyes. "So?"

"Are you really asking me for career advice?"

"Maybe." I chewed my lip. "Just a bit."

"This has to be the first time I can ever remember you asking me for my thoughts on your career or your talent."

"Yeah, well, you've given me plenty."

"Sure. But you've never asked. You've never really listened, either."

"So tell me," I said softly. "I'm listening."

"Alright," he said. "The truth is, no album Dirty has *ever* put out since *Love Struck* has done as well. But we're not exactly suffering. We've got hits on every album. None of them touched the success of

'Dirty Like Me,' but they don't have to. That song is a thing of its own. And the market is different now. The focus is more on single songs than the albums. We can't expect to touch the kind of album sales we could even five years ago. Worst case, with or without your involvement, the band cuts another album that, overall, ranks up there with everything they've done since *Love Struck*. Dirty isn't gonna shit the bed, no matter how much they've been struggling with writing this new album. I know that in my gut, in my fucking bones, Jessa." He gave me a squeeze. "You know what else I know in my bones?"

"What?"

"You belong with us. You belong writing songs with Dirty." His blue eyes scanned my face, softening. "Every great artist has doubts about their talent sometimes, Jessa. But what you did as a sixteen-year-old girl, unfiltered, uncensored, and without overthinking it, was magic. And sweetheart, I know you're a great model. You're fucking gorgeous. Sometimes I look at you, and it's like I'm... I don't know... looking at a dream." He shook his head, like he couldn't believe he'd said that. "Was that cheesy as fuck?"

"Let's just say you'll never make a living as a lyricist," I teased.

"Right. Well, my point being, you've been extremely successful as a model. I know it. You're beautiful. Like the kind of special beautiful they don't even have words for. Or at least, I don't. But I will tell you this. You're a better writer than you are a model."

"Shit, Brody," I said, wrapping my arms around his neck and molding my body to his. "You *do* love me."

"Jesus," he murmured against my lips, "she's a little slow on the uptake, yeah?"

I smiled and he kissed me, slow and deep. I melted right into that kiss, into the taste of him, as his warmth enveloped me. As always, I got the feeling he was claiming me with his kiss; that I was his. Always would be... always had been.

"You still haven't told me," he murmured against my lips.

"Told you what?"

"What I wanna hear."

"And what do you want to hear?"

"Move in with me," he said between kisses. "I want you here. Need you here... always."

I held him tighter, pushing back against the reactive fear. "What happens if I say yes?" I whispered.

Because I really, really wanted to say yes.

"We celebrate," he said, walking me backwards across the room, "by breaking in your new furniture." Then he laid me down on the couch, laying himself right on top of me. I loved the feel of him; his weight crushing me, forcing out everything else, even the breath from my lungs... everything but him. His strength, his warmth, his manly-woodsy smell. "Then we go back downstairs and call it a moving-in party, yeah?"

"Yeah. I like the sound of that."

He did too, apparently, because he had my jeans off in record time. "Jesus, you still wearing panties, princess? When are we gonna break you of this habit?"

I laughed and squealed a weak protest as he tore them off. I stopped laughing as he kissed his way up my thigh, wrapped my legs around his hips and smoothed the head of his cock against my pussy. I writhed in response, wrapping my arms around his neck.

"You sure about this?" I asked him as he filled me, gasping as I adjusted to the sensation—the fullness and the slight shock of it, followed by that familiar rush of heat and pure pleasure.

"What? Why?" His eyes found mine, a little dazed as the pleasure took him over, too.

"I own a *lot* of clothes."

"Okay," he breathed, but I was pretty sure his brain had left the building as he started screwing me slowly against the couch.

"We'll have to ship them up from my place in New York," I said as he kissed his way down my neck, and my body flooded in a wave of sensation... a tingling, buzzing warmth that shot to the tips of my nipples, the tips of my toes.

No man had ever made me feel like this. This alive...

This loved.

"No problem," he said, losing himself in kisses on my skin as he shoved up my shirt and yanked my bra askew. "You smell like heaven..."

"And I have some stuff down in L.A. that I'll need to get..."

He flickered his tongue over my grateful nipple and I momentarily forgot what I was saying. I arched beneath him, strung tight, wanting more.

"Cool..." he mumbled. "Jesus, you taste like sex..."

"And... over at my brother's."

"Uh-huh."

"And Roni's."

"Great," he said, kissing his way back up to my mouth.

"And I still have some stuff in storage at Dolly's."

His eyes caught mine. "Don't make me regret this, princess."

I laughed. Then I caught his lip with my teeth and wrapped my legs higher around his waist, urging him deeper. He groaned as he sank into me, settling his weight between my thighs.

"I won't," I said. "I promise." I lapped my tongue against his, making him moan. "Now fuck me," I whispered, "and make it good, so we can get back to our guests."

I stood outside, in the dark, just beyond the light thrown out the windows from the party room. I listened to the rhythm of the party within, the happy voices of my friends and family, as I gazed out over the city.

My city.

Here, just taking a momentary breath on the edge of it all, I felt right where I belonged.

A part of it all, but separate. In my own skin, my own space. Finding my way... but I no longer had to do it alone.

When I was a kid, I'd found music. And through music, I'd found a way to love myself. Over the years that love had faltered, but I was healing now, and finding my way back to me again.

I knew it wasn't going to be an easy road. Like Elle had often told me, hearts need time to heal.

I knew everyone was thrilled to have me back, but they'd also lost Seth, again, and it hurt. I knew it did, even if they'd spare me the sight of it. They'd feel it, when they thought I wasn't looking.

And there was still a void there. Seth Brothers had left big shoes to fill, and everyone in and around the band—Brody included—seemed to feel it was time they get filled, for good. I didn't envy them in that process. Seth had mad talent; that was never in question.

I just hoped they could find the right man or woman for the job. Soon. So we could all move forward.

The music and voices swelled as a door opened behind me. I turned to find Brody standing on the patio.

"You okay?"

He was worried; I knew he was. Still worried I'd start to pull away, even while I was standing right here. So when he came to me and put his arms around me, I leaned into his embrace. "I'm great. Just taking it all in, you know?"

"Good," he said, kissing my neck.

"Just thinking about my new room. I love it, Brody."

His arms tightened around me.

"You took a risk decorating it, you know," I teased. "What if I'd said no?"

"Then I'd turn it into a crash pad for Jesse, for when Katie kicks his ass out."

I snickered. "Bet he'd love the chandelier and pink furniture." I turned in his arms and looked through the window. I could see Jesse and Katie. He had his arm around her waist and he was listening, with a big, dumb grin on his face, as she told Dylan and Ash some story, her cheeks pink with excitement. "But she's never kicking him out."

"That's good," Brody said, turning my chin until our noses touched, his face tipped down to mine. "Because the room is yours." He kissed me then, sweetly, his lips lingering as he breathed me in.

"The house is yours," he said. "Everything I've got is yours." He drew back just enough to lock his blue eyes with mine, his eyebrows furled. "Don't leave me again, Jessa. I know I said I'd wait, but I can't really stand forever without you."

My throat got a little tight as I swallowed. Forever without Brody?

No fucking way.

"I'm not going anywhere, Brody."

Then I told him the words he'd been waiting to hear... the words I should've had the courage to say to him, so many years ago. "I'm home."

EPILOGUE

Seth

Six months later...

"YOU KNOW Dirty's looking for a new guitarist?"

Mark slid onto the barstool next to me with his phone in his hand, and my chest burned a little at his words; that creepy heartburn feeling I got whenever I heard mention of Dirty.

Davey, sitting on my other side, leaned over to look at the phone. "Fuckin' news site," he grunted. "You know they've got porn on the 'net, right?"

Trent cackled, stomping up behind us in his cowboy boots. "Yeah. We're gettin' real tired of all the videos of your old lady though. Seen 'em all."

Big Jake, behind the bar, ripped the phone from Mark's hand. "Who needs porn when you've got this." He touched the screen, spreading his fingers to enlarge an image.

"Hey, Big J," Trent said, knocking on the bar, "gimme the usual."

The bar had shut down for the night, customers cleared out and it was now just the four of us, sweaty and spent from a long night of playing music under the lights, and Big J, cleaning up. Everyone was drinking but me. And Trent, because he didn't have his beer yet. But Big J was too transfixed by Mark's phone to pull beers.

"Whadya say, Becks?" Mark asked me, and I felt all eyes converge on me. "You see yourself in the big time?"

No, I did not see myself in the big time. Or at least, Todd Becker didn't.

Seth Brothers had temporarily retired, and Todd Becker was now in the house; I'd appropriated the name from my dead father, just a regular name for a regular Joe. Though my parents were far from regular.

It wasn't forever, but it was for now and it suited me fine. Todd Becker didn't have to deal with lawyers and paparazzi and accusing stares wherever the fuck he went. Todd Becker was nobody. He played in a dive bar down south for shit pay, but no one really knew who he was or where he came from.

Which meant I could be left alone to do what I loved—play guitar.

As long as I kept my beard grown in like a thicket and my hat pulled low, no one gave a shit who I was. No one cared who any of us were so long as we showed up to the gig and played what was expected, which was CCR covers. So long as we knew "Born on the Bayou" and "Proud Mary" and "Bad Moon Rising," we were fucking golden. Around here, I was just the quiet dude who played guitar and slept in one of the tiny rented rooms above the kitchen, and perpetually smelled of barbecue because of it.

"What is it?" Davey leaned over the bar, angling for a look at the phone again and scanning the article. "One of those stupid reality shows?"

"Documentary series, whatever the fuck that means," said Big J. "They're filming the auditions."

"Gettin' thirsty here, J," Trent complained, still waiting on that beer.

"You're good enough, Becks," Mark said. "You should do it."

"Yeah. To hell with the guitarist position, though," said Big J. "They don't hire you, just take Elle to bed. I'll never get the fuckin' chance."

Trent, impatient, headed behind the bar to pull himself a beer.

I sipped my water. My heart was beating steady and slow, but hard, as I asked, "Rhythm or lead?"

Davey burst out laughing. "Jesus, you're cocky, you think you can fill Jesse Mayes' boots."

"I'd like to fill his ex-girlfriend," Big J mumbled, still thumbing through the article and drooling over Elle.

"You know, I met her once, in an elevator," Davey said, settling back on his stool. "'Bout five, six years ago, when I was playing out in L.A.. She's prettier in person."

"You didn't fuckin' meet her," Mark said.

"I *saw* her," Davey clarified.

"Dirty?" Trent snorted, pulling up a stool and taking a grateful swig of his beer. "The fuck is that? You wanna go play with punks?" Trent was a hillbilly, so in his mind Dirty was punk, Zeppelin was glam, Nirvana was noise, and all of it was trash. He only tolerated CCR because it paid the bills around here.

"Dirty's not punk," Mark said, then elbowed me, waiting on some kind of reaction. "You should try out, at least."

"Yeah," Davey said, "if they come 'round here."

Big J was shaking his head. "Says they start this week in Vancouver, finish in L.A.. Not comin' near here." He handed me the phone and I took it.

What the *fuck*.

I did my best to look totally unmoved as I scrolled through the article, my heart battering in my chest. But I couldn't fucking believe it.

At the top, there was a photo of Dirty, obviously recent. It was Zane, Elle, Jesse and Dylan. And yeah, Elle looked gorgeous. As always.

No Jessa in the picture, though.

I knew they'd asked Jessa to join the lineup, before they asked me. I knew she'd been writing with the band. I'd assumed she was filling the role, permanently, and I could live with that. It made sense.

But a fucking open audition? A documentary series? What were they, desperate or something?

Or was this some kind of publicity stunt?

If it was, kind of felt like it was tailor-made to slay me.

I'd accepted being asked to leave. Again. At least, I'd swallowed it as well as I could. I could step back and wish them well and not begrudge them a thing—mostly—if what they truly wanted was Paulie or Jessa or Ash instead of me.

But some random stranger, some nobody joining Dirty?

If it was wide-fucking-open, anyone had a shot at it. *Anyone.*

Even Todd Becker.

And that got me thinking...

Last time, I didn't fight for it when I had the chance; when Jessa gave me that chance. And that shit had been eating me raw for the last six months. I'd lost weight, lost sleep, lost a big fucking heap of self-respect. And I knew it, suddenly, with my next breath.

This was my last chance.

Third time's a fuckin' charm.

Maybe it was a chance I didn't deserve, but if that guitarist position was still open, it could still be mine.

The way I saw it, Dirty had been playing my songs, without me, for far too fucking long.

They'd also been my family during some of the best—and worst—years of my life, and that kind of thing wasn't shrugged off so easily when you were an orphan. I knew I'd fucked them over, thanks to my addiction, but Dirty was and always would be my family *and* my band.

I knew they'd wanted me back, too, before Jessa told them whatever she told them about me.

That I was a fucking rapist, apparently.

I stood up, so suddenly my barstool tipped over and crashed to the floor. I tossed some bills on the bar, picked up my guitar case and headed for the door.

"Where you goin'?" Big J asked.

"Vancouver," I said.

"You know that's in Canada, right?" Mark called after me.

I didn't answer.

"Hey, asshole. You got a passport?" That was Davey.

I didn't answer that either.

"You got two fuckin' dollars to rub together?" Trent shouted, amusement in his voice. "You know, case you get cold?"

They all laughed. I kept walking.

"Shit," I heard Davey mutter. "Think we just lost our guitarist."

"Good one, too," Mark mused.

I turned to shoulder through the door and took one last look at the guys I'd been playing with these last few months but didn't really know. They didn't know me either, and I liked that fine. Easier to disappear when the time came.

Well, the time had come.

I knew this wouldn't be easy; I just didn't care about that anymore.

I tipped my hat at them. "Later, boys," I said, and walked out the door. But I didn't plan on seeing them later.

I was going back to claim what was mine—and this time, I wasn't letting it go without one hell of a fucking fight. Which meant Todd Becker was about to give the performance of his life.

And Seth Brothers was about to make a comeback.

THANK YOU FOR READING!

Turn to the end of this book to read an excerpt from
the essential Dirty collection (double novella)
featuring Zane and Maggie's secret Vegas wedding,
Jesse and Katie's private wedding night vows, and more...

2 Dirty Wedding Nights

And an excerpt from the next full-length book in the Dirty series,
Seth and Elle's story...

Dirty Like Seth

They all thought they knew him, but only she knew his heart.

ACKNOWLEDGMENTS

I'd like to thank the following people for their support during the creation of this book:

All the reviewers and bloggers who've been so incredibly kind, welcoming and enthusiastic about reading and sharing love for my books—so many of you have given me BIG book love, both publicly and privately, saying amazing, beautiful things about my books and my writing, and I get warm, fuzzy feelings when I see your emails in my inbox. Sandra at Two Book Pushers—you win the award for giving first feedback on this book, always an important moment (for me), so thank you for making my day ("Fucking Seth"... lol, indeed); Erin at The Autumn Review; Sharon at Badass Bloggettes; Stephanie at Book Obsessed Chicks; Doris at The Book Enthusiast; Bec at Harlequin Junkie; Jennifer & Mindy at Hines & Bigham's Literary Tryst; Becky at Jo & Isa Love Books; Coco at My Reading Nook; Sara at Quesarasera; Sheena at Smexy Books; Beth at Tome Tender; Chantal & Rosa at iScream Books; Michelle, Kendra, Judy, Linda and Becky at Once Upon an Alpha; Angela and the ladies of the Wicked Reads review team; Sultan (blue clit!) and Dana, the Goodreads Smut-a-teers. If I've missed you, it's not because I don't adore and appreciate you, more likely the monster spreadsheet where I keep track of all of you occasionally makes me go crosseyed and something is bound to get missed. Hopefully I get my shit together next time.

Guin, thank you for reading this book and loving it and being so sweet about it. I'm glad you and my books have found each other! :) Chris, for your ongoing enthusiasm and support of my books; you're just awesome.

Mr. Diamond. OMG—for everything. Covers. Oh, God, the covers. And a million and one changes to said covers. Your big ideas. Your savvy. Your ability to see and believe. But mostly, for the dick in the drink and the piss in the cup. You always make me make it better, and because of that, I am a better writer. Oh, and for wearing no shirt and your ripped jeans while you brainstorm shit with me. Every romance author should be so lucky. Love you, babe.

To my readers: THANK YOU for reading this book. Your ongoing messages of love, encouragement and support always make my day. When you tell me that you read one of my books in a single, feverish sitting, or you just had to pounce on your significant other after reading a hot scene, or you can't wait for my next book ("please write fast!"), I'm elated. To know that my writing and the characters I love (and I mean LOVE—these people are crazy real to me) have made an impact on you means the world to me, for real. I'm so honored that you chose to read this love story; my intent as a romance author is to spread love. If you've enjoyed Brody & Jessa's story, please consider posting a review and telling your friends about this book; your support means everything to me.

With love and gratitude from the beautiful west coast of Canada,
Jaine

PLAYLIST

Find links to the full playlist on Spotify and Apple Music here:
http://jainediamond.com/dirty-like-brody/

Can't Change Me — Chris Cornell
Whole Lotta Love — Led Zeppelin
Never Gonna Give You Up — The Black Keys
Wild Horses — The Rolling Stones
I Belong to You — Lenny Kravitz
Wasted Love — City and Colour
Dreams — Beck
What's Your Fantasy ft. Shawnna — Ludacris
The Hills — The Weeknd
Hot in Herre — Nelly
Deuces Are Wild — Aerosmith
All I Want Is You — U2
And I Love Her — The Beatles
You Really Got Me — The Kinks
Just A Girl — No Doubt
I Put a Spell on You — Creedence Clearwater Revival
It's a Man's Man's Man's World — James Brown
Take Me to Church — Hozier

Don't Let Me Down — The Beatles
Never There — Cake
Why'd You Only Call Me When You're High? — Arctic Monkeys
I'm a Loser — The Beatles
Have You Ever Seen The Rain? — Creedence Clearwater Revival
Tighten Up — The Black Keys
Ring of Fire — Lera Lynn
Don't Cry (Original) — Guns N' Roses
Back Door Man — The Doors
No One Knows — Queens of the Stone Age
Best of You — Foo Fighters
Nothing Compares 2 U — Chris Cornell
Mr. Brightside — The Killers
The Lengths — The Black Keys
Save Yourself — Kaleo
I Feel It All — Feist
I Wanna Be Yours — Arctic Monkeys
Hey You — Pink Floyd
25.22 — Allan Rayman
Babe I'm Gonna Leave You — Led Zeppelin
One for the Road — Arctic Monkeys
All At Once — Allan Rayman
Jealous Guy — Deftones
Shake It Out (Acoustic) — Florence + The Machine
Dude (Looks Like a Lady) — Aerosmith
Heartbreaker — Led Zeppelin
Love Me Two Times — The Doors
Easy — Faith No More
From Eden — Hozier
Feel Like Makin' Love — Bad Company
All the Pretty Girls — Kaleo
Anybody Seen My Baby? — The Rolling Stones
Letting the Cables Sleep (Nightmares On Wax remix) — Bush
River — Bishop Briggs
Sleeping Sickness — City and Colour

In My Place — Coldplay
Heart of Gold — Neil Young
Halo feat. Linnea Olsson — Ane Brun
Yellow — Coldplay
We Found Each Other in the Dark — City and Colour

2 Dirty Wedding Nights

A Dirty double novella featuring
Zane and Maggie's secret Las Vegas wedding,
Jesse and Katie's private wedding night vows, and more.
2 *Dirty Wedding Nights* includes:

Dirty Like Us
*A sizzling friends-to-lovers novella
about a marriage of convenience—and a jaw-dropping
misunderstanding—between a notorious bad boy
and the one woman he's always wanted but can't have.*

A Dirty Wedding Night
*A flaming-hot, four-story collection about what happens when
a bunch of dirty-minded party guests are stranded overnight
at a remote, glamorous wedding...
and the clothes start coming off.*

DIRTY LIKE US

PROLOGUE

Maggie

The red carpet was worn beneath our feet. The altar was a single step, also carpeted in red, on which we stood, along with the officiant.

The officiant wore a black leather motorcycle jacket, a faded Steppenwolf T-shirt, ratty jeans and biker boots. A black leather bible decorated with silver studs lay open on his hands.

I wore a pink dress.

The room was small, and there were no windows. The ceiling was arched and the walls were black, strewn with neon beer signs and replica platinum albums.

There was a row of eight gunmetal chairs, four to the right of the aisle and four to the left, two of which were occupied. A woman I didn't know stood at the back of the room with a polite smile on her face. A man with a gun stood guard at the door.

Outside, traffic rumbled by, occasionally vibrating the kitschy junk on the walls.

In the next room, an awful song played faintly on repeat. A cheesy, sleazy rock song about a schoolgirl.

Near me, someone was talking.

But all I could hear was that old Steppenwolf song, "Magic Carpet Ride," playing in my head. I heard it the way Zane once sang it, as we sat around a campfire drinking Jäger from a bottle someone passed around, his voice so raw and smoky and beautiful it gave me goosebumps. I heard it the way my mom used to play it, loud, on her wonky old turntable, as she danced in the kitchen in one of her flowy blouses and a pair of cut-offs.

I could see her now, dancing in her bare feet, and looking so, so young.

And I wished she was here.

I was holding hands with him, and my knees were quivering. I could feel his heartbeat in his fingers wrapped tight around mine. His thumb smoothed back and forth across my knuckles, over the new ring on my finger, as I breathed, shallow and slow.

He was looking at me. I knew he was. I could feel the heat of his gaze moving over my face.

"Maggie."

I took a breath and felt his heartbeat, once... twice... Then I looked up into that gorgeous face. His arctic blue eyes held mine. He squeezed my hands slightly.

Zane.

Me.

Holding hands at the altar.

Holy shit.

"That's your cue, babe," Zane said, and I realized the man in the leather jacket had been the one speaking. To me. Everyone was looking at me and waiting.

And I just stared at Zane.

The corners of his eyes twitched. He smiled slightly and I couldn't stop myself. I never could, when it came to him.

I smiled back.

"Yeah," I said, in response to the man's question, but the word cracked and came out a whisper. I cleared my throat and found my voice. "I do."

Dirty Like Seth

Dirty Like Seth is a reunited-friends-to-lovers redemption story, featuring a fallen hero in need of forgiveness, a superstar heroine who knows how lonely it is at the top, and a secret love that flourishes despite the odds stacked against it.

CHAPTER ONE

Seth

I'd done some dangerous shit in my life. Stupid-dangerous shit.

Getting hooked on heroin.

Overdosing.

Almost dying at the age of twenty-two.

Yeah; those were definitely top three.

But this, right now, had to rank right up there on the stupid-dangerous list.

For one thing, I was trespassing on private property, on the lot outside a bar owned by a member of my former band, Dirty. The entire band was inside the bar, and while they had no idea I was here, they were about to find out. And I really wasn't sure how they were going to react.

But no doubt, they probably weren't going to roll out the red carpet for me.

For another thing, the bar was crawling with security, and the security guys who shadowed Dirty these days were mostly of the ex-military or biker variety. Which meant a whole lot of dudes who knew how to draw blood.

And last but not least, I was leaning on a motorcycle parked at the back of the parking lot behind the bar. A Harley. A bike that didn't belong to me but clearly belonged to a serious biker—one of the West Coast Kings, according to the skeletal black King of Spades insignia painted over the gas tank.

It was Jude Grayson's bike. Head of Dirty's security team. At least, I was banking on that being the case.

If it wasn't Jude's, I was banking on, at the very least, that it was the bike of someone he knew, and therefore I was not about to get murdered the instant the biker in question stepped out the back door of the building.

I was doing what I always did when I was nervous: playing guitar. But my mind was on that door. It was painted red, with a security cam on the wall above, pointing straight down. It wasn't pointed at me, but that didn't mean there wasn't some other one that was.

It was early evening and the lot was deserted. There were a few big trucks, the kind that hauled band gear and film equipment and stage shit, and several other vehicles jammed into the narrow parking spaces. But there was a high fence around the lot with a locked gate, and apparently no one in Los Angeles was stupid enough to climb that fence to get in.

No one but me.

I was halfway through Pink Floyd's "Wish You Were Here" when the red door cracked open and some dude's head popped out.

He kicked the door wide and stepped outside; he walked right over to me, winding his way through the parked cars as the heavy door swung shut behind him. And yeah, he was a biker. A baby biker. Couldn't be more than nineteen. He had an overstuffed taco in one hand, half-eaten, so I must've interrupted his dinner.

Could've been the dude with the earpiece who'd materialized on the sidewalk shortly after I'd scaled the fence; could've been someone on the security cams. But someone had tipped him off that I was out here. And since it wasn't Jude himself who'd come outside, whoever it was probably didn't recognize me.

Someone new to the team.

This kid, wearing a black leather Kings cut over his T-shirt, a badge stitched to the chest that read *Prospect*, looked more stunned with my idiocy than pissed off. I didn't know him, and whether he recognized me or not seemed beside the point. Either way, his eyes were stabbing out of his head in the direction of my ass, which was resting on the bike seat.

Maybe if I was really lucky he was also stunned by my musical skills, because his eyes kept darting from the bike to my guitar to my face.

"Do you know whose bike that is?" he said, his mouth open and full of taco meat he'd forgotten to finish chewing. Apparently, he was more concerned with my ass trespassing on the bike than with the rest of me in the lot.

I kept playing, looking him steady in the eyes, and said, "I know whose bike it is. You can tell him Todd Becker's here to see him."

The kid shut his mouth, chewed slowly for a bit, and stared at me like he was deciding whether I was dangerous, stupid, or just plain crazy. Apparently landing on the latter, he shook his head. He glanced at the plainclothes security dude on the sidewalk, who was pretending not to eavesdrop. Then he tossed me a biker-brat glare that said *Your funeral* and stalked back inside.

And for the first time today, I actually wondered if this was a giant fucking mistake.

Last thing I wanted to do was get Jude in any kind of shit.

When I first found out about the auditions for Dirty's new rhythm guitarist, I'd planned to head straight up to Vancouver to try out. But then I changed my mind. The auditions were only starting in Vancouver, but ending in L.A. the following week. And the more I thought about it, the more it made sense to wait.

Then I'd called Jude and found out he wasn't even in Vancouver. He was already in L.A.. And that sealed it for me.

I told him I was coming.

He laughed.

Truth was, I didn't think he really believed me.

But here I was.

All week, I'd hung out at the taco dive across the street. Each morning, I watched the lineup of hopefuls grow, winding down the sidewalk behind the velvet rope and around the block. Each afternoon, I watched the crowd dwindle until the last guitarist left the building. Most of the time I'd sat on the sidewalk, playing my acoustic, and even though I wasn't intentionally busking, people had tossed me cash.

That was weird.

I once had a number-one album. Now I had crumpled bills in my guitar case.

The end of each day, I'd bought three tacos and a juice. I'd given them to the old guy who lived out behind the taco place, along with all the leftover cash. Maybe that was just sponsoring an addiction, and maybe after all I'd been through with my own addiction I should've been wary of that. But the dude was seventy-six years old and living in an alley; if he wanted whiskey for breakfast, you asked me, that was his prerogative.

It was several days before I even glimpsed any members of the band.

On Thursday, just as the sun was starting to set, Dylan Cope strode out onto the sidewalk from the gated lot behind the bar—his bar—with a few other guys. The dude was crazy tall, plus his unruly auburn hair was aflame in the evening sun, so there was no mistaking him. He was smiling. Laughing.

Dirty's drummer was definitely the most easygoing of all the band members, and it's not like it had never occurred to me to appeal to his chill nature for forgiveness. Problem was, it would never be that easy. Dylan was a team player almost to a fault; the guy wouldn't change his socks without the approval of the other band members first.

Especially Elle's.

I'd seen her, too, that same evening. Elle Delacroix, Dirty's bassist. Also unmistakable with her long, platinum-blonde hair smoothed back in a high ponytail, her slim, tanned figure poured into a skimpy white dress and tall boots. She'd come outside with a small entourage—her assistant, Joanie, a stiff-looking dude in black who was probably security, and a couple of other women. I didn't even get a look at her face. She'd spoken with the guys, mainly Dylan, and after giving him a hug and a kiss on the cheek, she disappeared behind the building.

Were they dating now? I had no idea.

I wasn't exactly in the loop.

I knew Elle had dated Jesse Mayes, Dirty's lead guitarist, a while back; everyone knew that. So maybe anything was possible. But Dylan remained on the sidewalk with a bunch of guys, talking, some of them smoking, long after the SUV with tinted windows rolled away with Elle.

Today, the very last day of auditions, I'd waited across the street until the end of the day. Until every last one of the hopefuls had been dismissed and wandered away, guitar in hand. I could remember that feeling, vividly. Playing your ass off in hopes of getting noticed, of getting invited back, no idea if that was gonna happen or not.

I'd been in that position several times in my life. None more nerve-racking than when I'd first met Dirty at age nineteen. When their lead singer, Zane Traynor, took me home with him, to his grandma's garage, to meet the band. Once I met them and heard them play, I knew I had to do whatever it took so they'd let me stick around. I'd played with garage bands before. But these guys were something else. And they already had a killer guitarist in Jesse.

So I knew I had to bring something different to the mix.

I spent the next three years of my life hellbent on doing just that.

From that first informal audition, to the last show I ever played as a member of Dirty—the night they fired me from the band—I knew I had to kill it. To work my ass off to earn the chance they'd given me. I had to give them something back that they'd never seen before, never heard... something they couldn't stand to be without.

Just like I had to do now.

And to that end, I'd decided I had to be the very last person they saw today. The last person they *heard*. The very last guitarist to audition for the spot. *My* old spot.

So that no matter what came before, there was no way they could forget my performance in the onslaught of others.

Save the best for last.

That's what I was thinking, what I kept telling myself, as I sat here on the outside, looking in. Just waiting for Jude to come outside and *let* me in.

But I was no stranger to waiting.

I'd waited for seven long years for Dirty to come around, to ask me to rejoin the band. I'd listened to album after album, watched them tour the world, playing my songs, with guitarist after guitarist who wasn't me.

Then that day last year when I saw Zane at the beach... He asked me to come jam with him, just like he did so many years ago. And that jam turned into a meeting with him and Jesse, and that turned into a reunion show in Vancouver, at a dive bar called the Back Door, where we used to play. That was just over six months ago now. Me, up onstage with all four founding members of Dirty—Zane, Jesse, Dylan and Elle—for one song. Our biggest song. "Dirty Like Me."

Then they asked me to come back to the band.

Then Jesse's sister, Jessa, told them some ugly shit about me.

Then they fired me again.

For six months, I waited for a call that never came.

And now here I was. Poised to prove to them all how wrong they were about me, as I played my nerves out with the music. As the red door finally opened... and Jude appeared.

Big, muscular dude. Intimidating, if you didn't know him. Or maybe even if you did. Dark, almost-black hair. Black T-shirt, gnarly tats down his arms, jeans and biker boots.

And one hell of an unimpressed look on his face when he saw me.

He gestured at the plainclothes guy, who was still loitering on the sidewalk, watching me. Just a flick of his chin. *Take a walk*, that gesture said. The dude was gone, around the front of the bar and out of sight by the time Jude stepped out into the parking lot and the door slammed shut behind him.

I'd switched songs, so now I was just trying not to fuck up "The House of the Rising Sun" as Jude stalked over. He stopped two feet from his bike, from me, and looked me over like he was making sure I *hadn't* gone crazy.

"You kiddin' me?" were the first words out of his mouth. They weren't exactly hostile. More like he was mildly stunned, though not as stunned as the kid with the taco.

I stopped playing, flattening my hand over the strings to silence them. "You rode your bike here from Vancouver," I observed. "Took a few days off?"

He crossed his massive arms over his chest. "Like to do that sometimes. Hit the road. Alone. Tune out all the bullshit." He raked his dark gaze over me again. "You bringin' me bullshit?"

"Guess that depends," I said, "how you look at it."

"From where I'm looking, it looks like bullshit."

"No bullshit. This is an audition." I played a few lines from Jimi Hendrix's "Voodoo Child." Showing off, maybe. "I'm here to audition."

Jude still looked unimpressed as shit. "Auditions are closed. Invi-

tation-only. Pre-screened. And I never saw your name on the list...
Todd Becker."

"So screen me now," I said, still playing, quietly, as we spoke.
"What do you wanna hear? 'Fortunate Son'...? 'Roadhouse Blues'...?"
I played a little from each song as I spoke. "'Dirty Like Me'...?"

Jude remained silent, arms crossed, dark eyes watching me as I
played. The dude was tough to read, but the Jude I knew had always
liked listening to me play.

We'd established a game, early in our friendship, where he'd toss
a song title at me and I'd play it for him. If I didn't know the song, no
matter what it was, I'd learn it, quick. It was because of Jude and this
little game of ours, in part, that I'd become as good as I had on guitar.
Because if I ever struggled to master a song he'd requested, he never
let me hear the end of it—no matter that the guy couldn't strum out a
tune to save his life. And he'd made it a favorite pastime to challenge
me with the hardest songs. In some cases, songs I never would've
learned if it weren't for him egging me on.

"You still into Metallica?" I started playing "Master of Puppets."
Not my favorite band, but back in the day, I'd mastered "Master"—
no easy task—to entertain him.

He cocked a dark eyebrow at me, so maybe we were getting
somewhere. "You remember it."

"Hard to forget. My fingers actually bled learning it."

He grunted a little at that, which was about the closest I was
gonna get to a smile right now. I knew that.

"Or how about some Rage?" I switched to "Killing In the Name"
by Rage Against the Machine, another of Jude's favorites. At least it
was, years ago.

He shook his head, which I took to mean his admiration of my
guitar skills was neither here nor there at the moment. So I did what
I knew how to do: I kept playing. My talent was the only real card I
had to play here.

Maybe it was the only card I'd ever had to play.

"Killing" was another hard song—both heavy and difficult to
master. I'd mastered it. I'd played it for him enough times, long ago,

that it was in my blood. Any song I'd ever learned was in my blood; once I'd learned it, good or bad, I'd never lost a song. Even when I was fucked out of my tree on whatever junk I was on. Which was probably how I'd lasted as long as I had with Dirty.

Yes, I'd OD'd on the tour bus and almost died. But I could always get onstage at show time and nail any song.

Jude just stood there, that impassive look on his face; a look perfected over many years working security for Dirty and riding with an outlaw motorcycle club. But since he hadn't yet told me to take a hike, I knew what he was probably thinking.

It wasn't so much that he was considering his own ass—how this might play out for him if he let me into that bar. More likely he was considering how badly *my* ass was gonna get kicked.

"You want me to dance for you, too?" I challenged, allowing a little sarcasm into my tone.

Jude remained silent until I ran out of song. Then he said, "So this is how it's gonna be, huh?"

"Looks like it."

"Looks like an idiot playing guitar in a parking lot," he said. But then he uncrossed his arms with a small, inaudible sigh. He was looking me over again, top to bottom, seeming to contemplate how quickly the band was gonna recognize me.

I knew the auditions were blind. But it's not like I was hiding who I was. Other than the assumed name, I was still me.

I'd cut off my hair as soon as I arrived in L.A.; it was fucking hot, but the truth was, I was hungry for a change. A fresh start, maybe. No one had seen me with shortish hair since I was twelve, so that was different. I also had a short beard, but I'd been rocking a beard, on and off, for the past few years, and Dirty had seen me bearded. I had aviators on, but this wasn't exactly a glasses on / glasses off Superman trick. I wasn't masquerading as Clark Kent and planning to whip out my cape later.

This was just me.

Faded Cream T-shirt, worn jeans, snakeskin boots, bandana in my back pocket. Metal bracelet with the word BADASS stamped into it, which Elle had given me when I first joined Dirty and I'd never stopped wearing.

They'd see me a mile away and know who I was.

Seth Brothers.

Former rhythm guitarist and songwriter with Dirty. Fallen star. Pariah. And still, whether Dirty liked it or not, fan favorite. No guitarist who'd come after me was loved as much as I was. No one wanted me back in this band more than the fans. I knew that much from the messages I still received on a daily basis. It was the only reason I kept a Twitter account.

It was a big part of what was keeping me here, in the face of increasingly-bad odds. I was starting to feel how bad those odds were, given Jude's hesitation to even let me in the door.

I wasn't quite sure what to do about it. I'd never expected Jude to be my problem.

"You sure you want this?" he asked me, his dark eyes locked steady on mine. "Now?"

"You once said you'd have my back, when the time came."

"I say a lot of shit," he admitted. "Not all of it smart."

"Then we have that in common."

He grunted again. "Tell you what. You play Metallica for me, you've got your audition."

"Great," I said.

Not great. The only Metallica song I knew well enough to impress anyone—maybe—was "Master of Puppets," and that did not feel like the way to go with a Dirty audition. Dirty was not a metal band.

Clearly, that wasn't Jude's problem. He turned his back on me, a non-verbal dismissal, and headed back toward the bar.

I blew out a breath; kinda felt like I'd been holding it all fucking week.

I stuffed my acoustic into its case and picked it up, along with the other case, the one that held my electric guitar—my favorite Gibson. Then I fell in behind Jude.

It wasn't exactly a red carpet, but it would do.

ABOUT THE AUTHOR

Jaine Diamond is a Top 5 international bestselling author. She writes contemporary romance featuring badass, swoon-worthy heroes endowed with massive hearts, strong heroines armed with sweetness and sass, and explosive, page-turning chemistry.

She lives on the beautiful west coast of Canada with her real-life romantic hero and daughter, where she reads, writes and makes extensive playlists for her books while binge drinking tea.

For the most up-to-date list of Jaine's published books and reading order please go to: jainediamond.com/books

Get the Diamond Club Newsletter at jainediamond.com for new release info, insider updates, giveaways and bonus content.

Join the private readers' group to connect with Jaine and other readers: facebook.com/groups/jainediamondsVIPs

goodreads.com/jainediamond
bookbub.com/authors/jaine-diamond
instagram.com/jainediamond
tiktok.com/@jainediamond
facebook.com/JaineDiamond

Made in the USA
Coppell, TX
05 December 2024

41782658R00225